trevor english

PABLO D'STAIR

DOUBLE LIFE

First Printing

ISBN-13: 978-0692417157

Published by Double Life Press

www.doublelifepress.wordpress.com

Printed in the United States of America

CONTENTS

INTRODUCTION

When a writer of the calibre of Pablo D'Stair approaches you with an idea, you really have to listen.

It was about a year ago now that he got in touch with me to ask about another of his ideas.

Not content with giving books away for free, he wanted to serialise a book of his on the internet. To do this, he thought he might put up each chapter of the novella at a different site. Create some movement. Capture some interest. A bit like *On The Road.*

The novella was called *this letter to Norman Court* and you're lucky enough to have that in the book you're currently holding.

I said Yes. After all, he had me at Hi, would you be interested in...

My introduction to Trevor English was the same as you're about to get.

Within a page, I knew I was hooked. I knew enough about the guy to want to find out what was going to happen to him.

He's in a diner half-heartedly eying up a waitress. A man comes over and sits at his table. Mentions the wallet English stole a couple of days earlier. English doesn't bother to deny it, just listens to a proposal. $2000 to deliver a letter and the stolen wallet will be forgotten. Sounds fair. More than fair.

English is a grifter. A real bottom-feeder. He'll find opportunity in the human frailty of others and exploit it as far as he can. Anything to keep him in cigarettes and booze and away from having to work for a living in the conventional way.

The story is told through English's eyes.

In our introduction, he describes the man whose wallet was stolen thus: 'I didn't like this person. He looked like the clothes he was wearing and nothing else.' Which was the second point at which I knew I was going to help set up the blog tour. You'll read many descriptions of people in your time. You'll develop your instinct about when a writer is trying too hard to give you a picture and when it feels just fine. Describing a man as looking like the clothes he was wearing, to me, was brave and instinctive. It gave information about English, too, as a man too lazy to conjure up a better image while creating poetry at the same time. Poetry creation without intention. Now there's a skill.

So there goes Trevor, rattling along, his mind working at the cracks to find the best way to exploit his situation. And there goes Pablo tapping away at the keys. And off goes the novella on its journey around the internet. As I said, *On The Road*.

The Kerouac reference isn't accidental.

The English novellas flow with a real ease. Have an air of 'stream of consciousness' work about them. Pablo seems to let the character do the driving. Clever the way he gives us that illusion. Clever because I also feel that the stories feel as free flowing as rafts on a river, while all the time I know that Pablo has a paddle in his hand.

Before long I had a picture of the writer at work. Like Kerouac before him, I felt there was one roll of paper on which the story was typed. And there's a rhythm behind it. Not the speedy bop of jazz this time, more an urban dubstep. Shadows and edges becoming audible.

And I wonder how best to describe Trevor English to the uninitiated and can only shoot in the direction of the target. I see Ratso Rizzo, Hoffman in *Midnight Cowboy*. Which I shouldn't say, because now I've sown a seed, but I'm saying it and wondering who you'll get. Which flavours you'll pick up on as he moves from trick to splendid trick.

Now I have a new image.

At the typewriter sits Ratzo Rizzo. He's writing a story about Jack Kerouac and listening to *Broken Social Scene*, keeping a burning cigarette alive in fingers that poke through fingerless gloves (for he's too mean to pay for the whole things), who's morphing into Pablo D'Stair every now and again.

Which means that the only man not in the picture is Trevor English.

He's done it again.

Conned me into letting him slip.

Eluded my attempts to grab him by the collar.

Crept away into the darkness to catch the next bus home, drinking a beer and never looking back.

-Nigel Bird, 2012

for my family

Trevor
English

this letter to
Norman Court

Well the fat's in the fire and the water's in the tank
The whiskey's in the jar and the money's in the bank

BOB DYLAN, *Cold Irons Bound*

One of the girls working behind the counter—I think maybe the one who'd wrapped my burger, passed it to the guy working the register to set on my tray—she'd made sort of quick, flirting eye contact with me while I'd been in line, but she hadn't looked up to see where I'd sat down or anything. It had been flirting, though, like she'd for a moment, anyway, thought I was attractive, was probably even having a little fantasy about me, who I might've been, what I might say, do to her, but it was the sort of thing she knew it'd be ruined by looking at me again. I kept my eye on her anyway, kind of, not even so much thinking about anything.

I'd taken a large bite, was taking a drink to help me swallow it, when some guy sat down right at my table, nodded at me, smiling and it wasn't until I'd mashed the swallow down, caught my breath and was saying Can I help you? I realized it was the guy I'd stolen his wallet about two days before.

"Sixty, seventy dollars, it isn't much money," he said

I coughed into my hand, had another quick sip of my drink, wiped the excess from my lip.

"It was forty dollars."

No point in playacting the innocent for this guy.

"Forty?" He hardly seemed like he was paying attention, his saying Forty might not even've been a question.

"It was forty, forty-two, something. Look, it's gone, it's spent. And I'm sure you probably canceled your credit cards, everything, but I don't bother about those and I don't leave them around for people might take them."

"Why not?"

I didn't like this person, he looked like the clothes he was wearing and nothing else, that's all somebody would describe him by if he went missing or robbed a bank or something.

"Because. I don't know why not."

"You can't sell them to people or something?"

I shrugged, glanced over to the counter, behind it, the girl not looking up, still.

"Why would somebody buy a credit card someone's just gonna cancel?"

I knew there were reasons, knew what he was talking about, but I didn't know anything about it, in a practical sense—this guy'd probably watched a movie or some news magazine, had all sorts of little ideas about everything he'd picked up here and there. Thing was, he could chit chat it up, whatever he thought he was doing, I didn't care. There was obviously certainly nothing he could do about it, unless he was gonna shoot me, cut me down at the Wendy's or whichever place this was. The wallet was gone, it'd been forty-two something dollars, it'd been two days ago. Even if he was tape recording me, spy camera glasses, I didn't know what he thought, like he was being tricky.

"Well, forty dollars is even less money, then."

I nodded, back to my burger, the bite I took shoving wet bread up, wedging it up into the gum of the tooth I was missing and I dug at this with my tongue while he went on with his bit.

"How would you like to make some more money than that? How about we talk about that?"

I sighed, vaguely interested—at least it wasn't what I'd been thinking, wasn't so banal.

"How about we talk about it? Fine, talk about it."

"I'll pay you two thousand dollars to deliver a letter to my brother."

I grinned.

"A small fortune. But what else is it for?"

"It's not for anything else. Though, I suppose there's the stipulation that you don't tell him it's from me."

My mind drifted to cinematic pretend, trying to weasel around how he'd be edging me into something I didn't want into, but at the same time I didn't so much care, really, because it was going to be either he gave me the money, all of it, in front or there wasn't going to be anything about me delivering any letter to anybody and so I could just walk off if I got feeling something was askew, money in pocket, dust my hands of it all.

"What's he going to do with me I give it to him? I'm suppose to have a chat with him or what?"

"Just in case, just in case he asks you something. I just need you to put it into his hand, personally, that's the only important thing, no reason you have to say a thing to him after that, but just in case."

I ate my last bite, the girl wasn't even behind the counter anymore so I did a phony stretch to see was she maybe wiping down some table but she wasn't anyplace, was in back, employee toilet or something.

"And so how would this letter have gotten to him somebody didn't steal your wallet?"

He chuckled, very real chuckle, said he didn't know, he'd been thinking about it all for awhile.

So it was something, it wasn't normal, not like he could mail it from a pretend address—send it to a hotel inside another envelope, little note asks them to send it along so that the postmark is someplace strange—nothing that could be left to chance or have a straight third party involved with.

It was pointless, making it all a little mystery—I wanted to know about the letter, I'd say Yes to the guy, take the two thousand, open the letter and have a look. I was no more certainly reliable than a hotel clerk, this little scene must've just given the guy a kick, this little intrigue, maybe he was full of it.

And sort of mind reader, he out of nothing said "I like you, I think you seem the sort of person who could do this and know that's that."

"I seem that way, yeah?"

He nodded. "Yeah."

"You know you have to give me that two thousand, that's first, then I take your letter. What's your brother, gonna kill me I give it to him?"

He shook his head, face a scrunch, a real genuine expression of it's-nothing-like-that. In fact, I didn't think it was—the suit of clothes I was striking the deal with, it was just too earnest for that, it was just something I'd never decipher and it was right, I really didn't care and probably I would deliver the letter.

I said Alright, tilted my drink cup back, got an ice cube I broke and swallowed in two chews, looked over to the counter, behind the counter, the girl wasn't there, still.

***

Down to my last three cigarettes, enough to get me through the walk to the coffee shop I'd agreed to meet the man at, pick up the money, the letter. I more than halfway expected he wouldn't be there, still had some dull little anxieties he might be setting me up to do something, except all I'd done was agree to deliver a letter.

Two thousand dollars wasn't enough I could live carefree, but I couldn't think of the last time I'd had that much money on me at once, didn't know had it ever happened even back when I was working legitimate, checks every other week. Money goes someplace, always does, the same place, away.

As it was, what did I think was better: deliver a letter, get the two grand all in one handful or just stay the grind nabbing briefcases, wallets, whatever to make it enough to kick this friend or that enough to stay on in their apartment?

Not a question, really.

I was coming up on the coffee shop, the guy at a table outside reading some newspaper. Both the letter and the money, all neat in its own thick envelope, were inside of a Happy Birthday gift bag he set on the table, mentioning casually I would take it when we left, but I could go to the toilet, give the money a count if I felt like it.

"I don't need to count some money, there's not two thousand when I look later it'd be kind of a waste on your part, right?"

This'd obviously occurred to him, but maybe he wanted some antics, something to texture this all out a bit more for him.

"My brother lives in Mill Creek," he said and when I stared he smiled, added "That's in Maryland."

It didn't matter to me a bit, sort of made it nicer, a trip into the deal, but just to put it out there I said "How do I get to Maryland?"

"I think you might have two thousand dollars, right?"

"I didn't know some of that was cab fare."

"Then pretend it's yesterday and I'd said I'll pay you fifteen hundred dollars to deliver a letter to my brother, he lives in Maryland, though, so I'll kick five hundred on top for travel."

It wasn't sharp, nothing belittling or glib in his tone, but it still put me off his saying it like that, he didn't seem the type should be smug, but he was smug—though really there's no reason he shouldn't be except it put me off, I guessed.

"Alright?"

I puffed air out my nose, affirmative, giving my head a tick, peeked into the bag, the tissue paper open with scissored second third finger—the letter, the money pack. I asked was his brother's name, address in there and he told me Yes.

We settled this would be it, we'd be seeing no more of each other, he stood up to go. I kind of wanted to ask him how was he to know I'd delivered the letter, seeing as how the idea played out it was this guy's brother was supposed to have no idea this guy was the actual sender, therefore not something this guy could bring up in conversation, but thinking it over instead I didn't care.

Down the block with the bag, I ducked into a bookstore toilet. It was two thousand dollars—fifty-dollar bills, not exactly new feeling, not exactly old. From all I could tell, it was real money. In with the bills was a folded sheet of paper—the name Herman Flake, an address, another address for the office Flake worked at.

I left everything except for two bills in the bag, not wearing anything with suitable pockets, went out of my way eight blocks to a tobacco shop I knew the foreign guy working there always put a special pen to bills twenty and larger—not in a suspicious way, just something he always did and I'd remarked it. I asked for a pack of Daphne Durant's, watched him slip the pen across the bill I paid him, the ink acting right, not showing up.

Not that I'd thought it'd be phony, I couldn't think of anything more ridiculous than that, giving someone two thousand phony dollars to skip a few states over hand little brother a letter—I assumed it was little brother, anyway.

I smiled as I took in my first long breath of the first decent smoke I'd had in what seemed it was coming up on two years. I suddenly wanted to buy a new coat, something—some gesture to make the money a bit more real, something it'd got me a bit more substantive than a stump of filterless. So, I window shopped my way back to my friend Murray's apartment, where I'd been up the last month, sort of grumbling to myself that I'd had two grand for something fifteen minutes and already it was dribbling down—train ticket, theoretical coat, cigarettes—but did my best to reassure myself that at the end of the line I'd come out twelve, thirteen hundred up, easy, even with some frivolous distraction. Anyway, even were it a clean thousand that was something.

No one home, so I did my light packing, the money a bit bulky as a lump so I kept seven hundred on me, the rest wrapped up in a shirt in the middle of my duffle, I'd not let it out of my hand. I took the letter itself out for the first time, rolling my neck around, shushing coffee cheek to cheek, sitting on the arm of the sofa.

It was a fully addressed, stamped envelope, but obviously it'd not be sent, not been sent a good while back, just the wear to the creased up corners anyone could see that. It was addressed to Norman Court, written from a woman called Klia Flake.

I downed the last of my coffee, held the envelope up to the light, inspected it, completely layman, to see had someone got it opened before, didn't seem they had.

-You naughty girl, Klia I said, gave the thing a flick, then added Poor poor Herman Flake.

Though, thinking about it, that didn't seem to be his brother's attitude regarding the matter. Something like this, the caring thing'd be to get Herman aside, give him the hard news through a few shots down the bar, sadly show the letter off as the unfortunate proof.

I picked it up, again. Had it been opened? How would my guy know the contents?

But just as quick I tossed it back in my duffle—not only was it irrelevant, but it could easily be my guy'd found it out about whatever Klia'd been pulling behind Herman's back, there was this letter going to the fellow he knew she was off cuddling with, gave it the swipe, because what else could it be?

I grabbed some junk mail flyer, scribbled a note on the back for Murray—cryptic, just *Goin' to Kansas City, Kansas City here I come*—then took two fifties out of my pocket, set them on the note, added *Don't go letting the room out, the meantime.* I re-read it, took one of the fifties back, gave my duffle a final pat, inside and out—the money, the letter, etc.—went back to the note, took back the fifty and left down the change from my cigarettes earlier, instead. Just out the door, I turned back around, grabbed up one of the twenties, left just the rest—shouldn't be getting loose with the money, last thing I needed was the appearance I could be counted on for more than my usual next-to-nothing.

***

Train into Maryland takes day-and-a-half, two days for all intents and purposes, a little bit more expensive than a bus ticket, but I'd never been on a train before and I'd been on plenty of buses. Station was bleary and distracting, like I was stuck inside a dull cough wouldn't go away. Something—the lighting, the speakers, the people—was an irritant, so I wasted too much on two drinks and when I boarded was pointlessly jittery from the semi-drunk I'd put on.

It took an hour to dwindle back down to sober, needed coffee so wound my way down to a kitchen car on the lower level by the toilets. I kept my bag with me, even while I opened cupboards, must've had a lost expression on my face, because some woman leaving the toilet started up the stairs, peeked back around, asked me was I alright.

"There's coffee somewhere on this train?"

She didn't know, said I should try the lounge car, the sightseeing car, something. I nodded, let her go away before I went up the stairs, found the lounge, coffee, someplace to sit, looked out a window, sipping, duffle on my lap.

Bored with the passing landscape, I took out the envelope, pinched it, made a game of guessing how many pages. I decided I'd open it, could just tape it shut, after— I'd deliver it, taped shut or shut-shut didn't see how this would alter a thing. So the guy Herman'd know I'd probably read it, so what? I justified the technical betrayal to the guy'd paid me to deliver the thing with a mumbled Caveat Emptor—this was a guy, it couldn't be overlooked, was having the guy stole his wallet deliver a letter for dubious reasons to his brother, it should be expected by him I was opening it, our thing wasn't exactly housed between the four corners of a contract.

The letter was long, paper thinner than I'd figured, very long. I sighed even before reading a word, felt my eyes start stinging, the pages soggy from the ink, words on the reverse side of a page almost legible overtop words on front. For the first page-and-a-half, though very well written—women always write great letters, I'd always remarked that—there was nothing to the thing, it was inreferenced prompts, Klia writing in generalities to Norman about her life, her image of herself, all of it, things people write in letters to darling old friends who'll read them, make a point of finding time to respond to each question buried in the center of whichever paragraph.

I folded it shut in my bag, made my way back to the bar area I'd ordered my coffee, asked for a wine.

"White, red, blush?"

I considered, then dully said Blush, regretted it right away but didn't bother changing my order. The guy presented me with a miniature bottle, label and everything.

"How much is this running me?"

"That's six dollars."

I scoffed, getting the money from my pant pocket.

"I could buy a whole real bottle of wine six dollars."

The man seemed unimpressed and I got the feeling someone next to me was making a mocking face, got back to my seat and downed the thing, it really seemed hardly a glassful.

Back to the letter, I found it got quite lurid, all at once. This Norman, he wasn't her lover, some fellow called Lawrence was, an almost pornographic rendering of one of their early, quite daring, encounters presented with some self-analytic remarks parenthesized throughout.

I skimmed through the remaining pages, found at least one more of these full out reminisces as well as some various remarks about less carnal aspects of her dealings with Lawrence, though steeped in the obvious sexuality she seemed it impossible to separate from the two of them.

Leafing to the end, mind made up I'd spring another twelve, eighteen bucks to get a proper amount of wine in me, I saw the letter was dated more than two years ago. I just sat, not realizing it, nibbling on the side of my finger, staring at the rim of the window, lost in meandering thoughts, Lawrence, Klia, Norman, the gentle rise of the mouthful of blush likely smoothing me out. But I shook off the reverie, none of it my business. So she'd taken her tumbles with Lawrence not Norman, didn't make any difference, no difference to make.

Approaching the bar counter, the attendant smiling at me in an obviously particular way, I made an open, embracing gesture.

"I've changed my tune, entirely, you've made a convert out of me—stuff's worth every last cent. Three more of those."

My wit didn't seem to redeem me any, so I opted not to leave the two dollars tip, made my way back to my seat in the cheap compartments, but when I saw how vacant the place was moved to the seat furthest in back, the corner, propped myself in, bag pinned to the train side, downed my wine and fell easily to sleep.

Woke up middle of the night with a horrendous urgency to urinate and a two thirds erection, slogged my way down to the toilet and took a seat, not wanting to bother with aiming, the bowl a moving target, floor nudging up down under my feet more irregularly than I'd've imagined.

I recounted my money, disappointed, took out the letter and, rubbing my face, gave it another look through.

His whole name, Lawrence, her stallion, that was something—she wrote it'd impressed her, like something would impress a girl who didn't know better, impressed her all the more she did know better, something pointless like a name making her thoughts for him more easy, permanent, centered.

Lawrence Stephanie Glass.

That middle name, I wondered had she meant Stephane, figured no, it was more impressive as Stephanie, more fitting to her lulling it around in her thoughts, going behind old Herman.

Herman Flake.

Name-to-name it was a lost cause, poor little guy, I thought.

What was Norman to Klia, though? This level of detail—I settled on a particular bit, not a blow-by-blow recap of a particular tryst, instead her mentioning how after one encounter where Lawrence'd finished up on her face, she'd just dry wiped it off, nothing more, all day, all night, home with her husband, to dinner, to bed, had wanted to just put make up on over it next day but finally broke down and washed—this was something I don't know anyone someone writes so familiarly to. Not to her brother, nothing and Norman had either been a former lover or else must be a professional talk doctor. Except the salutation was *Dear dear Norman* and there was no closing *Sincerely* or *With Love* just her name, so obviously added out of rote, not necessity. I guess he could've been bent, but even that didn't seem to account for things.

There was light out the window I left the stall, some guy having a cigarette in the kitchen car, reading a paperback. The smoke perked me up a bit. I set my duffle on the opposite end of the table from him, was casually reaching for the pack in my pant pocket, decided instead I'd beg one off this guy if he'd be willing, my mouth lousy from wine and sleep, no point being wasteful of a cigarette I'd not be able to taste even.

***

I got down stiff from the train right about past three in the afternoon, lit up as soon as I'd made my way out to the street, scanning this way and that through a wince of cold.

It made the most sense to try Herman at the office address I'd been given, so I fished the sheet out of my duffle, went into a shoe store to ask directions—clerk seemed pretty unsure of just about everything so I tried the bank across the street, right after.

The building was a generic catchall, had to find the company name on the tack board in the lobby, rode the elevator to the ninth floor, antsier than I wanted to be. Better here than have to do this his doorstep, though, no chance he'd try something, even if there were elements at play I was unbeknownst about.

In the corridor just outside the closing elevator doors, I tucked the letter from my duffle into my coat pocket, chided myself for not thinking to put the thing in another envelope, phony little address, make it seem a delivery, nothing to even bother looking at me about.

Through a glass door, a reception desk, no obvious way to bypass it.

"I'm trying to get to see Mister Herman Flake," I said, briefly scanning were any of the business cards up on the countertop his.

The receptionist dialed a number, seemed to be listening to someone, nodded, but didn't say Goodbye or anything when she hung up.

"Mister Flake is away, just now, at a conference. Had you made an appointment?"

I lied about Yes I'd had an appointment, casually taking a look at one of the cards to get some context, but the man the thing belonged to was labeled *Assessor* and having no idea what this meant I admitted I might have got the time wrong.

"Maybe he'd meant he'll meet me he pops in after, any idea when the thing gets out?"

The conference was out of state, he'd not be back until

the day after next. I ducked a bow of thanks, down the elevator, stepped into a new cigarette, outside.

Two days staying in town, even as on the cheap I might manage, that'd be another sizable hit to the paycheck, this all amounting to some chump's errand rather quickly. It didn't make sense the guy'd've not known Herman was out, seemed as brothers they weren't on good terms—no surprise, maybe, but I couldn't figure my guy wouldn't at least know about some conference, anyway, when to expect the letter might be delivered.

No point to it, I decided I'd have a look at Herman's house, very least I could do the idea of leaving the letter inside a different package, trust no one would open it in the meantime, it'd be there Herman got in—added in to which, what did I care about the letter? I should really leave it with the missus, let her have a narrow escape, especially this two grand wasn't exactly making it worth my trouble—not my trouble to the tune of two grand, anyway.

Cab driver was nice enough to save me some money, told me which bus'd get me closest in to the address, said I couldn't find it from there a cab would cheaper by that point, anyway.

It was evening when I was through the bus, the walk, not unpleasant though the cold got considerably more physical around me, couldn't tell properly were my breaths out cigarette or me, which of the two more prominently thick.

Perfectly quaint little place and one car in the driveway, probably Klia herself at home, lights on throughout. Figuring I'd come out all this way, I should at least get a peek as much as I could at the principle players, I knocked at the door, hadn't even figured out what the thing was going to be I'd say I was doing there when it opened.

A woman, plain in clothes casual enough to lounge in,

proper enough to step outside, gave me a not unpleasant side tilted head, nodded a shy hello.

"Mrs. Flake, is it?"

Now she quizzed up a bit more, tentative smile. "Yes?"

"Sorry, just wanted to be sure the address was right, going by memory. I work with your husband, I'm handling something of his, he's out of town the conference a few days, was supposed to pick up something he'd left around for me."

She shrugged, seemed bored, said he hadn't told her he'd left anything, she could get him on the phone, maybe. I waved that off, started explaining it might've been he'd couriered it the office, instead, I'd not checked my messages right—I didn't believe a word of what I was saying even sounded plausible, but she just nodded through my polite hem hawing until I said Goodbye.

I got a cigarette up just down the block, started to laugh at myself—nothing to be worried about and anyway it was fun to have a look at her, get the general idea about the things I'd read in the letter. I had her painted less the fatale, now, more the quiet twig of a thing met the one guy rooted her right so her head was so addled up about it she'd write these book length letters out to Norman about she couldn't get shut of this beau and all of it.

I was cementing and cementing this idea about her as I got back where I'd get the bus back to the city, ducked in for a drink someplace first, do something about I couldn't feel any of my extremities.

It was a bit of a letdown, I got to admitting to myself, two drinks in of the off brand bourbon—not that she hadn't been attractive, but what'd I been thinking, Herman's out of town maybe I try on his old lady?

No.

Well, maybe a bit, couldn't be helped from the letters, to

go by those she'd be one to twist around backward and underneath about—and maybe she was, at least as far as it went with Lawrence. Still, I thought, third drink down at a hard mouthful, I needed something to pass the time of day with for two days, unless I was going to punch out, take my losses.

Losses.

I felt bone broke, meandered toward the bus stop. There must've been something the matter with me, I have a letter in my pocket worth two thousand it depreciates point A to point B, something about me I can sour even a quick buck into hardly room and board and meanwhile make a chore of it, on top.

Letter worth two grand to someone, I thought, but what else might it be worth, someone else? Two grand's what some guy I stole his wallet'd pay me to get it down the street two towns over when meanwhile he could've done that on his own—what'd it be worth to Kila to see that it didn't get delivered?

This never would've crossed my mind she'd fit the mental image I'd had of her reading the letter, but seeing her now, weakening her to someone'd had this one tryst, ever, no chance but Herman Flake other than that, flavored it different.

Gas station just up the way had a copy machine, didn't see how it could hurt for trying. The last of the last shot I'd taken slipping up around me warm, I paid out the two bucks something in quarters into the slot, almost felt it was the first clear profit coming my way this'd began.

***

Couldn't find a motel ran me less than thirty-nine for the night, so didn't want to just sleep through it, watched television until almost four, used up the free coffee and got a second batch the front desk. Woke up past nine, finally, showered with as much of the soap I could, even though it dried me out bad with the towels only making it worse, my skin rashed from drying off. I smoked in the room naked, dressed slowly in the one change of shirt and socks I'd brought, same pants, checked did I have everything in my duffel, recounted my money twice, made sure the photocopied letter was as legible as the original, left.

I took my time of it getting back to Klia's house—Herman working in some middling office in whatever capacity it seemed she'd be grinding a day job, as well, was sort of surprising to find her car there midafternoon, the house windows open as I made a pass, sounds of a radio talking, coming out fuzzy through the cold.

She came to the door, seemed she'd been doing something she still had her thoughts on, dressed grubby, took me a minute to notice her hands were spotted in various colours of acrylic paint.

"Didn't mean to interrupt you, you're painting?"

It made sense to me she'd've been, seemed like she painted.

My question briefly confused her, her face mussed, then like a blink there was the recognition. "You're here for something my husband left?"

I stared at her calm, no real gesture of getting my pack of cigarettes out, one to my lip.

"I'm here to see you, in fact, Klia. I can come in?"

I poked my nose a tap, started past her, right away her features growing irritable, not exactly telling me No but she pointed, said "Not with that."

"I think I will smoke, thanks. This's about a mutual friend, in fact—more a friend of yours, really, not mine so much—you know Lawrence Glass?"

Maybe it was the loping trot of my sentences, the smoke out my nose, it was a look of blah concentration on her, sorting out what I'd said, then a spot of colour to her cheek that drained just as fast—just the mention of the name, the thought in her head, it overrode the awkwardness long enough I was closing the door behind me.

"Is Lawrence, alright? You were here last night." She stammered, something clicking, eyes a brief skittish flare, she got the door opened and told me to leave.

I sat on the stair third up the case, let her leave the door open, her hand slip off the knob, waited before she was forming a word to talk over her, loudly the first two words, then dropping to even tones.

"I can give this letter to your husband, or I can sell it to you, I don't really feel like making a production out of this, I see I interrupted you, you're painting."

It really seemed she knew just what I was talking about, which letter in particular, I'd not even shown her I'd anything with me, yet. I wondered how long she'd wondered about it, wondered why hadn't Norman got back to her about this or that, how long she'd wanted to but never did ask him out loud—I wondered how many moods poor Herman'd had she'd interpreted as his knowing, grappling, forgiving, changing his mind and I wondered maybe it was this letter winding up gone had got the creeps in her, led her to end it off with Lawrence if that's how it'd gone or let him end it out with her, whichever.

"How is Lawrence, these days?" I asked, no answer but she looked like she knew, though certainly didn't seem at all like she'd been with him maybe in years.

I took the letter from my pocket, started reading it, the

dull bit, the bit about nothing, and she right away said Give me my letter.

"Going price to give you your letter's two thousand."

"I don't have two thousand dollars."

"That is either untrue or else very unfortunate, because the thing's this and it's with no games, alright? We can go drive down your bank and you hand me the two thousand dollars you certainly do have or else you don't have two thousand dollars, really, and I walk away from here thinking I'd better do something else constructive with my time."

"You wouldn't really go see Lawrence."

This paused me up, but not so much it didn't just look like I was taking a drag, indulging her a last moment.

"This is bargain basement I'm offering you here, I think you can guess that. Thing is this is something just fell in my lap and I'm looking for the quick thing it can be with no interest in it past this afternoon."

"You won't give me the letter."

"I'll give you this exact letter right here, that's just what I'll do—then you go do whatever you want with it, feed it to some pigeons, bake it in a pie, this isn't something where I want to see you again, ever, Klia, you're not my type. Last time I say this, it's two thousand dollars cash money, we're leaving right here, or it's I get my boot heel over as much of your life it'll cover and twist my full weight down—go get your car keys."

I was sweating heavily under my arms, down my lower back, between my spread legs, not nervous, actually just nearing giddy, all of it like a dream I was there on some stage in front of everybody able to say lines unrehearsed turned out they're the ones belonged there.

She swallowed, asked could she use the toilet. I told her leave the door open and only if it was a toilet downstairs. I did my best not to listen, but she didn't put on the overhead fan, blew her nose while I stubbed a cigarette out on the wood floor, felt like a rat about it, bent, took up the stub and wiped the spot clear with the cuff of my coat sleeve.

She came out from the toilet, it smelled like perfume or thick hand soap, went to the dingy green coat once probably looked something substantial, felt around until some keys came from the pocket, a few soiled tissues she let drop on the floor, said she wanted to see the letter. I told her she'd see it plenty all she wanted I'd got my money and she'd dropped me at some curb, driven off, wouldn't see one word of it until.

The drive to the bank, whole way she kept it on the same talk radio'd been going in the house. It grated on me, but I didn't see why I'd have her change the station, nothing to bully her over—a small price to pay she was going along.

I asked her was she doing alright when I noticed her eyes about to tear up, but she whispered Shut up so little girl, pitiful, right with the end of my question that I even said I'm sorry, turned my eyes down.

***

I stepped from the car, duffle feeling a grip heavier for Klia'd withdrawn the money all in tens, maybe just my imagination. Leaned to the open window, I handed the letter, the original, toward her, but she kept in profile, not reaching, maybe thinking I'd tease it away from her hand up for it, didn't want to go through anything else belittling. I placed it on the passenger seat I'd vacated, turned right up the block, not looking back till the crosswalk—her car was there lulling, window open still, face in profile.

Three blocks up I could tell I seemed edgy, legs all clunk

with each step, so I purposefully let my pace get sluggish, more-than-casual, strolled with still some vague anxiety on me. I don't know what I thought she'd do—if she called the police, what'd she say? Even if I was found with this money, I couldn't be because I didn't have to open my bag, anything.

I shook all thoughts like that off. Klia wouldn't do a thing at all, didn't for one single minute believe she'd seen the last of me, that I didn't have the letter in duplicate, the replica just as much damning to her as the genuine she'd just bought off me. I did still have a duplicate, she was right, nothing I was gonna hold over her, but she wouldn't believe that no matter if I'd told her.

I ducked into a fast food restaurant, ordered a burger, a shake, sat as much in the corner of the place as I could manage, waiting out the last of the feeling, for time to dull me out. I took the letter from my bag when I'd done eating, the photocopied pages still in the original envelope—I smiled at myself about that, what'd been the point?

Looking at Klia's address, it struck me it wasn't Herman's, not where they lived now, was someplace Pennsylvania. I pictured an apartment, they'd moved down to Mill Creek, someplace hardly any different except a house, Herman's job. It didn't matter. Norman lived in Virginia, according to the envelope, I kind of thought that was close, but then put the letter away, nothing left to do with it but get it to Herman, put it in his hand he got back in at the office, next day.

Something in that thought lingered with me up a few more blocks, into a bar where I took a seat in a booth, ordered a bottle of decent wine for myself, sipped at it looking at the empty space across from me, the shallow brown of the high booth back.

Nothing left to do.

Didn't seem Klia'd seen it that way.

What'd I said? Whatever, it'd been something to the tune of she didn't pay I'd find another use for the letter and straight off her thoughts'd gone to Lawrence and not her husband. Why'd that be? Well, seemed I was after money to her, of course, and why'd Herman be a viable source for that from I have a letter his wife'd been going around in back of him?

She'd thought of Lawrence as someplace else I'd go for money's what she'd thought.

I downed my bottle to halfway, looked at the envelope front, tapping this letter and that, little bugs, little crumbs.

It was she didn't want Lawrence to know she'd been telling the long and short of their thing to anyone, maybe, either just she thought he'd go sour on her because of it or because it'd put Lawrence in some kind of spot.

She knew he'd've paid, that he'd have to for some reason or another.

She'd not been with him maybe in the two years since this letter'd gone missing, maybe further back than that—it was way past her caring Lawrence knew how he'd affected her, she'd want him to know that, probably, more than anything. If there was a chance it'd lead even to meeting face-to-face with him for an I'm sorry or a How could you do this, she'd want Lawrence to have the letter.

There was something else to it if she was trying to keep me away from him.

Away from him where?

I looked at the addresses—Klia from Pennsylvania, Norman somewhere Virginia.

Where's Lawrence in all of that?

Bottle emptied, I made my way to the bar, asked could they leave a bourbon at my booth, break five dollars for coins and did they have a public phone. I was soft, head a heavy breeze, felt the coins grinding in my fingers, the phone just a wall mount in over by the toilets.

I dialed information, stammered through I was looking for a personal telephone number—really I wondered did they give those out, but they did, provided it was listed.

"I think it's in Pennsylvania, in Sandbar Pennsylvania, that's what I have," I said squinting at the envelope front.

"What listing?"

"Lawrence Stephanie Glass."

"Lawrence or Stephanie Glass?"

"Just Lawrence Stephanie, middle name's Stephanie. Lawrence S. Glass."

There was a moment or two, I rubbed an itch on the side of my thigh sort of, leaned around the phone, head tip tap tip tap tip tap to the wall beneath a reproduction advertisement for Calvert Whisky. I was staring at the slogan—*the Whiskey with the Happy Blend*—when the operator said there was no listing in Sandbar, but she had four listing for Lawrence Glass in Pennsylvania and one L.S. Glass Plumbing in Horton.

"Is one of the Lawrence's maybe in Horton?"

She checked.

"I have a Lawrence Glass in Horton, hold for that number."

I heard a click as an automated voice started giving me digits, padded around myself for a pen, but worse thing was I'd call back I'd heard things wrong.

Hung up, dialed, woman answered almost immediately, hardly the purr of a single ring'd gone off before a kind of short breathed clip of Hello?

"I was looking to talk to Lawrence Glass, given this number for contact."

"Who's this?"

"I'm with Nyborg Realty, calling back off a message he'd left?"

"I think maybe you were given the wrong information."

"It's Lawrence Stephanie Glass, is it? Horton, Pennsylvania."

I could almost see her blink, shoulders up down, saw her whole expression in the elongation to her first word "Ye-e-es, that's him." There was some muffled sound, her saying something to someone, not Lawrence though, then half a beat later it was "He's out just now"—another bit of her talking in another direction, not covering the phone this time, a bark of Pick that up, now—then she exasperated huff out her teeth said "I'm sorry."

"No no, not a bit of it, I'm sorry. I can just try him later, you let him know Nyborg Realty rang back—or nevermind, I hear you're busy, just I'll try back."

Not even stopping long enough to enjoy my little victory, I was slipping coins back in the slot, got the number for some motel in Horton, placed a call, asked did they know were there buses, a train station anything, how I'd get to them from whichever station.

"You're coming in on train? Commuter train?"

"I am," I said, smiling dumbly like the guy was there to make a face at.

"We don't have shuttles, but I'm sure a cab'd do it."

"Train stops in Horton?"

"No, commuter trains in to Darcy, but cab'd be the best to get here, no buses really."

I chatted back and forth a bit before just hanging up midsentence, bored with the pointless make believe, certainly not going to reserve a room.

I was surprised to find the bourbon at my table, glanced around to see maybe who'd left it, my mind catching up with itself it'd been me as I sat, lifted it, let some of it press up against my lip, swallowing nothing, inhaling deeply, tongue out for the little taste left over the scruff under my nose when I set the glass back to the table.

***

More than half drunk, managed to get the late commuter train, thing packed until almost half hour in—miserable situation, I just stood against the wall, duffle hugged tight to me.

I suddenly couldn't think why was I in such a hurry. Herman was back in town tomorrow, but who knows would he go in to the office and even if so, guy'd paid me to deliver the letter couldn't expect me to be there, the very first moment when already these extra days were his fault for not knowing about some whatever conference it was Herman was out at.

"Better just to get it all done," I mumbled, touching at my nose, raw from it'd started running awhile back, I'd been using napkins I'd swiped from the bar to clean it.

My thoughts were sloshing gently to the rhythm of the train, the sooner I was done with Herman, the sooner it was all done, the sooner I'd slip away more than a few bucks richer for my trouble.

But where did Lawrence live?

I rubbed at my eye with a thumb knuckle.

Had I been thinking I had his address, got it mixed in my head with Klia's old place?

Seat freed up, so I sat, knees impatient. No, this wasn't a good idea—no need to abandon ship, scurry back as already here I was on the train, but certainly I needed to sober out, get a handle on what was what.

Lawrence had his number listed, so probably his address was in the directory, or probably I could track it down through the number—anyway, there was L.S. Glass Plumbing, which it'd be a bit much of a coincidence that had nothing to do with him, guy named Lawrence Stephanie in the same town as an L.S. company shared his surname.

It was well past dusk by the time I got out at Darcy, stomach a mushy knot, in no shape for anything but a trip to the toilet yielded nothing but making me cramp worse from the effort, then a fit of sneezing made me feel a wrung rag.

Town was still operational, for the most part—some bookstores, smaller coffee places were closed up, but a convenience store got me some cold and allergy tablets and a number for a taxi, had to walk back to the station for a public phone. I smoked even though it was a lost cause, swallowed the soiled phlegm that kept either rising up from my gut or else slimed down my nostril back, told the cab Take me to any motel in Horton and asked what was the matter with the air it was turning me inside out.

"Take a stiff drink before bed, clear you right out."

"That's what to do about it, yeah?"

"I didn't used to believe it, but some rum, it'll sort you."

"Rum'll do that?"

"Rum, bourbon, vodka—make you sleep warm, too, good hard sleep, you'll wake up like there's never been anything the matter with you in your whole life."

I nodded, not wanting to get too chummy, feel pressured into leaving the guy a tip for medical consultation on top of the climbing fare, asked a final Where's Horton, anyway? slunk my soggy head to the door window, vibration helping things.

"Horton's no place, that's right where Horton is. I'll take you to the Super Eight, though, I don't like any of the others."

I made an affirmative noise, eyes closed, getting my head back to Lawrence. Nothing to do for the night except maybe have a look at the plumbing shop, whatever it was, hope my medicine did the trick. This was no state to get a couple thousand dollars off some guy, fact that I could hardly motivate myself to blow my nose more than enough proof of that.

"Or is it allergies?" the driver asked me, asked again when I guess he thought I hadn't exactly heard him.

"What's the difference, it's cold or allergies?"

"Just that rum won't do anything for allergies, nothing does anything for allergies."

"I took some tablets," I said, asked could I smoke a cigarette and were we almost there.

The light had gone away outside when we came up on Horton, it was just an odd cut in the midst of nothing, Super Eight's raised sign the tallest structure around.

"Jesus Christ, is this a place?"

The driver laughed, told me Good luck about my allergies, if they were allergies.

The motel lobby was air conditioned despite the weather, got signed into a room no trouble, made sure the clump of buildings up the way was Horton, proper.

"You know L.S. Glass Plumbing?"

"Sure. That's by the movie theatre."

I nodded, took my key, started to walk across the lot right away, ten minutes to the city and it was impossible to tell how I felt, was it the come down from my drunk, the medicine getting on me, or just the next phase of my head clogging up.

Place was a store, sink fixtures, toilet fixtures on display in the window, been closed since five o'clock even though there was a glow looked like someone'd left a portable television on at the cashier's desk. Place'd open next day, eleven o'clock, which was fine with me—I could sleep in, take care of things, hopefully take the last commuter train out of Darcy. But this seemed off—train'd leave Darcy early, that made sense, but I wondered how often did it head out, again after that?

I tossed my duffle on the bed of my room, stripped naked and shut off the air conditioning that'd been blowing hard since last time the room'd been let, it seemed.

How much was this jaunt costing me?

Train, room for the night, cab, cab again, tomorrow, then the train back, if there was a train back that time of night. Worse case, I'd have to stay in Darcy, get the train day after next, letter off to Herman, but that'd be another room, lots more headache.

Clock showed eight-fifteen. Local directory was right in the drawer with Gideon's, I recognized the number I'd dialed for Lawrence before, was practicing what'd I say to get past his wife she answered again when a man said Hello.

"This Lawrence?"

"Who's this?"

"This is someone needs to talk to Lawrence, rather do it on the telephone than I have to come knock on his door. This Lawrence?"

"This is Lawrence."

"Need you to come out the shop, talk a few minutes about Klia, if that's alright with you."

I ran the hairs of my forearm over my dripping nose through a pause.

"I don't know why there's thought involved in this for you, Stephanie, I'd honestly save us both the hassle of making this a house call, unless Klia' a particularly happy subject with your old lady."

He apologized, voice hushed, but enough normalcy I guessed his wife was near enough he had to make a play pretend who he was speaking with.

"We're putting the kids down, right now."

"I'm happy to let you do that, you tell me when's a good time you'll be out here, tonight though."

He sighed, seemed pathetic how he was unsettled trying to keep his act up, explained he didn't know could he get away just then.

"How about we say by eleven, then?"

"What am I supposed to tell Emily, I'm ducking out on a Thursday night?"

He said that maybe like to sound he was talking to a pal was inviting him for bowling.

"It's I'd be more concerned what I'm supposed to tell Emily, that's how I see it."

I sneezed three times into my elbow, wiped my face into the raised shoulder of my free arm.

"Make it before eleven," I said, hung up, another fit of sneezing, to the sink where I popped three more tablets on my tongue, swallowed them with a mouthful from the tap.

***

Before I left to wait around would Lawrence show up, I ducked into my room with the new photocopy I'd made of the letter, the motel office. I debated should I slip it in the original envelope, or how exactly should I play it? With Klia, it'd been almost obvious I'd give her the original letter, at least some hope at peace of mind, but the thing was different here as flat fact I was only gaming Lawrence with a replica. It didn't mean he was any less in tight he didn't pay me out the two thousand I'd be charging, but this little tick of propriety held me up, especially through the blur of the second handful of medicine tablets getting up over me.

Shouldn't I save the envelope for Herman, some connection to the actual—yes, I decided finally, touching at my lip to find it wet, a sleeve of mucus over it, if there was someone to keep up appearances for it was Herman, Lawrence more a sitting duck I just needed to give the spook to, nothing much of consequence.

I took a seat on some shop steps across from the movie theatre, the plumbing shop in view kind of peripheral, mostly obscured by a shut closed kiosk set to the sidewalk. I smoked and shivered, any chirp of wind a bit different in pitch taking my attention.

It was getting ten past eleven when headlights came up against the theatre face, over the kiosk, little ugly car parked, shut off, the driver keeping put. When no one'd emerged after five minutes, I made a casual stroll to the plumbing shop door, gave it a tug, started to walk away after a glance at the car window I couldn't see through—behind me heard it open, thump shut a dull crack kept mute by the chill, was around the corner, new cigarette just going when Lawrence wandered around.

"If I'm to believe everything I read, you're quite the kisser."

He seemed terrified, not at all the sort I'd pegged him for, easy flab to him, relaxed into his role as husband and daddy.

"How old's the youngest?" I asked, a little tense he'd not gone ahead with so much as a What do you want? in the minute already he'd been there.

"She's four."

"Thing here is I can have as many of these made as I feel like, print them up one a week enough I'd get quite a following I managed to get place let me leave them around."

I handed him the photocopied pages.

"Klia's good with words, don't know if it's flattery or what, but she knows how to fill a page—page five's a real example, you get there yet?"

He hadn't even looked through them, so I suppose he had the idea. I stifled a rising sneeze, sucked phlegm and spit, a long string of it thick from over my chin to my coat sleeve, didn't bother with tugging at it, just took a bit in with a slurp and went right on.

"You can see I'd rather be taking sick time, just today, so we'll do this easy—you get me two thousand, it's the last you'll have to think about it."

It was like it hadn't occurred to him this was going to be the thing, he seemed at a loss.

"When?"

I wiped my palm up over my nose, roughed it into the coat over my ribs.

"Anytime works for you, Stephanie, or what else it'll be is right now, what do you think when?"

"I don't have two thousand dollars."

"Even I have two thousand dollars, it can't be that hard to come by."

"Not in cash."

I spit a long dribble down onto the pavement, made a real thing out of leaning forward, stubbing my cigarette in it, tapping down on it dainty with my shoe toe.

"This town have a bank, cash machine?"

"I can't take out two thousand."

I sneezed, two lines of mucus I felt them slick out my nose, a sheet over my upper lip, didn't touch to clear the mess, stepped in close to Lawrence.

"You might think it's something people'd think

charming you're out getting some dowdy housewife to feel she's found that secret someone while meanwhile your own wife's at home growing your kids up, but I don't think generally it'll play off that way. You think I think you own a shop and there's not some two thousand dollars cash you can get your hands on in a pinch? I'd start thinking with your head right, because that's just exactly what this is, understand me?"

And sick to death of the words tasting of wet salt, I scooped at my face, a loose handful, wiped it a streak across Lawrence's coat front. This seemed to put the matter to him a bit more pointedly, because like a light had gone off his arms came up appeasing.

"Alright, yes, I hadn't been thinking that. There's money."

"Golly, is there? You keep that here or the store?"

"The store."

I nudged my nose he should turn and walk and as he got the door open, just after I told him I'd wait in front, he said "I don't have money, this isn't my money, really, this is payroll, I wasn't thinking about it."

"That sounds like it'll be a real headache, Larry—hey, maybe I'll put a rock through the window to make it look suspect for you, alright?"

He seemed he almost thought the offer was serious, probably he'd swing back by later, do just that very thing except he seemed just smart enough it'd occur to him someone probably was watching us one of these little town windows and that was bad enough, some gossip might make it back his wife's way, no need to give himself any more to dig up out of.

The whole time he was in the shop, I was sneezing, both hands over my face, warm bursts of breath up over my eyes, spilled over my cheeks, three sneezes I'd have a good fistful of slop, kept roughing it on the brick by the glass of the window.

He handed me the letter back with the money, so I gave it back across, but he stepped away, head shaking, wanted nothing to do with it, didn't even want to chance getting rid of it himself in case some little sliver would set off an alarm.

"There's over three grand in there, you'll see, alright? There isn't anything else."

I eyed him, peeked in the bag he'd given me, just as quickly knelt and trundled it into my duffle.

"That's payroll, right, nothing really to do with you. There a cash machine around?"

He looked like he was going to cry. I thought of Klia, but really the comparison was ugly—she'd at least seemed devastated, this guy just seemed a kid I'd outsmarted him he thought he'd drink one soda already while reading the magazines then just pay for another to take with him.

"You said two thousand, there's almost four in there."

"Then I'm sure another five hundred'll make it four and'll save me even thinking about a return trip any time soon, right?"

He said Klia's name, but it was a weird blurt, I couldn't catch any tone of context in it, might've even been he'd been telling me Go get the rest from her. But he fell in to step, I followed him up the way to a cash machine outside the bank, snorting and feeling my stomach loose and ready to turn, hand to grit my teeth and clench my buttocks.

He practically slapped the money at me so I struck him across the mouth with the side of my fist, not hard enough it'd hurt him, I didn't think, but he just kept there, face to the wall like he was seething but knew what'd happen he lost check.

"In fact you put your head against that little wall and you

count two hundred, Steph. I'm walking that way, but I give your house a call twenty minutes, it'd better be you picks up."

I ran my hand over his shoulder a last time like I was using him as a tissue, though I wasn't, sneezed in to that same hand by the time I was half block off in whatever random direction I'd went.

***

I'd ducked into my room just long enough to throw some water on my face, place a call in to Darcy about a taxi, told them I'd be out front of the Horton Super Eight, agreed no problem about paying meter-and-a-half considering the trip out it'd be for their driver.

I could hardly picture some police car rolling up on me, but kept in the bleak, back behind the buzzing sign, sat on an overturned shopping cart full of rocks, figured it was where someone sat their smoke breaks, stubs all around the litter of dead grass.

Regretted not having taken some of the tissues from the room, roll of toilet paper, but it seemed the worst of my cold, allergies, whatever it'd been was now subdued by the tablets I'd taken, my head a wet sock rolled up in another by the time I was in the heated cab, dozing as the driver kept tuning the radio between commercials on various stations.

"You know when the commuter train out of Darcy goes?"

He thought it was at just past six. I looked at the clock—sneaking up on one—asked if there were any cheaper motels inside five minutes walking or so to the station.

"Not five minutes, no. Hotels're all kind of outside the city."

So I told him never mind, he could just leave me at the train, I'd wait.

There was a convenience store open, down a few blocks, bought a nice sturdy document envelope and a book of stamps, more cigarettes, noticed the copy machine so made one more replica of Klia's letter, nothing particular in mind for it, just something to do five minutes, warm pages spit out, glow of the scan crisping against my eyes in stabs.

There was a train left out at quarter past five, boarded that one, saw that a certain compartment had a placard it was a Quiet Car, no talking allowed, lights off, business people listening to whatever on headphones, most of them also either nodding off or else reading paperbacks illuminated by little blubs clamped to the back pages.

By the time I was back in to Mill Creek, my head'd cleared enough air actually passed clean in through my nostrils and drinking a hot coffee too fast settled me back more or less to even, except the sour glaze of fatigue, my eyes hurt to blink against the coming sun changing the sky bright.

Wondered was there some way I could get a buck or two off Herman for the letter, but couldn't come up with an angle'd make it someone would pay me money out to get a letter proved their wife had gone around on them.

In a sandwich shop toilet around midmorning I counted what money I had left—seven thousand three hundred thirty-five dollars, counted it off eight times to be sure. I breathed a long sigh out, proud of myself, though really it meant I'd managed to spend through something seven hundred dollars in two days, calmed myself by calling it all return on investment.

Across the street from where Herman worked, everything seemed strange to me all of a sudden—really there was nothing left to do, nothing but hand a man a letter and that'd be it, nothing left but what I'd been paid to do, only, to begin with. Probably, the feeling was worse for I'd not slept since bleeding the money off Lawrence, that still seemed like where I was though at the same time ages ago, nothing that could ever find me no matter how bad suddenly it might want to. Lawrence'd be having to explain about why he'd not be able to do paychecks that week to his staff, though maybe not even, I'm sure he had enough in the bank to cover it, really he'd just be fretting in the shower, thinking how he was gonna float things this account to that, keep the wife from knowing something was off or else barring that what he was gonna say to keep it had anything to with Klia out of it.

"Klia Klia," I mumbled, looking down at the business envelope I'd prepared, eight dollars worth of stamps in the corner, Herman's name and office address, a name from out of my own imagination as the return.

I had two last cigarettes, put a stick of gum I'd bought in my mouth, got on the elevator up to the office, same receptionist from before, she looked up she'd recognized me.

"For Mister Flake?"

I nodded, started to ask Is he in, but already she was on the phone, saying to probably Herman that a gentleman was there, had been in earlier in the week. She nodded, hung up the phone, took a sip from the fast food drink she had there by the phone, told me he would be right out.

The man who came out of one of the two doors off the waiting area few minutes later looked nothing like his nondescript brother, this one portly but only in the arms and legs, face with a beard shouldn't be on it, easiest guy in the world to describe later only everyone would think you were describing something out of R. Crumb instead of anything actual.

-"Mister Flake?"

He eagerly extended his hand, I gave it a dull, gripless touch.

"Sorry I missed you, was out at a conference, really thought I'd cleared my appointments up better."

"That's fine, it might've been my fault, nothing really except to give you this."

He took the envelope, a grinning nod, I could see his eyes tick on the return address, narrow a bit and he started turning the thing he was gonna open it right there.

"Do I need to sign anything for this?"

I wished I'd thought of something like that, something to've given me a brisk reason to appear and just as quick disappear, instead had to shake my head No, asked did he have anything for me to take back. It was stupid, but the moment of his confusion then his face shake No, no validated me nodding and telling him Thanks again then. I got in through the closing elevator probably just as he was recognizing his wife's handwriting, body shifting a squint, looking up to see maybe was I still around.

I found subway stairs right up two blocks, got down them in the midst of all sets being used by people coming up, fished a ten dollar bill out of my pocket to buy a pass, got on the first line pulled up, set my head to the window then when no one took the seat in front of me to the top of that. I laughed, it hurt to do in that position and kind of my head clogged back up, but I laughed and let myself, rubbing and rubbed my eyes each with three fingers of a hand.

I switched trains, rode to the end of some line, out into the cold afternoon, into a cigarette I hardly bothered to smoke, into an hour spent drifting, reminding myself why the bag I was holding hurt so bad on my wrist.

Noticing a menswear shop, I remembered how I'd wanted to buy that coat before, fondled lapels of suits along the racks until I found a checkered top coat, closed myself in a room to try it out for size. I made the deal that if it didn't drop me below seven thousand up, didn't drop me below seventy-one hundred up, I'd take it, frowned when I saw it cost five hundred, just kept it on and rearranged the insides of my duffle.

I'd forgotten really about the last photocopy, took it up, read some of the boring stuff from the first page. I folded the pages shut, stood up to look at myself, closing the buttons of the coat up around me, slipping the pages into the deep of one side pocket while I touched my thumb to my nose, gave a nice little sniffle.

***

Middle of the night, I woke up from my leg cramping, stood teetering weight down onto it, hopped on one foot to the sink and drank handfuls. I walked to the door, made sure the chain was in place, the blot, gave a tight push with my hip to the recliner I'd moved in front of it.

It was only three, I'd had the room since eleven, watched television awhile, must've fallen asleep just short of one o'clock—it felt I'd be out for hours, days, indefinitely, heavy, blank dreams and I was sweating out whatever the medicine tablets hadn't dealt with.

Woke again at twenty past six, long enough to see it was twenty past six, woke again coming up past noon to the phone ringing, front desk wanting to know did I need the room another day.

"Overslept, no, be out half hour, sorry."

They said if I was out by one, they'd leave it without the late checkout fee.

"I'll be out twenty minutes, do I need to come down the desk?"

"No, housekeeping'll be by at one, long as you're out by then."

The shower was torture to leave, but once dressed, even in my clothes that had a soiled breath of me to them from being worn days in a row, I felt good, different. Got my new coat around me, did it up only center two buttons, scratched at the back of my neck where it seemed there was still a tag, though I knew they'd removed it and had checked dozen times already, too.

It was a good walk down to a larger train station, had two glasses of wine in a lounge after I'd bought a ticket'd take me through Virginia. Deal I made was I wasn't going to think about it until I got off at a main station, no idea was it even remotely close to the address I remembered exactly from Klia's handwritten envelope—one five seventeen Pillowgreen Glen, city'd been called Door, which is what'd stuck it in my mind—but if it was, I'd take a pass at Norman Court, himself. If not, station in Virginia was good enough a place as any to disappear from, awhile.

Being honest with myself, provided there was a place even called Door, close to the station or not, I'd take a turn through it, no point not even trying.

Closed in the train, feeling the most away from everything I'd felt, I leafed halfhearted through the creased up photocopy of Klia's letter, stopped on some passage— her wondering about herself, if she needed to know she was being wrong to feel so much of herself and what did that make her, what did it make her she knew she really didn't care.

By now, Herman'd read this, too—everyone'd read it

but Norman, though I'm sure he'd read the same thing hundred times, other letters, heard it over the phone, across the top of a table they'd met up for lunch, sometime.

I wondered what she'd think of most, Herman confronted her with his replica—him, herself, Lawrence, Norman, me.

Why was I so certain he'd confront her?

Seemed he had enough brain in him to hold some measly office job, didn't take any more brains to know there was nothing between you and a woman you sleep beside her and there's that nothing every night of your life.

Why'd his brother care so much this letter got to him, other than just it was so obviously cruel, some way of proving himself up as something superior in his own mind?

Didn't care, actually, not about that—wondered though was Herman more likely to turn on Lawrence, track him down the yellow pages two minutes flat like I had, put the poor guy through it, drown his life out. Because what was likely to get at him more, his wife'd gone in back of him or some guy'd got sounds from her he'd only dreamed of getting up from anyone?

No, didn't really care about that, not so much anyway, except what'd get back to Klia if it went like that—felt kind of rotten, hoped it went just that way, Herman takes it out on Lawrence, maybe grows one big enough to have some on the side himself, Klia just left alone, out of it, nothing else except what I'd done to her coming her way.

It was Virginia station before I knew it. I'd settled in, must've gotten it confused in my head the trip'd be overnight like the last train, that or just the motion is what'd had me feeling even, because first foot on the platform a tangle of uneasiness got up me, knew what it was I was thinking—like until I'd looked at a map, saw Door as a clear point on a certain bus route, had a cigarette gone two thirds down, every breath out my nose—some muscle somewhere in me was trying to get me to consider just moving on.

It was nothing different than I'd just done twice over, but it was also true those were the two times ever I'd done something like that—the letter now with Herman had took the steam from me, the urgency, Norman was an afterthought could just be kept that way, I let it.

This was a just-now proposition, though, whole thing'd been since the guy'd sat down, hunted me down over I'd made off with his wallet, there wasn't the full taste still in my mouth, it was true, but there was taste enough I couldn't ignore things that were facts.

I got on a bus to Door, the heat inside getting me sweating wet under my coat, the air when I stepped off bringing just as wet a shiver to me, cold through quick, like to my gut.

"Anyone know there's a place called Pillowgreen Glen, something like that?" I asked generally of three people working limply behind the counter of a coffee shop I'd ordered an espresso from.

Turns out it'd be another bus was the quickest way, one I caught down the block, came into a neighborhood more inside a small town than I'd thought it'd be. Address one five seventeen turned out to be an apartment above some shop sold billiard tables.

Not the best feeling, I saw right there on a call box Nor. Court, the black of the type dusted long into grey almost looked like half erased pencil—had no idea why, but I'd pictured something bucolic, a porch, walking up a stone drive and having to pull a screen door back before knocking on old wood, cracked paint.

I hung back the other side of the street, smoked a few cigarettes down, trying to get a feel for whether I thought there might be someone at home, if even someone still lived there, the old brick of the windows, no curtains, giving the place a look of disuse. But customers seemed to go in and out of the store, even when the door opened there was music coming out, place probably was an active hall as well as the shop.

Inside there was a bar area, so I had a bourbon, ordered another just to be able to ask "Some guy Norman Court supposed to live upstairs, here? I rang but no one was answering."

The guy taking my old glass away, pouring my second drink into a new one, said "Norman's up there, always up there, didn't answer he's probably busy calling the cops on us, right?"

I said "Right," guy not even bothering to ask why I'd asked, like everyone asked or at least somebody did, every day.

***

The door to the thin stairwell up to Court's place wasn't locked, but I pressed the callbox button down anyway, heard an odd cackle of static, silence, then a gravel of someone going Was someone there?

"Is that Norman Court?"

I paused, good fifteen seconds went by before the speaker voice saying "This is Norman Court, yes."

I chuckled, kept my finger on the button, leaning in. "Hi, my name's Alain, you don't know me, I know Klia, said I should look you up since I'm in town for something."

Another pause before the speaker told me "Yeah, the door should be open."

"Then I'll come up then, okay?"

No answer. I waited through the rest of my cigarette then got in through the door. It smelled something like chlorine up the well, less and less though as I got to the corridor, found there were three different apartments, one label Fitz Studios, LLC, old applique letters half peeling, half stuck to the door forever.

No one answered the first door I tried, neither had a label, took a moment to bolster myself and tapped gently on what I figured had no choice but to be Norman's door.

A man opened it, genially, stood in the opening and smiled. "You know Klia?"

I nodded, hands folded behind my back, duffle dragging them down, causing me to up more on my heels than I'd meant to. Guy's teeth were off, not horrible, but a peculiar misalignment made it so when he smiled I felt particularly conscious of the fact he was a skeleton down underneath his face.

He invited me in, asked "How's Klia doing?"

I was saying how she was quite well, how I'd been out of touch with her myself the last while and as I went on with this he made a show of locking the door, leaned back against it.

"You're the guy thinks you got rights to her money, isn't that who you are?"

I paused just a beat, set my duffle down, bounced on my toes while I got my cigarette pack out, struck it in my palm a moment, smiling to accentuate this was meant to be applause.

"Great at pretending, aren't you? I guess, yes, that's just who I am and so figure you know just what it is brings me here. Glad to know Klia and you haven't drifted out of touch, these years, good you keep up your pen pals."

He just stared at me, eventually frowned, like he was truly disappointed about me, in particular.

"You're some punk aren't you, graceless kid just comes along thinks you can take what you want, is that right?"

I sighed, long breath of cigarette down my nose, blew it off to one side, lips puckered and bent, sort of wondered how old did he think I was, though he'd probably not meant Kid like that.

"That's just what I am, Norman, I suppose it is. Not that I see much difference that and who anyone else is, but you see my point in things and you know what's gonna happen you don't pay me, here, alright?"

"What's going to happen?"

"Without even using my imagination, I'm gonna have to mail this letter of yours, or else think of something a bit more clever. Looking at you, I'd rather it'd be I take something's yours than I have to go back Klia's way, hate to have to bleed her and bleed her and kind of hate even more what else I have to she gets dry, you know? Really does seem to me she's a good person."

He walked past me, out of the room, rounded the corner into another. I was just starting to get uneasy, squinting was the door chained or what in case he came out with something irrational on his mind, was honestly startled when he threw a number of bundles of money, rubber banded, there on his floor, one sliding just about up to my toe.

"That's a start, Norman—why don't you tell me how much of one, not so much in a counting mood."

"Take it and get out."

I was aware of the touch of my chest to the inside of shirt, felt how dirty it was at the collar. I knelt, took up the first packet, didn't stand, went for the remaining four, got them into my duffle.

"You know what it'll be this turns out it's funny money,

Norman, not that I disagree with your showboating or anything."

"Just get out of here, go off someplace and die."

I lit a new cigarette.

"Someplace and die? Sounds like maybe we're not exactly on the sort of terms I was thinking. You're mad I took a peek at your dirty letter, that it?"

He went back into the other room. I felt myself tense, blood hard in back of my eyes and audible at my temples. Just as quick as he'd gone he was back, threw another two packets at me, told me Klia was a good woman, I had no right even knowing her name.

I took up the money, knelt back at my duffle, put both packs in, then took one out. I tossed it at his feet.

"Klia seems she's a fine woman. She seems she's a fine woman, Norman."

He kicked the money back at me, told me Take it and leave. I looked down at it, at him, his glare, some kind of disapproval I didn't know what it was going on in his mind.

"Alright, you feel that way you can buy up all the she's-a-good-woman you want, far as I'm concerned—I'll take this and she's a used up old hole, far as I think, doesn't know how to take a thing for herself, alright?"

He didn't move, say anything, just looked at me while I put the last of the money in my bag. I zipped it shut, let the weight of it catch hard my arm going limp at my side.

"Get of here, go be your bag of money."

Used the wall to tap out my cigarette, undid the latch he'd closed, keeping my eyes on him, but he wasn't going to move, whatever it was he was just standing there for his little reasons.

"Then I'll do that, piggy bank, you enjoy your piece-of-paper-good-woman."

There was some kind of music from out through the door marked Fitz Studios, now, it got louder somehow, the way it echoed I scuffed my way quick down the steps and outside around a corner.

Wasn't until I'd gotten into what was like a whole other part of the world, wider lawns, a park, some community center people playing games of touch football all around I sat down, used the tree I was leaned against to scratch the base of my head, counted one of the packets it was nine hundred thirteen dollars. I didn't bother with the rest, closed my eyes all the way through two whole cigarettes, even lighting one from the other without looking at anything, flat grey of the sun getting through the clouds getting onto me, convinced myself I could see some difference out through my lids when I'd blow smoke out but didn't know really.

Wondered as I got a cab from a line I noticed all in queue outside some restaurant if Norman'd already been on the telephone to Klia. What'd he told her? I'd been by? He'd paid out money, things'd be fine, nothing to worry about, I was some punk nobody?

No, I didn't think so.

Norman'd keep it to himself, not want her to know a thing, that when I'd given her that letter to burn it hadn't made one tick difference, that I was still out floating around, who knew what was in my head.

Who did know?

Really did hope he wasn't telling Klia anything then pretending there was nothing to tell when she asked.

***

There was a university campus, short walk from where I got off the train, a certain building towering high turned out it was the library, lugged my way up stairs, landing after landing, found a table to sit at, buried in some corner, unzipped my duffle and hardly knowing what to think counted everything.

Just short of eleven-and-a-half thousand dollars.

I sat and hours passed, nobody coming anywhere near me, nobody, nothing, sat there with the duffle, the money, stared at wall, ceiling, shelves with wheels affixed to the ends would spread one away from another.

Eleven thousand three hundred seventy-two dollars, plus I had five or six dollars between all my pockets.

The little area I'd tucked into windowless, I sat until the clock on the wall showed it well into evening.

Outside it was flat with cold, felt darker than it was. I found a coffee shop just closing up, asked didn't they have any left in some pot, they said it was cold, got them to give it to me for nothing.

Three mouthfuls into the cup, five drags down my cigarette, it struck me I'd no idea where to go and couldn't go anyplace I did think of. It just wasn't a good idea to be anyplace, not for awhile—though at the same time I couldn't just stroll around forever, a duffle bag of my dirty change of clothes and the money. I'd need a room for the night, which already felt a drag, but anyway I'd do some laundry, have that little problem solved, was beginning to feel especially unwashed under my new coat, like grime was transferring inside to out, didn't like how there was some spot of coffee, something, already on the cuff, when was I ever going to clean a coat?

Grit my teeth through the price of the first hotel I came to, didn't want to keep walking around, though--was most annoyed that to wash all my clothes it'd cost for two runs of the washer, the dryer, ridiculous considering it was only one pair of pants, underpants, two shirts, four socks, but unless I wanted to wrap up in a bed sheet down the hall it was the two loads, one trip to the machine in my boxers.

Just undressed, holding a cigarette I wasn't smoking, the actual implications got all over me, sulfurous side concerns not enough to keep me distracted. I'd no place to go and eleven thousand wasn't something I could set up home and hearth on—any hump a part time job a pizza parlour made twice that a year, now it was absolutely all I had, everything, it and a change-and-a-half of clothes.

What was I thinking I'd do—get to someplace new, find a place to live, get set up and what's it cost to do that?

Added on top, I'd only been able to support myself as I had on suitcases, stolen wallets, little grifts and franchise pawnshops because I knew some ins and outs of the town, had sofas, floors of people I could impose on, become a kind of fixture, harmless although everyone'd more or less the right idea about just what I did, day to day.

New town, what'd I know from what?

Nothing.

I got into any sort of comfortable groove, necessities sorted out, what'd my little nest egg've dwindled to?

I was neither infuriated nor numb, just pacing, insecure, felt abnormal, thoughts miles behind where they should ought to've been.

Before I knew it, I was waking up eight in the morning.

Didn't bother to shower, collected up the clothes from how I'd arranged them for the two strategic trips, put on the shirt visually seemed the cleanest, under my coat it wouldn't matter, either way.

Middle afternoon by the time I was on a full bus, random middle aisle seat, trying to keep my calm, nodding off, chin to the duffle my arms wrapped around, not understanding why I couldn't keep awake. At some rest area I could see a decent sized town an easy walk, wandered away, ate cheap hamburger, downed a coffee too hot to get a refill straight away, sat in the toilet to straighten my thoughts, get things in order.

Already it was down to eleven thousand two hundred something—this couldn't be maintained, just moving burned this fuel up. To keep from torturing myself, I drew a line under eleven thousand flat, understood the two hundred or so on top needed to be sunk on one more room, one more night, whatever was thriftiest from the Goodwill—that and enough to rent some cabinet out someplace at least a month, take care of I'd have someplace to put the money. Week or two wandering around, professional loitering someplace innocuous, see how things'd fell.

Had an awful sleep after two hours with the phone book comparing prices, storage lots over P.O. boxes, woke up to outside it'd snowed but now sleet was dousing itself over top that, everything ugly, upturned scab looking.

Picked up the room phone to dial Murray's place, puzzled through how to get a non-local call to go out. Very least, I'd maybe get Murray to pack up some stuff of mine, clothes, whatever he thought of, I'd meet him on a quick swing through town, step down the train, get the bag, move on.

Murray answered, said "How's Kansas?" after we'd traded Hellos—he was obviously a bit put off it was me calling.

"It's swell. You let the room?"

He sighed, I knew he was rolling his eyes, probably had a movie on pause he wanted to get back to. "No, man, your deposit has reserved your perpetual spot, worry not. Policeman was here looking for you, though."

I stared at the hotel painting above the bed, watercolor western scene, horses and no people, sun the same color as the hills of field it sank in.

"Which policeman, what do you mean?"

"A policeman, I don't know which."

I could tell he was walking with the phone.

"Left a number, card?"

"A number, wrote a number you should call him about whatever it is."

I leaned in toward the painting, tried to get an idea of my reflection in the darker spots of it under the glass.

"Policeman didn't have a badge, a card right? What'd he look like?"

"I'm sure he had a badge, something. Plainclothes, detective somebody or another."

"He just wrote telephone number on a sheet of paper, that seemed straight with you?"

There was a pause, didn't know what I was bothering Murray for, knew who it was, guy I'd took his wallet and'd given me the letter to deliver to begin with—wouldn't be able to describe him either except he didn't look like anyone.

"Alright well, either a real policeman or else a pretend policeman wrote a telephone number down, said you should call him and so you want that number or not?"

"What did he look like?"

"Guy in a suit, looked like someone either was a policeman or else pretending to be a policeman and said he was with the police, he wanted to talk to you about something. You want the number?"

I wrote it in the margin of one of the local restaurant menus left by the lamp, asked Murray could he get a bag of my stuff all together, but I couldn't come up with an answer when he asked what I wanted him to do with it, told him I'd call him back and could he do me a favor, not tell anyone I'd called.

"You need your twenty bucks back with everything?"

I told him Yeah, if he still had it, but he said he didn't, laughing, told me to call him when I wanted to pick everything up.

***

Spent the start of the day with checking out of my room, getting directions from the desk clerk to a storage place few blocks down, renting out a small storage unit, like half a closet, bit heavier in cost than a bus station locker but I couldn't make myself easy with one of those. Didn't want to have to come back any time soon, so took out eight hundred dollars to get me by, told myself consider it all I had in the world and treat it accordingly, tracked down a commuter train got me well away by nightfall and took out a room a motel advertised weekly rates made the seven days equivalent to three nights regular, parking lot lined with tractor trailers and vans, place just down from a freeway entrance.

I walked to the end of the line of strip malls—mile, mile-and-a-half of nothing but them—bought myself a squat bottle of vodka someplace as I went, kept on a bit further getting myself warm with it, smoking cigarettes from fingers I couldn't feel. Eventually I settled on a particular public telephone, out in front between a veterinarian office and a shoe store some shopping center closed down for the night, already. Took my time arranging the coins I'd broke a ten for, set them on the shelf there used to a phonebook someone'd made off with for whatever reason. Took another swallow, dropped the coins down and dialed the numbers out.

Few rings in, guy answered I could tell he was in someplace public but could tell also that as soon as I'd said You left this number for me he'd excused himself, was moving out away from whoever he was with, sounded like in a restaurant.

"Trevor," he said, getting his breath, "well there you are, was worried you wouldn't get my number."

I knew who he was and more or less where, knew he was standing outside someplace just as cold as where I was, easy to picture. I hated he knew my name, or that he'd said it, anyway, obviously he knew it.

"Thought we'd settled on we weren't seeing each other again, ever, now it's been what a fortnight?"

He laughed, a chuckle I could tell was out his nose, he must've been lighting a cigarette his own which reminded me to take a tap off mine before it went cold.

"That's funny and you're right, you're right. Though we're not really seeing each other, right? I don't think really we're going to ever have to, we just need to find out some way for you to pay me the money it seems you owe me."

I'd taken a mouth of vodka he'd been talking, took my time swallowing, the rise of what I'd downed before getting me loose, rocking while I spoke, uneven from on my toes, flat, on my heels.

"I owe you money now's how you've figured it out? That's interesting. Don't have a math book on me, but counting things off my fingers I don't come up with how that's supposed to work out."

I'd emphatically raised my middle finger while rambling this out, really amused with myself, leaned against the brick and had another swallow, deciding not to bother with starting up another cigarette.

"Terrible thing's happened, Trevor, unfortunately

something though that we have to act accordingly about—not to say it wasn't something'd crossed my mind was a possibility, though can't say it was exactly expected—it seems Herman got bent out of shape with things so much he decided he'd go and shove a bullet right out through the top of his head."

I smiled, rubbing my neck, reached to the phone top to take my bottle back up from where I'd set it, surprised it had maybe just one more tilt left in it.

"That's really quite a thing, something else, I guess, though like you say it's not outside the realm of what to've expected might go happening someone reads a letter wrote all in detail like that and all the time it's their own wife's the one who wrote it."

"You're absolutely right. Like I said, it had occurred to me, couldn't say the news was so surprising to me, but what I must say did give me a bit of a startle was that Herman went ahead beforehand and shoved four other bullets right into Klia while she was relaxing in her evening bath."

I tapped my forehead on the side on the phone enclosure, closed my eyes hard enough I heard a kind of rumble in my ears, got the screw cap off the bottle with one hand, heard it hit the cement, swallowed what was left inside, looked at the empty a moment before dropping it, giving it a gentle kick out down the curb into the lot.

"That is pretty terrible, I see what you mean there. Though seems it doesn't keep you feeling just tickled pink with yourself, the whole thing, right? Same time, too, interesting all as it is, seems beside the point to I owe you some money, doesn't it?"

There was lengthy pause, maybe him finishing his cigarette, maybe waiting while someone passed.

"Trevor, just what is it you think you've been doing?"

"Don't see why I'd feel like answering you that, man—you want to know about doing things, go do them."

That gave him a kick or else he was good at fake laughing, really seemed I'd put a smile on his face.

"I honestly don't think I'd even know how to begin doing things, not as industriously as you, for sure. And look, not wanting to keep you on the phone too long and I've got to get back in here a minute—way it turns out is that what sounds pretty open and shut about Herman and his wife, one minute, gets complicated just the next when someone gets in touch with the police, thinks there might be more to the two of them going dead than appearances would indicate."

I didn't want to listen, didn't care, didn't respond and he let it keep silent just long enough I got a beat breath out my nose before he went on to where I already knew it was he was driving.

"Guy named Norman Court, you might've heard of him, he seems to be convinced that someone blackmailed Klia off a couple thousand dollars, then did the same to him, on top, and so now that's got everyone trying to be clever thinking Why would someone go and do that? and Isn't it funny that'd be something happens right before this other thing?"

"Yeah, yeah," I said, rolling my head around my neck, "as fascinating as all that is and of course we both know that you know it was me bled them off some money, that's money not one bit of it is coming to you so I'm going to tell you just it's been great chatting but then I think it's time we say Goodnight."

"Trevor, you hang up and we haven't decided to get square on this—where, when, and to what dollar amount—it is not going to go nice for you and I'm being missed at dinner so let's get these finer points sorted out."

I hung up, vodka hitting me I'd not've said much coherent I had kept on the line, got around a corner and just couldn't manage getting a cigarette lit up for my fingers, the steady pinch of breeze to the night.

Heard the payphone back behind me ringing, perked up, made my way back to it and took back the coins I'd set on the shelf, shoved them in my coat pocket, watched the receiver as the ring groaned, sounded like frozen tin cans clattering in a bag.

Felt soft and feverish, my palms actually hot, didn't seem to be sweating when I touched them, just hot, points of heat all through me from the alcohol, I supposed. Phone had stopped ringing, didn't start again. I picked up the receiver, hummed along with the dial tone under my breath a second, set it down.

***

I drank coffee in the dark, listening to television in the slaps of it blue and grey to the wall, the ceiling, then laid still half listening waiting for my drunk to wear down—I ran the shower a few times but never stepped in despite I was shivering even with the heater on, likely needed steam to get all through me to feel even a handful better.

If I closed my eyes, all'd happen was after a few minutes, thoughts corkscrewing, I'd come to realize they'd opened and I'd been putting both hands to my face, moving them away, putting them to my face, something I'd done as an adolescent, little habit I'd only ever catch myself doing now I'd gone under a few shots too many.

A few times I got anxious, couldn't force myself to recall the full telephone conversation with the guy—I'd drift asleep, wake up going over some dreamed version the talk, try to get it sorted, fall back asleep and this'd repeat.

By nine in the morning, I was waking, felt I'd gotten stable, shower had me feeling normal except I was sniffling, head clogging up if I sat or even stopped pacing. Once the four-cup packet provided free in the room, literally labeled *Budget Coffee,* had heated and I could swallow hot sips from it, I didn't feel like doing anything but pacing, anyway.

Whatever it'd been with the guy on the phone, all it'd really done was cement I had to get lost, no chance of resettling back in town, not with he'd be able to track me down whenever he wanted without even much effort. Other than that, didn't see what he could do. It wasn't something he was going to turn me in, as this'd at the very least bring some scrutiny to him, have him having to explain himself when I explained myself—seemed he had a regular life, couldn't see it he'd be going out of his way hunt me down for some few thousand dollars'd do nothing but be a headache to him, all things totaled.

No. His thing'd been a little chance, bluff of sorts, I'd called it and now things stood just where they stood.

Two o'clock, I'd settled on I'd have to get back by to grab my money out of storage, grimed my way back into my unwashed clothes and made up my mind I'd spring for something off the ready-to-wear rack JC Penny or wherever, not bother about thrift stores the hassle of finding something'd fit—best to think of things like I had ten thousand dollars, clear, everything above that just consider it spent, price of getting myself out.

Went down the front desk, told the woman working I'd had a sudden change come up, wouldn't need the week and could I get back the remainder of my money. She explained I was already there my second day and since I was leaving those two days'd be charged out the regular rate, not the pro-rated cost based on a full week's stay.

"I've been here just the one day, last night this morning."

"Housekeeping's gone for the day, past checkout—you're here two nights, last night through tomorrow morning, if you want the third day back we can get it to you."

Two days was practically the week already, and as she wasn't budging I doubted the manager'd deal anything better. Decided I'd stay until next morning, maybe even stay out the week, catch my breath.

I bought a brown suit on special some shop up the row of strip malls, bought three colored t-shirts, set of four pair of socks and two pair of boxer briefs came bundled, got back to my room just coming up on evening, started some laundry going.

Took a lazy shower, not really scrubbing myself until real quick the last minute, sat dripping on the edge of the one of the two twin beds I'd not laid in, had a cigarette, starting another just flipping the television on when there was a knock at the door, deep toned thup thup thup. Figured it might've been the manager about the room rate, I'd just go down the desk a little while, but there was another knock, exact same tone, duration, rhythm.

Eyed out the peephole, there were two uniformed policemen there, recoiled, cigarette rolling across the floor, knelt to get it up before something caught fire, tossed it the sink basin and got a towel around me, briefly glancing a look in the mirror—panic, blatant panic. I stared at myself and there was another knock.

"Sorry, just finishing up the shower, wasn't sure it was my door."

Both officers nodded, one asking was I Trevor English.

"I'm Trevor, sure. Everything alright?"

"We were wondering if you had a minute to come with us, some questions they'd like to ask you."

"They'd?"

"Some detectives."

I nodded, meeting eyes with the officer standing behind the one talking, back to the talker.

"Questions about what, sorry? I'm just in town, last night."

The officer talking shrugged, said it was something better to go into with the detectives, re-asked did I have time to come along but with a tone that every single little thing I was doing was being run through some filter they get the academy—best bet to just say Yes, worst bet at the same time.

"I'm just getting dressed, give me one minute?"

They nodded, let me close the door, I made certain not to lock it and just started getting in my clothes.

If it wasn't here, it've been somewhere they'd've found me. Whole line seemed pretty clear—guy I'd made the phone call to him he has the number, this gets him the general area, he goes and drops some tip the authorities some sly way, whatever. After that, how long is it supposed to take track me down, all the time I'm using my own ID anyway because why should I've been thinking I shouldn't?

Nothing around the room to incriminate me, though, so easiest thing'd be play it straight like I don't know anything about any of it, other than they'd been given my name I couldn't see what else they'd know I couldn't just deny it.

Getting my coat done up, I reached to the pockets for cigarettes felt the last of the photocopies of Klia's letter there, froze.

What was best, though? Stash it in the room really quick—did that and they got some reason to search, it'd be found out—or keep it on me—again, anything went they had reason to detain me, my pockets'd be turned out, there it'd be.

Knock at the door, very polite, not like before, I got a cigarette to my lip, patted around on myself no real point, opened the door with an apology for the wait.

"Not under arrest, right? Was thinking about early dinner, maybe do some bowling up the way, later."

"We're not arresting you. Thank you for cooperating, hope to have you back in no time."

I smiled, the officer letting me walk ahead of him and I could hear his partner lingered back a few steps, was saying something down into his radio I didn't know what.

I was sat in the back of a patrol car, left there, officer who'd escorted me walking across to the hotel office. He's the only one got back in the car, but I noticed there was a second patrol car, saw the other officer having a smoke leaning on its hood, like he'd nowhere else necessarily he had to be.

***

Station I was sat in was more a kind of substation, looked like a carryout restaurant from in front and in back looked about what I expect the offices of such a restaurant're like, thin hallway, five or six doors down along it. I was sat at a table in the third door down, told a detective'd be in shortly, that it'd be fine I wanted to smoke.

I stood when the detective entered, shook his hand to a brief little nod from him sitting down asking me did I know someone name of Klia Flake.

"I don't know her, no, no one like that I said," sinking in behind my cigarette. I'd been really hoping things weren't going to take this tack at all, let alone straight up in front, now just like that, one question in, I'd settled into the version of things I'd have to keep up, no room to get an idea what angle was being presented, bide my time.

"You don't know her husband, maybe? Herman Flake?"

"I don't."

There wasn't an ashtray, kind of made a face was it alright to ash on the floor, detective slid across a sheet of paper he nabbed up from on top the small filing cabinet behind him, my flick to cigarette dotting a broken bunch of grey across the blank page, still some bits getting on the table.

"What brings you to town?"

"Nothing particular, really couldn't even tell you what is this town. Came in the train, took out a room."

"For the week."

I nodded, it clearly hadn't been a question. "For the week, yeah."

"Except something came up today you need to leave early?"

I ashed, most of it missing the paper, one bit burning a tiny hole, brief flag of smoke vanished before it'd dwindled up two inches.

"Told that to the clerk, yes, but no, nothing came up, just the room is crumby and I'm only wasting some time no reason to it, on the outs with some friends, figured I can do better, no need to take a week out in a dump on impulse."

"Okay," he said, made some note of something in a paper out of his file folder. "What about someone named Norman Court?"

I tensed, mind churned for anything, but he didn't even wait for a response, leaned back rubbing his eyes, genuinely looked sleepy.

"I should tell you you're here because Mister Court

alleges that somebody bullied him for some money, gave a description, a picture was done and somehow we got informed by someone that the picture looked a lot like you, like someone named Trevor English—in fact it does look just like you—and got told at the same time that you're in town here, supposed to be meeting this someone who placed this call to us, instead."

I nodded, my cigarette nearly down to the stub, held it like a dead bug making a face I didn't know where I should put it out, detective smiling, sighing that the floor'd be fine. I stepped it out, set my pack on the table, offered one the detective and he took it eagerly. I lit his from mine, handed it over the table, said I had no idea about was I meeting someone, I really was just on the outs with pretty much everyone I know, taking a trip around to keep my head clear.

He nodded, took a few drags like he was just enjoying his own little thoughts about something unrelated, then took a drawing looked just like me from his file, asked me could I have a look.

"Looks just like me, sure does."

I moved it back in his direction, he just letting it stay on the table—I wished I'd turned it, thing looked it was giving me the eye, straight on.

"It does look like you. It does. And the drawing at least, it looks exactly like someone stopped by Herman Flake's office two times, week or so ago, claimed he had an appointment, at least it does according to the receptionist."

I could feel my thoughts getting knotted around each other, part of me trying to figure who else might've seen the drawing or where else I'd given my ID they might've already checked on, but with no time for these thoughts while at the same time responding, pretending like this was all out in left field as far as I was concerned, I had to concentrate to just keep up a nonchalance didn't come off as distracted, come out with just flat answers suggested nothing, either way.

"It does look like me," I repeated. "Someone looks like me, I guess."

Detective took up the paper, put it away, repeating that it looked like me, but adding almost as though it was something he wanted to emphasize in good humor, that it looked Exactly like me.

"What happened between you and your friends?"

I blinked, asked what did he mean.

"You're on the outs about what?"

I made a face it was none of his business and just as I thought maybe I'd vocalize that, as well, there was a knock on the door, the detective excusing himself, coming back in just thirty seconds after. He sat, leaned to stub the cigarette I'd given him out on the floor, tossed the extinguished stub into a small wastebasket—my own was still just mashed in a dark smear of soot by a leg of the desk. He looked at me, really earnest.

"Trevor, I have to tell you it's thin, what you're saying is coming across as thin to me. But one thing I know from this life is You never know—could be even though it sounds thin, it all might be fine. But I've just got my information and so'm not seeing your version of things as clearly as the picture I've got, already. That's fair, right?"

"It seems fair, sure."

"I'm going to ask you—unless you have something else to say to me—to step outside here in front of the station, there's someone is going to have a look at you. Now, if this person says they know you, I'll have to put you under arrest and we'll have to press into all of this a bit more at odds with each other—and remember, this picture it looks a lot like you, so if you have something else you maybe forgot to tell me about anything it might be time to think about telling me what that is."

I knew exactly how guilty I looked, knew the detective had me pegged full on, couldn't even bring myself to say anything—I was done as far as he was concerned, no matter who was out front to give me a look said this or that about it. There was a disgusting urge to confess, or not even that, urge to blubber and just ask him leave me alone, but I got standing, mumbled could I have a cigarette I went out, or would that slant the looker's ability to identify me.

"You can have a smoke. You want to take a minute, have a smoke here, then we can step outside?"

I was shaking my head even while he indulged himself with his fatuous little question.

We got back down the corridor, out through the front, uniformed officer who'd brought me down standing middle of the lot, his patrol car in a space about twenty paces further on. Detective stopped me, positioned me. I flicked my cigarette out into the lot, upset I'd done so, watching the blue and grey smoke from it tangling in scraggly billows about third way between me and the uniformed officer.

Stood there what seemed a few minutes before the patrol car flashed its lights, flashed them again. Stood there another minute, the detective holding up his hand, keeping it elevated, then the lights flashing once, twice, detective's arm slowly lowering to his side, hanging there limp like it was an empty sleeve the wind was enough to sway, same wind now rolling my dead cigarette in hobbling little rolls down along the lot.

"What's that mean?" I asked when no one'd said anything or looked at me another minute, nothing else from the parked car.

Detective turned to me, smiled, eyes tight like fists.

"It means it wasn't a picture of you, turns out."

I kept his eye a moment, switched to a quick squint at the patrol car, hands down in my coat pockets, one gripped around my cigarettes, other flat against the pages of the folded letter.

***

Dropped back at the motel by the officers, it was dark, mist to the air made it seem it'd snow, orange tint to the sky. Some kind of impromptu parking lot get together was going on, rooms on the lower floor had their doors open, televisions on in each room barking out and people wandering in and out, room to room.

I went right into the office, supposing I'd ought to show myself in case something'd been done to the room, needed to sign something—also still thought I might ask for my refund of one day since I wasn't staying the full week, definitely.

Skinny older guy was rubbing his eye, hard, three fingers, don't even know he registered the electric bell of the door opening, though he didn't seemed startled at my being there. I kind of shrugged, told him I'm Trevor English, there was a thing I had to go with the police earlier, just want to be sure everything's alright the room.

He nodded, concentrating on something, made a gesture of both hands like he was shaking something, then said, bit of an exclamation "English, yeah somebody called for you. Trevor English?"

"Yes." My stomach felt bloated and ready to sink. "They leave a message?"

"That you should call him."

He handed me a card, I took it, not even giving it a glance.

"Room should be fine. Have your key? What was it happened, the police?"

I doddered my head, excused myself I was beat, he didn't seem to care.

Entered my room tentatively, but straight away got the impression not anyone'd been in. Checked under the bed though, checked the windows were locked, found it didn't seem they even could open.

Remembering about the letter in my pocket, spent awhile at the sink burning it, tearing it into little squares to minimize smoke, doused each bit quick in a trickle I kept from the tap. I was done five pages, three cigarettes smoked, when the room phone rang. I let it ring out, hollow aftertone of it seemed to fill the room two minutes.

I knew there was a chance it'd been the guy who'd paid me to deliver the original letter to Herman'd been the one hadn't identified me down the station lot, stood a better chance it was Norman Court, though. Meant I needed to think up something clever to do about that, just didn't feel up to thinking about anything at all. He'd obviously some reason in particular to not serve me up, especially he'd spent the time'd come all the way out a moment's notice the police'd gotten the tip I was in the area. Not likely he was driving back to Virginia—and to punctuate this, the room phone went off again, rang until it went out, I was just through the ninth of the photocopied pages, fifth cigarette, pack just about spent.

Best thing wait until morning, call a cab, have it waiting—even have it wait the other side of the motel so it didn't give anyone away the idea it was me getting into it. Cab drivers didn't care about sneaky things like that, I'd ask for the car to park other side the motel ten minutes, pay the meter for that on top of the fare, leave the room like I was off for a walk, someplace for a drink, make the quick break around, cab'd have me up onto the freeway one minute.

I smiled at my reflection, but the smile looked patronizing back toward me, so I narrowed my eyes at myself, muttered something about I'd like to see you come up something clever, then.

Same time, it struck me if it was Norman calling, why'd he do that not just come up the room?

Police might be watching me, maybe, meant they see him coming around they'd get to wondering why didn't he put the finger to me he had the chance, officially—the detective knew no problem I'd something to do with everything, served to reason he's just as iffy about Norman, every reason to be.

I waited for the phone to ring, but it didn't another hour, another hour.

To put myself in better spirits, I considered that Norman getting me off the hook more or less freed me up a good bit, the final analysis. Definitively, a man who'd been blackmailed'd said no question I'm not the person'd did it, while meanwhile I actually was—since no one else with any authority existed'd be brought into things I didn't much have to fret being stopped or tracked down, at least not by authorities.

Get on a bus, get a ticket I'm sure no one's getting on the same bus with me to be bothered about, then lose myself again the first stop someplace, weave back around to the storage locker my money—locker at least I'd got under a made believe name, storage unit rentals are good that way.

Soon enough it got to be next morning, I'd not slept five minutes solid. Put a call into a taxi could they send a driver out, wait out in back I'd throw twenty dollars on top the fare—dispatcher had no problem about it, said driver'd head out, wait around until middle next hour.

"Tell him leave the motor idling."

"No problem."

Commonplace request, it seemed. I hung up feeling almost normal with everything until there was knock on the door. Looked out the peephole it was Norman—he wasn't at the ready, looking for some change the bulb of the peephole his side of the door, was just leaning on the railing, kind of his back halfway to me.

I was through my last cigarette he knocked again. Sat to the bed, wondered was the cab in back yet. Norman out there didn't seem it changed anything really, just I'd have to literally make a fast break, hope he wasn't just gun in his pocket set on cutting me down broad daylight, lost to caring about anything.

Another knock went on comically long, like he was tapping a song but I couldn't pick up any tune if he was.

"What do you want, Norman?" I said, mouth to the door, then moved a little to the side in case he really did have a gun.

"I didn't know your name was Trevor, I wouldn't have thought it was," he said, not even raising his voice to be sure it'd get through the door plank.

"That's interesting, yeah? Guess I've never really thought it'd be my name either, just's been my name. What do you want?"

Sound of his voice changed, like now his mouth close up the door, maybe side of his cheek to it, he was more audible but at the same time seemed he was keeping more hushed, maybe hands cupped to contain the direction of the words.

"I want to know who gave you that letter."

I stared at myself leaning against the wall by the door in

the mirror, just looked at myself. Finally sighed big, watching me move, said "It was Herman's brother, alright? So can you get lost?"

"Which brother?" he said, the words awkward, like drips to the floor of something melting.

"The non-descript one, didn't know there was more'n just him. One doesn't look like he's anybody"

"Herman doesn't have any brother."

I watched myself in the mirror close my eyes, really felt like I saw myself do it.

"Who gave you the letter?"

Opened my eyes, looked straight across at myself was like I'd been watching back the whole time.

"Please, Trevor, could you open the door?"

I walked to the sink, scrubbed my face with wetted palms, dried it a damp towel smelled off even though I'd only ever used it just once, earlier.

Norman'd moved a pace or so off as he heard me getting the latch open. I told him there was a taxi out the back, go down give the driver thirty dollars then we'd walk someplace for a drink.

***

Asked the waitress did they sell cigarettes, tried to not think about she'd said No but there was the gas station across the street. Norman'd gone to the toilet, which time I'd considered slipping out, but as I hadn't already and Norman seemed tame, if peculiar, figured I'd do best to figure out where his mind was.

Back to the booth, Norman sipped his coffee while I stared at the bourbon I'd not touched, played at the side of the glass with my thumb, tapped my fingernail. Tired of it all, Norman not talking, even looking at me, I told him I appreciated he'd seen fit to do right, get me off the hook with the police, but other than that there was nothing to do with anything me and him, me and Herman, me and Klia—said that name, he gave a look right at me made me slow through the rest of my list, dribbled to a stop, took a sip of drink.

"I could tell you were an awful person the moment I saw you."

Cleared my throat a bit, leaned back, said "Could tell you were a pervert got off reading how other guys're humping the gal of your dreams second I opened that letter, your name the front."

He casually reached across, took up my glass—I tensed a bit, thought he was going to give it to me in the face, instead he drank it down, set it empty next to his coffee, nothing I could have a word with him about with him the one paying.

"You didn't have to deliver that letter to Herman, but you did. You'd gotten everything you wanted."

This bit made me think I'd pegged it right early on he was some talk-doctor. Looked around, caught the waitress' eye, did some pointing gesture she nodded at she'd bring another drink over next free moment she had.

"I was hoping you might kill the man who'd given you that letter."

I grinned. "Can't think of a reason I'd ever do anything like that, Norman, sorry that's what brought you out this way."

"I thought perhaps the reason could be you feel indebted to me for realizing that you're just an awful person, scum beside anything to do with what's happened, and realizing that I let you go."

"Played that hand a bit silly, didn't you? Also you've got the wrong idea about I'm awful—go kill someone yourself that's what you're so interested in."

He shook his head, easing the messenger bag he'd been wearing since the hotel off his shoulder, setting it on the table.

"I couldn't make myself so dirty. I wish I could. And I'd have no idea how to find someone so ugly as you, again, a person who could do it."

He pushed the bag across, cartoonish in the drama. I got the idea he was someplace else, had a half asleep look inside his eyes for all the intense way he kept them on me—sad look, I believed him about not wanting to be dirty, that he was somewhere inside some story his own and things like that were actual.

"Got the wrong idea about me, that's the only thing, alright? I'll take a bit of money get a letter place to place, take a little money don't take a letter place to place—yeah, then guess I'll just do what I want. That's all, though. Don't want your bag, whatever's in it."

Soon as the waitress put down the new drink, Norman nodded thanks at her, took it over and downed it between three tilts of it back, cheeks bulged full from the third, first two sort of to build a momentum.

"You don't have to tell me you've done it, I'll know. All I need is you to tell me you promise."

"I don't promise. Want me to take some money in some bag, I'll take the money you don't need it, that's all'll happen here. I'll be honest with you that far because you did right by me, that's all you'll get from me anything like I promise."

He pushed the bag all the way over the lip of the table, my end, fell onto the bench next to me, a little way on top of my leg.

"Look at you, Trevor. You'll never have anything because you're nobody."

I leaned in over the table top, got my head a bit

sideways. "Look at you, Norman. Never had anything, nothing now, only got someone you think's nobody to go crying to about it."

His face seemed asleep, like all of this's just what he'd daydreamed hundred times the ride over from Virginia, felt I was smoothed into his script no trouble, got thinking maybe he knew just what he said he knew about me, that he knew what I knew about him was the truth and didn't care.

"I don't promise and your make believe girlfriend is dead for you couldn't keep her not dead, can't do anything about it now, so you want your money-bag back you ask it back, otherwise I'll take it you paid it to me for giving you things straight, then you can go off someplace and die, yourself."

When he stood I went a little bit cold, felt my gut shut in tight like I'd swallowed something heavy enough it'd dropped straight down me, stuck. Not even looking at me, he moved by, gave my shoulder a touch, the hair of my head—I'd not even noticed he'd left money on the table cover the drinks until after he'd gone out the door.

Waitress came around, asked her did what was on the table cover enough her tip and one more drink. She eyeballed it, said it would, so I asked her to leave another for me I get back from the toilet, she could keep whatever else on top.

Both stalls were open, so I closed myself in the wider one, sat sideways on the seat, eyes to the door, not trusting Norman wouldn't be through any moment some pistol he'd left his car, wherever, still had a spook to me from how he'd just wandered off.

Undid the three buttons the bag, first thing my eyes set on was the pistol then there beneath it however much money it was, rolled in those awkward bundles just like

Norman'd thrown at me before. Short little gun, way I always pictured a gun, compact, almost alive like it'd wrap itself around the outsides of someone's fingers itself. Gun looked so heavy made the money beneath it seem soft, tissues'd been used over and over and waded.

I downed the bourbon waitress'd left without sitting, made my way to the motel office at a trot, waited behind someone checking in, woman from the first day working, giving me a nod.

"Not past check out, is it?"

She shook her head.

"Like to get my third day back, then, before I'm charged the week."

While she rolled her eyes, explaining she'd go get some form I'd have to sign, I scanned around the suddenly empty, dust white lot through the glass of the office door, nothing except a snapping from the plastic bag the trash bin over by the newspaper machines, faint shush of the freeway traffic up the hill.

I signed the paper, she gave me back the one day in cash minus some cancelation fee I didn't bring up my qualms about.

"Hank gave you your message this morning?"

I'd turned to look out the lot while she was talking, slowly turned back making a long M sound before the actual word Message. "No. Yesterday. Someone'd left a number, Hank told me, yeah."

"Called again this morning, wants you to call him."

She handed me the number she'd jotted on a card. The lot outside'd just gone grey from white, sun on it now down through stiff line of clouds.

***

Couldn't relax right the whole time on the train back toward where I'd got the unit to store my money. New money I'd transferred into my duffle, arranged it the way I liked it to look—gun was in the duffle, too, I'd checked was it loaded and when it was left it that way, wrapped it in two shirts, very uncomfortable the thing'd go off, something'd get its trigger down I let it bounce around loose.

Taxi'd out to the storage unit right away, mostly because I didn't know what was I going to do about getting a room, anything, without using my ID, wanted to go a long while, get myself lost far away before I chanced using it again—if I could manage something smart, never have to mess around with it again that'd be even better.

It was with thoughts in my head weren't getting me anywhere on the subject of fake identification I came up to my unit, took the key for the lock I'd bought out my duffle, stared at the shut up mound of the gun a moment, zipped the bag.

Everything was fine, old money right where I'd left it, separate plastic bag of trash inside a larger bag of trash, just paper, nothing'd go off sour—really I thought the whole ruse was silly now, someone bothered to break in some storage unit saw it's just a trash bag they're gonna look in that bag.

Toyed with the idea could I sleep in the unit, just the night, maybe hole up a good week—vanish without going anyplace, no one'd expect I'd just stayed around—but there didn't seem to be any way to lock the thing the inside.

Added to which, who wouldn't expect? Who'd I think it was looking?

It was nagging thoughts of things left undone I knew was keeping me from just getting a train across the country, couldn't shake that too much was going I'd no control over it to let me relax. Same time, didn't know how to close anything out—Norman and the guy'd given me the letter to deliver the first place, they both wanted something, now, had money from one of them kill the other, other one wanting money from me I'd bled off everyone else.

I laughed, but then stopped myself because it seemed like something a person losing control of his wits'd do, laugh when certainly there wasn't something to laugh at.

Smoked down half pack of cigarettes, gently pushing the duffle full with everything around the space the side of my foot. No, couldn't just take off I had this money someone'd paid me I'm supposed to go kill someone else—though at the same time, why not? If I was gone I was gone, couldn't picture anyone being able to track me down.

Thing was though, again: eventually I'd need to use my ID for something, eventually I'd come up somehow someone'd be able to find me they were looking, not like I could live forever in hotel rooms on the spoils, the sixteen thousand in the duffle didn't buy me a new me and I'd no idea how go about being someone else.

Did I want to go living back on Murray's sofa, whoever's, back to petty theft get myself through the day to day, nothing else but that?

Gave the bag a hard kick, tensed down like that'd been a bad idea, gun'd go off I behaved like that.

That's all I had to go back to, either way—except I could get a job, figure out some grift maybe, except even to do that I needed name, social security number, needed everything like that, everything that'd keep me situated one place anyone could come along find me.

Locked the duffle down in the unit, kept out a solid thousand, took a minute to go through my pockets, discard whatever little scraps and loose coins'd collected.

Two cards both with the same phone number written on them, same number as the guy;d given me before— thought it must be some gas station cell phone he'd bought, maybe I ought to get one instead of always sniffing around for payphones.

It was this guy who was the real threat, really, Norman'd been playing his hand wanted me more his dirty little helper, didn't have anything on me except I'd his money and money'd never seemed to matter to him. I could walk away and Norman wouldn't follow, but this other guy'd already tried to put it to me, calling the police, shown himself actively set on taking what was mine with all his cleverness tracking me down, phoning in a tip.

Was a row of phones outside a liquor store, one of them in use, some woman bulked up around it keeping her conversation as private as a parking lot phone'd allow. To be polite, I loitered across the street until she'd finished, got my coins down the slot, dialed.

He picked up after two rings, casually said my name.

"What's your name by the way, except it isn't Flake, is it?" I said, sounding hasher that I really meant.

"You gave me a scare, Trevor. They said at the motel you'd got back to your room, but when you didn't call I thought maybe they had it wrong and you'd not talked your way out of things. Good for you, breathing free."

I was tonguing the space where my missing tooth'd used to be, letting him talk mostly because I wasn't ready to make my pitch, didn't know did I want to so much hearing his voice, it hitting me full what he'd tried to do to me.

"What's it gonna cost to end this?"

He seemed unsure how to respond, made me wish I'd

just skipped out of town, that I'd been wrong he'd keep it up coming after me.

"You're calling to make me an offer?"

"It seems that's just what I'm doing."

"I don't understand that."

I chuckled. "Something you have to understand about it? I get it, gave you a headache with my thing, you think it's the least I can do pay some of that off and I'm not really interested this being the narrative of my life until whenever you feel like it's not, but think maybe you're the sort I can say Let's do this it makes us square and you let it do just that."

Awkwardly fished a cigarette up to my mouth while the line kept silent, then while he made a long breath into his end of the receiver made crackling sounds like wind in my ear.

Finally he said "I figure you went down to see Lawrence, too, you're not telling me otherwise, are you?"

Breathed smoked down my nose a bit, last of the breath out my mouth while I said "Lawrence paid through the teeth, mostly because I guess he was more at fault than Klia, the thing."

"Then I want five thousand dollars."

I knew the way he was figuring it, that according to his numbers he was asking for half—all things totaled including the original two thousand he'd given me deliver plus counting what I'd said about Lawrence as he'd paid double the letter into the deal.

"Four thousand."

"Five thousand you want us square. I don't have time for this, either, so that's how it is."

Screwed my cigarette up into the coin slot, tube of it spilling a few cinders then dry flakes of tobacco, just broke open a mess, was about to talk again but realized he'd hung up. Left the phone to my ear, quiet until it rang a few times, recorded message came on I'd need to hang up I wanted to place another call, let the message go half dozen times before I set the receiver the cradle, completely done, crumbs and old air left in my head, not a single thought.

***

It was strange stepping out off the train, into the station close to four in the morning, strange recognizing immediately and deeply the city I lived in, nothing specific, just the laziness I could walk with, the unconscious understanding how far I was from here or there, feeling I'd not had since stepping on the train originally, letter from Klia to Norman not even open.

Went down the storage area the basement of Murray's building, reached in through the hole in the wire fence of his little cubby, took the spare key from under the towel on top the boxes I knew had most of his books in them, elevator up to his floor, let myself in. He wasn't around, supposed he had the night shift as it was just midweek.

Took a long shower his body wash, shampoo, conditioner, used a new one of his disposable razors to shave. Smiled that my Kroger brand pizzas were still in his freezer, tucked to the side of the three half empty boxes of popsicles, only grape flavored ones left, heated one of the pizzas and drank a two thirds full bottle of cold water the fridge, refilled it from the tap.

I dressed in some of my old clothes I saw Murray'd packed up in one of his old suitcases for me, put the clothes I'd been wearing I showed up in my duffle, poked around the apartment generally to see had I left some little knick-knack of mine around maybe I'd miss later, didn't find anything, turned on the television and smoked. Turned the television off as soon as whatever show I'd stopped on got to commercial, dug through my duffle, carefully took out the gun. It was a funny weight in my hand, I didn't even loosely curl my finger around the trigger or even put it alongside the trigger, held the handle odd, way it'd be the gun were a banana—I pointed it around variously, put my coat on unbuttoned to see what did the weight feel like down the pocket.

Struck me I didn't have an extra duffle to put the money I was bringing the guy in, rooted around through Murray's things until I came up with an old backpack I'd seen in the same corner forever, full of old school notes and some miscellaneous garbage which I piled neatly—not like I exactly planned to see Murray again, but if ever I did he asked I'd tell him I'd took it, which he'd already know.

Locked up behind me, kept the key for when I'd come back for my bag as I'd aim to do so I knew Murray wasn't around anyway, got to the street with the old backpack around one shoulder, hands in my pocket, tensed when I touched the gun, but kept walking until I was to the phone outside of the post office.

Guy picked up, said my name then right away in with his bit how the money was to be delivered. I frowned, his plan more clever than the ones I'd been thinking. I was to go to a hotel he'd rented himself a room out, give whatever it was I had the money in—a backpack I said over him, but he didn't acknowledge me—to one of the desk attendants, say it was for Mister English they'd be expecting something delivered for him and would take it to the room, he'd go ahead and call the place in the evening, make sure they'd only taken the bag and I'd not gone to the room, meanwhile I was to get on a train to Henderson Crest, give him a call I was there and when he recognized the proper area code from where I called he'd go up for the money and we'd be done.

He hung up after making sure I knew which hotel and he'd had me repeat the procedure to him, nothing else.

It was only just past nine thirty in the morning, so I got some coffee, careful to remove my coat, set it over the chair back when I sat, padded the outside of the pocket to be certain the gun was as down in the pouch as it'd go.

It got under my skin more and more he'd had such a neat and clean little plan, smugness all over his voice I replayed it, like it was all some dreadful yawn for him, it was I'd done the leg work and he could just ho hum up a plan I'd slip into like a cog, give him his payday.

Even more annoyed because he was right, why not be smug?

Spun some pointless little ideas how could I get at him after the money'd been dropped when I couldn't even begin to come up with how would I fake a call from Henderson Crest, but all of it amounted to nothing but some limp thing like try to call the hotel and get out of them some sneaky way which room'd been the one had a bag left for it—trouble was I didn't know which room, which name, no way to finesse the question. Short of getting a job there, getting a whole list who'd taken out rooms then spend forever trying to match them up with my guy I was blanked, and even that nonsense only worked in fantasy land had he used his real name, real address.

Felt pretty terrible about myself, mind wandered to what maybe Norman was thinking I was up to. He must've known I'd just split with his money, I'd even told him that was just what it was I'd had my mind set to do—but I wondered, anyway. He crept all into my head, whole little scene of him forcing the money on me, the gun, how I really felt he'd ignored me saying I don't promise, pretended the words into I had.

I perked up a little bit it struck me maybe if I explained it right I could get someone to keep an eye on the desk, see who got the bag, pay them a little bit of money follow the person, but just as soon I slumped into stepping outside for a cigarette, saw about a million ways that this'd never stand a chance of working even if I could come up with someone'd do it inside the next hour or two before I'd have to be on the train out.

Guy was as smart as me, clearly lot smarter on top.

Ridiculing myself, it occurred to me he wouldn't be going to the desk to get the bag, bag'd already be up in the room. But maybe I could see if I could hang around, see which room the attendant took the bag to, have someone stake it out.

No. Just as much nothing, but I wouldn't stop thinking no matter how much I told myself stop.

I was tired, realized I just drifted to the side walking down the street, was leaning against a wall, hand around the gun in my pocket.

Only thing I could do was to not leave the money, but that was more something I'd be doing to myself than to anyone else.

Got on a bus, seat in the back, extra vibration because I was just above one of the wheels, or at least it felt that way in my head. Found myself thinking how when I'd been younger, high school, I'd like to walk around in the cold, holiday lights up and things especially, pretend I had a gun in my pocket, was waiting to walk past a certain person, pull the trigger—always'd wondered would the shot cause a recoil, make me hit against my leg, leave a bruise, wonder could I just keep walking after the trigger'd been pulled or would it be evident what'd happened, people rush down on me. Those were the games I'd played. It seemed sad and pretty at the same time, smiled not quite able to make that out in what there was of my reflection the window.

***

Due to the weather'd gone bad, the train out to Henderson Crest was packed grotesquely with people, I'd managed to worm my way into a corner, at least, still standing but able to lean back with my eyes closed. Adding to the discomfort, the train'd continually pull to a halt, some fuzzy announcement coming on that due to something or other these delays were unavoidable, apologies for any inconvenience—each time these announcements sounded the same few people'd vocalize their irritation in the same sarcastic asides or sniffs down their noses, each subsequent lull boiling them more ferocious.

I felt lost not holding any kind of duffle and hadn't exactly recovered from the reality of I'd absolutely just left five thousand dollars off a hotel for someone—it wasn't mine anymore, five thousand dollars. The numb kept me from focusing on the fact that it'd been money I'd been paid to kill the person I'd left it for, paying him out instead out of anxiety he'd never leave me alone.

Would he leave me alone, I'd paid him?

Honestly, I thought he would. His victory here, he'd just enjoy the prize, even if he knew Norman'd paid me to kill him, if somehow that ever came out to him, I didn't think he'd take pains to track me wherever I wound up, grind another few bucks out of me—probably he'd just be oddly proud of me for angling such a thing, it'd give him a grin and that'd be all.

Was buzzing arguments in my head like at Norman, that even had I said I'd kill this guy, how was I supposed to?

Even had I promised, all I'd promised is I'd see what I could do, turned out that wasn't anything.

When my stop came up, didn't bother with moving along in the crowd, just sat on a bench, after two minutes of noise, people queuing for escalators, the stairs, place was empty and wet, stank of ozone and whatever smell it was drifting from the restaurants across the other side of the street.

Just in case the public phone at the station wouldn't show the right area code, I walked along until I found a tucked in bar, ordered vodka—changed my mind to bourbon after the bartender'd turned away, didn't bother getting her attention, whispered to myself how vodka would be fine.

There were phones back over by the toilet, the jukebox. It was only just five o'clock, figured the least I could do was wait until six, quarter past six, make the guy have to wait around a little, if nothing else.

"Nothing else," I said, took my drink up, just touched my lip to it enough to get the sting, flavor, thick of the air up from it in my nose.

I had coins in my pocket already, but broke five dollars just to have something to do, asked for another drink, downing mine right after the order, this eliciting a smile from the bartender, though I didn't know this meant did she think that was interesting, charming, or just an obnoxious thing to do. Saw her leaving the new drink down, taking up the four dollar tip I'd left, all quarters she'd just brought me from the broken five, fished the card with the telephone number on it up from my pocket, dialed it out as slowly as I could.

Line connected, but nobody said anything. "Hello?"

"What's the name of the bar you're in?"

I stammered, said I'd have to ask but right away the guy was chuckling, said "Never mind" and then "Goodbye, Trevor."

Wasn't sure had he hung up, just waited until there was secondary click, ringing started, put the phone down, went into the toilet. I spent a minute or two washing my face, trying to ignore what I figured were the looks I was getting from the other patrons in and out as quick as they could, some of them not even turning the tap to get their fingers wet after the urinals, just yanking a paper towel the dispenser, blowing their noses, dropping the used thing the ground and out the door like it was all one gesture for them.

I was walking out the door, hand curled around the gun, remembered my vodka, had to fight my way back to my spot, took it up, getting a hard look from someone like they'd been planning they'd take it no one showed up the next minute, I'd come just under the wire—even thought they might try to protest it was theirs, so took it all a mouthful, still swallowing it I got outside.

Thinking it over, I was glad I hadn't mentioned to the guy Norman'd asked me to put the trigger on him I'd decided against it—not glad because it'd've made me look weak, glad because had I said it this guy'd probably have come up with some other slant to play things at, get me in to something else.

Reassured myself that no, Norman wouldn't come looking for me. He'd even said I didn't need to tell him I did kill the guy, it'd all been some weakling gesture on his part giving me money, the gun—that's the thing, he figured I'd play remote-control-him and go do whatever awful he could only get up to in his imagination, same as he could only get up to it with Klia his own mind.

Waited until the last train back to town, rode it more or less myself except some young guy buried in a paperback up a corner seat—he'd pop his head up every stop, squint to see what was the station, look at the map, odd little compulsion, sort of amused me, made bets myself would he do it the next stop, the next stop, next, would he get off before me.

Some hideous bleat of thick rain started I was good five minute walk out from Murray's, waited it out in a drug store reading magazines, leafing through them anyway.

Couldn't get shook of thoughts about Norman, especially now the money was gone and he wouldn't hear from me.

Why'd he say I wouldn't have to tell him, he'd know?

Only way it seemed to make any sense was he had someone following me, someone could just as well've a bag of money their own and meant to put a bullet up me either after I'd done the guy dead or else if it looked I wouldn't be able to accomplish the thing.

First lull of rain, I dashed to Murray's and still wound up pretty soggy. He was in, as were two guys I only loosely knew from someplace years ago. I said I'd just get my stuff go a hotel, the two guys hardly paying any attention, Murray getting me aside just to ask was I alright, did I need something.

"I'm fine."

He looked at me—must've seemed pretty pathetic to him because he told me let him give me something for a room, anyway, it wouldn't be such a good idea for me to stay over. Don't know was that last thing because there was a larger get together coming, some lady on his card for the night maybe, or did he just not want me around, offered to stave off some awkward weaseling into things my part—either way, I told him I'd appreciate it, couldn't really promise I'd be able to hit him back, though.

***

Since it was Murray's dime, took a room the night right in town, bought myself a few packs to smoke and a modest bottle of vodka when I couldn't find bourbon anywhere near as cheap, the same size. Had the television on, volume up too loud I couldn't concentrate right but I didn't turn it down, just sat on the toilet the door closed it got I wanted to focus.

Couldn't leave it with Norman'd just wandered away we'd had a drink he'd put a gun my hands kept telling me say I promise.

Nothing thoughts clogged me up, idiot things really— like find some report about someone dead, say that'd been the guy, or even as far as thinking I'd shoot myself the hand or something, say a struggle'd gone down, I'd got the worst of it now had no way I'd ever find the guy, again.

It was this meandering finally got me to unscrew the vodka, poured some in one of the plastic cups wrapped up at the sink, added a little water just to convince myself I'd more than I did and maybe it'd keep me paced. It really wasn't I wanted to get drunk, just couldn't only keep up the cigarettes with nothing else in me and the thought of food was impossible.

Getting the first swallow down, hissing from it tasted excruciating, it struck me Give him back the money, give Norman back the money it'd be done.

Doing vague math in my head, even after the five thousand I'd paid off the guy with, I had something twelve thousand—eleven thousand, twelve thousand, kind of'd lost track of incidental expenditures, so say eleven thousand—which meant I could give back the whole six thousand something he'd given me with the gun, this'd leave me five, then even I gave him back what I'd first took off him I'd have three, two or three, something.

Got caught up it was funny if I'd only have three left,

meant I'd spent more than the original two thousand I'd been given deliver the letter—if I'd only be left three, or say even I was left four, it meant that still didn't account for the four thousand something Lawrence'd paid me out and neither the two I'd bled Klia.

This was all immaterial, but still it got my head in a fuss, wanted to be at the storage unit to give things a count, couldn't be satisfied with the figures I was coming out with.

Switched back to cigarettes off now a straight, waterless glass of vodka, took the room phone and sat it in my lap, puzzled out did I remember the address right to Norman's place—town was called Door, address something like one two three, but I couldn't get it right, odd combination of numbers seemed normal but wasn't.

Figured out to dial information, hung up, stared at the cigarette I hadn't smoked, stubbed it and poured a vodka, just a half inch high of it, downed it.

One five seventeen Pillowglen, it came to me I looked at the bed, my congratulatory handclap dull and pudding sounding, more the sound of slapping a plump belly.

Dialed information, again, relit the cigarette I'd stubbed but stubbed it right back it tasted odd, got a new one going while I answered the woman asked City and State.

"Norman Court I'm trying to call, address fifteen seventeen Pillowglen in Door."

"Pillowglen?"

I nodded, didn't bother saying Yes, smoke out my nose, mouth, nose, mouth all from the same drag.

"I'm not finding any listing for that."

I scratched my neck, answered "There's a bar with something the same address, don't know the name of it, but almost the same address, Pillowglen."

"I have listings in Pillowgreen Glen."

I nodded nodded nodded, cleared my throat. "That's right. Norman Court in Pillowgreen Glen."

She made a kind of whisper sound, but didn't say anything.

"I'm not seeing a number listed for Norman Court."

I stubbed my cigarette, grimaced at myself because it'd be thoughtless, thing still more'n halfway good.

"How about there's a bar that address?"

"I have a number for Eastwick Pub, one five eleven Pillowgreen Glen."

"Should be it, I think."

Before I could ask would she just tell me the number she said she'd connect me. My instinct was to hang up I wasn't ready, but as I didn't feel I wanted to go through it with information get the number again I got a new cigarette up, stubbed the two I'd just stubbed all the way out because they were leaking scums of dark smoke was sort of annoying me to smell it.

"Eastwick."

I coughed, apologized, said Hello.

"Can you hold on?"

I didn't answer, figured he wasn't waiting for me to.

Half minute later someone else was on the line, a woman. "Hello?"

"Hi."

"What can I do for you?"

It didn't sound so busy, woman's voice was even, undistracted.

"I'm trying to call for Norman Court, guy he's upstairs I think. Left me his number a message I lost it, thought maybe you all would know."

"You're calling for Norman? Who are you?"

There was something to the tone, I got uneasy and the vodka seemed all of a sudden it was scuttling its way up in my ears.

"My name's Murray Flake," I said, almost chuckled at the freeform combination. "I've just been trying to get through to him a few weeks about something, finally got he gave me his number. Maybe I got it wrong. He said he lived above Easwick's, though, I remember that."

Another odd pause like I was saying something didn't make any sense, but then I could tell she'd cupped the receiver, was saying something off to the side someone.

Suddenly back in my ear, same even tone, she said "Norman Court died few days ago on Thursday."

While I blanked on anything to say, heard her confirming off to the side Thursday? then I guess someone'd corrected her she said "Wednesday night" in my ear.

Man's voice broke in, "You say it was Norman you were calling for?"

"Yes."

"He swallowed his medicine cabinet on Wednesday, what are you calling us for?"

Got the idea from his tone the man was standing up tall as he could, waiting for me to say something else he could swat me down.

"Well, it was just he gave me his number awhile back, I'd lost it."

Swallowed odd, abruptly, coughed once then just stammered a minute, said I'd call back, then—didn't mean to say it, but right away the guy was in with "No, don't call back here, don't have anything to do with him."

I said Okay, but he'd already hung up.

Sat, phone in my lap, moved it back to the bedside table, looked around for my vodka and when I didn't see it stood, heard it tip over my foot knocked it, stared blurry watching it glug out into the sand green of the carpet.

Counted off on my fingers—Wednesday was day after I'd seen him.

No.

Yes. It'd been Monday I'd got out from the police, then next day'd seen him.

Realized the television volume was still up high, shut it off, but when the quiet got thick all over me like water spilled from a mop bucket I turned it back on, went to the sink and started washing my hands, my face—wasn't until I'd scrubbed hard a towel, was feeling around for my cigarettes, it hit me I was crying, sniffles and burps. Tried to take in a drag, it made me sneeze. Sat to the floor, leaned a cuddle in close the heel of the bed.

***

I'd consolidated everything down to what'd fit in my duffle, figured there was enough room for the money on top, but if not I'd be able to sort that out. Thought about unloading the gun, but then left it, slipped it back my coat pocket.

Got the train station still headache ridden from the vodka the previous night. I didn't let myself sit down the train, worried I'd drift off to sleep, wake up missed my station, even more of a headache. I walked end to end of the compartment, when I'd get to each door peer through at the people milling the attached compartments, noted only one of them'd look up each time I did, was probably putting them off.

Thought about going into the storage rental office to officially close out my unit, kind of think I thought it just to stall going in. Something in picking up the money and being able to wander off still hadn't hit me as reality, part of me thinking I left the money alone I could just have back the life I'd had.

Life I'd had.

Real pause maybe was because the money into things or not, leaving meant I had less a life than I'd had, not had much of one to begin with—but not taking the money didn't mean a thing along those lines, it was all a fact now, it'd already happened just needed to do it, now.

Stale air came out the room a gulp like it always did the unit first opened, pulled the bulb on, closed myself in as best I could. Tore open the garbage bag I kept the smaller bag in, just dumped the money, smoked a few cigarettes looking at it.

Only nine-and-a-half thousand, including what I had on me I'd taken out last time.

It was kind of a jolt. I emptied my pockets—put the gun back in, removed my coat and set it off to one side—dug through the paper debris I'd filled the bags with, turned out the clothes in my duffle.

Not even nine and a full half—nine thousand three hundred sixty-four dollars, that even totaling in the loose coins I'd accumulated from all over.

As though any amount of thinking would change things, I paced around through a few hardly used cigarettes, turned things over and over. Even had it been ten and half, ten four hundred, I'd've believed that.

Wondered could someone've found out what I had in here? The staff of the place? Gone through the trouble to undo the trash bags carefully, just clip a bit, put it all back neat?

The crumbled paper strewn around, I really had no way of knowing—maybe they'd even torn through the original bag, found the money, just replaced other bags, other paper, even.

Sat down a last few minutes, repacked my bag of everything except five hundred dollars in my pocket—first same pocket as the gun, then I switched it, then I switch pockets, the gun the money, because I reached more naturally into the one, was tired of feeling the metal there, tired of the sink in my gut every time and my fingers giving it pulps, tapping it like maybe there might be some reason take it out.

Didn't know exactly what about anything I was down the street, nothing except I just wanted to get someplace I could squirrel the money away again, but same time had no interest on focusing what that'd mean. I wanted to go far, though. I wanted to go away.

Stopped a gas station, asked was there a bus depot, girl working told me there was one in town, pointed out a bench other side of the street, said transit bus would take me in, though she didn't know which line. Because I felt a little bit guilty I bought a coffee and a random candy bar, halfheartedly flirted enough to get the idea she wasn't interested—had the feeling she kept looking out to the bench I waited for the bus, worried I wouldn't get on.

Depot was ugly, looked like it'd been recently painted but whoever'd done it'd done so poor a job looked it hadn't been painted ten years—floor inside was the same concrete the walk outside. There were a few people didn't seem transient sleeping on the benches and I noticed the two public phones didn't have receivers, one of them had just a space where the coin box'd go. There was a television on way over in one corner, below it a dirty fan on oscillate, but this all a corner the benches weren't near it, just like these two thing's been discarded over there, casting their mix of shadows no one ever noticed.

Part way I didn't want to get a ticket, but the bus service was a national chain, figured it was immaterial what the station looked like.

"Hi, need to get a ticket back out Colorado, you have anything leaving that way?"

Woman working made a face it'd been a stupid question—probably it was, why'd they only have buses to certain places?

"I lost my ID, though," I said and was going to go on but, same tone to her voice as her eyes rolling'd had to her face, she told me I wouldn't need to present ID, just fill out a form she didn't hand me until another minute clacking at the computer, numbly naming off departure times.

Some reason I didn't take the earliest bus out, walked into town a bit to have lunch, vaguely of a mind to get rid of the gun. Thought most about this I was using the toilet the fast food place, thought I'd drop it down in the bowl, give someone a real startle, maybe even wait around to see the police show up—but just as quick I got the creeps, because say somebody put two and two together it'd been me dumped the gun, what a pointless bit of trouble that would be. Seemed there was the same trouble anywhere I'd lose the thing, felt eyes all over me heavy as hands all over me, coat pocket seemed the best place to keep things subdued and in secret.

Got back to the station, sat, noticed the woman working the desk was smoking so smoked, too.

The husks of the telephones struck me, suddenly. I felt around, found I still had the card on me the guy's telephone number.

"Are there phones around here actually have phones?"

The woman told me across the street or back in town,

across the street a convenience store but she said guy owned it would make me buy something.

"Buy something to use the public phone?"

She stared at me.

"That's awful," I said, a little bit giddy for some reason at her blankness, her cruelty toward me, her proper disbelief, her knowing I had my ID on me was just some loser needed to disappear like hundred losers she gave tickets under made believe names to everyday.

Guy just stared at me I said I needed to use the phone.

"Woman the bus station says I need to buy something?"

"Minimum two dollars."

"How about can I just give you two dollars?"

He shrugged, I left him five dollars on the counter, didn't get the feeling he was going to be interested in making me change.

Put my coins down the slot, squinted at the card and dialed, phone just rang and rang—I leaned there, listening, listening. Eyes closed, scratched my chin the receiver bulb, hung up. It was funny he'd not smashed the thing, removed the battery, shut it off, but at the same time what did it matter he had or he hadn't done this or done that some cheap telephone?

Took up the phone again, straight off, the thought was I'd dial Norman's number just to hear it ring, listen. Same time I heard the dial tone to my ear, I realized I didn't know the number, probably if I did it wouldn't ring, would beep dull and insistent that it wasn't a number anymore, at all.

Mixed in with the tone, don't know what brought it on, why I'd want to bring it to mind, I spent a minute pretending like I could hear Norman, hear him telling me I was an awful person. He'd told me already before, but for some reason wanted him to say it again I could answer him—I could tell him how he was absolutely right, how same time he had absolutely no idea.

Mister Trot
From Tin Street

Feel like a broke-down engine, ain't got no drivin' wheel
You all been down and lonesome, you know just how a poor man feels

BOB DYLAN, *Broke Down Engine*

I'd almost forgotten I'd wanted to keep an eye out for this certain customer after having seen him at a restaurant with his wife and kids two week prior—he walked into the store and I nodded Hello before I'd even looked up. It was him, certainly the man from the restaurant. He lingered around the new release wall, then slyly ducked through the curtained partition into the adult section.

I let Teresa take her break before me, waited almost half hour for the guy to come out with the usual stack of six pornos—three newish ones, three random older ones. Wynol Trot—he looked just like his name, smelled like his deodorant and the fabric of his sweatshirt. Wedding ring still on the hand, which I'd wanted to confirm, then I got a glimpse in his wallet there were photos of his kids, younger than they'd been at the restaurant, two boys and a girl in department store portrait.

As soon as he was gone, I pulled his account back up, scribbling down his telephone number, address at the same time I pulled up his history, hit Print, nervous Teresa might ask What's going on? she noticed the machine spitting out papers before it got through. Ducked the printout into my duffle back in the office, waited out the shift kind of jittery over nothing, left without renting anything for myself.

It was thirty-three pages long, Wynol's history. Considering he'd been a customer many, many years, this wasn't staggering, but the weight of the papers in my hand made the whole thing seem dreadful and immense. While I leafed through the pages on the bus going back to the basement I rented out a house next town over, I noted a few repeats of certain titles, highlighted these once in my room, heating coffee my six cup maker, eating a few slices from a loaf of white bread.

Wynol was what I learned from the other clerks to refer to as a clockwork jerk-off, had his little life built around stopping in, getting his six pornos each week—there were other people who took out six a night, seemed to go overboard with it, those who not only rented but bought and bought when the films were new and high priced, not even waiting two weeks for the first fifty-percent markdown—Wynol was just a clockwork jerk-off, made me chuckle.

Thing was, even the fact he rented six was so middling, store was set up that way, rent-three-get-three-free, it was so commonplace he used the freebies to grab random material. In my heart, I figured he only wanted just the one, maybe two, but knowing three'd get him six, it was just four dollars more and so who could turn down such mathematics?

Saw he lived on Tin Street, town next over but in the other direction from the video store than the town I stayed in, didn't know exactly where was Tin Street this town, but I'd figure it out day after next I was off from work entirely.

Had it arranged with the people I was renting from I could use the guest bath and even though they didn't mind me using it or even hanging around the kitchen, living room for awhile, they were home, I liked to take care of grooming things the evenings between six and seven-thirty, noted they were seldom around then.

Smoked while I took a walk around the neighborhood, gotten used to not being able to just light up indoors whenever the mood struck me, had with me the handwritten list I'd copied of just the six titles Wynol seemed to rent out most frequently, one title seemed he took out with every third rental batch or so, *Street Legal Rides volume thirty-five*, figured he must have a crush someone particular in there, twenty-eight times he'd rented it last two years, second most repeated title only'd taken out thirteen.

The nights were mostly sickly warm, lately, and I'd had to move my bed around, get it away from the end of the basement room with the window because some thick bugs would gather around the pane at night, mulch and bushes out there always seemed damp despite the bushes hardly had leaves or anything grown to them—one night one of these insects'd been on the wall, crease of the corner, it'd put me off, I'd sprayed the sill down inside and out. It was ugly the way the bellies of the things'd look, the ones trying to crawl up the outer glass or else just kind of stay put, suckle on it, especially when the jabs of the television cast all over them scribble scrabble, room dark otherwise, like they were twitching, moving in shakes, vibrating.

When it got to be four in the morning and I wasn't asleep, went for a walk, bought some document mailing envelopes, photocopied Wynol's whole list seven times, closed one copy in each envelope, bought a little can of alcohol, a mixed drink cost only dollar fifty but had a kick to it and beside they sold them just at the grocery store open all night.

It wasn't pleasant to walk around holding all the

envelopes, even with them all in a plastic bag, wasn't pleasant to sit a bench or anything with the buzz on from the drink so got home, could already hear the husband and wife I rented with up, chatting and could smell their coffee brewing but knew they wouldn't drink any of it until they were back from their jog.

I poured myself a cup into my own mug while it was still brewing after I heard them lock up the front door, leafed through one of their magazines while I drank at the counter, realized rent'd come due top of the week I'd maybe go into the store for my check, get it cashed, leave the rent early like I preferred to do, get it out of the way, like a game to keep me from instead trying to toy out ways to skip out on it altogether.

So dressed and bus had me to the store good timing, mail'd just been dropped, I had some chit chat one of the clerks I earnestly liked, opened my check I got outside started off in the direction of the cashing place shopping centre about five minutes walk. And waiting with the sad lot of folks I always waited with, sighed a little bit it was almost two weeks worth of working almost full time the video store just to keep this basement apartment and I'd lucked into that beside, if not for it I'd've been dipping into my reserve of a few thousand dollars—the job was enough to keep me sheltered, fed, keep me in smokes and dollar and half cans of liquor almost whenever I felt like it. The last month or so I'd kept myself burning through every free cent and'd squirreled away few hundred dollars.

Pocketed my money said thank you the cashier never said anything back, had a smoke while I walked to the bus stop. Wynol's address well in my memory, just needed to figure out just where Tin Street was—I'd ask at any shop along by where the bus let out, worse came down I'd ask a cab. This was just to give me an idea of Wynol, make sure it'd be worth any trouble—there was a hive of other Wynol's just like him he didn't feel soft enough and even if he did this'd just be to get my footing, tap few hundred dollars off him, five hundred, just to feel out the rhythm.

Paying for a day transfer pass, I got an odd jitteriness, felt like I had to hiccup, kind of, didn't know what I'd call it, rocked in my seat the back of the bus, could see myself, titled, slant in the circle mirror by the center door.

***

Tin Street was a fine neighborhood, little community tucked off by walls with no gate, walking down the street looking for Wynol's address seemed I was miles away from the city, though all the major commerce was really just out across the street outside—supposed the wall was to muffle the sound of traffic and all.

His address, eighty-eight two, was last house just at the lip of a public park. I sat on a bench to have a smoke, causally watched his closed front door, empty driveway. Chuckled about what a headache it'd actually be, now I was set to it, to find out anything about the guy—couldn't follow him, obviously, with him having a car and me dependent on the public transit. I wondered why I wasn't just going ahead with things, what'd it have to do with anything where he worked, who he knew, any of it. Knew it was better to get a feeling for some soft spot, though, figure the best way to leverage things against him, which right turn of phrase'd get him to just hand over the money—added to which, this being the dry run something I still thought I might make a regular play out of, I'd ought to give it concerted effort, make a real go.

As an afterthought, hit me it'd also be important to know things about him it turned out I'd have to go through with my threat—I got a new cigarette going, thought about that. Chances were thin it'd go off that direction, might even've been jinxing things with all the prep work. Idea was I threaten, he pays, I hadn't even quit my job at the video store and he knew it's where I worked.

Went for a walk around, came back by the neighborhood the evening, car in the driveway, couldn't tell anything about who'd come home. I made a long loop around, gave the car a good look I came up past it—number of bumper stickers, *Proud Parent of a Fieldway High Honor Student*, another same sort of sticker but for *My Kid Is An A Student at Cauldwell Elementary*. One for the boy one for the girl, kids I'd seen at the restaurant, older girl, younger boy.

Family alone should be angle enough—just to keep his voluminous pornography habit from his wife'd be worth five hundred no thought, then I put in he'd pay me or else I'd send it to the kids on top, send it his own girl in high school, send it to every kid in her class same time, the faculty the school, the parents. Five hundred dollars wasn't a thing—pluck a guy form thin air has something to hide make it easy for him keep that thing hid, always a way to play it.

Self-conscious how long I'd been around, went across to one of the shopping centers, found a place to buy cigarettes and a pocket bottle of vodka as I was dry back home the basement room. Waited around thumbing through this and that a secondhand bookshop, it was getting dark out, temperature settling I decided to make a last pass, this time two cars in the drive, nothing new to learn—would've jotted down license plate numbers, even though there'd be no point in that, but didn't have anything to write with.

Had a few swallows of vodka getting back to the bus,

nodded off a little the ride, got off rubbing my face groggy. Was strolling having a smoke, taking my time with it I'd not be able to have another without leaving the house, it struck me why would I have to show myself in person to this guy? I was treating the whole thing like a doodle some notebook, enjoying it but nothing of thought to the matter—really I could just give him a call, threat I had the material and what I'd do, get him to drop the money somewhere.

Took the printed history out of one of the envelopes, mouthful of a day old, half cup of coffee was left in the base of the small pot, smelled food cooking upstairs so held off having any bread, man or woman likely to call down to me I could help myself to leftovers of whatever it was like they often did.

Only a work telephone number with extension on the print out for Wynol. I snuffed a shush down my nose—it made perfect sense just the work number, why'd he want to chance getting a call to the house the wife picks up some movie'd wound up late or something? He was already conscious of he was hiding this all. Same time, not like he's going to use a phony number, buy a separate phone about the thing, we require a number he jots down his real one from work.

Went straight back out, ten minutes out to the phones inside the grocery store, dropped coins and dialed just to verify it was real and get an idea about things. Three rings in, recorded voice came on *Thank you for calling Fieldway Highschool. Reception is open from Six AM until Four PM, Monday through Friday. If you know your parties extension, please dial it now. To leave a general message, please press pound sign. For information regarding—*

I hung up, coughed into my hand then gave a little bow in the direction of the phone, fished a cigarette out my pocket to my lip and gave myself some soft applause with the pack, stepping out to get the thing lit. In fact, I was very near giddy from the call, congratulated myself in a loping walk around the back of the stores, down some street I'd never gone, got myself a booth some restaurant's bar, really felt I'd proven something, some knack I had, quirk of understanding the subtleties of human nature, something. Guy Wynol, I'd just figured him he was some hump, give him a shake see what'd fall out, but this was more perfect, nuanced than that, guy like him's not even just got to worry about being ashamed, sleeping the couch, not worry just shaming the family name and all, this is his profession'd be on the line into it.

Almost figured I'd twist him for more'n the five, but it was more delightful to me just hurt him hardly at all, give him a close call, see at all did it even change his ways or would he still be down the shop once, twice a week?

Skipped a shower next morning to sleep in, woke enough time to dress and get the latest bus'd have me to work on time, still twenty minutes until my shift started. I was a bit paranoid that the fact I'd printed Wynol's account history would show up someone looked—say I started putting it to him, he complins to the store they investigate how is it someone could've got the information, it'd be my employee numbers as the person who'd printed it up. Figured worst thing came of it's I'd lose my job, claim I'd agreed to print it up for someone a few bucks, nothing'd be able to tie me to blackmail, extortion, whatever it'd end up being called.

Nothing though, no indication that sort of thing was kept track of.

Couldn't think how could I delicately ask did it show up on some other report or could it be tracked, somehow, even if it wasn't regularly—figured the twenty year old system our computers ran on, it wouldn't be anything to worry about, but stayed tense, didn't feel I was at work the whole shift, kept bringing Wynol's account up compulsively, would pay attention I was scanning things in was it his account number'd rented them out.

Out of a sense it'd make me seem less out in my own orbit, I ordered pizza for me and the two other clerks on, pattered back and forth small talk, even rented out something on the recommendation of Pela, though it was something seemed nonsense I'd not care about one minute of.

***

Didn't sleep really night before my day off, spent it over-rehearsing imagined calls to Wynol. Gave in about three in the morning, walked the grocery store, had two dollar-fifty cans of Long Island Ice Tea thinking it'd lull me off I lay in the dark, but it just got me swimming. Dressed and out the door by five, still feeling the mild soft off the alcohol, eyes irritated from me rubbing them all night long, face getting sweaty, unwashed still.

Took the bus to the end of a certain line I'd never ridden it, had fast food breakfast just squirmed around in me especially on top of the drinks, had coffee some franchise place I'd never heard of, then found a phone I liked top floor of an indoor shopping mall.

"Fieldview highschool, how many I help you?"

I sniffled a pause, not having expected an actual person then asked could I be put through to Wynol Trot, gave the extension number.

"Mister Trot is in class at the moment, would you like his voicemail?"

"He gets out of class what, three?"

"School lets out at two forty-five, but Mister Trot might not be available."

"Voicemail's private? He's the only one can listen?"

"Only Mister Trot has access to his voicemail, yes."

I said to go ahead with putting me through, then, didn't know why I was asking all of this stuff, apologized and the receptionist just said "I understand, I'll put you through". Voicemail message came on right away, generic thing, computer voice then Wynol saying his name at a certain point, computer voice finishing things out—while this was going on I leaned back, squinted at the phone booth, smiled when I saw it did have a little card with a number on it.

Started right in the beep, bit of an affect to my voice, not so much, though, didn't want to seem cartoon.

"Hi Mister Trot, you don't know me but I need to have you to call me about a matter of some urgency regarding all the porno you really probably don't want it getting out all over the world you spend your off time having your jollies to. What I mean is we need to discuss you paying me out a little something, keep every single person in this world I can think of to send a tick by tick breakdown to, just in case you don't get what I mean Urgency."

I left the number, said Thanks, hung up.

Straight off, I wanted to go have a cigarette, rolled my eyes this whole I'd left a number the payphone. Gave it up a lost cause after half a minute, not like he was going to call me during his office hours or whatever, have a chat with me he's in his classroom—convinced myself it was better, even, because maybe he does call, phone rings and rings, he gets a spook in him good I was serious about the whole Urgency tack.

Popped in to a drug store, picked out a little notebook

and pen, thought better about this before wasting the few bucks, instead found a copy shop, took a pen, tore some sheets of coloured paper into squares and tucked them down my pant pocket.

Next telephone I came to, dialed information and got Wynol's home number, also got that his wife's name was Sandra, jotted that down because I'm always awful keeping names and it'd give some flavor to my eventual phone call I could use it, give an extra tinge to how I was coming at him, make me seem peculiarly un-anonymous.

I'd catch some late bus back to the town I kept my room, I decided, use the town I was wandering around in for my call. Teetered around outside a movie theater, considering maybe it'd help pass the time better to just shut myself into the noisy dark awhile, nap or else actually get interested in whichever movie I'd pick, instead I just smoked and tried to keep myself from every two minutes looking in through the window of a bakery café every I could see a wall clock.

When it was dark, I used a telephone the parking lot of a car wash, dialed Wynol's house. Surprising me, it was a kid answered, very casually, like it was he'd been expecting a call from someone.

"Yeah, can I talk to your dad?"

"May I ask who's calling?"

I could hear conversation in the background, the kid saying away from the phone Dad, it's for you, then kid asked me again who was calling. Wanted to say just Get your dad, but as kid'd repeat this verbatim and it'd make it probably more awkward than I wanted it to be I told him "It's Herbert, I'd tried your dad earlier at his office, must've just missed him". Heard the kid say It's Herbert something, from school, rolled my eyes at this translation, glad when a man's voice I recognized was Wynol came on, blinked, realized I'd forgotten to use an affect my voice the kid'd picked up, grumbled my voice up more low pitched.

"Wynol, what's the matter you don't check your voicemail?"

"No no, sorry I just got caught up it slipped my mind."

He seemed to be overacting this, so I didn't get edgy with him, figured it was for show in front of the family, told him we needed to talk and now was when I was free up for that.

"Can I call you back from my office, give me two minutes?"

Took me a minute to find there was a number on phone, sticker on the side of the box.

"Got something to write with?"

"I'll remember, go ahead."

His tone was starting to grate on me, didn't like his casual I'll remember thing, seemed a little too much he didn't think I'd do anything he happened to mix up this number for that and not be able to ring me back.

"How about you give me your number, Wynol, you got a special number I can call work better for you?"

"Sure do, sure do. You have something to write with?"

Squinted my eyes, phone pinned to my shoulder my ear, getting pen and a scrap from my pocket, told him I sure did, he should go ahead.

To give myself back a sense of menace, soon as he'd finished saying the number I hung up, lit a cigarette, did my best to smoke it casually, but after what felt like two minutes just flicked it out the road, dialed him.

He picked up, half ring, right away started off, voice thin, tight, like he'd fit a wet glove around it.

"I don't know who you are or why exactly you think you can threaten me, but whatever your joke is it's done right now."

I smiled, one eye shut a bit more from the grin tilted up more that way. "Wynol, sure I agree with you, that's very good, good for you—only thing is, there's no game and this's gonna be very simple, quick as can be, too, five hundred dollars out of your pocket you can rest easy."

"Don't call my home again, don't call my work again. I will press charges against you for harassment."

It was too much, he seemed so earnest, tough guy teacher man sitting in his swivel chair the study—maybe I didn't know just what he looked like this persona'd've given me two seconds pause before I'd sniff it out, steam roll over it, but given I was the guy he handed over money to twice a week rented him out the visuals for his morning shower, it actually just made me laugh.

"Laugh laugh," he said, "you won't think it's funny if I have to get the courts involved—this isn't cute and this isn't something I'm going to put up with. Do not call me again, and you'd better understand."

He hung up. I was smiling too hard even to care, got a cigarette started, leaned to the wall next to the phone.

***

Ride in to work, wondered would I be able to tell had Wynol been up the store, asked how his history could've gotten out—he'd seemed so matter of fact about getting the courts involved, even though doing so seemed it'd leave him exposed to having to let at least his wife know what was going on, didn't seem likely with he was so secretive about his little habit. He'd been cocksure I was bluffing or something, though, maybe thought I was some kid pranking him, a student maybe'd seen him go in the store or something just trying to toy with him. Might be he didn't even think in terms of there was a print-out of his history, just thinking it'd be innuendo I'd bring down, something he could paint as bullying, nobody close to him getting on his wrong side.

Everything seemed same as it always seemed I came in, just had some chit chat in the office, set my stuff down, leafed through some magazines before it was time to go out.

Was in a position I'd either have to abandon things with Wynol or else push, actually go through with my threat. That or I'd have to find some way to twist some pressure on Wynol, get him understanding about there was actually some trouble coming his way he kept up with being stubborn and how reasonable it'd be to pay out just five hundred dollars keep it from happening.

I felt good with this all in my head, less distracted than I could get, had a kind of jaunt to me while shelving movies back, cleaning shelves when it was slow time for customers—I played out variants on what I might do, recalled Wynol's stiff insistence I leave him alone and what else I might've said, how he might've kept up the tough guy shtick. Funny, it was funny how it'd gone that way.

I was back from my break, had spent it just wending circles back behind the store, drifting through half dozen cigarettes and a bottle of some fruit drink. Evening shift'd officially started, so it was just me and a young kid called Scott on, he made sure it was alright with me he took his break, worried it was around the time it'd get busy.

"Go ahead, I'm sure I can handle it."

Pulled what'd accumulated in the return bin, caught up in my idea how I'd even let it go a week before taking another step, noticed that when I scanned a certain film it was Wynol's account information showed in the corner. Scanned through everything else in the stack, quickly, five more belonging to him, one of them *Street Legal Rides volume thirty-five*. At my register, I punched up his account, now had the eleven digit number down to rote, showed nothing else rented out, stared at the partition to the adult section, a line three customers forming.

Wynol joined the line, rolling his head around his shoulders again and again and sniffling, seemed really peculiar to see this back behind the other customers who were just milling regularly, reading the backs of the cases they had with them. Got his turn, he let a long, long breath out through tight lips, set his movies down, told me "Hi, sorry, long day". I shrugged, smiled, took the cases with me around the corner to put the discs in them, Wynol leaning on the counter, arms folded, patting his hands and making puffs of breath out.

"Worked here long?" he asked me while I was scanning his card, handing it back.

"Since a few weeks after I moved to town, worked here something two months, two three months."

Another excessive breath, this time down his nose, little whistle to the end of it, rubbed his eyes while he asked me if I liked the work.

"It's fine, beats real work, I guess."

"Is that right? You go to school?"

I felt compelled to lie, said I was going to start taking some design classes later on, maybe take some sound design classes.

"Community college?"

"Yeah."

"Community college is good around here, don't listen to people if they tell you skip it."

Just nodded, told him his total. He didn't say anything else, even Goodbye, took his movies where I handed them to him around the censor, was clearing his throat harshly he got out the door, could hear him doing it still the glass swung shut.

I tapped his account open, closed it right away, walked a lazy kind of circle of the area behind the register, could hear another customer picking up cases and setting them down back in the adult room.

Returning the discs'd just been returned to their places, I gave a long look to the case for *Street Legal Rides*. This'd be now almost thirty times Wynol'd taken it out last two years—thing looked pale and generic even for the type it was, mid-list little production company, all amateur girls even though most of them'd probably been in dozens and dozens of scenes by now.

First thought was I'd have Scott rent it out to me, but then got spooked about that—things eventual came around to any sort of someone looking in to Wynol's account information getting out, I wouldn't want the only adult film I'd ever rented to be one he'd rented every other week. Probably it didn't matter, but it was enough to make me just lift the disc I'd bring it back in the next few days no one'd ever've missed it. Simple enough, I slipped the disc my pant pocket, left the cover case for it in the stacks—unless someone came asking for it by name, there'd be no reason to think odd of it. Just in case though, I took the store sleeve out of the rental case, put that in my pocket as well, put the empty case in with all the others the bottom shelf.

Scott came back I ducked to the toilet, transferred disc and paper to my duffle, oddly paranoid any time Scott went to the office the rest of the shift that he'd go rooting through my stuff some odd reason, just happen upon I was stealing.

Wondered where exactly Wynol stashed his rentals, did he leave them his office the high school—did he watch them there, when did he watch them?

For a minute, I thought maybe his wife watched them

with him, maybe that's why he hadn't seemed nervous exactly I'd had him on the phone, but that only made sense I was threatening I'd tell his wife, which I hadn't done, or at least had only done so bundled in with everything else.

How Wynol'd just come in, huffing and puffing, it made me want to put another call to him right away, just to poke him, but it'd serve no purpose until I was ready to apply some torque, wondered would I get to that point, even.

Had he chatted with me as a way to feel things out, or just to release the nervousness he must've felt coming back in, playing things overly casual same as any kid stealing'd do?

On my walk to the bus, I ducked in to a shop, bought a cheap pair of headphones I hope'd work with my television in the basement, usually just watched with the volume down, usually didn't watch much, didn't so much know why was I going to now, just that I was.

***

Gimmick of *Street Legal Rides* was the same as umpteen other porno series, girls purporting it was their first time—at least on film—and that they'd just turned legal age to consent. "Can we have some proof of that?" voice'd prompt from behind camera after each girl'd introduced herself, girl'd coyly nod or say Yeah, hold up her I.D., camera'd zoom in on the thing—real name, address'd be blurred, but age, height, all of that and the girl's picture'd be perfectly legible. After camera lingered a moment or two, some commentary from the guy holding it, shot'd zoom back, girl'd look right down the barrel of the lens and in whatever attitude it was the particular girl had'd say

"Isn't someone gonna take me for a ride? I promise I'm street legal" or some version of the line.

Stuff itself was pretty straight forward, uninspired even if I did find one of the girls cute—no zest to the performances, not a lot of variety to angles and the guy the girl going position to position seemed neither were particularly in to it—to top it off, whoever was holding the camera also prattled way too much, trying to coax something interesting from the girl's mouth but this paid off so seldom it was really just a distraction.

Eighteen girls on the collection—another part of the gimmick maybe—didn't understand why there were multiple volumes of the series let alone why Wynol had such a passion for this one, seeing the store carried at least two dozen.

Disappointed with the thing as pornography, I took a walk, smoking, knew it was obvious Wynol got the same one on account of one of the gals just made him feel specifically pleased with himself. Didn't see as how I'd ever solve which one, though—one looked like his daughter, could be, or looked like a friend of hers, one maybe looked like kid of some friend or a girlfriend he used to have, there were only so many things it'd be but even still it was a cipher.

Didn't feel like keeping the disc around, would smuggle it back I got on shift, but turned it on a last time and started going through the girls, just the bits they introduced themselves. Noted a girl introduced herself as Daphne had a driver's license from Colorado—fourth girl in, went back through the first three, two from California, one from Washington, went through the remainder, more California, one Utah, few from South Carolina.

Daphne.

I squinted at the paused shot of her license, blur over

her real name absolute, nothing to make of that. Counted off from the birthdate on the card and considering she really was eighteen like she said it'd been three years, three and half years something the thing'd been made.

Shut off the television, went out for another smoke, can of Vodka Martini from the grocery store.

So she'd been his student, had to be it, or at least she was a girl'd gone to the school he taught—much to his surprise he's going through his porno one day and there she is. Daphne. Only he knew what was the real name. Daphne. There she was, the little flunk out or teacher's pet, the one who he'd heard rumors about weren't meant for him to be hearing as a member of the faculty and then Pow—Daphne.

Strolled back to the store for another can, clerk asked me "These actually work?"

I was tipsy, in fact, nodded far too friendly, gave a ringing endorsement.

"If you had a card with us, you know these are only a dollar."

"Is that it?"

"Do you have a card?"

Shook my head, asked what a card'd run me.

"Card's free." He scanned one, handed it to me with a thing to fill out. "Bring that back, you're good to go."

"Does it make this one only a dollar?"

"Sure does, just fill it out and it'll keep working."

Told him Hold on, bought two more as a celebration, only drank just the one of them, the others hung in the plastic bag dragging down around my left wrist I smoked with my other hand.

For one minute I wondered why'd Wynol not just go ahead and buy this volume, must've spent time times the fifteen bucks whatever it'd run him, but blew a scoff of smoke at myself, actually whispered to myself Don't be a dolt, liquor had me loose enough to mumble, not enough to fully vocalize such things.

It must've be a real kick to him, like sometimes it was there, sometimes not—sometimes she was there, sometimes not—an added bump to the reality of his fantasy, fit with his generalized idea of what it'd really be like to've taken a chance with her, got her.

"Got you, Wynol," I said, aloud but on purpose, opened a new can and downed it, no point in sipping as it tasted kind of awful I did that but went down like nothing I just turned the can over let it all down me.

Slept for a solid while, woke about one in the afternoon. House was empty, so took my time in the shower, lounged in the living room awhile. All totaled, I was impressed with myself, really had spotted Wynol from nothing and had him mapped out I could draw him on the wall a perfect likeness, now. Put me off he'd given me the hard guy line I'd called, that didn't seem to compute, but I wrote myself some allowances on that, no accounting for every idiosyncrasy some pervert—beside, it was just he'd been nervous, bluffed his little peacock feathers up high, now it was a joke that it'd given him to thinking he'd scared off anything.

Got to work, waited until it was just me in the store to slip the disc and the store sleeve from my duffle back into a case, took a particular pleasure in putting the cover back in the adult room. As a little joke, I put it up on the New Arrival shelf, though it wouldn't last long there, either a customer'd nab it or if I wasn't the one straightened the room after close whoever else did would put it back in category.

Work drifted by alright, bit of a loud altercation with someone over some fees—I egged them on for no good reason, eventually took off the fees and let them rent their current selections for free.

It was a woman I seldom worked with closing up with me, she took forever to do the paperwork and insisted on walking the floor to verify it'd been vacuumed thoroughly—revealed herself she was just full of it with that, because after her five minute walk around the store she praised the job I'd done while all the time I'd not even touched good half, three-quarters of the place.

Waiting for the bus, I really, really thought about hopping on the other line would take me to the town I was going to use to call Wynol, again, give him a real jolt calling middle of the night, see how he liked it when I lost some of the politeness I'd shown him, originally. Guy wouldn't pay five hundred dollars to save himself being exposed just what he was deserved whole handfuls of whatever I could come up with to get him unsettled, make him stew.

Note on the outside basement door reminded me rent was two days past due. I tensed, for a moment felt real indignation because I was sure I'd paid it, but went in my pocket and, no, everything from my check was still there. I closed the cash in an envelope, left it in the cubby slot the husband and wife had set up on the kitchen wall, a kind of hanging basket, then stood listening up the stairs, didn't hear anything, heard maybe the general hum of things in the house, air moving in the walls, sighed and closed myself back down in the basement.

***

Called from a payphone would it be alright I stopped in the high school, the afternoon, told the receptionist I'd been a student there number of years back, was just in town a few days, hoped there might be yearbooks I could have a leaf through, made a whole charming thing out of it, I thought. Seemed it'd be no problem, I'd just have to check in at the desk—this made me nervous, but I figured I could just use a ploy of saying I'd been the guy called on the telephone before but dolt that I am'd left my wallet at home, they'd just let me sign in.

The bus in to town, started thinking I should maybe've disguised myself somehow, what if I had to walk right past Wynol I went into the school, wouldn't take him long at all to figure it was odd my being there and then what it meant. That all seemed a bit much, cutting or coloring my hair or something, didn't know what else would disguise me, really, so I just hoped for the best, wasn't thinking I'd have to be there that long and I could keep to a corner, luck held up for me even a little.

Drank a coffee, smoked a cigarette halfway, flicked the rest and chewed some gum until my breath felt good before I walked past groups of students milling around, faculty members, parents moving around, got in through the main door and up to reception.

"Hi. I'd called on the phone before, just wanted to take a look some yearbooks? You mentioned signing in, it hit me now I've left my wallet on the dresser, never think to grab it I don't drive or anything."

"You just need to look through some yearbooks, I think that'll be alright."

She told me sign in and what was my name, wrote it out on a guest pass I had to keep hung around my neck.

"I'm Lionel," I said, then spelled it when she asked me spell it for her.

Did a charming thing of it'd been too long, which way was the library, she pointed and I asked a few kids I came across, too, school a massive thing, like a grounded boat.

Scanned around just in case was one of the study groups

at the tables being proctored by Wynol—struck me had I said Lionel because it sounded something like Wynol, way I pronounced it—quietly asked some student was shelving back books from a cart which way were the yearbooks.

Figured it was the same year, year previous as it'd been Daphne'd done the movie she would've been in school, started with the year previous. Flipped through the book, overly glossy pages, sweating much more heavily under my arms than I wanted to be—it was tricky focusing and seeming casual all at once, kept tensing anytime a faculty member went by or even stood up, spooked they were going to ask me who was I exactly, what exactly was it I wanted.

Junior class, girl named Rene Spree looked a dead ringer in her portrait, a few candids, and some group photos she appeared in. Gave a quick look through the following year's senior class—no mistaking her, there, must've been just the summer she'd gone in front the camera, bell'd rung last day of class and there she went.

I would've rather tore out the actual pages had pictures of her, but library wasn't built that was possible to pull, noticed there were copy machines but got worried someone'd tell me they were fine to use but then would ask for the books from me and which pages. Nothing to do about it, though, went up to the main desk, whispering more than I had to, asked "It's alright to use the photocopier?"

"Do you need coins?"

I nodded. "How much per copy?"

"Fifteen cents."

Woman broke five dollars for me, I nodded my thanks to her then spent another few minutes going through the two books, some reason wanted as many images of Rene as I could find. I copied a few random pages as well, put them at the top of the stack just in case when I went to return my visitor badge got cornered in to chit chat someone and they wanted a casual look what was I holding—nothing like that happened though and I got a few blocks away from the school, ducked into a grocery store, asked where was the toilet and sat in a stall until my knees stopped bouncing.

Leafed to one of the candid shots—Rene and a group of friends eating lunch, all sat up on a table.

"Well hello, Rene Spree," I said through a calming breath out, heart rate getting down to where I couldn't feel the heat out from it up against the inside of my shirt. Second later, I corrected this to "Hello again, Rene Spree," stood up, flushed for no reason, roughed water all over my face and up and down my forearms the sink until I felt a bit more comfortable, had to use toilet paper to dry myself, towel dispensers all empty.

Suddenly felt drained, not at all up to riding back by my place, changing for work, called from a phone by the grocery entrance to see was it possible get someone's number would cover my shift.

"I don't mind, I'll take a double," same woman I'd closed with night before said.

"They let you do that?"

"Sure. It's fine."

"And you don't mind?"

"I can use the hours."

Said an extended speech of Thank you, I'd owe her one, hung the phone up.

For two minutes I was refreshed feeling, then when I was other side of a crosswalk got back sunk feeling, went back to the grocery store. Bought an envelope to put the photocopies in, looked around did this store sell the little cans of alcohol like the one I tended to frequent. It didn't, so I left, walked until I found a decent coffee shop, instead.

Knew I needed to be making a plan what exactly was it did I think these photocopies were going to get me, but just felt altogether too fatigued to think anything. I wanted things to hurry along, got irritated at the flat fact it'd have to wait two days until I was off next for me to make another move, wanted to just go to Wynol's door, show him one of the photocopies, look at him, shrugging, ask just what was he thinking, how did he think this was going to go for him he didn't just pay me out the simple little five hundred dollars.

Gave myself a real laugh, thinking I could find someone, some girl, pay her twenty bucks leave Wynol a message on his school voice mail, pretend herself up to be Rene, leave him something breathy and blue game at first, but then turn it vaguely like she was the one on to him for the money. Sat until my coffee was cold thinking alternate versions of this up, then thought maybe it'd be better rent the disc out again, get a recording of the audio, Rene as Daphne saying *Is someone going to take me for a ride, I promise I'm street legal?*

Got such a kick form this, actually, I borrowed a pen off one of the guys behind the counter, took out one of the pictures, junior year portrait, Rene fourth over a row of five, wrote the question in the margin, drew a bubble around it, a line connecting it to her mouth. Was standing about to return the pen when something else struck me— sat and wrote out *Oh, thank you Mr. Trot. Now ride me again and again and again* wrist started hurting but I wrote out twenty-nine times *and again*, print getting less legible and smaller each time, circled the whole bunch of text sloppily, again scratched a line from the circle to her mouth, then circled the picture, then scribbled out the name Rene Spree and up in the top margin, all capitals, wrote *Love Daphne XOXO*.

***

Used a computer at a café to print out a little letter onto the back of one of the photocopies of Rene, put it in an envelope I then posted from the same town I'd been using to call Wynol from. Sent it right to his house, I decided, not from the school, just to give it more of a stab—even if his wife happened to open the letter, which I couldn't see why would she do that, it didn't take the curse off I could give his history and all to anybody I felt like—letter wasn't even specific enough anybody except Wynol would know what I meant, thing instructed him to be available for a call, late, three days from day I sent it, figured that'd be enough time not only I'd be sure the letter'd arrived but if he had to wrangle an excuse for free time he'd have every chance.

I had a day off one of the three I had to wait, it went by like half asleep drool, moved but seemed to stay in one place, just spreading out more of itself. Trouble was with this thing, I was letting it go too long, it was putting me in a headspace I liked but wanted it to lead someplace—felt like I was treating it more of a hobby. Got I'd get more and more listless during work shifts, my breaks'd go by in what seemed a few blinks and a walk to the curb and back—same time, if I'd focus on how much time'd gone by, really it didn't seem any of it really had.

I daydreamed ahead, thinking I'd refine things out a bit I used this idea on someone else, less with all of the personal interplay, just letters with instructions where to drop the money—someone went ahead and paid me off, great, someone didn't, what harm did that do me? Real idea was I'd collect a good handful of people seemed from their accounts they had something I could convince them they'd lose if they didn't pay me off, quit the job, take another in some nearby town, wait a good enough bit of time and then start in. I could whittle the method down, smooth it, get it so that it was something portable, workable—daydreams, daydreams, things I saw plenty of holes in, but then in little flashes I'd find a way to plug one up.

But Wynol, he was a different kind of bug now, he was something'd taken a life its own, research for the future aside.

Night I was to make the call to him, I had work off the next day and because of the bus schedule had to take out a room, that or else wander around the night until buses started whenever they did. Figured a night a motel'd be worth it, kind of a reward to myself. It made me chuckle, Wyonol paid up five hundred, already expenses into it I'd only be collecting something less than four.

Walked a good thirty minutes from the motel I'd booked at, went to some phone outside of office buildings with shops along street level—bars and restaurants here and there were alive and mumbling energy, everything else just seemed bloated asleep in the humidity, the soup of the morning's air got dark was all night seemed like lately.

Dialed Wynol at the number he'd given me last time, home office I supposed, let it ring six times the machine came on. Hung up. Loop of the block, cigarette, cigarette again leaned to the phone, I dialed him back up. Machine clicked on after the six rings in, hung up.

Either meant one of several things: he'd gotten such a startle in him he'd been beat to the point thought he could ignore me away—I doubted this—he'd not been able to free up time—maybe, I'd try back off and on until midnight, eventually if this was the thing his wife'd say "Who is it calling you, answer, it might be an emergency"—or else he was being belligerent, fully knowing I knew he'd read the letter and caught the drift full in his face, just being the little brat about it.

"Not a good idea," I whispered as part of a long blue grey exhalation a new cigarette.

"Benefit of the doubt though, benefit of the doubt," I added on the next drag, walking in the direction of one of the bars had music coming from it.

"What's a good vodka?" I asked, girl tending bar had nothing going on and didn't seem interested in the band like everyone else did.

"Good cheap or good good?"

I considered it, she was getting a shot glass set up.

"Good good."

She smiled like I'd been the first person'd said the right thing in her direction all night.

"Chopin," she said, "good good composer, good good vodka."

She watched me take up the glass, told her I'd get her one it was alright, not to worry, I wasn't trying to press anything on her and otherwise I'd generally mind my own business.

"You're not here for the band, I take it?"

She poured herself a shot, refilled my glass—I wondered was I paying for both, for either—I swallowed the second shot back as soon as she'd turned hers up and was swallowing.

She told me "Hold on a minute, don't wander off alright?" went to the other end the bar and had to deal with making what seemed an awful lot of drinks for some group'd all come up the counter the same time.

The vodka was wonderful, actually, had me turned over and over, realized I'd been poisoning myself ugly with what I'd been drinking ever since getting to town, since having to spend such a cut into my savings to get set up. Didn't like thoughts about anything before that getting on me, though—Norman, didn't like thinking about Norman—wished the bartender'd pour me another, that or at least give me a look.

Soon enough, the rise of the second shot must've hit me and I was loose, not thinking about a thing.

"I've left you dry, I'm so sorry."

Bartender practically slid back over, poured me a shot, her a shot, told me "Don't worry, you can afford it," to which I smiled because I was drunk enough to know it's what I was supposed to do.

"Are you around later?"

"I'm around later tonight, usually I'm not from around here, though."

"Oh no."

"Well, from around here, just not this town. I'm just here I need to make a phone call, tonight."

"Phone call, huh?"

I didn't understand the overtness of her posture, her flirting, figured I was making it all up, that I was a typical mark and she'd be rich as she could get off me I'd not even know it'd happened.

"Phone call, yeah."

I started to stand and she seemed genuinely worried, went a bit straighter before leaning in.

"When's your phone call done? I'm off kind of late, so maybe you wanna stop back by, if that's alright?"

I promised I'd swing back in awhile, but honestly by the time I was few blocks up and third shot hit me I got focused on the call, nothing else.

Found a phone a gas station lot, dialed Wynol, it rang to the machine. Tried again right away and again right away, machine machine.

Impossible—what'd I pick the one Wednesday he goes out of town all of a sudden?

Could be he had his office phone the ringer off, it struck me, mellowed me out a bit. But few more cigarettes in I was fed up, got the idea he was having a long thin grin over it, either heard the ringing or else could see how many missed calls'd come in on some display.

Machine took up.

"Wynol, this's a big blunder your part, typical you've gone mistaken my kind patience for something other than that. Going to have to flay you now, I'm afraid to say. Rene must've been a real A student of yours she's worth all this."

Hung up weak but furious, lumbered off whichever direction my momentum'd started me in. Was more than halfway back toward my motel I remembered about the bar, the bartender—somewhere'd run out of cigarettes, but kept patting around myself for one each time I remembered there weren't any.

***

Miserable, got back to my basement room early next morning, had woke still drunk in the motel, but antsy drunk, couldn't get to sleep so found the first bus running.

Knew it'd come down to either forget it with Wynol or else go through with it giving his information around—go through with ruining him over five hundred dollars. It wasn't really the thing, to follow through, it was supposed to be threat didn't work it could be easily forgotten, move on to something else. Thought for a few minutes it'd be worth it maybe go through with it in stages, up the amount I was asking for, but deflated quickly from, drank some cold coffee left in my pot—if Wynol wasn't budging here, who knew what'd he get up to I leaned on him more.

I'd developed a cough sometime while I'd been asleep, it seemed, almost choked twice on my coffee, little sudden burst of my throat spasming, me trying to resist making it worse.

It all of a sudden felt so silly, so overly elaborate a game to've been playing, just still I couldn't so easily let it go, like breaking it off with some girl or having it broken off, thing stayed in my thoughts, couldn't get shut of it.

I skipped my shower to instead walk down the grocery store, get some cigarettes, got back to my room, changed into work pants, shirt in the duffle to put on once I was there, otherwise I'd sweat through it five minutes in the humid overcast it was becoming outside, suffered through coughing and two cigarettes while I waited for the bus.

Guy owned the video store was having a laugh with Scott when I came in through the door, right away he saw me, expression changed, asked me how was I doing and could I come back to the office for a word with him.

"Sure," I said, big smile and playacted rolling my shoulders like my neck needed a rub, owner giving a nod to Scott who busied himself with stuffing insert coupons in with the sleeve art the new releases.

We got in the office, owner closed the door, told me could I sit down.

"Should I get changed first, quick? I'm on in five minutes."

Shook his head, I sat, he turned the chair at his desk around.

"Trevor, we've had a rather serious complaint from a customer come up—a regular customer, I've known him many years, says he's been receiving some harassment and he believes it's an employee here or someone who knows an employee here who's responsible for it."

I'd no idea was I managing to hide my tension or if my

little shift of position and look of earnest concern I mugged on just made me seem a clown, obvious I'd been pegged dead bang.

"What kind of harassment, what do you mean?"

"It's not something I necessarily want to go into details of—and I'm not saying that it was you, Trevor, but this customer has been rather emphatic in his belief that you have some role in it or else are the one actively doing the harassment."

I nodded. Shrugged. "I've no idea what that could be about. I can talk to him, maybe apologize if I said something or whatever it is."

Owner cut me off, gently raised hand, seemed he was hoping I'd see where the talk was going—I did, actually, but I guess he hoped I'd just slip right along there for him, save him the ordeal.

"I just want the matter dropped. The one thing I know for certain is that none of the other employee's—I've worked with these people for years, some of them since I opened and that's a long time—would have anything to do with what it is this customer is alleging. And I'm not saying I think you do have something to do with it, I'm not accusing you of anything—but he's intent on pursuing legal action and I've decided it'd be best if I just let you go, he's willing to forget it."

I rubbed my eyes, leaned back a bit, then forward. "I really need this job," I said, and it was true as much as it was me doing my best to act how I'd ought to act, give off that I was innocent.

"I'm going to put it down that it was voluntary, not that you're fired—you're not fired, I'll be glad to be a reference for you."

"I'm not harassing anybody, man. I mean I have to tell you this puts me off, alright? It's great you'll be a reference, I mean sure I appreciate that but doesn't it kind of make it out to this guy he's right it's me bothering him or whatever?"

The owner had a very genuine on my side look, now, nodded nodded nodded.

"I understand, that, I understand about that. It's not an easy decision and I promise you that when I speak to this person I will be emphatic that no investigation or anything led to the decision, I will emphasize that we did not fire you, that we have no reason at all to believe you are responsible for what he is alleging."

I sighed, almost aggressive. "So why fire me then?"

He looked at me a long minute, I moved a little bit uncomfortably. No point pressing the matter at this point, even if I was innocent, didn't even know what outcome I personally preferred, keeping the job or this'd just be it.

Owner stood up, said because he knew the circumstances were unfair he was cutting me a check for these full two weeks and two full weeks, on top.

"You don't want me even to work through this shift?" I said, taking the check—personal check from his own account—and the paperwork went along with it. He said it was fine, that he had all my shifts covered, walked me out to the parking lot and apologized, shook my hand.

I was already almost to the check cashing place by the time my thoughts caught up to me. Rolled up against a wall down the side of family restaurant, between it and a bank.

What was this guy Trot about?

It didn't make sense. Now I'd escalated it with letting on I knew about Rene Spree was one of the girls on the dirty movie he goes ahead and threatens the store, out-and-out lets on he thinks it's me blackmailing him?

My stomach was unsettled, wondered what was the best

move—certainly not to keep up with the thing, best absolutely to just take this and roll with it, but maybe was it also best to get out of town?

I fumed, looked at the check I'd just received. People I lived their basement weren't likely to give me back some prorated monies if I left right away, so all I had was this check and my money I kept in storage—all totaled maybe it was six thousand now, six and half thousand now. Travel, setting up someplace new could cut into that sharp, pointlessly, but staying around I could maybe find another job, keep up what I'd been doing with the video store, saving a bit, keeping my eyes out for some angle, finding some grift I could work.

Got distracted from this consideration though, it hitting me that Wynol knew my name, knew what I looked like— according to the owner he'd straight up accused me of harassment, and I'm sure he actually told the owner about everything, steady customer, maybe even a friend.

Wondered how much of it could Wynol have actually put together, not theoretical, but concrete.

The yearbook pages?

Described me to reception the high school, learned I'd been by there.

How long had he known my name and been poking around, seeing was I maybe behind it? Since right away?

I wanted to stop thinking, to run, but there was no way around that for all I knew it'd be irrelevant to run.

Couldn't he find me? Track me?

My usual defensiveness at the improbability of this stoked up, the ungodly difficulty must come in tracking someone they vanish some random spot in the country, even if I did keep using my name and ID.

Then the moment I rounded the corner, back to the sidewalk to get down the rest of the way get my check cashed, it hit me full that someone might already be watching me, if Wynol had the sniff of me from the get go, it wasn't difficult spend a few bucks on a private investigator see what was what with me.

Walked right past the check casher, realized it, kept walking though, like it was impossible I could do anything but.

***

Swung through the grocery store, as it was right where the bus left me off, took up three cans of Gin Martini, was numbly paying out the four dollars fifty the clerk asked it hit me it should be only three dollars.

"These aren't just one dollar each?"

The guy, middle aged, didn't seem he particularly cared or didn't care, asked if I had a savings card.

"I got one last time, yeah. I forgot it, though."

"Phone number?"

I closed my eyes, wobbled my head, opened my eyes. "Yeah, I didn't fill out that sheet, that's the thing. It's alright, just the four whatever is fine."

I'd said that thinking he'd only charge me the three dollars because what'd be the difference, but he took the five dollar bill from me, handed back fifty cents, reminded me to bring the sheet in next time.

Drank the first can down in the grocery store toilet while I threw water on my face, the other one out in the parking lot, felt cloudy and vague by the time I was unlocking the door to the basement room.

Right away, there were the several sealed envelopes of Wynol's history I'd have to do something about, opened the drawer with them, stacked them on the bed mattress.

It'd take just as long to destroy them all as to destroy all but one, so decided I'd head down to the storage unit I kept, leave them all in there—I wanted them either completely obliterated, not a trace, or else keep them secure, just throwing them in a dumpster, down a gutter was something I didn't want to take any chances on, the storage unit was out under a different name, no one could know which one even if someone was following me and saw me go into the place.

I turned out my pockets, went through everything, proud of myself for finding a few receipts from convince stores in the town I'd been calling Wynol from, but then it hit me I'd taken out a room in that motel—even if they couldn't necessarily give out guest information, anyone halfway clever'd find another way to get it out of them I'd been there.

The owner of the video store, he'd said that Wynol had agreed not to press charges if I was terminated or left the job. That's cooled me out a bit, initially, but seemed ominous now, seemed something he'd said to give politic appearances about things, just meant he wouldn't press charges against the store, nothing about me—but nothing changed that if he pressed charges against me everything'd come out, it wouldn't stop me being able to send all my information to whoever I wanted or else if there were proceedings I could stir up as much clamor as I could manage.

I flopped on the bed, not as drunk as I felt, but overacted I was completely inebriated so I could have excuse for these rambling lines of thought.

All I needed to decide was should I head right out of town, or should I stay on a bit, then out.

I had no way of knowing Wynol had a private detective following me—I tried to out-and-out deride the idea, but couldn't quite, just couldn't dismiss it—so my leaving town might be clear and easy, even if it cemented to Wynol he'd be right about me.

As long as I didn't out him, why'd he have reason to make expenditures to figure out where I was?

"Well," I said aloud, "because how's he to know I wouldn't just come at him another angle, another time?"

Closed my eyes, felt trapped and at a loss.

Woke up not too long later, overheated from my clothes and mouth thick with old saliva, throat stuffed with paste I'd kept my mouth open through the sleep.

Threw the envelopes and receipts in my duffle bag, slung it over my shoulder and stepped outside, the stink of ozone pinching me between the eyes, sky an obvious bloat of it'd rain in an hour or two.

How was I supposed to know if someone was following me—how do people follow people?

That was the only thing, because if Wynol didn't have any witnesses that I'd literally done anything or made a call or whatever, there was nothing he could do by calling in the authorities except make a headache for me—which he'd already made, I kind of suspected he knew that—and it'd be a headache for him, too, that was the other thing.

So, he postures up, gets me out a job, figures he's turned the tables and all of it so very neatly, had me marked as a punk and he was right, knew he was right.

Except, he knew I knew what I knew about him, his habit, and now Rene Spree into the bargain on top.

Bus was air conditioned and perfect, I was shivering by halfway through the ride, transferred to another line, this bus more packed I had to sit with someone right next to me leg against mine all the way until one stop before mine.

My panic, I rationalized, was getting the better of me—Wynol Trot was a high school teacher, obviously had some sort of complex he was better than his contemporaries, but not like he was someone wanted to exact holy vengeance on me for sleuthing out what his particular kink was—so he came across a porno had a former student of his in it, so what?

I mean, obviously I could make that look plenty bad for the guy, no sweat—but I mean So what on his end—he's gonna hire an assassin, he's gonna see me drop over dead his own hand?

It had to be something—not like he could trust I'd be tormenting myself around like this and that was how he felt his weight'd been thrown around proper for his trouble—had to be something, because costing me my job didn't a bit change his position and if he had no way of knowing had it jostled me to back off or else had it just upped the ante, generally, it didn't make sense why'd he even gone through with it.

For Less Self Store-It was set up you were given two keys, one to get into the maze of corridors, one to the unit, even if you supplied your own lock which I hadn't. Mine wasn't a walk in unit, more or less just a cubby about the size of the freezer part most refrigerators above another just like it, did out my combination, swung the door open.

I unzipped my duffle, knelt quickly, taking up the material I'd brought, rummaged open the thick trash bag I kept in the unit, transferred the things in, my hand touching against the bundle of cloth I kept the gun Norman'd given me in. I leaned in, breathing the confined air, the flat odor of plastic, stagnant cloth, money. I gripped the wrapped gun, took the bundle, setting it quickly into my duffle, then locked up and out the door into it was now bright and biting hot, lit a cigarette, glanced up and down the road.

Wynol had nothing to call the authorities on me over,

nothing in the world would hold up in legal terms and unless I did something else that well was dry for him.

Gave a look back once I was down the street, kind of wanted to count up my money, but I knew what it was, at least enough it wouldn't change things I was wrong by this or that amount, over or under. I'd get packed up, keep to my room, figure out some method of leaving—no need to do it blind, that'd only lead to spending more than was necessary. Take a breath, be out of town by end of the week, top of the next.

***

I got back to my room late, exhausted, found an envelope taped to the door, tore it open as I sat on the bed thinking it'd be something from the people I was renting the basement out, though no idea what.

Five hundred dollars inside. Twenty dollar bills. Twenty-five of them.

I put the money on the bed, stared at it there in the dark. Made sure my shade was all the way down, locked the door and sat on the floor, tense for a few minutes but calm once I figured there was no reason to be.

Nothing else in the envelope, nothing written on it. I counted the money to be sure it was five hundred—not that I could think of a reason any other amount would be in an envelope outside my door—absently put it down in my pant pockets.

Troubling for two reasons, didn't know which more than which—why would Wynol be paying me out of nowhere and how did he know where I lived?

Following me, he had someone following me. It was stupid that I was almost excited about that, that I'd sorted it out ahead of time, actually had to concentrate to reason straight.

Could it be anything else?

If Wynol was friends with the owner of the video store, could've gotten my address that way—other than that I couldn't figure it, I didn't get mail, had no friends, acquaintances.

Maybe he knew the people I rented from, they'd mentioned offhand having a tenant, thought he worked at such and such video store?

Supposing Wynol'd told the owner everything, though, supposing the two of them were friends or that just from hearing what I'd threatened owner'd thought it'd be fair enough to give out my address, because how would I ever prove it, besides?

Didn't matter, just irritated me to still have two options, each just as plausible.

I was just distracting myself from thinking on Why would Wynol've come all the way out to deliver the money, envelope it to my door?

Crept upstairs, sat in the dark of the main living room area, sunk in one of the large chairs looking at the cold television or the soft of the closed windows I could see out but doubted anyone would come peeking in.

Leaving the money was an escalation, or either way wasn't something I could grin, feel a champion about— technically it was what I'd asked, so there was an illogic to my being upset at Wynol about it, an illogic in my thinking I'd go asking him Does this mean we're even, or should I be worried?

"I am the blackmailer," I whispered, "he is the pervert, I am not the one under any thumb."

Almost stood up to pace around, mutter to myself all sides of this like it was simply rhetoric, instead sank lower where I sat.

When I heard the sound of shuffling from the top floor,

quietly as I could got in through the door to the basement, sat on the steps, leaned to the wall, closed my eyes. I'd wait until morning, pack everything I could in my duffle, swing by the storage unit and get out of town. Whatever Wynol had or didn't have planned, doubted very much it'd be for crack of dawn a school day—certainly he knew how I'd interpret the money left on my doorstep, knew it'd jar me he'd even found my doorstep, but nothing I was going to run scrambling off middle of the night about.

Lost track of how long it'd been I'd be running the same thoughts around my head, heard the couple I rented from coming down from the upstairs to the main floor, chatting, heard them starting the coffee. Stood, stretched myself out, touched at my clothing then went out to the kitchen myself, nodded at them very politely.

"Did someone stop by for me yesterday? I got hung up, didn't get in until late, but a friend was supposed to drop something off for me."

The man looked about to say something, woman started in before him so he turned his attention to some casual stretching.

"Not when we were here or he didn't come to the front door, anyway."

"Alright."

"You want some coffee? You can always help yourself."

"I might, gotta get a shower, but yeah thanks for that."

It'd been largely a pointless interaction, but I'd wanted to verify that leaving the money had been purposeful, that whoever'd left it knew for certain I lived in the basement—I'd never mentioned this, not at work, had only put down the full address of the house on my application, meant I'd been observed going in or out, no one just going to guess about taping an envelope of cash to a basement door someplace.

It couldn't've been Wynol personally left the money—or he could've left it, just it for certain wasn't him who'd ever followed me. So, he'd hired someone or asked someone to follow me around, probably still had them following me around—why?

Heard the door open, shut, lock, went up to the kitchen just as the coffee was finishing its last hisses through the filter, poured some in a mug from a cupboard, set it on the counter and stared at the heat up from off of it. There wasn't yet any real sun outside, watched through the window how already the air stood thick, plump and waiting for sunlight to tip it into being a misery.

Choice I had was same choice as always, run or stay around, run or stay around—things'd gotten away from me, didn't even know exactly what outcome I was after with the circumstances.

Walked to the grocery store, tense halfway through about I'd left the gun in my room and how hard could it be to break in, got caught up in little fantasies of returning home to find it gone.

The air conditioning of the store was pleasant, I walked odd loops of the aisles, trying to seem just like I was loitering but also trying to keep track of who else I saw, could any of them be following me, knew I was nothing near observant enough, better not to get caught up ferreting out my shadow—even if I thought it was this person or that, what good'd thinking so do me, no way to confirm?

Walked back to my room, packed everything I could into my bag and went out again, got the first of the two buses'd take me out to the storage locker, each mile of road feeling more comfortable, my neurotic tension lifting with the realization that I'd be gone, soon, on a train, bus, whoever it was Wynol was paying wouldn't follow me forever, couldn't.

Transferred buses, fell asleep in my seat coming awake each time it stopped, little pelts of anxiety I'd been out too long, but soon enough it was the stop a few miles walk from the storage facility.

I smoked a cigarette, looking around—nobody could be following me, no cars parked nearby, no odd milling pedestrians—the way down to the unit, it seemed more and more I was alone—isolated little road, no one at all within eyeshot.

I used my key, let myself in, walked around the corridors randomly awhile before getting to my unit, unlocking it, letting the weight of my duffle from my hands, itching my palm where the skin was all pushed awkward out of place and into divots.

The unit was empty. I didn't even register surprise, rubbed the back of neck, looked around, looked back into the unit, closed the door, looked at the number, looked at the adjacent units and the locks. Closed my eyes, funny that anger didn't even start to rise, no thought of pestering the manager did they steal from me, did they let someone in—whole reason I'd picked this place was it was tiny, no cameras, out of the way, didn't require ID, every reason made it obvious it'd take no more than fifty bucks slipped to whoever was on duty the front to get in, get the unit belonged to so and so, maybe five bucks more they'd hand you the key, ten bucks they'd empty it for you.

***

I sipped gas station coffee sitting at a table in a bookstore, had my cigarettes out, absentmindedly turning the pack around and around by nudging the corners. Felt a little bit like I was inebriated, cares kept off just at the slightest distance, close enough my fingers out at arms length knew there was something there, just not close enough to scrape my fingernails across.

Between the five hundred Wynol had left in the envelope and the uncashed check from work, I had just a touch more than one thousand dollars. It was gutting, especially I doubted Wynol'd even thought for a minute there'd be any money into the bargain for him—whoever it was'd followed me had figured it out easy the unit was where I kept what I had to hold over Wynol, Wynol'd told them See about getting in and they had. It was basically my own five hundred dollars I'd been given, though not literally, didn't think Wynol'd've known what was in the unit until after he'd had the envelope left.

What did it matter?

I stood, sat back down, had a mouthful of coffee I could feel crawling around down in me.

What did it matter?

Asked someone was browsing a shelf right by me what time was it, they said just shy of three, I nodded, then went outside, crossed back to the gas station to a line of three payphones. Called to get the number for Feildway High School, dialed the number, muttering it over and over, reception picked up.

"Hi, I was hoping to speak to Mister Wynol Trot, if he's available?"

"No bother," reception just said they'd try putting me through to his office, it'd be his voicemail if not him. He answered a casual Hello after just one ring, pleasant and half distracted sounding.

"Hi Wynol."

He cleared his throat, I could picture him shifting in his chair, a grin, maybe lifting a cup of coffee to have a sip each time I talked.

"Is that Trevor English? How are you, Trevor English?"

"I think you've got just the idea about how I am, Wynol Trot, so how about we get to the thing what we're going to do about it?"

I heard him speaking away from the phone, asking a student or a colleague could they come back five minutes he was just on a call.

"Whatever do you mean, Trevor? Is there something left to do?"

"I'm sure you're feeling proud about it all, Wynol, that was high school teacher clever of you, but I keep a copy on me at all times, don't think you want to be pushing me into doing something clever with it."

"I think if you had something clever to do you would have, by now, that's what I think, quite honestly."

"I don't just shrug off someone spirits my money away—games aside for the moment, you do know that right?"

"It wasn't your tuition money for those community college credits you were talking about, was it? I'd feel just terrible about that."

"Wynol, I'll put this stuff in the hands of your kids, your wife, your principle, head of the PTA, might make it just a point use this five hundred you left me print enough I can get a copy into the mailbox of every parent the school, just leave them under windshield wipers—now I don't know about what it is with perverts like you, fronting off makes you feel big and bad next time you hit the pause button or what, but you're taxing my patience."

He made a sound, not a proper laugh, just the sound he was smiling so fat it had to be audible.

"I don't think you have a copy, being blunt—and all the more being blunt, go ahead and get clever if you do and I'll have you brought up on charges in a heartbeat, seeing as I know someone who knows where you're standing right this second I don't think it'll be tough. I'll tell you, I'm almost of a mind to call the police right now, say you delivered one of these envelopes to me, have a friend say you delivered one to them, as well, in person, describe you down to the fleabites and then I'll gladly explain how you've been harassing me and share with them everything I have that proves it—there's only one reason I'm not going to that, in fact."

I'd gotten out of breath listening to him, the implications of what he was saying pressing down over me, hardly registered he'd stopped, seemed like he noticed it, been waiting for me to catch up.

I didn't know what to say, except ask "What reason?" like he so clearly wanted me to.

"Because you're going to pay me not to."

"Very cute, very very cute, man. I get you're a lofty guy, but even reading you like I do we both know you wouldn't put your family through that, bring yourself down low in with me."

His voice changed, a sigh like he was bored, just indulging me because if he didn't we couldn't get to his next thing.

"You think you're going to get to give a press conference? I'll tell my wife myself—sure I watch dirty movies sometimes—what do you think she's going to leave me, tell the kids all about it I'm subhuman, I'll be tarred and feathered? Listen—that grocery store you like getting drunk at, three dollars at a time, you're going to stand in front of it, tomorrow morning, a nice gentleman is going to say Hello to you, shake your hand, you're going to put one thousand dollars in his and then we'll be all done."

He spoke away from the phone, again, something like That's fine, Anthony, come on in.

"You only left five hundred."

"Think of something clever, I have to run, student's here."

I caught a muffled word or two he was saying to the kid'd shown up before the line went dead.

When I turned my eyes out to the parking lot, they stung, went to rub them realized how much I was sweating, sopping wet, pulled up the front of my shirt, padded my eyes with it, could smell the sour off from in the fabric.

Tried the toilet door inside the food shop attached to the station, it was locked, had to wait in line for a key.

I looked almost I was going to cry in the mirror, washed my face over and over, my arms, my hands, dried myself with paper towels then ran more of them over my body, under my shirt, undid my pants and wetted towels to wipe down my legs, between them, dried off. Flattened my hair down wet, combed it with fingertips, tried to part it this way, that way, just mussed it, added more water, suddenly spit in the face of the glass, growled, spit on the floor, then took some steady breaths before I wet my hand to rub away the splotch on the mirror glass as best I could.

Kept slow and calm, got another coffee, gave looks to every customer, but figured whoever was following me was out in a car. Wondering if my observer had some device he could've heard my end of the conversation got me wondering had Wynol recorded my call to him at home, before—made me call back to his office because he was equipped to do that there.

The question Who would do that? popped to mind and it right away sounded so ludicrous, so hobgoblin, I laughed, spilled a few spots of coffee on the tile, rubbed at them with my shoe before getting napkins, sure the clerk at the register was giving me squints.

"You have the key?" woman asked me I got to the counter to pay.

"Key?"

"For the men's room, sir?"

I put my cup on the counter, touched at myself.

"Does it lock automatically?" I asked, felt a clown the way she just stared even at me.

"You left the key inside?"

"I wasn't even thinking. I'm so sorry."

She rolled her eyes, told me coffee would be dollar twenty.

"It's a refill," I said, pointing vaguely in the direction of the machines where a sign advertised refills for a dime.

"You took a new cup."

"I didn't take a new cup. This is the cup I bought I was in here half hour ago, just went to the bookstore."

She stared at me, finally tightened her lips, shaking her head and didn't meet my eyes the rest of the transaction, me handing her a quarter, she handing me back fifteen cents.

***

I didn't exactly hurry to get to the check cashing place, made sure I was there with plenty of time before it closed, but didn't hurry. It was just me and some woman paying her utility bill, half asleep seeming—I couldn't tell was she trying to flirt with the guy taking care of her or what.

When I put my thumb print on the check, handed across my ID, it struck me I'd no matter what need to find some way to go without that, my name was getting sagged down with things could be traced back to it— it made me uneasy to identify myself, uneasy to be myself. Didn't count the money after the clerk counted it out and tried not to do the simple math of adding five hundred to it—or four hundred seventy-six and change—but automatic I knew it came to eleven hundred dollars at the most, if anything more not enough it would matter.

Didn't even walk away from the shop front, leaned there like nobody, like any nobody did any day with nowhere else to go. It was dark and the air hardly moved for its thickness.

Let myself in the basement room, undressed completely and lay on the bed with my feet draped over onto the carpet. Part of me wanted to think about what I was going to do to get Wynol, how I was going to arrange a smooth revenge, but a larger part of me knew it wasn't anything, nothing to do, nothing that he couldn't hurt me more than I could him, not even enough we'd go down together or something cliché.

Wynol hadn't done anything wrong. It was strange that the sentence was both a surprise to me and something remained foreign even though I recognized it. I couldn't do anything to hurt him, because he hadn't done anything wrong.

I'd have eighty-eight dollars and some handful of change maybe even amounted to a few more dollars once the thousand I had to hand off in the morning walked away from me.

Walked around the neighborhood smoking, kind of looking around all the time was I still being watched, didn't see why I would be, though at the same time Wynol might've got a kick out of paying the guy to watch me around the clock, considering the money from the unit must've more than paid for whatever it'd cost.

Or had the guy watching me mentioned the money?

No difference, but it was funny to wonder about something like that, to wonder what was the incentive in it for a private investigator or whatever the guy called himself, what did he care about getting into a storage unit, for example, why side with some pervert just because he'd been paid to?

Briefly fantasized about giving the guy the scoop on Wynol, maybe even puffing it up, winning him over to me, but it;' never happen.

Took everything out of my duffle, dull little inventory of what was about to be everything was mine in this world. Got to the bundle of clothes around the gun, I unwrapped it carefully—odd how the thing didn't look the least bit familiar, not that I'd spent any amount of time with it, but it looked almost like it'd been replaced, something redrawn in a clumsier hand than the original. Realized I was staring at it, I set it on the desk, fiddled around in the dark with getting some coffee going in my pot but knew I was thinking about it—nothing in particular, nothing sensible, just pointing it at Wynol, pointing it at him.

I got dressed, packed everything in my bag, including the rewrapped gun, sat on the ground and drank coffee waiting until I either fell asleep or the sun started to come up. Two cups swallowed, I stood, slung my bag over my shoulder, made a last pass around the room, didn't even lock the door behind me, trudged, immediately sweating again, through the dark hum of air to the grocery store.

No one was at the customer service desk, so I asked the one teller on duty and the night manager milling around with him was there a telephone directory, could I get the number for a taxi. Manager nodded, but instead of a directory he just went around to where the clerk was, patted around under the counter, came up with a business card.

Though I doubted it, one of the cars parked in the lot could've been the one the guy I was to meet in the morning was sitting in, maybe asleep—maybe I could go peer in to every window, except even if someone was in one, what'd I do about that?

Cab said it'd be out fifteen minutes, so I went and bought two last cans of Vodka Martini, didn't bother about the discount card, drank one down and tucked the other into my duffle, it'd be my victory drink I knew I was in the clear.

Waved when the cab pulled up, told the driver I wanted him to pull out onto the highway, I'd tell him which exit once we were going. Radio burbled something odd sounding, songs that were being interrupted by the disc jockey talking then starting again, music interrupted every fifteen seconds by some sort of a commentary.

I watched the grocery store lot move further and further away, no one seemed to leave from it, watched the road behind us, empty, empty. When we were just about on a particular exit, I told the driver Here. Area was not really developed, kind of put me off because I wanted to at least be near someplace, so when we passed a dead-for-the-night strip mall I told him pull in, instructed him to go around behind the shops to let me out. Driver took it in stride, was most ordinary thing on earth, so I felt guilty I didn't leave a tip except told him keep the twenty from the fare being eighteen and something.

Sat on the steps of a loading area, smoked a cigarette, let what felt twenty minutes pass before I took out the can of liquor I'd squirreled, downed it, lit up another smoke. Sat there nodding, reassuring myself I could not possibly've been followed, reassuring myself this was better—better to have to get myself lost awhile, hide it out, live transient for whatever a few days, a week or two than pay out my last dime and be nowhere with no way to get away from being nowhere.

Didn't take long before burbles of paranoia took up in my ears—couldn't any investigator half a brain think about calling cab companies? Could only be so many, after all, couldn't they show my picture around, get I was dropped off wherever this was, then door-to-door with my picture, get at me a foot print at a time?

But that'd leave me no worse than I'd been, say I was tracked down. Certainly I didn't have any particular advantage now, didn't have any particular plan, but still had money in a bag, even if not enough to live indoors a week.

When my buzz started wearing down and I needed to fight how I wanted sleep, knew sleep wasn't coming, started walking along, stopped, drifted back to the shopping center, stood in front of a telephone until I was beat under my fatigue enough to fish the taxi card up from my pocket, dial out the numbers. It took a few minutes to arrange the ride back, because I didn't know where was I—explained I'd been dropped off not three quarters an hour back, something, gave the address I'd called from, said I'd be going back right to that same place.

***

Traffic started filling the lot, began getting an odd feeling when the dozenth person'd seen me out smoking on their way into the store saw me smoking on their way out, carts full with bagged goods. Wynol'd just said I was to wait around in the morning, no specific indication what time or that I should be doing something special—I'd decided to pick as conspicuous a spot as I could, but one I was still able to chain my way through three quarters of the last pack of good cigarettes I'd be able to swing for a long while, no worries I'd be shooed away some ordinance. If somebody lingered a tick too long giving me a glance, I'd feel my stomach tighten, I was some kid at the bus stop, hoping somehow the bus didn't show I'd be free.

I was wrapping myself up in thinking Wynol just wanted me occupied for some other reason when a man waved at me casually, stepping out from the car he'd just parked. Small man, tight weight to him, dressed in shorts, shoes with no socks, hairy upper halves of his arms. He gave a second wave to confirm my tentative hand lifted was appropriate.

"Hello," he said, extending for a handshake, stepping right up to me.

"You know Wynol?"

He smiled, raised one shoulder, titling his head in its direction, heard a little crack of his neck.

"I know Wynol, yeah. You know Wynol?"

"I'm trying to understand, for my own curiosities' sake, mind telling me just one thing then I'll get you this money?"

"What's that?"

He didn't seem in any sort of hurry, to have any particular animosity toward me—my thoughts of maybe getting him in my corner stoked, ebbed, I stepped out the cigarette I'd taken a last drag from.

"You tell Wynol you found that money in my locker? Just out of curiosity, because I've always wanted to know something like that, what'd a guy do he found some money's none of his business."

"No, didn't tell him about it, nothing he needs to know about."

I took the money out my pocket, I'd made a packet for it out of some loose sheets of paper and invisible tape.

"Don't suppose there's any point asking Why don't you do me a good turn here, then, give it back or else just cut the thousand from it, give that to Wynol?"

He sniffed, didn't look impatient, just looked he had no inclination to respond.

"You're okay with that you're the one robbing me, right?"

"I'm okay with it. Why wouldn't I be?"

I wanted to give him a stare, but found I was averting my eyes any time they'd touch him, handed the packet across and watched him turn around, get back to his car, drive off. Whole thing'd been like nothing, my heart wasn't even going fast, it was what I figured dying in one's sleep'd feel like.

Walked back in the direction of my basement room, mostly just to be out of the heat, get some sleep. I toyed with what Wynol's thinking with leaving me that five hundred was if he hadn't known a thing about the thousands of dollars'd been in my storage unit with the copies of his account history and the photocopies of Rene Spree from the yearbook—guessed it'd been because he knew he was going to charge me this one thousand, just a joke, pirouette my little blackmail back around, all things taken into account it wasn't so aggressive a thing to do. He'd get his thousand, that'd be that, would figure I had the scare in me, nothing either of us'd want to go escalating.

Unless the guy I'd just given the money to kept that, told lies about me. What would it matter to him? Maybe doing that'd keep him on payroll another little while, pretending to be hunting me down—this gave me a smile, I wished he was doing that, opportunistic, making a big fat imagination out of other people's intrigues and noias.

That's what I'd do.

Two cigarettes left total by the time I was to my door, smoked the last of the one I had lit, flicking it against the outside of my window, it bounced back against my shoulder before to the ground.

How long had it been since I had nothing more than sixty dollars in my pocket?

Long time, but not so long. Not so long and what difference really had there been I had a bag full of money someplace?

For awhile I lay on the bed, wanting to sleep, but I just wouldn't. I felt lost, even any steam I'd built to go against Wynol spent—he'd only taken five hundred dollars from me, if not for my own having to secret my money away I'd be fine, just take this as a lump, something to learn from.

Everything I'd lost'd been lost incidentally.

Should've left last night, or anytime—Wynol'd never've chased me, he was snuggled nice in his security that he had enough to keep me from ever going against him, didn't care about anything else. I don't know what would've given him more of a giggle, even, getting the money off me or knowing he'd got me to scamper away all a mess.

Not even sixty dollars. I counted out my money, only had forty three and some coins, math in my head'd never caught up with the second cab fare.

I woke up it was night, deep night, could tell right away I'd been out for more than twelve hours.

Used the toilet upstairs, got back down to my room and finished off the pot of coffee I'd brewed the previous night, started another one, drinking down the last bit of warm water left in the gallon I had sat on the desk for coffee making.

Waiting with a cigarette in my lips for the coffee to brew, wanting to drink a cup before stepping out, I thought to myself how it'd been a mistake to go after Wynol when all the time it was his wife I should've been leveraging—Wynol I'd been playing with too much, it was just me against him, animals in a dark room not even knowing which parts we were biting off each other, hoping just they were the ones'd end things fastest, but with his wife it'd've been Wynol was the bad guy, the one doing it to her, I'd just be an extension of him, she'd have to protect her family and he'd've cleaved himself off from it, been made interloper by his actions.

Took a hot swallow of the new coffee, wished I'd kept a pour of the water I'd just drank to dull the temperature, took a few more sips to numb my lips to the sting of it, drank the full cup and it groaned sharp, made me cramp, the cigarette I lit as I locked the door behind me doing nothing to help.

Wynol's wife.

I chuckled through my nose, congested a bit, couldn't remember what'd she look like the restaurant that night.

It was Friday night, so whatever I was going to do one way or another'd have to wait through the weekend.

Got back to the room and must've fallen asleep, like the previous sleep hadn't meant anything. Woke to the sound of a lawnmower someplace, rolled over, stared at the ceiling, listened, not sure which part of last night was real—had I thought things or dreamt things, which parts were the parts all in my head, weighing me to place, easing me slowly back to focus, which parts were thing actual real.

***

Read magazines the grocery store until I felt comfortable enough to pocket the non-prescription reading glasses I'd settled on I wanted, it'd been awhile since even so simple a shoplift—kid game, really, hardly counted as theft. Outside I put them on, not so much a difference to things, nothing

I wouldn't get used to inside five minutes. Decided to splurge on some cheap cigarettes at the gas station, walk a few loops of the neighborhood around where I kept my room, then closed myself inside, undressing to hurry up the cold of the air conditioning.

Only had the one off the ready-to-wear rack suits I'd bought awhile back, everything else'd been in the bag the storage unit. I laid the pants, jacket out, fingered the wrinkles. Only had just the pair of shoes I was wearing, but probably I could polish them up halfway decent, heel hadn't flopped loose, bottoms hadn't worn thin near the toe which was the eventual fate of all of my shoes due to some odd way I had of placing my weight and how I'd forever be scuffing my toes on the pavement on the phone, standing, even just waiting at a crosswalk.

When I heard the couple I rented from come in, I popped up the stairs, met them in the kitchen.

"Do you have clippers, do your own hair?" I asked the guy, he and the woman smiling.

"You need to borrow my clippers?"

"I was hoping to. Getting rid of this mess for a job, hopefully for a job, interview anyway."

They both congratulated me, said that was terrific.

"Just some office thing," I said when the woman pressed me, "but better than grinding the retail, part-timer some shop you know?"

"When's the interview?"

It was a hot topic, I even relaxed into the charade due to their inquisitiveness was so earnest, without weight.

"Monday, mid-morning on Monday, out in Fieldway."

"You know how to use clippers? If you want I can buzz you, later on, little bit easier than doing yourself."

"That'd be fantastic, I'd appreciate it. Doing my best to look like I've at least heard of respectability, right?"

The woman touched the man on the back, kissed his shoulder and headed upstairs, wishing me good luck.

"You have something to wear?" guy asked, getting a sports drink from the fridge, having a swallow while I explained about my suit. Still getting his breath from a quick second mouthful, closing the fridge, he told me he had some suits'd probably fit me, if I at least wanted to try one on. I nodded thanks, said it was worth a shot and he went upstairs.

Sat in my room for something around two hours, smoked one cigarette just standing in my open door, an odd smell of upturned soil to the darkening air—had a long, lazy thought about how dozen of animals, dogs, cats, squirrels had all of a sudden started furiously clawing up the earth, pulling it back down over themselves.

The man called down the stairs, I heard him sound the clippers a harsh buzz, called I'd be right up. Sat with my shirt off, a little bit self-conscious due to the guy's physical fitness and the woman popping her head in every so often. Fielded questions about a past I invented a little bit with each answer, didn't take a look at myself until all the hair was gone, then looked down at it in a pile, said I'd sweep up, the man telling he'd get it, I should go take a shower and he'd get out a suit for me.

I lingered in the hot water, soaped myself repeatedly, every time I ran my hands over my head they'd come away with speckles of hair in the grooves of the palms.

Knock at the door, man said he was leaving the suit just outside. I almost asked did maybe he have a fresh razor, some foam, but then just re-used one of my three, only tough spot caused me any bother was the underside of my chin.

Suit fit better than mine had when I'd tried it on—I'd

lost more weight than I guess I kept track of. Fine light grey suit, appropriate for the heat, another plus over the rather thick discount brown one laid out in the basement.

It felt good, the man the woman, their little show of Didn't I cut the smart figure? and all of it, but this didn't last long because they were on their way out for a night of it. I thanked them, again, man pointed to another tie I could use if I liked, a mute green one folded into a loose square on the counter top.

With my stolen glasses on, the borrowed clothes, I hardly felt myself—best I'd felt in a long time, aware of myself but only conscious of how different I seemed, looked forward to how it'd be for the first day or so, how it's always be a bit of surprise, seem there was a sharpness to my features I'd catch a glimpse of reflection somewhere—day or two, few days before my mind dulled to it and this became just how I looked, not how I didn't.

I tried out some versions of introducing myself into the mirror, into the air.

"Hi, Mrs. Trot, I'm a friend of Wynols, well he's helping me something at the school."

When I remembered Wynol's wife was called Sandra, I tried to get comfortable saying it—it'd work better than Mrs. Trot.

"Hi Sandra, I'm a friend of your husband. Hi Sandra, I'm Frank—I'm Theo, I'm Duncan. I'm a friend of Wynol."

Looked like I could be his friend, could be a clean cut teacher of high school physics, maybe, but didn't think I'd have to get around to explaining where I knew him from, just needed to seem pleasant enough to be greeted with a smile, seem appropriate enough to belong knocking on a door.

Not thinking I'd really keep it on me, I got the gun out

of my duffle, gently tried it in the suit coat pockets—it seemed to fit them all, best of all at the hip.

Got back in my own clothes, decided I could go get myself a drink down the grocery store. For a change it was a different clerk on, so I asked could I sign up for a discount card without it seeming off. Clerk scanned one, gave me the paper to fill out. I left with three cans of Gin Martini.

Was still awake when the man and the woman got in, heard them trying to keep their giggling subdued, get up the stairs. Turned on the television and laid in the bed not even facing it, just liking how it actually seemed I could feel the licks of the jags of light, volume on loud enough only that nothing was distinct, one thing recognizable was the tone of laughter, applause on the sitcom repeat must've been showing.

Sunday came and went I didn't even leave my room, smoked out the window, most of the time spent on my belly or with sudden fits of pacing, slipping the suit coat on and off until I was used to having to tick this shoulder up and back a bit at just this moment to compensate for the weight of the gun down the pocket, keep it from bringing the fabric down too sharply, one sleeve up showing my whole forearm.

Middle of the night coming to Monday morning I sat, coat off, just undershirt and boxer short, gun on the bedsheet in a pinch of wrinkles all around it. Wrapped it back up in the bundle of clothes, same as always, buried it down in my duffle.

Hadn't polished my shoes, I noticed, but overall look of things probably no one else'd notice either. Licked my middle three fingers wet and ran them all around one, did the same, same three fingers other hand, other shoe.

***

I left my duffle on a bench, good view generally of Wynol's house front, bushes groomed nice but not really seeming like it in the damp humidity, everything looked it'd recently been crawled over by insects.

Too early for anything because I'd caught the first bus—anxious to be away from my room, same time not wanting to go anywhere else and have to come back, even any of the cafes, convenience stores in the area the bus'd left me—I walked a distance along into the park area, rounded back to the bench every few minutes, doling out my cigarettes, throat tight with each drag to the point I'd take every other just in my mouth, hold it, blow it out a formless mess.

Both Wynol and Sandra's car were parked outside the closed garage, hoped it wasn't Sandra left first, was going on the assumption that since Wynol taught high school he'd have to be out early—even Sandra having a job with typical hours she'd be alone for a spot.

First time the door opened, I tensed then went loose, same sensation through my body as I'd stubbed my toe, turned my back, counted off ten before casually starting to stroll, giving a peripheral look who it was leaving. Young kid left the house, the boy, Wynol's son, walked in a bumpy, clumsy way a kids walk with a backpack. He went a good way down the neighborhood and I idly followed him until I got the idea he was joining a group of other waiting kids, handful of parents, at a certain corner, school bus probably just few minutes off.

Took my time getting back by the bench, sat down for a minute, stretching my legs out, digging my shoe heels into the grass and soil, both pulpy with the morning wet and plump humidity. New smoke started, scanned around for were there any trees I could use for a toilet—no, but a distance off next to the backstop of a flimsy little baseball area was a portable toilet. Made me sigh to look at, but went over, gave uneasy looks around like I wasn't meant to go in, that some neighborhood patrol'd come give me a citation. Finally, couldn't actually work up the nerve to go in. Absurd. Even more absurd, just to give the impression to anyone might've been looking out their window over breakfast at me, I milled around, gingerly having my smoke, did a pantomime of reaching into my pocket, taking out a portable phone, turning around toward the fence to disguise my hands were empty.

Didn't think I was in the shape for this deal, not this morning, slugged my way back to my duffle, grim with knowing I had less than forty dollars and my room was only my room until the top of the month, short short time away.

Tightened when I saw Wynol leave the house with his daughter a few steps behind—her hair was long and only towel dry, shirt looser than it needed to be—Wynol addressed some remark at her, but she didn't seem to make a response and I noted Wynol peeked into one of the trash cans at the corner of the garage door, gave a long look in there going on tiptoe.

Purposefully turned my back and wandered into the field until I heard the dull clap of car doors one two, engine going and soft slow rough of wheels backing out, watched the vehicle move off in the same direction the boy'd gone, a quick little double beep of Wynol tapping the horn, obnoxious attempt to be cute or something, kid probably cringed from it, had to ignore a few jabs from his friends.

After the school bus'd left with the son, I watched the house front for any sign what Mrs. Trot might be up to, any sign she wasn't in the shower, something, still laying in bed, maybe her work didn't start until a bit later on she could have a sleep. Way the house was made couldn't even tell were lights on behind the blinds, no upper level window in the front at all.

Overcast made it hard to keep track of time, each time a car from a neighboring house'd take off, I'd get antsy, move toward my duffle, then squint at the house. Got it must've been an hour since Wynol'd left, argued a last time I could just wait and see, get a more or less exact time she'd be out the door by, come back the next day, but no.

Took off my glasses to give my eyes a rub, set them back, duffle over my shoulder, crossed up to her door and gave a quick four five knocks. Did my best to seem casual, look the part I needed to play at least a minute or two of, could tell from the sound of the latch moving a little then all the way she was having a look out the peephole at me before committing.

Didn't let her get the first word, made a sheepish kind of head bow looked a mild apology and began "Hi Sandra, hi I'm Arthur Davies, I was hoping to catch Wynol, looks maybe I missed him."

She nodded very politely, didn't seem on her guard. "Wynol just left for the school."

On top her talking, said "I was just on my way there, actually, was meeting with some people about a possible position, Wynol'd said he'd have some papers for me. I'd meant to stop by last night but got caught up some things."

"I'm sorry."

I kind of made a head bob, purposefully let my speech get meandering, shrugged. "Anyway, my fault."

"I'm sorry," she said, again, genuinely seemed she was— but also had a look I'm sure meant Wynol hadn't mentioned anything about it.

"Do you think I could use your toilet? Sorry, great question for first thing out of bed, right? I'm sure I can managed."

She smiled, stepped back while she said it was no trouble, that she was just finishing coffee before heading out, was glad at least someone'd been around for me.

I followed her into a dining room, she pointed toward an alcove just to the side of the kitchen, asked did I want coffee.

"Would it be trouble?"

"No trouble."

"Then if it's not, alright—already missed Wynol, now I don't have to be anywhere till past noon."

She nodded, looked at me like maybe she thought I'd seemed about to say something else, then just as I was turning she asked did I just take it black or how?

"Black's good or anything you want to put in it's alright, I'm not the creative sort, just know how to order it black."

"I'll come up with something, then."

After another dull smile, I actually went into the bathroom, hit the overhead fan, removed my duffle and adjusted at my coat shoulders, necktie. Wondered if Sandra found me attractive, felt disarmed and sure of how I presented myself because I struck her as handsome, well put together.

Sat on the closed bowl, ran my hands over my head, interlaced the fingers shushed them together through the fuzz. Noticing my shoes really still look shabby, I took a length of toilet paper, removed left shoe, wiped it down, right shoe—probably wasn't any difference really, but it made me feel better.

Enough time passed, I flushed the toilet, ran the faucet, cleared my throat.

***

Set my duffle down as I rounded to the kitchen dining area, Sandra sitting with her coffee, reading from a book she turned over, still open, smiled at me.

"Do you know a girl called Rene Spree?" I asked.

She right away said "Gloria's sister?" and I felt some tension ease—there was something, anyway, little way in I jumped at.

"That's right, Gloria's big sister—I suppose your daughter must be in the same class with Gloria?"

"That's right."

I took a seat opposite end of the table, Sandra leaning in her chin to one hand then went straight, got an apologetic look, asked did I still want coffee and moved to stand, stopping at my gesture could she keep where she was.

"You're aware of your husband's proclivity for the dirty movies, or aren't you?"

She didn't lift her cup, but put her fingers tentatively near it, kind of hummed "Proclivity for?"

"Dirty movies."

She looked at me, something on the fence between considering it a joke she was missing the rhythm of or a slight she should be defensive against. I used the pause to just continue.

"He has a six a week habit—I'm guessing you don't know. Flinn Video, it's in a town called Fordham. You know he goes there once, twice each week?"

Could tell she'd never heard of a Flinn Video, also could see she'd caught on the tone was threatening, my little speech an invasion.

"Six a week for a long long time, years back. Don't know where does he watch them except seems it isn't here."

She started to rise, I told her not to, she did, so I did, too and told her to sit.

"I'll stop with the sneaking up on things, don't want you to make a mistake before you've heard this, alright? No art, here's how it is—about three years ago, Gloria's big sister graduated Fieldway, made some choices got her in with the film crowd."

"I want you to leave."

"I know you do—and sure, none of your business girl wants to spread gets it mixed up with talent, except about two years ago Wynol came across one of her movies, Rene'd done a Norma Jean now she called herself Daphne but Wynol knew the thing."

I'd slowed, expecting another insistence I leave, even more aggression, but she gave a slight tick to her head, seemed she got the picture, kept quiet.

"Become his personal favorite, thirty times he's watched it two years, takes a romp with it something like every other week."

"Please leave," she said, but conviction was lost, it was a whisper, more like she'd wished I'd never showed up than she wanted me to go, now—still, I got a bit sharper in posture, kept my lips thin like I was talking more just with how I stared her down than the words.

"Thing is but I'm not leaving—stand up sit down, however it's more comfortable on you, talk again and my tone'll have to change bit more ugly, alright?"

She moved back toward the counter enough to rest against it, still standing.

"Leveling with you, I'm not a good guy in this, don't want you under the impression that's what I'm posturing here. This information came my way, I go to Wynol I tell him it's going to be he pays me a reasonable sum or else I go ahead let anyone I can think of in on this."

"You're blackmailing my husband?"

I ignored the question, seeing as I'd just answered it.

"Showed him a print out his porno rentals, showed him picture of Rene the yearbook—dot-to-doted it how life'd not be so good people knew he had his jollies and all with some video a girl he used to be in charge of uniform code with and all."

I took a pause more to get my thoughts straight than anything, worried I was drifting too far from the thrust. Sandra shifted where she was, nothing else.

"Wynol tells me take a walk, not gonna part with a penny about it."

She started to talk, I raised a finger, quickly pressed on about how it seemed to me only natural let the man have a second chance, he wasn't making good decisions on account of it being all out of the blue, but he turns me down again I get miffed.

"I don't understand," she said, couldn't tell was it about my explanation or just about the thing why I was blackmailing him to begin with.

"Told him think what he's doing—pay me off five hundred dollars or copy of my little file ends up his boss, copies in the mailbox the parents every kids at school, copies to your daughter and Gloria, bulletin board the library, any place I can think—do you understand me now, Sandra? You understand what that'd be?"

She nodded quickly, eyes closed, then wide, then closed. "I understand, yes."

"Wynol isn't as quick on the uptake, obviously he's married up—he tells me how he won't pay, even in mind of all that, so I get to thinking Well this man just doesn't care."

Felt my breath should've been more forced than it was, talk getting motorboat, but each breath placed nice, didn't stumble and she got the hint she didn't get a turn to voice an opinion unless I said.

"You care, though, yeah?"

She stared at me, didn't say anything which was just enough.

"Normally that'd be all for a guy I'm asking just a few bucks off, I'd put him down as not the generous sort and settle up otherwise—only it's not my thing I want to ruin you, Sandra, don't go and think I particularly relish the thought your daughter wondering Well does daddy think that way about Gloria? or what else, you understand?"

She said "Yes," eyes closed, a shake of her head like she was well beyond my needing to keep painting.

"Thought one last chance, see if you can see matters the proper perspective, not get mixed up you're something larger than everything else all together."

That was all I had, just like that, speech ended, just looked at her.

"You want five hundred dollars?"

I walked to the coffee she'd left when she stood, had a swallow, sweet, cinanaom, something else I couldn't place what.

"Only thing is Wynol had the chance at five hundred, blew that down. This isn't something I'd a mind to be around more than the day about—headache all into it, thing's five thousand and it's this happens right now with no more squirming."

Like I knew the script, obvious script, she went how she didn't have five thousand dollars. I could feel I was going to start fidgeting we didn't get out the house, so I put it to her then how much could she get her hands on in the hour, quick trip to the bank, the two of us.

"I have maybe two thousand dollars, maybe three I don't know."

She had trouble getting good sentences out, odd mix of information about checks clearing, days of the week.

Picked up my duffle, told her Three'd do just fine and how she thought of anything interesting she might do in the bank instead of cash withdrawal I had a scheduled pick-up for the packages going out so I wasn't there to tell the delivery man Forget it, that'd be all.

"I'll get you the money," she said it like it was just me badgering her now with tough-guy speak, like I was still in character while she was off the stage on to real things.

Titled my head and she right away went to her purse on a table by the door, eyes wide like things were something else for her than for me—took me until I was closing the car door to realize that's just exactly what they were.

$$***$$

Sandra drove bit under the speed limit this street, bit over this other, was a longer drive than I'd anticipated, kind of wondered were we heading the right way, was something strange happening—didn't ask, nervous to break the silence.

"Do you know Rene?" she asked while we were in a line of traffic, light'd changed green, changed back red twice we were still in the same line.

The question was curious to me. I made a pause out of scratching at one of my eyebrows to think, just went noncommittal with "Do I know Rene?" space between each word, not a full tilt of questioning inflection.

Traffic moved a bit, we made the turn we needed to make, came a stop behind more traffic, another light.

"Do you know if my husband slept with her?"

She was looking at me, nothing aggressive. I looked away when I answered—didn't want to be having the conversation, but what'd it look I was the one clammed up about it?

"I don't know Rene. Found out about her I was looking for incentive get your husband to pay me out—looked and there she was."

After that, nothing from her.

We parked on the street, told her when she went inside I was going with her, she was to take out the money in twenties and then she'd walk out, I'd walk out right behind, she'd hand me the money and that would be it, even added in something about I promised her I wouldn't be back.

She lingered a moment before getting out of the car, I was at the curb about to lean down, tap on the window the passenger door when I saw she'd stood, closed her door.

Bank was one of those the whole large building belonged to it, but the service area no larger than any branch—only two people in line, three tellers active, I watched her join the queue while I took up a deposit slip, doodled on it with a pen.

Even if she said something, there was nothing she could say—even her handing me the money and she'd managed to whisper to someone That man is robbing me, even they got word to security to somehow nab me once the cash'd changed hands, how could that go?

Guess it could pretty bad, really, except I'd just say she was paying me money she owed me, it was all nonsense about anything else so she could keep the money. Couldn't see how someone could be arrested for someone handing them money and be held, made to explain themselves.

Came her turn in line I tried not to stare, did a show of crumpling the slip I'd filled, made faces like wasn't I a dolt for writing down some wrong figure, took another slip and started doodling in nonsense information again, vaguely wondering could such things help incriminate me off chance things did take a turn toward the unforeseen.

Sandra finished out—I saw when the teller started to count the money, kept my head down the count of twenty—when I looked up Sandra was already moving out through the door. Kept the deposit slip I'd been filling, shoved it down my pocket, was out in the sponge of air, sun out all of a sudden but getting covered up again by the time I caught up with Sandra at the car.

"I can get you more money," she said, not having handed me the withdrawal envelope yet.

I tightened my eyes. "Don't have time for you can get me more money, you said at least two thousand—I'm granting you a bit of grace, with that, how much are you giving me here?"

Her expression was even, gave the envelope across and told me "It's twenty four hundred."

"Twenty four hundred's alright," I said, slow, tense this was a stall out I should give the whole packet right back to her.

"You said five thousand's what you want, now—I can get you that, another twenty-six."

Nervousness got the better of me, smiled big, made a phony laugh and put the money on the car hood, both hands up, stepping back.

"Hey, alright whatever you say, but I don't know anything about any of that, alright?"

Saw a flash of confusion, worry to her just while I turned, then felt her hand on the same shoulder my duffle strap.

"You can find out about Wynol, if he was with that girl?"

The sidewalk out in front of me was mid-morning thick with people, mostly folks worked around, everything looked old like it'd been pulled up after being underwater a long time. I reflexively went to get a cigarette, didn't, turned around. She had the money in hand, casual as could be, looking at me, nothing else—the proximity to the bank I felt I'd just robbed had me uneasy and knew it showed. She could ask anyone find out about Wynol some romp—then again, maybe as I already knew the score about things she'd rather that than go through explaining herself. Maybe she just wasn't thinking right, flat.

"Can't say I can find that out for certain, to be square about it."

"Can you try?"

I relaxed when she moved some of her hair behind her ear, hair came out she didn't move it back.

"Sandra look, I just don't know exactly how you mean find out, okay?"

Could tell she didn't either, the same time felt now I'd seen a glimpse of she'd pay me out, even if it was suspect, might as well not talk her down from it.

"I can try to find out, yeah, but I mean I don't know something a few days don't go thinking I'm of a mind to make it a hobby."

"No."

Told her did she want a call at home, her cell, want me to send it in a letter, what?

She put her purse to the hood of the car, dug through it for a pen, wrote a telephone number in the margin of a receipt. I took it, slipped it down my pocket—meanwhile she'd set the envelope the money on the hood, too and I snatched it, started walking off not another word, felt stress on my back for wanting to take a glance back, got around a corner and then into a random office lobby door on purpose just to keep myself turning and see her still there.

Actually was stiff, worked out something funny with my hip—no check-in desk the lobby, figured it'd be a good idea kill time, get my breath, so took the elevator up as high as it'd go, got out, slowly walked down a flight or two of stairs before I stopped to sit, stomach ache creeping up to my shoulders.

Realized I was tapping the envelope on my knee, hadn't put it in my duffle, tapped it slower, slower, looked at it. Twenty-four hundred dollars. Counted it ten times, different breakdowns of the piles, kept two hundred out in a tight fold, the rest burrowed down into my bag.

The stairwell was comfortable, didn't see any kind of cameras or anything, none I would be seen by, so kept where I was a few hours, every now and again'd hear a door open, echoing conversations or footfalls up or down, no one close enough I worried about it.

Went back into the lobby, saw it was raining horrendous, spills of it, wished I knew about where was the nearest bus station or were their trains, though at the same time I worried about that's where people'd be looking for me were there people looking.

***

Bus pulled out away from the city, moved onto the highway, dark out the windows, only sounds of the wheels under me, stray music that got away from ear phones, bus lights off and nobody using their own to read—nothing, a little sleeping pill being swallowed by a mostly empty road.

I slept, too, would wake time to time but softly, duffle heavy on me, watch out the window—it got lighter with each time I'd doze, was a powdery kind of orange sky I wandered away from a rest stop, something I didn't have to do, I'd not had to show my ID for the ticket, but it made me feel immediately vanished. Not that Sandra'd called the police, nothing like that—rested and away, felt an imbecile for my flare of panic after getting the money, she'd probably not even have let on to Wynol she knew a thing or even that I'd accosted her, gotten the money off. Wondered had she even made some purposefully vague excuse for its absence from their account, what thoughts something like that'd stick in Wynol. The whole thing was a gnarl, but now nothing I was concerned with.

Except for maybe Sandra would pay me money for this thing about Rene.

Maybe.

Or honestly, I'd no doubt she'd pay me were I to find out, but had no idea how I'd find out—just the puzzle of it, the distraction, it kept me occupied though, felt good. If it'd get me back to five grand, it was the cleanest line I had on something like that. The two thousand plus I had was nice, a relief after having dropped to absolutel zero, but in itself wasn't enough to set me up someplace else, not the way I liked, didn't give me wriggle room, cushion to relax on.

Had a bite to eat some fast food restaurant, broke five dollars for a payphone outside the entrance door, irritated I'd not bought myself new cigarettes yet, let a low breath down my nose, a grunt.

Information gave me numbers for five different Spree families in Fieldway, had to call back get the numbers a second time because of nothing to write with.

First number was an answering machine, made a little note of this, used the release of nervous tension to give me inertia enough go buy cigarettes, walked back to the same phone, lit up, gave the second number a dial.

Woman picked up, I asked just said flat "Hi, is Rene in?"

"I'm sorry?"

"Is Rene in?"

"No, got the wrong number."

"No Rene Spree there?"

She hung up, made me chuckle—even though I was up to something didn't seem there'd been call to be rude with me, far as this lady knew I'd misdialed a number and just wanted to be sure.

Dialed the same number back.

"Hi, I'd just called, wanted to make sure we hadn't just got disconnected. There isn't a Rene Spree lives here?"

"This isn't the number you want."

"Okay, sorry."

But she'd already hung up, real character, found I was smiling and still even thought I'd call her later on, middle of the night, make a recreation of it.

Third number faired no better, except for the person, some young guy sounded like, was perfectly fine with it, like what did it matter at all, even seemed there was some sincerity to him saying Sorry and offering me Good luck.

Was well into the afternoon, so decided I'd get a cheap room someplace as long as I was fixated on this and besides had nowhere particular to go. Wound up a smoking room, two queen beds, some Extended Stay— looked like renovations to it'd been abandoned mid-stream, some point, areas of carpet missing, signs warning of wet paint taped to walls obviously long dry, no hint of odor the corridors, every other light fixture missing, exposed bulbs not turned on.

Had a rest in the air conditioning, watched television, smoked and watched myself smoke the mirror—by now I'd gotten used to the way things looked my stolen glasses, even seemed strange when I'd take them off.

Got dark out, I walked until I found a patch of phones, these outside of an ice crème shop, in front of some discount clothing warehouse.

First number went to answering machine, again, kept

myself off calling the third one, fourth was a number either I'd wrote it down wrong or genuinely was now out of service.

Started another smoke, but was distracted, stepped it out after just three, four drags, dialed the last number, facing away from the street, my view a service door and a light bulb, dead, closed behind a grate.

Call connected, pleasant sing song of a woman saying Hello then saying off to the side how she was just getting the phone, repeated her Hello.

I made as pleasant a chuckle as I could, started "Hi, sorry I just want to be sure this is the right number, I was hoping to get Rene Spree?"

"It is the right number, yes, but Rene doesn't live here."

"Oh no. So sorry for the bother, I'm just coming to town a week, Rene and I were in class together Fieldway High, was hoping to look in on a few people she's one."

"She's moved to Maine, awhile back."

This made me grin, thinking of *Street Legal Rides*— though I supposed they could get footage for that, wherever and beside it was years ago, that.

"Maine, yeah? I guess that's her off the list, then."

"I'm sorry."

"Don't suppose do you have her contact information would you, or her number at least? I know it's an odd question, just in a nostalgic headspace, had a mind talk to everyone, at least, if not see them."

"I can't promise when I'll speak to her next, but if you leave your number I could pass it along to her—I'm sorry, I've forgotten you name."

"Nathan Frisk—we were in Mister Trot's class together."

"Oh, Wynol."

"Wynol?" I said, bit disappointed in her enthusiasm,

though didn't know why that'd be—not like I was hoping Wnol'd been with Rene and either way the kid sister was friends with Wynol's kid, served to reason families'd be close.

"Mister Trot, I'm sorry, Wynol is his first name," she said, a smile to the explanation.

"No, that's alright. I guess I'm allowed to call him Wynol, now, too right? Anyway, yeah if you could say to Rene it was Nathan Frisk called and I guess you can leave my cell phone."

She asked me wait just a moment, got something to write with, had me repeat the invented name, spell it, laughed that she'd thought I'd said Frist—I chuckled, too, bored with the call, made up a number she also asked me to repeat.

For show, hoped it might jog any last crumb out of the woman, I said "Gloria must be about in high school now, right?"

Bit of a beat passed, probably didn't mean anything, probably just something'd caught her attention.

"She is, yes—not in class with Wynol, though, not until senior year."

"Oh, sure—look, I won't keep you, thanks so much. Do tell Rene I'd love to hear from her, alright?"

Some pointless back and forth and then Goodbye.

Kind of dug at me, finding this little line to investigate then it cutting short like that, doubted very much Rene had a place her own, doubted even more she'd have a listed number, cell phone was most likely thing and even with that who knew she still called herself Spree.

Can't promise when I'll talk to her next, woman'd said— the mom I supposed—could easily've been coded talk get through thing, my call had a pretty random nature to it, after all and now thinking about the pause when I'd mentioned Gloria, whole thing might've been a kind of defensiveness due to she knew what her daughter was up to, on guard, didn't like the mention her other daughter.

Maine. I doubted that.

***

Even though I was ready to leave well before checkout, waited in the room an hour past the scheduled departure time, told the desk when they called up that I apologized and would be right out, waited until housekeeping knocked on the door to actually go.

Thing with Sandra was I couldn't figure it right how I was supposed to get the money away from her, but didn't want to think it wasn't a possibility—been her idea, after all, if it was some ploy to catch me out she'd've just turned me in the police. She must've known I'd take the same precautions with the material I alleged to have things came to a further handoff I'd told her I'd taken this time.

More, I was nervous about I didn't know how to fabricate evidence it turned out she wanted some, felt I should have something at least without her even asking, but nothing substantive came to mind. Maybe even the better play'd be telling her I'd come up blank, tell her something like that I might come off as honest—or not that I'd come up blank, but find the right balance I had something, just nothing'd ever be something she could substantiate.

Thing was, it'd been only yesterday she and I'd met, a call not even hardly twenty-four hours'd passed, what'd it seem like, no matter what line I tried to draw?

Started thinking about Wynol, got me something more focused. He'd robbed me, thought he'd won the day but'd come up broke, now, was a softball lobbed just hanging there I could have a good smash at. Didn't matter so much did he deserve it or not, thing was he'd earned it—not my fault his head was too big to see around itself, something like this'd sucker up on him, just showed him for the bigger chump, which was what he was.

Beside which, Sandra didn't know how I was connected to anyone, didn't know only way I could try to get information out of Rene was same as her, same as anyone, give a call and ask—and even couldn't do that.

Other option was leave, everything hung up—Sandra waiting, Wynol all bloated, me less than half what was rightfully mine.

Spent a little while milling in a bookstore, read the back cover synopsis of this and that, abject and feeling each and every slight movement of time.

Phones across the street from the bookstore, one to either side of the door a thin taco restaurant, this on the hip of a long storefront window covered with For Lease banners. I found the receipt with Sandra's number, looked at it, fatigue in strings all over my eyes—hit me I'd had no coffee, not even brewed the pot in the room before I'd left.

Dialed.

Took five rings Sandra picked up, knew she was staring either at the unfamiliar number on her cellphone display or the words Unknown Called, Restricted, Unlisted. When the line connected, she didn't say anything. I waited almost half minute until she did and it was just Hello?

"That Sandra?"

Could be the pause was something her getting a tape recorder, someone else giving her a last minute whisper in the ear.

"This is me."

"So look, I'll just get at the point about this—but you have to understand something and that's I didn't get Rene herself out on this subject, couldn't get in touch with her direct, this is something from a guy close with her, or he knows her anyway, knows the sorts of things like what you wanted me to find out, understand? Friends with her from the low side of thing with her."

"I understand."

"So it's your business now, but this is what I heard from this person—also this is something where he doesn't know about why is it I wanted the information, this particular reason versus that, I just got him talking, got the talk around to our question, he isn't going to be anything to do with you."

A pause and then, even toned, braced, Sandra said "Okay." I looked at my shoe, made some tip tap tip tap sounds with my lips, quiet, used the base of the phone stand to rub an itch'd developed on my knee, balance funny. Knew she was waiting, just figured I'd let it go some weird amount of time, no effect one way or another in mind about why.

"He's been with her, few times, never was a solid thing or whatever you'd call it, didn't hold hands or anything on top of it. When she was at school two, three times and since then only twice more—he paid her for those, but didn't pay or anything like that when she was in school."

Breath caught strange I'd said this, like it curlicued up me, pressure stayed at the base of my throat. I rolled my neck side to side, felt my skin crease up from pulling my face in, trying to shake the sensation.

When she hadn't said anything, another full minute, I told her to forget about anything about the money, especially it wasn't anything I'd be able to press anyone more on without probably causing more a headache— someone else got the idea I had an angle to play about Rene and Wynol, they might decide to play it instead of me, be a lot less civil about it, I explained. She said she understood and I told her "So that's it" and added in I was sorry about it, knew it wasn't something she wanted and least of all something she wanted to know from me.

"That's alright," she said.

I nodded pointlessly, even kind of rolling my eyes that the phone wasn't hung up, yet.

"I want to pay you."

Coughed, still couldn't get the odd spot my throat right.

"I mean don't worry with that—I'm out of town, anyway, just that's something you don't need to bother about, I won't come back."

But she repeated she wanted to pay me—wanted to see me—asked could she.

"I'll bring the money, just tell me where."

Told her I had places to be, so she wanted so bad to pay me we could arrange that, I'd call her with some instructions how to get the money to me would make things simple on the both of us, nothing about seeing each other was a very good idea.

Then it struck me probably she had it in mind to give some of her own payback toward Wynol, have a playdate with me—even seemed a good idea in the first burst of it being clear to me, grinned.

"You're looking for something else, Sandy, I can't imagine you'd have a hard time finding that."

"I would have a hard time finding it."

Laughed, hadn't planned to, didn't even know why, just a blat of me laughing.

"Is that how it is, yeah? Because I'm not going to keep saying No forever, you're so enamored of the idea but I'm out of town and'll be way out of town by tomorrow— don't think I'm not flattered, but not so much I'm making an extra trip for it, okay?"

"I'll meet you."

Didn't sound she was in control of herself or she wasn't, figured if she brought the money that'd be easier than arranging some kind of drop off I'd just give myself the creeps about, anyway and this'd be no more or less safe.

Took of my glasses, set them on the phone top, turned and looked across at the dingy windows of the bookstore, told her that's where she should come—named the town, the cross streets I could see--explained it'd have to be as soon as possible and it turned out I wasn't there that's just how it'd be left.

"Alright."

"And you need to bring the money, this other thing's a favor I'm doing for you, don't get the idea I consider it has cash value your side."

Thought I heard her breathe like she'd smiled, maybe not, didn't matter.

"How much?"

I just told her "All of it," hung up, right to a cigarette and rubbing at my ear with clammy fingers.

***

Hadn't chewed my fingernails since adolescence, smiled, nibbling at my thumbnail to get the line of it even from how I'd made it crooked. Sandra showed up the bookstore past nine o'clock, climbing toward ten. I watched her go in, leaning forward over the little table I was sitting at behind the window of a bakery café. She was in there twenty minutes, wondered if she'd made a circuit of the place, taken a seat waiting—seemed she was sharp enough to know I was wary, wouldn't just be waiting around, greet her with a hug.

Now she was out here, was still up to me I was just

going to take the money off her or go off to some room into the bargain—I was not altogether certain the second thing was a sound consideration, other than I guess she'd get a kick out of it I was the guy her husband'd put the whole family at risk about, have a roll around with me. Even there, couldn't see what the angle might be—with a good enough amount of time since the initial jolt of my showing up, getting the two grand off her, seemed she should've thought the better of things, like what'd keep me going against her with it, what was trustworthy about me I was obviously heartless, a thief?

There was phone up the block, lit a smoke, called the number Sandra'd written on the receipt, she answered ring and a half in.

"Have the money in an envelope, I'd hope."

She started answering, her voice caught, cleared her throat. "In an envelope."

"Go ahead to the ladies room the second floor, there's a trash bin, bury it down in there, come on outside, turn left, start walking."

"Leave it in the trash?"

"I just told you, and we stay on the phone you do it."

"Where am I walking to?"

"You're just turning left and walking, I don't like to confuse people too many specifics. You in the toilet?"

"I'm getting there."

"Get there and you tell me it's empty or whatever, someone's in a stall that's fine, you don't have to wait that's going on."

It was empty, heard her breathing different for the various activities involved with going in her purse, depositing the envelope—told her take out bunch of paper towels, dry, then some wet ones, put them on top of everything.

Once she was outside the store, I repeated she should go left.

"Am I meeting you?"

I hung up, watched her react, take a pause, then just start walking, not even a glance around see maybe was I across the street like I was.

Made clicks of my tongue against the back of my clenched teeth, bounced on my toes, kept eyeing the bookstore, sides tight. Dropped more coins in the phone, dialed her, glances to the paper for every single digit just form my jitters.

"Hello?"

"Go up another block, turn right, three blocks down and wait."

"Another block?"

"At the next cross street."

"Can you see me?"

I hung up, had timed it with the crosswalk signal to the bookstore going for me, was in through the doors and walked up the escalator two steps at a time. Wouldn't've mattered to me one way or the other'd there been people around, pushed into the ladies room, no one at the sink and didn't care about the rest. Envelope was thick, green envelope like it'd been ordered specialty, such a particular shade—words Brick Green occurred to me as I was already through the door again and thup thup thup down the escalator, both feet on each descending step.

Outside and swung the corner, felt my motions were getting awkward, stilted for their quickness, felt like I was a coin just kept spinning after it seemed it ought to've spun flat. Raised a hand to more than half dozen taxis before one pulled over, I told it pull onto the freeway, driver nodded, turned his radio up, music I kind of was familiar with, but not enough I could sing the words in my head.

Just gave a glimpse in the envelope I got the adhesive tore—it was money—then stuffed it down into my duffle, closed my eyes with my forehead hard against the lukewarm window glass.

Some exit I saw signs for various hotels, motels I told the cab pull off and it left me at a diner. There were some payphones I eyed before I went in, told the hostess I'd just sit at the counter, asked which way were there toilets.

In the mirror I looked exhausted, purple to my eyes like they'd been walked on.

"Poor Sandra," I whispered, then forced myself to say it out loud—"Poor Sandra."

Wanted my tone to be more mocking than it was, my expression more or less just beat, almost embarrassed.

Money in the envelope was exactly the twenty-six hundred made it a total of five grand she'd paid me out. Probably by the time I'd been served my omelet she'd gone back by the bookstore, found the money gone.

What'd she do? Wait around like probably I'd still be calling her or scramble to her car, start back home?

Or neither—take a random room a random guy, take a random room all alone and spend the night feeling a sucker about it all?

Didn't matter, far as I was concerned, just sat and downed coffee, ate too much, walked toward a motel feeling sick to my stomach, like I was dragging my full weight around with the base of my tongue.

Reception desk, asked could I sign in without presenting my ID, some story I realized I'd left it in the other car with my brother, his girlfriend, that they should show up sometime by morning, we could present it at check out. That all went through seamless, felt dancing inside, like I was coming up with reasonable stuff with no planning, grifting through even with mind not more than halfway made up about any decision—couldn't go forever without an ID, but could muddy the waters behind myself enough with little patter like with this desk clerk, later on figure out about swiping the wallet some guy I looked a bit like, no need to rush.

Brewed more coffee in the room, drank it from one plastic cup while I also drank tap water, cold as I could make it, from another.

Too worked up to sleep, went out for a walk around, rocking in place anytime I'd stop. Came up on a liquor store all by itself, empty lots on either side, unlit traffic light at the next crossing—went in tentatively, found just some old woman working there, sitting bare footed on a stool, reading a news magazine. Was fondling a cheap bottle of vodka, just size enough keep it in my pocket, when I noticed a display for Chopin brand, smiled, bought a thin tall bottle of it.

Took a drink out in the lot, looked straight up, breathed out the stinging scent of the alcohol, pretending it was a relief of air pulled all the way up from under my heels. When my head bobbed down, I said into the air like to someone walking away from me "Hey, don't count your money for a few days, you just get where you need to get, don't worry until you're settled, there'll always be something." Then when I started to walk, I turned around like I was now the guy I'd just been saying that to, raised the bottle, took a swallow.

***

About a mile down from the motel I'd let for the night there was a patch of larger franchise hotels, slumbered my way along toward them, road empty but still careful to keep in the shoulder. Closed up my vodka bottle tightly, obsessively so, turned it upside down a few times to test it wouldn't drip a thing, then laid it on its side in the grass behind some of the front bushes a Marriot Suites, rubbed my eyes with a knuckle a long few minutes before I went inside through some automatic doors.

"You have a telephone I could borrow or are there payphones?"

He pointed, asked did I need coins when I nodded thanks, took me a few steps to realize I did. Brief jolt of panic about I didn't have my duffle, sour breaths, gurgle in my gut, but recalled it was back in my room, safe and warm—I was more under than I'd thought, kept touching my nose and cheeks, sensation like I'd stepped through a few strands of spider web.

While the clerk banged open a roll of quarters, asked also were there toilets. I'm waiting for my brother, I explained quickly, even though guy hadn't seemed bothered by the question.

"Just around the corner."

"Need a key?"

"No."

Took my coins, went to the phone. Sandra didn't answer—phone rang and rang to her voicemail, rang and rang to her voicemail, finally just right to it.

She'd be driving home, now—maybe not, maybe laying in a room, maybe even she'd wanted to answer, thought I'd leave a message she made it clear she wasn't picking up.

But I wasn't meaning to call Sandra, anyway—drunk, it was just I had that receipt in my pocket so I'd dialed.

"Sorry to bother you, again—pen?"

"Sure."

Clerk handed me one, some paper along with it. Information got me Wynol's number, scribbled it, went to the toilet. Washed my face, half expecting it'd do something to make me feel sober, but the vodka wasn't anything near to peaking, yet, water against my face, under my hands, just felt like I was rubbing wax into wax.

Misdialed three times at least, fingers mashing two keys at once or else I'd hear a double tone of something, push down the cradle lever, start again.

Wynol answered quickly, but not a rush of breath, just like maybe he'd chanced to be near the phone, could be he was waiting for a call from Sandra based on some story she'd laid out for him.

"Wynol," I drawled, "Wynol Trot how are you? Hey what is it you teach again?"

"I'm calling the police."

I laughed like I'd swallowed something wrong, a sneeze out my nose of a chuckle. "Come on, never mind, didn't realize that was such a sensitive subject, with you."

He hung up.

I put in more coins, dialed, he picked up right away, again.

"This is costing me money, Wynol—I don't hang up on you, so show me some courtesy."

"I have the number you're calling from."

"Well, I have the number you're answering from."

He hung up.

I was smiling I could feel it even with my face thick and numb. More coins, dialed, he let it ring to the machine—at least I hoped it was a machine, but even if it was voice mail I knew he'd check it right away.

"Wynol, look—I'm just calling to tell you we're even, alright? You just go and check your bank account—you, your wife's bank account—everything's nice and right between us, now, we're ten times even and then some on top. Some on top and underneath and kind of various angles I don't know what you'd call them. Sandra says Hi, by the way—sorry I kept her so late and she might just be letting calls go to voicemail, taking a nap get her land legs back before she heads on back. Apparently there's a whole ton of things you just don't do with that girl, yeah? Maybe if you asked her something what're her interests you wouldn't need to pay the rental fees—peculiar and inventive lady, your missus."

I started coughing, said "Excuse me," but couldn't stop coughing so hung the receiver to the cradle, doubled over for a minute, then went back to the toilet, probed my fingers down my throat until I belched. Spit thing strings were hand to break off, took handfuls of water, washed my face, kind of, glanced in the direction of the mirror but not really at it, got out the door and into the lobby area, took a seat at one of the tables.

There was free coffee, so I sat with a cup and watched the rerun of some old medical drama the clerk had the television in the dining area set to.

As the alcohol continued to rise over me, I thought of other things I wanted to've said, wanted to mock at Wynol—yeah, he's gonna what? call the police, give them a telephone number, tell them go out and arrest some guy?

"Sure you are, Wynol," I said, getting to my feet, waved to the clerk at the desk, getting a nod in return.

Was well down the road back to my motel I remembered about the vodka out in the bushes, kicked the air and tottered to the side, fell, rolled onto my back. Got sitting up, patted around for my cigarettes but didn't seem to have matches. Just sat in the road, breathing whistles through my nose.

Seemed maybe an hour later I got in my room, undressed, threw up into the bathtub a few times, ran the shower and then lay on the floor, room lit just by the cut from through the three quarter closed bathroom door.

"You're a mess, Trevor," I said, pointing at the ceiling, pretending to laugh at how humorous I must seem, naked, splayed in an ugly little hotel.

In this vague drunk, spent most of the night early morning concerned about what sort of identification it was I needed, actually—travel I could handle without it and the thing was I didn't want to travel, wanted to hole up, get going again like I had, job like at Flinn's.

Got dressed as far as my socks, sat on the bed, dialed the front desk.

"Hi, is there a shuttle service this motel, like to train station, airport sort of thing?"

"No, not here. Across the street, the Holiday Inn has a scheduled shuttle to Bradley."

"They let me use it I'm not a guest there? I just pay them out something or what's the thing?"

"You just use it, we send people over all the time."

"When's that?"

"I think it leaves seven, seven fifteen or something."

Told the guy thanks, looked at the clock, it showed coming up to four.

Only wanted the shuttle it was cheapest way to get furthest away, but still had little fantasies about getting on a plane, really, floating back the whole way across the country just a few hours—but there'd be no difference, I'd land the same noplace as anyplace was for me, only thing was plane ticket'd drain me down quicker than anything else. There must be other shuttles to bus transport and stuff a big airport, little bit of luck those'd run free of charge as well.

Finished dressing in my suit, did my best to do up my tie, couldn't seem to get it and my fumbling creased a wrinkle down across it, the tip bent up a flimsy triangle, as well.

Holiday Inn turned out was back in the direction I'd used the phone to call Wynol—smiled I could grab my hidden away vodka, but found when I got to the bushes it wasn't there. Checked around every place, but it was just gone.

***

Ride out to the airport went quite awhile, shuttle stopped at must've been a dozen other hotels, morning went from mild and dark to pinching heat and unfiltered glare of sunlight down. This all made my thick dry mouth feel thicker, drier. Eyed a water bottle some girl reading a book had in the pouch of her backpack, finally leaned in, asked could I have some, I could give her ten dollars—think that came across to her as flirtatious, because she smiled, biting unnecessarily cute at her lower lip.

"If you're that thirsty, you can have it, you don't need to pay me."

She got the bottle out, asked if it'd be alright she took one more swallow.

"Sure, but I definitely got to pay for it, now."

That was enough to get her blushing, drinking with her head ducked off to the side like I wasn't supposed to be noticing only I was supposed to be, even more.

She closed up her book in a way it was obvious I'd been cornered into this chit-chat—last ditch to get free of it I pointed at the book where she'd shut it, laid it on her lap.

"What's that you're reading?"

"It's Cheever, you ever read him?"

Shook my head, explained I'd not meant to distract her from it, said I felt rude, now. No luck, she totally ducked the book into her backpack, shifted posture like presto we were deeply involved in something took precedence.

"I can read it on the plane. Where're you flying to?"

"I'm actually just abusing the shuttle system to get around on the cheap—we get the airport, I'm gonna get another shuttle some hotel further up the way, so forth, all the way until I run out of airports and hotels."

She wanted to know was I really doing that, told her Yes I was and she called me crafty, introduced herself as Dorance.

"Well," she said, "I'm going to Utah, so that's not quite as exciting."

"I agree."

Then an awkward pause, my thoughts'd already wandered, pretended to be squinting intently toward the front of the bus like at something curious and specific going on there.

"What's your name?" she asked it as a whisper, the whole little girl game of it all getting well past my last nerve.

"It's Philip, sorry. I'm Philip."

She did a little indication I should lean in more—dense, it seemed, to the fact I was not charmed by her deal—then when I did she kept the whispering bit up, asked did I want to have something to eat with her at the airport, her flight wasn't for a little while.

"You're not in a big hurry about the shuttles, right? Those go all the time."

Fake grinned, closed one eye, tilt of my head like I couldn't argue with that, but said I did have to make some phone calls, that was the first thing, and that anyway I couldn't go into the terminal, either.

Rest of the trip was misery, her eventually going back to her book, but I could tell she turned up her eyes anytime I moved, until I just closed my eyes.

Could only somewhat remember I'd called Wynol, was

glad I'd done it, that something'd prompted me to get a last blow in—anyway, whole thing totaled, hadn't he come out the upper hand, swiped my job, place to stay and wasn't I the one still down a few thousand dollars even for all of this scrambling, last minute?

Wondered would Sandra play it she'd gone around with me a bit, wondered was she confused at all about that whole aspect of it, trying to figure had she put me off or what could it've been.

Either way, they seemed a pointless group of people, nothing I'd be worried about very much longer—at least I hoped not, wanted them to drift out of my orbit. They'd been like stepping on a bomb, everything was like that.

Had to go ahead and walk along into the main area of the airport with the girl—I'd already lost track what her name was. Spotted a men's room after she told me she was going to get some coffee and sit in one of the larger chairs some corner.

"I'll meet you? You want a coffee?"

"Sure."

I did, actually, so she wanted to go buying me coffee, that's fine.

She added she'd also get me a water because coffee wasn't hydrating, so it was actually more a headache than it was worth—didn't matter, she'd be off on a plane ride, might as well nab coffee out of it.

Took the stall down the end, went through my pockets, my duffle until I found my ID.

Trevor English.

Thing was more than five years old, picture certainly didn't look like me, even seem like me—not just for the new haircut and stolen clothes.

When I stole a new ID, I'd make it a clean shaven guy, meantime I'd grow a beard—it wasn't something I'd have to flash around all day long, but there were ways to do it better than others, or I figured there were, anyway, I'd never done anything under a stolen name, whole thing had me kind of antsy. Whatever way it was debated, though, being tracked down pretending I was Johnny Jones or whoever carried with it less risk of the shackles coming down than getting recognized out as Trevor English, as me—name was toxic, something I'd blown my nose into too many time, now it was soggy, viscous, give it a few minutes it'd be hardened to jags, just needed to be discarded.

Bent the card in half, in half, in half until the soft line forming across the middle broke it in two, did the same for the pieces, put one piece down in each of the two trash cans the men's room, another in a trash can just outside it, the other in a receptacle I passed on the way to the payphones.

Stood there, duffle at my feet, fidgeted it this way a kick, that way a little tap with my foot side.

Nobody to call.

Nothing.

I felt void of other actions, though—could go have a cigarette, I supposed, then remembered about the coffee.

Strolled past the kiosk the girl'd indicated, scanned around all the chairs, couldn't make out where she'd gone. Stood ten minutes on the thought she might've had to use the toilet, then made a circuit around. Went up to the kiosk.

"Girl come through here something half hour ago, buy a coffee?"

I laughed even while the woman's face made a hopeless expression.

"I mean, she'd've bought two coffees—light brown hair, backpack?"

Woman nodded. "I think so—was she wearing sort of a light green top?"

"That's her."

"She only bought the one coffee, I think."

"That right?"

I gave another scan around for her.

"Was she supposed to get one for you?"

I nodded, slowly—she wasn't anywhere, gone.

"She was supposed to, yes, but seems she thought the better of."

"She was cute," the woman said, leaning on the counter.

"No she wasn't," I answered, a purposeful sniff, ordered my own coffee and made it a point not to say anything else.

Spent as long as I felt like on a bench out in the passenger pick-up area, smoking, making slow progress down my coffee. Every once in awhile I'd think I recognized somebody—the girl, some guy. Nobody. Every now and again, someone'd look at me like they might've been thinking I was somebody, too, quickly able to discern I wasn't. They'd look away and I be glad about that.

Helen Topaz,
Henry Dollar

Hey! Who could your lover be?
Let me eat off his head so you can really see!

BOB DYLAN, *10,000 Men*

I'd really fell in love with the name of the sixteenth, seventeenth guy I stole his wallet to get his ID based on he looked pretty much like me—Henry Dollar. Must've smiled all really full of myself all day that day and a month into it being my name officially, even there on the name badge I got for the security job, it still gave me a kick.

Was breathing into the hot of my coffee, fogging the lenses of my stolen reading glasses, leaned against one of the pillars the underground garage, not ready yet to make my full round. Down the way, coming out from the elevator, I saw that woman'd been going out of her way to have cigarettes with me, chat a little bit more about me out of me at a time. Hadn't asked her, but she'd volunteered she worked up the fifth floor of the building, offices for Kolfax Company, Ltd. Nothing better to do I got her full name, wandering through the offices middle of the night—Helen Topaz.

She caught my eye and started right over, I took a swallow and met her—when she'd seen I'd started walking had stopped, lit herself a cigarette, asked me did I want one, I told her No thanks.

"Your wife doesn't miss you, all night?"

She'd said this on another occasion, that time'd made a thing of pointing to the wedding band I wore—this'd been something tucked in a pocket of another stolen wallet— but this time just said it on a breath of smoke out, obvious she knew she'd asked before and so now the question was moving on to indicate other things.

"She does, but it works out better I take a second job awhile, just she's got some classes to finish out."

"Then it'll be your turn?"

I shrugged. She made a face like Was I sure I didn't want another cigarette? so I took out my own pack, lit one.

"What else did you say you do?" she asked.

"Don't know I had, but nothing so interesting. Some filing work—actually a lot of the time I can even do it at home, just bring home these boxes."

"Filing?"

"For a loan company, house loans and stuff, sorting all these papers out how they like them."

And then we back-and-forthed about Did the company make me sign something about having the papers off premises? or whatever, I said Yeah, made up some bit about how inane it all was, added but it was good I could see my wife she popped home for lunch or something.

Like I knew it would, that got a pause from her. Could tell in the quiet tick tock tick tock of her next two drags she was analyzing that out—did it suggest happiness, indicate my imaginary marriage was a solid one? or was it a tag for her to pull, get a step further along where she was getting at, little conversation this night, little conversation that?

"You get evenings too with her, though? Or that's when you sleep?"

Since I'd played along with it all long enough, no point letting it go loose, I answered her "It's usually when I sleep, yeah," then went on my toes took a breath in, let it out I went back on flat feet, asked "Did you want to grab a bite maybe sometime, just something—talk without it being in a parking garage?"

She said Sure, eyes wide and an unnecessary rise of both shoulders, but I was scratching my head, acted like I hadn't heard.

"It's I know you must be beat from work, like I'm always pestering you, feel I'm taking advantage, right? I've got to be here, so I shanghai you into chit-chat you're going to your car."

Even while I'd said all that, fake shyness, random shifts of weight foot-to-foot, she was trying to get in again, emphatic, that Yes, yes she'd love it.

"What's your shift, anyway?" I asked. "You get off eleven, midnight from coming on at four or something?"

She sighed, rolled her eyes already like we were especially intimate. "No, just for these next few weeks I'm working extra, getting some things finalized—come in whenever, leave whenever."

It was a cue line I didn't take, lit a new cigarette, let her add in herself Good thing, though, or otherwise I never would've bumped into you—been shanghaied.

Still didn't give her the direct confirmation, no reciprocal Yeah good thing, just matter-of-facted how my schedule coming up was rough all week through the weekend, but maybe the upcoming Tuesday we could do lunch.

"You take lunch around here?"

She did, but said if I had the day off she could meet me wherever.

"It's fine, no I'll just meet you out here, come down after I sleep in, right?"

Waited until dead center of my shift, two in the morning, to take an extra stroll around in the doors of

Kolfax, poked around offices I knew weren't Helen's before I key carded my way in there, let the door shut, took a seat, place lit by the night out through the windows and the computer on some abstract screensaver.

Looked the same as last time, pretty blank, only photos of her and some girlfriends, nothing to show she had a boyfriend, a lover, even a former one or a crush she kept photos of. One or two of the pictures she had up did have a guy in the mix, but another clearly showcased this fellow with his arms around one of the other ladies, Helen in the same photo hugging a girlfriend, all big laughs on the faces.

Work stuff was neatly filed, candy jar that said Don't Touch—but this turned in her direction not out to anyone else might have a treat her expense—few secondhand-shop paperbacks on display by some postcards of vaguely European places, nothing written on them.

Night went by, got cigarettes my way to the train'd take me out to the apartment I was letting a room out in—bit of good luck I'd fallen into, the guy actually owned the apartment on opposite schedule of me and hadn't asked any questions about anything due to I'd offered half year rent in front, cash, which'd set me back a bit but security job'd just about got the investment back and with no sort of record at, no signed agreement on a napkin even, I was well eased into feeling alone, clear.

Had bought a lockbox I kept in my duffle all closed up in a cardboard box in the closet, every night before I left I'd check it, every morning I got home—money in a growing lump, gun all covered in cloth, stack of IDs I could use in a pinch. My entire life.

Had a long shower, realized I'd not used soap I was toweling dry, getting dressed in my lounging clothes.

Thing with Helen was on my mind, how to play it if I

was going to play it—knew I had her attached, but needed the whole thing to be her idea it came down to anything or else I was just shooting myself in the foot.

Fell asleep trying not to fall asleep, trying to play out scenarios, how much to play it I really just liked talking, how much I was making a pass just slowed up by guilt about going behind on my wife.

Had two nights off in a row, actually found I was getting anxious for Tuesday. I shaved my beard growth all the way down and cut my hair.

First night back, Helen didn't show up in the parking garage, maybe her working late had come to an end. But almost like it was meant for me, now she had an obvious calendar set to her desk, Tuesday circled—thing was brand new, not a mark anywhere else, the previous months just flipped out of the way this one.

***

Guy assured me some cheap little video recorder thing I bought'd save video it took to disc, make still photos out of it, bargain at less than sixty dollars—showed me what discs to use, that the thing just basically plugged in most computers. It recorded a total of thirty minutes footage, more than enough if I could just figure out how my little plan was to actually work in the real world, out of my meandering head.

Sat at the desk in the break-room testing the thing out—all very straightforward, filmed myself looking into it, set it on the floor filmed myself walking the corridor.

I needed a confederate, but that'd be impossible, so needed to think how could I get the equivalent from just myself. It'd be simple enough get some images of Helen and I talking, having a smoke on the premises or something, but that wasn't exactly the stuff of blackmail, wife or not. Needed us out in public looking chummy some time there's no reason I'd be talking to her, needed us at least walking into a motel, hotel, even better walking out again, the morning. Ideal would be get some image in through motel room window, she moving to shut the blinds, me in behind her, cupping her breasts, even getting her shirt over her head.

There were problems in all of this, but it was a fun puzzle to cigarette my way through, loops of the parking garage, mumble about to myself the elevators up and down.

Main trouble was having the whole night around me, loose and rumpled and so comfortable to get lost in, lose perspective on everything, think the night and the garage and the building floors were everything, it kept my focus warm, distant. As soon as I was off shift, shivering my way to the train, things crisped into place.

Took a trip out the convenience store I realized I couldn't find what I needed poking around through the apartment—some duct tape was all, really, the owner of the apartment only had invisible around, that or a glue-stick. Cut a square of fabric from the bag, thumbnail size, lined up lens part of the camera the inside of it, taped it firm to spot.

Did a test the bag to the kitchen counter, filmed myself leaving, coming in through the door—watched the playback on the screen in back the camera, not wanting to trouble about untaping it, taping it back.

Got to be my Sunday overnight, Glenn, middle aged guy I relieved, said his usual Hello and did his usual dull salute I limply returned, squinting to see was he leaving a paperback behind like always, something to read in case nothing else.

"That's for you," he said, pointing at a yellow envelope, name Henry Dollar on it.

"Who left it?"

Figured it'd been Helen and it was—I opened it, took a peek the note without reading, meanwhile Glenn said he didn't know who'd brought it.

"Some security guard, right?" I said, tossing the envelope the table corner. "Folks leave suspicious packages, you don't see who about what?"

He chuckled, but was obviously more interested I wasn't going to tell him what it was with the envelope.

"Bad news?"

"Just nothing," I said, took a seat, adjusted the chair as low as I liked it.

Note started *Sorry for the note* which couldn't be anything but interpreted as with a flirty tone—no need to leave a note, let alone do it in some greeting card. It went on she was sorry she hadn't been able to pop by, just some things kept her in lately, but I should feel free I wanted to call her anytime I got a moment, make plans for Tuesday. *Anytime* meant even overnight, said so specifically I could ring her up I was on shift I got lonely, bored.

Took a smoke out front the main doors the building, looking for a place I could conceal my camera bag, someplace I could leave it down long enough get some footage I could make stills of, someplace it wasn't going to be run off with I left it. Nothing across the street—wanted a café, leave it a window table, tell someone on staff I'd be back just a minute, leave, they'd take it behind the counter.

Best thing available was a ledge of brick, some bushes. Ducked in, got my bag for a quick test out, be sure it got images of people head to foot, nothing unexpectedly obstructing the view.

Everything fine when I squinted in at the playback.

Supervisor showed up around three with paychecks, showed me a polaroid of another guard another site'd been caught sleeping, having a laugh about it but mentioning the guy was on his last legs, one more offense'd be it.

"You do this with everyone? I pass out from the excitement you get the scoop, paparazzi me out of a job?"

He waved me off, said I could sleep all I wanted, flicked the photograph said how Saul, this other guard, was some kind of professional bum, really needed to go.

Always got tense a knot I chatted the supervisor, worried he'd bring it around to some of the paperwork I never did turn in properly, that or he'd once mentioned how owners the company wanted everyone to get licensed, which'd mean I needed a class, get registered properly, something I couldn't well do.

Nothing like that, this time, just he left after asking did I want maybe an extra day shift or two end of the month, I told him sure and he said he'd try to swing my schedule I wouldn't end up grinding doubles for it.

Phone rang, which was a rare occurrence this site. It was Helen—clock showed just coming up on four.

"Are you awake?"

She didn't even identify herself.

"Helen?"

She laughed. "Yes, Helen. Were you waiting on another call?"

Ignored the prompt, said I just wasn't sure from her whispering.

"Funny you mention it about being awake—my supervisor showed me a photo he got some other guard asleep at the switch. How are you?"

Didn't want to bring out the hour of her call any more than let it stand obviously I knew it was four.

"I'm good. Woke up, couldn't fall back asleep, worried you didn't get my note."

"Your note?"

Odd pause from her, I didn't fill it.

"Didn't you get it an envelope I left?"

Looked at it there on the desk, turned to look out the tall glass the building door, my oily reflection all warbled up in it.

"I got your note, I'm joking. Glad you called though. Hey, how about I just meet you out in front, Tuesday, around whenever you want?"

She thought it sounded good, we planned to meet eleven, beat the thick lunch rush.

***

I was up and moving around the apartment already, guy owned it coming out his room doing up his tie, waiting out the last coughs his coffeemaker, nodded did I want a cup.

"Glad I caught you, too," he said. "I'm having a kind of party, get together thing here this weekend—don't know if you're at work every night, but you're either more than welcome to partake, otherwise wanted to give you the heads up about the noise."

Poured some coffee, riffed something about it'd be nice, thought I was off but my schedule changed all the time.

Only bathroom was still warm with his shower, smelled of his cologne and soap even though I'd waited an hour before turning on the shower.

First thought'd been to wear a suit, get nice and shaved up, but tinkering with the idea, decided I'd keep my stubble growth, dress casual—seemed if I did have a wife and she saw me with some woman in town middle of the day, no one she knew, no reason I ought to be there, something about my dressing casual, seeming so relaxed'd be oddly more unsettling.

Bit paranoid, tested the camera another time before I was out the door.

Train ride was a hollow sound, heat seemed up too high against the mild morning, felt buried down in my head, not thinking about anything, eyes stinging from how I'd not slept since previous day before work.

Smoked a few cigarettes while I positioned my bag, couldn't resist giving it a last test for the angle, but it got me antsy—no one was really around, but still felt I should trust myself better.

Knew I'd've shown up the building ten-twenty, the latest, so when it felt it must be crawling up on eleven I stopped someone, got from them it was ten forty-two.

Another cigarette—watching the door nervous she'd come out early—then I hit Record, strolled to the other side the main entrance. Another cigarette, tried to get loose, threw a few punches and things, thought about I really needed to buy a watch.

Helen walked out, coughing into her hand, looked around but not wide enough to see me, yet. I took the moment to take a few large strides, made a wide, arms up and open gesture of Hello—idea was the camera'd catch what seemed an obvious, comfortable meeting, something chummy like it happened all the time, same time idea was I didn't want to act out-and-out loverboy for Helen, wanted to keep things nebulous another little while.

She stepped right into my act and I made sure to come around we'd be in profile the camera—didn't hug her, but leaned in, gave her arm a tap, big smile on my face and she touched her hairs away, touched her arm, did a kind of push in my direction her shoulder.

"I haven't kept you, have I? I really need a watch."

Said this kind of leaning back, still a big smile, roughed my hair and asked could I borrow one of her cigarettes.

"You can borrow one, but I'll need it back."

I stood for a moment at her side, facing camera, tilting my head curious like peering in her purse after her.

"So, where were we heading?" she asked.

"Anywhere, you know the terrain, I entrust myself to you."

Last bit of my playact, I did an overly large bit of gesturing, pointing down this end the street, that end, like which way to go, squinting one eye closed when facing camera, look more flirty.

She said we could just walk, didn't have anything planned. We headed off, me chatting her question about her job and a quick mention of how I liked the colour of her shoes—a comment I didn't let stand even long enough her to say Thank you, directed comments back to her work, routine, all of it.

Once we'd turned a corner and got down two blocks, I stopped, drooping my head, fake frustrated clap of my hands.

"Forgot to grab my paycheck, meant I would pick it up before I met you but got running late. Wait here? I'll just be right back."

She offered she could walk with me, but I didn't really give her the chance, shook my head no no and started off, stammering I'd be back two minutes and she should remember her exact thought.

Broke into a jog, even, glancing back I got near the building. Bag was there, I grabbed it up—for a moment was thinking I'd leave it at the security desk, decided instead just untape the camera, balled it in the shirt I had in there, put the pair of pants on top, slung it all over my shoulder.

Caught up to Helen, she didn't even mention the bag's appearance, pointed at a thin little restaurant across the street and we started jaywalking while she asked was it alright to go someplace only served salad or did I need something else. Shrugged anyplace was fine, as long as she didn't take offense I only wanted coffee.

"I'm just more here to talk, actually—not weird, you know? Just feel cooped up, haven't actually been out, like out-during-the-day in forever."

So she ordered some salad and I poured myself coffee the pumps. Found a seat, not even thinking I'd moved back to the furthest corner until she laughed, cocking her head to me she sat.

"You're so clandestine."

"I'm sorry—you're right, it's stupid. Do you want to sit out front?"

She shook her head—could tell she was glad she'd said what she'd said, that I'd reacted as I did, but could see also she was anxious it'd put a spook to me.

Told some story about how I'd lost my one tooth forever ago, then she went on how her roommate had crumby taste in movies but was always having movie nights—caught myself almost mentioning how guy I lived with was having a party coming up, the near slip-up getting me ill at ease, quieting down, leaning back.

Server took Helen's salad away.

Started to ask her when did she have to get back to work, she cut in over me.

"I'm going to tell you something because I think I can tell you and I'm sorry if it's something I shouldn't say— I'm going to try to kiss you, probably really soon. Is that okay?"

She was staring. I kept my features even, long enough seemed natural not too long.

"Is it alright with me or in alright-in-general?"

Apparently the correct thing to've said, she blushed, leaned in, whispering.

"Generally I know it's not okay. But, we're already being clandestine, right?"

I was leaned in, too, let my forehead touch hers, felt she was turning her head, little nuzzle, mimicked this and then touched her nose with mine when she moved enough that was obvious to do, made her be the one to lean up into my mouth for the kiss, soft, quiet.

We kept like that I counted off twenty in my head, then I leaned back and she did the same.

Rubbing my brow like I was at a loss, keeping close eye on her expression, waited for her to start to say something else—she got as far as getting a breath in and the word Okay out before I moved three fingers to her chin, leaned in to kiss her mouth that'd immediately changed shape for it.

***

I got antsy choosing which computer to use make the stills from, first thought the computer the guard station'd be fine, then thought it'd be better use a particular office I could access—wasn't until past midnight and I'd slow poked through my first set of rounds I finally plugged the camera into a slot, tensed my way through the program set up, certain to the point of doom the thing wouldn't work how I'd thought, the nothing I knew about computers dead weight, making me want to sleep.

All worry turned out to be nothing, soon I was sipping cold coffee and watching myself approach Helen. Seeing her on film was the first time I spent considering was she at all an attractive woman, found I thought she was—she'd that sort of plain look video of regular people always had, however much she was pretty or not kept in odd dimensions, seemed smaller than any kind of generalize idea of an attractive woman'd go. I liked to look at her, and even more liked to look at myself, head-to-foot, fascinated that I moved like that, especially it was playacting, me fronting I was cool and nonchalant about going out in back of my wife. It really looked that's the way I'd be, that's the way I was.

Could click through frame-by-frame, also could enlarge so it was even better, the grit to the video quality made more cliché by the blow up, my face next to Helen's taking on dimensions could easily be construed as incriminating. And the context so easily peeled clean from reality—just a shift of angle, cropping out the image of her hand in her purse, making it just in close her looking down, me squinting down after, it looked we were in love, were embraced.

Found myself chuckling at the stories I'd invent to each still, even more when I stopped in a convenience store get them printed out. Made two dozen, decided I'd choose the six worked the best, but couldn't make the cut down from eight.

Took the train out to the main office of the security company I worked for, slipshod company used the upstairs of a row house for offices, the downstairs space'd been unrented since I'd had the job. Supervisor working the desk didn't know me on sight, though we'd met more than a few times, thought I was an applicant until I corrected him.

"I was wondering were there other sites available—still overnight if there are, but even middle shift might work out."

"Everything alright with Delmore Street?"

"Sure, no problem, just was kind of wondering."

Supervisor looked to the guy working the reception desk—guy was a guard, too, but now just dressed in grubby clothes like he was caulking a toilet or something. While this guy was leafing through water warped papers on a clipboard I was already getting a cigarette out for when I left.

"You can smoke that in here, no problem," supervisor told me, pointed at some books of matches in a pencil holder.

Lit up, had a few drags, guy at the desk set the clipboard down said there was nothing until someone called Ford left middle of next month—shift'd be overnight, but out in some area called Weld.

"Train'll go out there, though?" I asked, body language to show it'd be fine.

"Long ride, but sure."

Pretended a little nod like I was weighing that factor, then said it'd be great I could take it, but it didn't matter at the same time. Left after they set me down for it, tentative.

Relaxed just walking nowhere a bit, then got back to my apartment, laid around, looked at the photos of Helen and I. Before I left for my shift, I put the photos in with my money, the wrapped gun—just stared at the box as I re-taped it shut. First squirm of anxiety got in me, worry about how if this'd go off wrong I'd have to start again, ferry this box to some other living arrangement, worry at what it'd take to even make it back to even with the expense of the change factored in, let alone the trouble in that.

I didn't like the thoughts, had lost a good tight grip on what was mine, felt I was being bullied.

After a minute, knew it didn't matter—nothing was even at risk with the scenario done like this. There was no victim, no upper hand or under hand on anyone, there was no Norman, no Wynol, nothing like before. Even if it didn't go off, it'd just flat tire, I'd be fine right here, hidden in these rooms, enough money to pay through the whole year even if I didn't pick up another dime, now until then.

Had three swallows of vodka from my flask the way to work, bought a coffee to half-hearted cover this up, same time doubted Glenn'd care, probably was he did the same even though he was on part of normal business hours.

"Another card for you," he said even as I was crossing the lobby from the closing door, like this was something he'd been waiting all night to tell me.

"Another card what?" I said, feigning I had some kind of head cold, glancing back at the doors, my reflection jumping from the door getting full shut.

He nudged the card my way, I asked he get a look at the leaver, this time—he shrugged, said same thing as last time, it was just there he got back from the toilet.

"Secret admirer, I guess," he said, leaning a bit forward like we'd have a good chat about it

"They say everybody has one, right?"

Didn't wait for him to answer anything, took the card with me the break room, gave it a read.

I've been importunate, it began, something I had no idea what'd that word mean. Then it went on how she hadn't the nerve to ask me in person, but I could call her let her know was I mad, said how she'd taken a room out for next Tuesday night at someplace called the Xavier Suites. *If you're mad, forget I ever even wrote this, please okay?*

Closed the card in my duffle, left my duffle on top the lockers, took my place the lobby desk, Glenn giving me his little salute Good-night.

Started out my first round late, kind of was waiting for the phone to ring it'd be Helen, didn't happen. Took the elevator the fifth floor, right off, keyed into her office, took a seat in the dark, absently opened up drawers, looked at the same photos she had around.

Calendar had upcoming Tuesday marked, same as the Tuesday where we'd just met'd been marked. In fact, calendar had the next several Tuesday's marked, which I didn't exactly know how to interpret, right off—that she wasn't sure about her thing working out this next Tuesday, so those were she'd try again? or she had something planned out for every Tuesday the next little while, in case?

Didn't matter, really, but I stared at a phone number she had on a Post-It stuck in the corner of her computer monitor, kind of wanted to call it.

Lobby phone did ring just past three, a whispery little Hi.

"Hey, sleepy pie. Why aren't you sleeping?"

I let her have this flirt from me, mostly because I then made dumb about her latest note, no relenting like I had before.

"You didn't get it?"

I even looked around the desk as though I had to account for myself visually.

"Sorry, no. I'll ask Glenn, tomorrow. He's an idiot, so that could account for it, probably. You don't think someone took it—no one would take an envelope, right?"

"I'm sure maybe it dropped or knocked into the trash on accident. You want another date, is that it?"

I'd put a perky up step to the question, in response got a long quiet followed by "You really didn't get my note?"

Looked up at my reflection the inside door glass.

"Really didn't," I said. "What'd it say?"

***

Xavier Suites had a garish hold message, someone in horrendous mock-up of a hipster voice, swinging music going in the background, explaining specials and things—had to wait through the bulk of this three times before clerk connected, voice almost erroneously plain after the recording.

"I'm trying to be sure my reservation for Tuesday's all confirmed," I said. "Mine and my girlfriend's."

The girl I was speaking to asked me the name'd hold the reservation—first time it occurred to me could be this particular place'd been chosen by Helen on account of she knew someone worked there and could get a discount rate, but I grit past the paranoid tick, said Last name is Topaz.

Without my needing to prompt, girl ran down the whole thing—Yes room three-two-two was reserved, Tuesday night, held under this or that card, but I could change that I wanted at check in.

Slept in later than I wanted after hanging up, was midafternoon by the time I was showered and felt together enough to make the trip into the city. Didn't want to take a cab to the hotel, already felt I was on a meter myself, profits dwindling down as costs floated up—there was only so much I'd be able to wring out of Helen, if anything, so each smoke, each coffee, each train fare, all of it now felt a coin at a time, few bucks at a time less I had to show for my little scheme.

It was a long, bitter stroll I hadn't dressed right for, weather damper and piercing, then in the end it was like I'd feared, that Xavier Suites wasn't a motel with outside room entry, was in fact a building set back sort of in between some others. I milled on the pavement out away from the entrance to have a last smoke, but got the idea from so many people exiting already lit up that the place was cigarette friendly, so with as much authority as I could, strode in the door, past reception with a nod, got in an open, waiting elevator.

Walls of the third floor were blue, almost felt pink—lobby hall'd been pink—cinnamon candles in the halls, everything done up posh, but at the same time a weird ring of franchise to it, like the doors were props could be folded down and tucked in a backseat.

Room three-two-two, stood in front of it nodding. Corridor was nothing could help me plant my camera, walked the length of it though, like maybe out from nowhere some hiding spot might become evident.

Time limit to the recording was a bigger bother than anything, only real idea made sense was to rent the room right across, three-one-nine, see if I could get the lens right up to the peephole for a clear video—good idea if it'd work, actually, took care of I'd have to retrieve the thing and it'd be easy to get as en flagrante an image as I wanted.

I left out the stairwell exit, made sure it easily slipped around to the front but in such a way if I knew Helen was in front, the lobby, I'd not be spotted, could get down the street, make an innocent re-approach. In fact, exit door opened out into an alley, little jazz bar cut into it, ducked in there for a vodka.

Even if the peephole thing didn't work, there was always something—could buy some flowers, some package, tape it the outside of the door, camera going.

I liked that, had another drink to celebrate, then got some coins, asked the bartender did he know the number the hotel just outside, he gave me a card with a discount coupon for a hamburger at the Xavier lobby café on back.

Thankfully, someone picked up only ten seconds or so into the hold message, I asked was it possible to reserve particular rooms for particular nights.

"As long as it's not already reserved, no problem. You want one of our upper suites?"

Coughed into my hand, throat stung like I was getting a cold.

"Nothing like that, no. Just wondered about could I reserve three-nineteen for this Tuesday, coming up."

"Three one nine?"

"If it's free, yeah."

It was and I roughed the hair the base of my skull the guy told me room ran two forty-nine the night. Told him could he hold on one minute, put the receiver against my leg, tapping it—I could affix something to a door without letting a room, only hassle would be to nab it off, but also I remembered the peephole thing, which might work best, got back with the guy on the phone, said I'd take the room, then, reserve it under the name Kilpatrick.

"Do you want to guarantee that with a card?"

Blinked, did a big, quiet, ugly fake chuckle up my nose—no cards, almost just muttered Nevermind.

"What happens if I don't do that? I just check in by a certain time, things're good?"

"Un-guaranteed, you have to pay by eleven or the room can be let—might not be, but it can be."

"Eleven in the morning?"

"Eleven in the morning."

Finalized arrangements, got myself another vodka, almost left without paying by accident, guy politely calling me I'd made a few steps to the door—there was no kind of accusation, but still it made paying seem twice as harsh, like it was a punishment.

I'd forgotten about the party in the apartment, got in to find it was already underway. I was introduced around to a few people by the guy I rented my room out from, all seemed nice enough, one woman in particular seemed to strike up a liking to me and I fabricated my way through a conversation with her, standing in one spot and going through a glass and a half of someone's rather pricey bourbon.

Loose, even enjoying myself, I was completely taken out of things when someone walked up to me and said You do security at the Norton building downtown?

I didn't, didn't even know what was the Norton building, shook my head, but must've showed an obvious perplexion, even irritation on my face because the guy burst out a laugh, promised he wasn't stalking me, that the apartment owner'd mentioned I worked security, said it was in some big building, guy laughing just had a friend once worked the Norton building was why he asked. I laughed, too, said drinking got me suspicious of everyone, poured the laughing man a shot then another, just to be as sure as I could the memory'd be sunk, drowned, forgotten.

Woke only mildly hung over, early, heard some people who'd stayed overnight milling around, chatting with the owner. Tried to shut my eyes, but if I did some swirl of distracting half memories from the night got in—think I'd kissed that woman, but didn't know, thought I'd thrown up, but then wasn't sure, mouth didn't taste like I had and because I vaguely remembered the decision to close myself in my room, the lack of concrete images of being hugged to the toilet the shared bathroom discredited the idea.

Ducked my work clothes into my duffle, just spent the day out until it was time for work, surprised to find Helen smoking over in the same area I'd left my bag to film us, huddled into herself not wearing a coat.

"Working late?"

I did a silly show of peering around, then leaned in and gave her a quick kiss, put my hands down my pockets, shy shrug to my ears both shoulders. She just smiled, took a few more drags, asked did I want to see her office.

"Have to get signed in, do some things, but sure."

She laughed, finished her cigarette, gave my shoulder a quick kiss, said she didn't mean just that minute, that she actually was working late, I could get the tour before she left.

When I started toward the door with her, she laughed, looked at me flirty, asked wouldn't it be better if we went in separately, that I was practically holding her hand.

"I'm losing that clandestine touch, looks like, right?"

This got another of her smiles, teeth long over lower lip as her head turned. Turned my back from her, lit a cigarette, made a point to glance over, see was she waiting for me to.

***

Laid out diagonal across the bed in the Xavier Suites, three nineteen, staring at the curtains I could close around me, canopy. Since I'd had to check in at eleven'd just spent the afternoon lounging—place was a hotel made for one thing and a gaudy version of it, made me wonder almost how'd Helen come across it.

Peephole shot with the camera worked beautiful, had the thing affixed to the inside door with duct tape, just a matter of tapping down Record, walking out—image didn't even seem fish lensed, just an image straight of someone standing there.

In a little fit of inspiration before I'd left my apartment, took one of the various pieces of jewelry I'd come across tucked into some stolen wallet, I'd got a few odd rings and necklaces got that way—would use it to be sure get Helen right up the room, tell her I had something for her, play the tease I showed up to the lobby café. Not that it'd take much convincing, truth of it—taking stock the room again, it was an obvious and bold advance she was taking, moving from sneaking a couple kisses, here and there, to renting out some room for the night a married man, let alone this swank set up. Stubbing out a last cigarette noticed for the first time short cut bath robes hung to the side of the television cabinet—the His one same length as the Hers, strawberry red the one, green zebra print the other.

Took my time down the stairs, out the side alley, ducked my head past the line waiting outside the jazz bar, hurried the way around to the Xavier Suites entrance. Helen saw me just when I looked up, coming into the café, waved just a bit with her fingers up off her one knee, other hand lifting her drink for a long swallow, the whole thing.

"Hope you don't mind I got you a bourbon?"

Nodded, something about the noise around me making me forget with the ruse of giving her some ring—all of a sudden, in the moment, it was less a misdirection, less a gameplay.

"It's fine, yeah."

I took a sip, set it down.

"Everything alright?"

Rolled my head around, took the rest of the bourbon down.

"Stupid, maybe, but I was thinking could we just up the room?"

She right away blinked like it'd been a mistake her part about the drink, told her Don't worry even though she hadn't said anything, and while I reiterated it might be better just get in the room she nodded and was saying Yes, no, no don't worry.

In the elevator I went to my toes, long breath out, chuckled like it was supposed to be a shy apology.

Waited for her to start like she was going to say something and talked right over her with "I've been thinking about getting my mouth on you for about a week, would that be alright?"

She blushed and pretended to stiffen, uncertain. "Mouth on me?" she said, schoolgirl, then was starting in with "Whatever do you mean?" but I leaned and kissed her long—long enough the door opened, closed, elevator up another two levels, passengers getting on.

She held my hand hard and we both bounced on our feet. Mind a flap back this way then that, thought about slipping the ring into her hand curled so stiff around mine—it'd be a waste, unneeded, waited for the urge to get past, rode in quiet, letting her be thinking about whatever it was she was.

Three two-two was down almost end of the hall, could feel my blood up for each step nearer in, like a drunk coming on, anticipation I was about to scream for no reason, laugh too loud at something I'd wonder why.

Didn't even wait for some sign from her, pressed myself into her back, her chest flattening to the door, back arching, turned her around rough, her hair in both hands, kissed her mouth, bit her chin turning her profile to the camera, latched three fingers of one hand into the waist of her pants, pressing her back to the door.

"Let me get the key," she said, giggling and breathy.

"No," I said, lifting her hands above her head, both her wrists gripped in one of my hands, the other a grope of her breasts, tugging at the fabric her shirt. Let her go, turned her profile again, shirt up over her head—left her like that, arms up, fabric pulled odd and her face covered, went to my knees and kissed her stomach, crotch of her pants, undoing the three buttons, lowering them quarter way down her thighs, pulling down one side her panties, mouth on the protrusion her hip, then got her shirt all the way off, cupped her ass lifting it hard.

She was pawing me as feverishly, if not so methodically, so I rolled my back to the door, pressed down enough force top her head she understood I wanted her down her knees—lifted my chin high, closed my eyes as though she'd taken me in her mouth, even lolled my eyes a second straight like at the camera, then right away pulled her hair mean, stood her up, both palms to her face made her look at me long enough the camera could rest on us, get the image thorough—Helen and Henry more than halfway undressed, a mess in the hall.

"Let's go inside," I said, lips by her nose.

Her mouth moved something like Okay, no sound.

The actual sex was awkward, seemed too long—once the room door was closed, my euphoria tilted low, subdued. I've no doubt I was serviceable, she seemed well sated, but laying splayed on the still made bed, Helen reaching one foot across to touch it my chest from where she'd wound up head by my shin, I just wanted a smoke, to pace, think. It got a bit much, the little Mmns and things from her, the odd whispered Gods after we'd been done already five, ten minutes, so I stood, went into the toilet not saying anything.

Strange to see myself naked, face flushed, even exhausted—poked at my eyes, tightened my jaw and looked at myself various angles. After a few minutes, flushed the toilet, wet my hands, brought one across my neck, thumb worming in with some sweat caught in the space behind my ear.

Saw my cigarettes on the floor, leaned to take up the pack, one to my lip. Was looking for my book of matches,

Helen giggled at something, an on purpose giggle, rolled from her back to belly and wriggled to the end of the bed mattress.

"You used to be big."

Didn't register what she meant at first, saw the matchbook.

"And you had a beard."

Tensed, but played it off she couldn't've noticed, struck a match, lit my cigarette slowly, shook the flame dead, smiled at her. She was holding my wallet, gingerly touching at the face on the Henry Dollar ID.

"That was forever ago," I said, casually reaching for the wallet but she scooted out of reach, as though this were the game and I was playing, too.

"I like you all big and caveman," she laughed ugly and long, like she didn't even care I'd laugh too or not, maybe even didn't want me to.

"That was a short lived look," I said, "saw my photo it came in the mail right away stopped with the sweets and started a regiments of karate. Knew you planned all this out to swipe my pocketbook I'd've stayed home, you gypsy."

Had to lay on top her make her finally give the wallet up, tossed it over toward my pants where they'd wound up by the television cabinet.

"When did you move?" she asked, tracing some picturing on my side, rubbing her hand like erasing it, tracing something else, maybe the same thing.

"Year or so."

"I never get around to changing my license either, still have one from Vermont."

Kissed her hip, moving myself down over the bedside, positioning her legs open in front of me.

"Remember how I told you about wanting my mouth on you?"

She made a sound, kicked at me.

"Give you my former addresses, references I finish with that, good?"

***

Helen'd made it a thing to call me every night since we'd been together, even just five minutes she was groggy like already asleep. Wondered when would she bring it up about making Tuesdays a regular thing like the circles on her office calendar suggested, but it got all the way through the weekend she hadn't even brought up about another lunch.

It'd taken me awhile get up the nerve go in a place to print out the photos of Helen and I outside three two-two, but I did. I'd spent two nights manipulating the images—it was arousing to do, crop out this, zoom in close my face, hers, too close, just playing, zooming in until the image grained, pixilated, was just an abstract spill of light and shade. Finally I had a dozen, put them and the eight from our other filmed meeting into an envelope, printed my name out some label the security desk computer, affixed it.

This was mid-shift, Monday night technically Tuesday morning, was just about to leave for my rounds—thought'd been to give it another few days before another move, but when the phone rang I knew it'd be Helen, just felt compelled to move things forward.

Let the phone ring. Let it ring.

It stopped, but I kept looking at it. Stared.

I rubbed my eyes, flicked the envelope across the desk top, pushed the chair back and was getting to my feet the phone rang, again. Took it up immediately, glancing around, but didn't say anything the receiver to my ear.

"Henry?"

Made my voice low and dark, underwater and someplace else, "Hey."

She laughed, and unsure wet sound like a garden snail, wanted to know was everything alright.

"You tell anyone about us?"

Even with the question coming out, still considered had I ought to start in yet, was there some wrong ground I'd step on, queer the thing up—could still play it into a joke, forget the whole thing.

"What do you mean?"

My voice was broken porcelain, a handclap, hoped she cringed a little the seethe I gave to the words. "I mean did you tell anyone—anyone—about us?"

Line went quiet, the confusion palpable, something like I'd punched her but then right away kissed her and laughed, left her she didn't know had something happened or not.

"No. I didn't tell anyone."

"This isn't a joke, and I think you need to understand that. So what are you doing?"

"I don't know what you're talking about, Henry."

She sounded offended, but the tone was clearly just a defense—after all, she didn't know what I was talking about and I didn't know did my anger sound it had conviction or did I just come across lunatic.

So I just stayed quite, didn't say anything to her saying my name three times, minute long pauses between. Took that long, but her tone cracked, she said, scared "Why do you think I told someone about us?"

Could almost see her recoiling from the sound of my slapping my half-tense palm to the desktop.

"Because someone sent me pictures of us, Helen—because I have an envelope of photos of us."

I started another sentence, but broke it off into an angry chuckle—she was stammering something about she didn't know what I meant.

"Pictures of us meeting when you wanted to meet, pictures of us outside the hotel room you reserved—come on, Helen. Or's this one of your flirts—you being importunate?"

Tensed at that, head swam—wasn't supposed to've read that note she'd called herself importunate, tried to think'd maybe she told me what she'd written, scrambled to have an explanation ready she asked, but if she remarked it odd I'd used the word back at her didn't say anything about it. Didn't matter, I'd lost my bearings, just vaguely sputtered, kept making her tell me she wasn't trying to get over on me about something. Wanted to ditch out, shut the phone down, instead just went silent, let it stay the hum of phone connection and my breathing, looked at my knees, hand tightened hard around one.

"Can I see you?"

This got me back focused, charged—she'd swallowed the thing, had got the import even though she didn't have the whole thread.

"No, Helen, you can't see me."

"What pictures?"

That was it, last question last syllable of it her breaking off almost in tears with confusion.

"I'm hanging up."

And I did. Avoided the desk rest of the night, a precaution against myself—didn't need any more improvisational bravado, wasn't even sure the effect this call'd have. For one, hadn't brought up the money, the blackmail which'd been the entire thing, ask her to meet me and bring it up I was being wrung for money. But looping the parking garage through however many cigarettes, actually came around to praising myself for this tack—I'd wanted to meet her, present the photos to her all a whisper, but that'd make it all seem the sham it was, that behavior was storybook, didn't gel with the banality, the panic some guy'd feel being messed around over stepping out on his wife, made sense to treat Helen as the enemy, not to plant her firm as confederate.

If it came to it, I'd have to approach her, again, but no harm letting it go, see how she played it next.

It was exhausting, the tread of it round and round, unable to step clear of the thoughts. Didn't leave my apartment room, called out sick from two shifts. The time away was good, got me feeling flat and un-invested again, distanced me.

First night back, I was ready to call Helen but found a note from her she was up in her office I got in from my first rounds.

Stared at the elevators.

Stared.

Smile broke out my face—I was getting caught up, realized I was thinking about what'd it look like I went up to her office, what if someone was still watching me. Ridiculous. Whole ride up the fifth floor I wobbled my arms, my face around, made myself light and loose. I was too used to being anxious, it was seeping into the invention, it was peculiarly easy to get lost in the false paranoia of the part I needed to act.

Knocked on her door, she opened it right away, looked at me like she was terrified.

"Is it okay I came here?"

I touched her hip, moved her in—she didn't back-peddle to pace and so I pressed myself against her, let her put her head on me like it was her had some problem going on, all laughable.

She sat on the floor, knees up, chin on them, then chin lifted so her head'd touch the door, then chin back to them. I sat the desk chair, rubbing the sides of my nose two fingers both hands.

"Look, sorry I can't call or anything. I know you don't know anything about it, alright, but it's not just someone wants to give me a scare, they're asking money out of me and I don't have it to give them so I'm really in something tight and I just don't know what about it, okay?"

She looked at me.

"I can't see you anymore, Helen."

"Okay."

Looked at her awhile—she didn't offer anything else, turned her eyes down after not too long, so finally I stood sluggish to my feet, went for the door. She didn't move, still, still wasn't looking up.

"What's going to happen?"

Took a breath in, finished opening the door.

"Don't worry about it."

"I mean, if you don't pay them, they tell your wife, give her everything?"

"They'll do that anyway, you know?"

I sighed, leaned to the wall, roughed my hair and made a defeated croak.

"I don't know, Helen."

She said Okay, again, but still didn't move.

"I'm sorry I thought it'd anything to do with you, really. It's my own fault for it all, okay? I did it, this is what I did all myself."

She didn't respond, but did scooch to the side enough I got the door open, stepped through—heard the slow click of it going shut behind me by the time I was pressing Down the elevators.

***

Training shift came up, from nowhere, out the site in Weld. Supervisor hadn't been kidding about the train ride—Weld was nowhere. I'd been thinking somewhere in the city or the surrounding town just out the opposite direction from Delmore Street, but place off some tangent the commuter train, not even the metro, thicks of wet tall grass all around it few miles, humid even in the stiff cold.

Site was an offshoot building some discount printing company, wasn't much to train me in. I strolled the rounds with the meek little guy I was on with—not the guard leaving I'd replace, just someone else—and even when he poured himself a little lump of whisky into his Styrofoam coffee cup I kept my flask to myself, took swigs in the toilet, then had a few good mouthfuls I told him I'd do the next set of rounds myself, get the idea.

Place was twenty minute walking from where the train let off. In the morning, I shivered my way out in the glaze of sunlight, eyes felt mugged, glad I'd kept a few swallows of vodka to keep me warm. Turned out the earliest train I'd ever be able to get coming off shift was one hour fifteen minute wait. It didn't bother me, actually enjoyed it for the sense of nothing and nowhere it lent.

Thing with Helen'd been just a mumble from time-to-time in my head through the night at work. Took a hot shower, brewed some of my lousy coffee my little pot my room, paced around blowing cigarette out the window, thinking maybe I'd queered the thing all up. Big joke was, reason I was having trouble pushing was the make-believe to the whole thing—putting some pressure to someone else was one kind of thing, manipulating it to make it seem I was being come down on kind of bored me, I knew it did, was a blasé disinterest kept me from engaging right.

I just wanted the money, so it came to it I'd have to ask for it.

Hour into thinking this way, my blood was more up, seemed to have someplace to go around in me—it was I'd been thinking too much to play the weakling, need someone like Helen come on to my rescue, but really was no reason I couldn't turn it to more of a demand.

"This is as much your fault as mine, Helen," I said, long breath of smoke out my nose into a sudden clatter of wind scrambling itself into the building front, smoke almost back in my nose.

By the time I was giving a nod Good-night to Glenn, getting seated the desk at my regular site, the simple reality that there was timeline to contend with took center stage—if the thing was going to be someone was holding it over for me the money, they'd want it today much rather than whenever, few days from now, a week. So, I needed to press it that way to keep it seeming legitimate.

Wasn't surprised, more disappointed a call came in just twenty minutes into I'd sat down. Looked around uneasy I picked up—until it got into the night I felt the building occupied, felt watched, unready for myself.

It was Helen.

Tried to put on a pleasant voice, but then couldn't even get a turn to say Hello, she just, barely slow enough to keep it cleanly legible, said "I know I can't call, I left my office door propped open, just go look in the middle desk drawer."

I sighed at the sound of the call severing, lilting my head back and a long breath out through tight lips. Caught a peripheral glance the motion of my reflection the front door glass, rubbed my face, now conscious of myself, that even though no one was looking I needed to look how it'd be right for me to look someone was.

It was getting a drag though—thought about this up the elevator—the constant thinking I had to perform. I'd asked for it, sure, built myself the boards I was posturing across, but I felt distinctly unsettled with myself, my head trying to get ahead all the time just getting ahead into nothing, like coming up every ten seconds with what someone'd want me to go like then nobody cared.

She'd propped the door with one of her paperbacks, I kicked it in the room, let myself in my keycard, little snarl at my lip, like kind of mocking her for propping the door when all the time I have a key, but maybe she wanted to be sure about things.

Full three thousand dollars in an envelope, two page note in with it.

Sat in her chair, counted the money, tossed it her desk, looked at it.

Letter was about what I'd expect as accessory piece to this—on about she really insisted I take it, we didn't ever need even to talk about it, just she was worried, then like almost negating the first part saying how of course she'd rather hear about how it'd blown over, things were okay, in that case I could leave the money or return it to her.

Honestly just scanned the thing at first, only read it in detail it occurred to me I'd obviously have to call her, didn't want to get caught off guard some reference she'd make. Ridiculous.

Dialed her from her office phone, she took up after waiting five rings then didn't say anything even after I'd said Hello and I can't take your money.

"I can't take your money, Helen."

Still nothing.

Squinted hard over my shoulder the shut office blinds, face a scrunch of rolling my eyes and a shrugging gesture up with both hands, phone pinned to my shoulder my ear.

"Helen?"

"Is everything alright, then?"

"I mean, nothing's alright or anything, no—but this isn't something I'm taking money off you, okay?"

This was out without my thinking, half regretted it as it seemed alright I could've played relief, thankfulness, just didn't for whatever reason feel like it.

"If you need the money, use the money. I don't know why you think I don't have something to with it, Henry, I don't even know what you mean by that."

"I'm not insulting you, Helen. Just seems why'd I want to get anyone else in it. Listen, I gave him what I had, I'm sure that'll be it. Whoever it is got what they're after, and not then I'll deal with it another way or otherwise it'll always be I'm owing somebody."

Silence on the line—was actually kind of proud of myself over that little drift of illogic, could tell she was upset and I actually grinned a bit, flicked the pile of bills.

"You don't owe me, Henry."

"Even I did take it I owe you—not something I can say that money'd be back to you in a month's time, you know? Had to pull money out of the joint account already, give some story my wife about friend got into something, already that's not sitting well—gotta get the money back in savings but I'll get you your money, right after."

"You didn't tell her about me, right?"

Looked at the picture of Helen hugging her girlfriend, her other girlfriend hugging some guy.

"Telling her'd kind of defeat the whole thing, but she's not an idiot so it's I've got it in my head now with my friend, gotta keep that up, gotta hope this guy wanting money's gonna take what he got and let it be all done—I don't know what it is, right now, alright?"

Made a breath of pretend exasperation like I'd run down on things to say.

She asked me how'd it go I got money to the guy.

Defensiveness, stalling clogged my throat, coughed. Told her it didn't matter about that, said guy'd told me to leave it the desk some hotel, made me get on a train out someplace, give him a call.

"Probably to be sure I couldn't see who he was, I think."

She was quiet, my mind drifting into the past— Norman's money, money he'd paid me, that's when I'd left money a hotel.

Helen asking me if I was alright made me realize how long it'd been since I'd spoken, couldn't quite remember the thread of what we were saying.

Told her I wanted to see her, seemed nothing exactly better to say.

***

Met Helen someplace three blocks up from where I was actually living, waited around out in front a furniture store smoking three lazy cigarettes, saw her coming up to all bundled some coat seemed a whole other person covering her.

We took a booth a restaurant was more-or-less just a bar, but it was quiet enough and she seemed relaxed, right away ordered herself wine, asking the server did they have salad then shaking her head No thanks she was told what kind they did.

Made a few awkward smiles, face drawn, breathed into my hands, palms flat to each other like at prayer, tapped nails of both thumbs my nose, finally told her how grateful I was about that money, I'd figure out how to have it back to her soon as could be arranged.

"I don't want to talk about the money."

"Okay."

"I don't want to talk about it—that's done, it's just done."

"Okay."

"Okay."

She nodded like I'd indicated I agreed much more than I actually did. Something felt off.

I said "Look, I still have it, you know? I don't know even will I need to use it, might not even be I'll need it."

She sighed, actually seemed sad I'd said something.

Drinks came, I said I'd have another vodka, shook my head about anything to eat and Helen didn't even take her eyes off me to answer, was looking at me kind of tight, even while she took a swallow her wine.

"What if he does ask for the rest of the money?"

Blinked, took a sip more like a nibble my vodka, lowered my brow like I didn't exactly get what she'd asked.

"Then I'll pay him, I mean, and I'll get the money to you, after."

Was starting to tell her if she wasn't comfortable with the thing we could forget it, but she shook her head, emphatic, dismissive, quick, said that's not what she meant.

"What would it mean if he asked for the rest, for more than you gave him?"

Didn't want to play it too bewildered—didn't think she'd that—so I took my whole drink and still out of breath from the swallow said It'd mean he was serious about the five thousand, I suppose.

"Why would he stop there, then?"

She said this very pertinently, my attempt to deflect out of it with forced levity—chuckling "You trying to cheer me up?"—not even registering.

"Do you still have the number, he gave you a number to call?"

Not precisely where, but knew she was moving toward someplace, felt my legs go locked, curled around the booth seat, scratched under my lip too hard my thumb knuckle, no idea how my expression'd gone.

"I think you should try to figure out who's doing this," she said.

Knew I was smiling, but not what the smile'd seem like to see.

"I don't think I should do that, not for one minute."

"You could call him—say you know you didn't leave enough money, but you got the rest."

"No, Helen."

"Or maybe not call him, but if he calls you, when you arrange another drop."

I lifted my glass, actually feeling annoyed, hardly the presence of mind to act it was about something else, put my glass down looking around for the server.

"I think that's a very bad idea—you should take your money back, really. This isn't something I'm trying to turn tables around on someone, I'm not in the shape for anything clever."

"Why wouldn't he always be able to come back for you—you do one thing and he can hold it over you, forever."

Thankfully, waitress'd taken note of my squirming around, asked did I want another drink and while I said Yes, Helen downed hers, asked another wine.

"I'm not trying to catch anyone, Helen—I don't think he'll try to get more money, if he does, I'm done, I guess I'm done I can't figure out how I'll get it. But same thing'll happen I get cute on him, right? What'm I gonna do, muscle him up and even something like that he just makes one call has some buddy drop an envelope with the postman."

She looked like this last thing was a new consideration for her, she lost momentum, nodded like it was a fair point, started touching at the napkin around her silverware.

"You could do something," she said, quietly—it was kind of like to herself more than to anyone, certainly more than to me. "Why did you want to see me?" she said, not a full turn to her mood, but clearly she was making an attempt to get off the subject, had a look she was doing it more because she knew I'd want it, but still.

"I just wanted to see you."

"I wanted to see you, too."

I nodded and so did she.

"Wanted to tell you sorry, something, I don't know, tell you I'm not going to be security the building, getting reassigned some reason, so wanted you to know that— don't worry all of a sudden it's Glenn or someone answering the phone four in the morning."

"I wouldn't call you, if that's why you're leaving."

She'd made a face, one cheek up, too big a smile, eyes down a pout.

"They're just transferring me, nothing like it's about you calling me or not."

"Okay."

I nodded, squinted, glad the drinks came, all of sudden morbidly tense, excused myself to use the toilet after drinking half my glassful.

In the mirror, washing my face, couldn't remember last time I'd seen myself so shook up—I tapped the glass it seemed so much like I was actually in it, permanent.

Didn't actually use the toilet, so two minutes into being back in the booth of course now felt the urgency of needing to urinate, kept me even stiffer, head more removed from things than I was even trying for.

"I think I wanted to let you see my face I told you how I'm not going to be able to see you again, alright?"

Smart girl, she knew well enough it was coming, didn't make some wordplay dodging around it.

"Not like I'm going anyplace gone, but it's not something I can be seeing you."

"I know, I'll wait, I'm not going anyplace either."

"It's nothing about waiting or not waiting—I'm not asking you to wait, alright?"

"Alright."

"Not asking you anything about that, just that I appreciate your helping me and wanted to say good-bye right, or as right as it's possible, okay?"

Didn't understand her face, it seemed somewhat like I'd said something wrong, she wrinkled her nose, said "Of course I helped you," then kept the expression a few more seconds too long, sighed her shoulders up against her ears then down.

"You can call me if ever you can or you want or anything," she finally said, face into her wineglass right after.

"I won't."

"I know. But you can."

Finished my drink, vodka had me swimming a little bit, the conversation interminable, the urge to just stand up, laugh, leave. Chewed the inside of my mouth like something actually was ending, something actual had something, anything, to do with me.

***

Got in off a second training shift from out in Weld—completely unnecessary—was undressing, moving to check my box in the closet it struck me how it was I felt trapped. Thing's'd been itching me wrong, especially since last time I'd seen Helen, put it off to general nerves of getting away with something new, but now I got it was just really I was trapped. For all I'd set up, this little pantomime'd gotten me clean maybe two-and-a-half thousand profit, nothing else—Helen's three thousand minus all it'd taken to wrangle it, then I had to subtract into that she'd gone three thousand when I'd only been after two-and-a half, so if not for that slip of luck I'd only really be up two thousand.

Nothing.

Nothing.

But worse into the bargain was that I honestly had no choice but to stay around, now roil in these fits of unease I'd get—even if I knew for a fact they'd all pass away, I was still nowhere other than where I'd been before the thing. Even say I used the two grand to move away—it'd cost the whole thing even to do that, and then the problem of getting set up someplace, again. Here, I'd established myself into a nook, no worries about a job, place to live, what I'd call myself—each place I left, it was someplace I left forever, so it made sense I should've been paying more careful attention to see about making sure I'd only leave if out-and-out I'd no alternative, but this'd been like I'd tricked myself out of something and couldn't rid myself of thinking how I'd be stuck paying the toll a good hard while.

Little bit more money in a box, little bit more money not to spend or else it'd be all gone.

Shifts at the Delmore Street building sat miserable the week, stayed away from the front desk, roamed the parking garage behind cigarettes or coffee getting thick from being drunk so slow.

It was a laugh to think how I'd thought I'd find some

other woman pull this same game on, like I'd be able just walk a few blocks over and start it all up again there, a theatre engagement with a regular paycheck, a vanishing act after'd leave no one looking for me, wondering about me.

Whole thing with Helen, like everything, it'd fell in my lap, I'd cuddled it up in my arms and run, only this time I'd not gone anywhere.

Supervisor'd brought paychecks around, made me kind of ridicule myself all night how three paychecks—three and half, really, but that hardly mattered—that'd earn me the same as I'd got this whole thing and for basically the same result, sitting no place in a building closed for the night going no place else it got morning.

Middle of the week following I'd last seen Helen, I popped into her office, sat in her chair, looked at the circled Tuesdays her calendar, flipped the pages all the way through see had she marked anything else and could I puzzle out why.

No. Nothing. Didn't know at all what maybe I'd thought there'd be, but whatever it was wasn't there.

Was getting my cigarette ready for my stroll around the garage few more hours, saw the candy dish labeled Don't Touch, hesitantly reached for one, squinting—wondered did she know how many there were, some little ritualized thing, count them every day. Pretended to take a drag my cigarette, clicked my tongue myself for being a moron, took a candy, chewed it hard and swallowed like one movement.

Then saw a Post-it note the corner her computer screen, stuck halfway on top the one I remembered seeing before, this new one written in same thick red marker the calendar days were circled.

Don't Call.

Cleared my throat, staring at it, trying to smile about something, coming up empty but felt like I was managing a smile, regardless, skin going tight up and creasing all across my face.

Very least, I thought better of using Helen's office phone, copied the number down, made myself hurry down the bottom of the parking garage, give myself the time it'd take to get back up to get myself convinced I'd ignore the note—wait out my shift, anyway, call from someplace else, last thing I'd need is it'd turn out to be Helen's cousin Phyllis or something idiotic, Phyllis wonders What's this number, asks Helen on the strength it's the same area code and it wouldn't take too much figuring out the thing from there to get back to me.

Same time, what'd it matter?

That was a far stretch, knew I was just stalling—placing the call from the lobby some movie theatre wasn't going to make much difference I wanted to be that paranoid about it.

Just had the sunk feeling I'd had too often before— there'd been that conversation with Helen over wine, that peculiar eagerness she'd shown, all proud of herself coming up some smart idea then the obvious frustration, deflation, disappointment I'd not rubbed my hands together and decided to play loverboy sleuth with her.

Three times before I dialed the full ten digits, rocked hard in my chair, having to scoot it back in to the desk by the time the answering machine took up.

I stopped, flat, dead—stopped.

Ugly sort of woman's voice went "You have reached Beaker and Turnover Investigators—if you have a mailbox number, you may dial it at any time to be connected."

Voice went on about if I was calling for Martin Bleaker press X if I was calling for Desmona Graves press Y—I just let it talk, receiver rested in a curl over my shoulder, stared at the paperback Glenn'd left by the rolodex, dog-eared, misshapen like it'd bloated from being rained on.

Hung up, dialed the number slowly, reading off each digit I'd written on the little scrap I'd torn from a piece of crumpled paper in Helen's wastebin, let it ring just once, hung up, started rocking in my chair hard, forced clicks, again, staring at the paper.

I grabbed a pen, started scribbling out the number, rubbed my face.

Helen's note, the number, it said Don't Call.

Don't Call.

Must've been up since the night in her office, I'd left her sitting there.

So, seemed she hadn't called, had been waiting for the say-so from me and I'd not given it.

"Done," I said, standing, waggling loose arms and shaking my face. "Done."

It'd been some little fanciful idea of hers, she'd shown restraint to not just do it—note was an artifact, now, not like all of a sudden she'd start an investigation and what'd she investigate, anyway?

"And you can give back the money," I said, nodding as I lit a cigarette not even out the front door, yet.

Nodded, nodded.

"I can do that," I said, shouldering into my reflection, empty cold air squirreling over my shoulders, sound of a moan, the lobby echoed, too loud like it always did.

The money was the only thing connected me to Helen—money the only thing really connected me ever to anyone. I wanted done, simple as telling her I'd not heard from the guy, wanted her to have it back, insist, say if he ever did call it'd be another thing and then of course he'd never call.

Nodded. Felt relaxed after two more smokes.

Needed to remember that none of it was real—no wife, no blackmail. None of it was real. Nothing about me was. Nothing about me mattered, anyway.

***

Made arrangements to have my last set of shifts covered, Delmore Street, before I'd start permanent out in Weld. Last night on shift, I let myself in Helen's office, put a wrapped gift box with her three thousand dollars in the same drawer where she'd left it, before—also put in with it some nonsense, short note of Thanks, things'd turned out alright. Used one of her Post-Its, stuck it to her computer screen, let her know her present was in the drawer, signed it HD.

Used the whole of that day to get sleepy drunk in my room, woke into the evening, went out to get the drunk back up. The idea was keep the sense of having been beat from getting on me, let the entire matter get behind me—it stayed on my mind, certainly, but I was able to treat it as an object, a carcass to examine for science, see if it gave indication how it might be made viable were I to get the chance for something like it, again.

Didn't know, couldn't figure how I'd done anything wrong, just I'd wound up some nut wanted to be clever there was no need for it.

Got glum for awhile, it hitting me how actually I'd come out underneath, things analyzed—had paid for the room, spent money this and that—it was like a slow, bored whistle wouldn't go quiet, after awhile even I knew the drinks were just making me less able to articulate how much it got under my skin, did nothing to actually make the wheeze of it stop.

Turned out I was allowed to start the Weld site a night early, wouldn't've known if not for a call in to the office about would my paycheck be at Weld or was it left at Delmore—supervisor told me it was at Delmore, but he'd bring it out that night he made rounds.

On the train ride out that evening, near empty compartment, looking at some piece a discarded newspaper, I realized I felt comfortable the more barren things got around, the more I felt elsewhere, nowhere— the walk along from the station to the work site was pitch black, even the tips of my cigarettes hardly seemed to smolder enough to light. It was like even though nothing'd gone through with Helen, still my body, something, some element of me was ready to move, get someplace else, the shuttling of the train and the quiet cold of my walking felt like that, felt like motion.

It was the supervisor sitting at the guard desk, gave him kind of a puzzled nod as I entered, flicking my last cigarette back behind me to the lot.

"Let Mitch leave early when he asked," supervisor said, sighing himself standing.

"Good of you," I said, palms to the counter window separating desk from lobby, doing a few abbreviated pushups, shaking my shoulders around.

"Your check and this was left for you few nights ago, figured I'd bring it along."

Took the check, asked "Left?" while narrowing my eyes on the second envelope.

"A man left it for you, I think Glenn said—would've just put it in the outgoing mail, but figured you'd be back by, slipped his mind until earlier tonight."

Also there was no address, but figured supervisor was just talking to talk, tossed both envelopes to the desk, a light remark about Glenn, few minutes chat then supervisor drove off—I walked into the dark lot for another smoke, seemed to be able to watch the taillights his car forever they went.

The envelope'd be Helen, but still I tried to think what guy would've left something—or it could've been a guy, why not? Absentmindedly started a second cigarette, sighed, stopped short tossing it into the lot, leaned to the wall, took three slow drags, abruptly tossed it away.

Just my name—just Henry Dollar—typed on a label, label affixed to the plain-as-can-be envelope.

Computer typewritten note *Hi, Please give me a call, it's very urgent.*

Thing was signed *Douglas.*

Just stared at it. No telephone number, because that would be—to Helen's way of trying to be careful—a risk.

Douglas.

Shook my head and muttered a Jesus Christ, sat in my chair then got up straight away, went around down a hall to a break area for employees of the company—a coin coffee machine, a vending unit with sandwiches and microwave burgers—didn't get anything but sat at one of the long tables.

At least it meant she hadn't hired the private investigators—she'd done that, this would've come to the apartment I rented the room in, something like that, wouldn't't've come at all someone was looking in to me.

Two minutes after this thought, struck me that it'd be best to give Helen a call specifically because of that—already this letter'd been meant for me few days ago, could be she's sitting around with all manner of phantasm in her head, could be I don't respond she decides to hire someone and who knows the trouble that could lead to.

It's important.

That'd kill me, I tried to ignore it—I'd not be able to

relax until I knew was that something meant anything or just some random way she'd decided to go and phrase this nonsense little letter of hers.

Stalled through ordering a coffee, pouring some it out to add cool tap water, thing still too scalding to take a proper sip from, kind of blew enough to hardly ripple the surface after dialing, the purr of three and half rings before she said Hello, tough to tell what her tone let on.

"Everything alright?" I asked, purposefully quizzical if not dubious, but not wanting to sound dismissive, no need to put her off like she'd have no reason to get back in touch with me, just also didn't want to give an impression of I'd been waiting around for it.

"Is everything alright with you?"

"Everything's fine, Helen, yeah, you know as far as fine goes, considering."

"Okay."

She said it, but odd, obviously wrong, something so heavy in her pauses they practically leaked.

"You don't sound okay," I prompted, felt my shoulders tensing.

"He didn't send the pictures to your wife or anything, did he?"

"No. No, I think he took what he could and it's all done."

Started to say I'd never be able to tell, was something I'd live with, but she talked over me.

"He called me."

Genuinely asked her to repeat herself from the confusion of I'd still been speaking.

"He called me at work four days ago, Monday."

Tried a sip of my coffee, it was bearable, swallowed half a mouthful.

"Called you why, about what?"

"He said you hadn't paid up, he wanted me to pay, now."

I leaned back, quick sip of coffee, one eye closed like if she were in front of me I'd be giving her a look was she joking.

"Why would you pay him anything?"

"He said he wanted five thousand dollars or he'd send the photos to your wife, he said he wanted it right away."

Coughed into my hand, the end of the sound coming off almost like a chuckle.

"That doesn't make sense. You didn't give him any money, did you?"

"Not yet. He said you were supposed to drop it for him, like before."

Scratched the hair the side of my head, brushed some of the flakes of dandruff wound up on the table to the floor, scratched a little more.

"He wants his money, he said he didn't care where it came from."

"Well, I paid him twenty-five hundred," I said, just feeling the thing out—a movement of my arm across to get my coffee made me realize my armpits were sweating thick.

"It wasn't enough, he said it wasn't enough."

"Don't give this man any money, Helen, this doesn't make sense, okay? Let me worry about it. Do not give him your money, it's nothing to do with you."

Line went quiet—I'd caught myself on those last words too late, winced and mouthed a growl.

"Helen, I just mean don't pay him. Look, I'm on a schedule this site, not as lax as your building, let me call you in an hour."

"I have to get to sleep."

Rolled my eyes, my head shoulder to shoulder then

nodded tip tap tip tap to myself, leaned forward, head to my wrist-back, elbow the desk.

"Alright. When can I see you, we'll sort this, okay?"

***

Just from how she was sitting, her purse on her lap still slung to her shoulder, both hands the strap right where it attached to the pouch, I knew she had the money on her, five thousand dollars. Waved as I crossed to the table she was sitting—booth in a regular franchise restaurant just like I'd told her over the phone, said I'd seen no point being secretive, was obvious he'd either be watching us or knew quite well we'd be seeing each other, not like additional photos'd make it any worse.

Decided I'd take a measure of control, early on, give me the best idea where her head was at I didn't let her choose the weather from the get.

"Did he send you the pictures, show you the pictures of us?"

Shook her head tight, "He said you knew which ones."

Waiter popped up, actually startled me, told him just I wanted coffee, Helen shook her head same way she just had at me he asked her did she need something else and was anything wrong with her salad.

"I know which ones, or whatever, it's no difference he has worse ones whatever, ones I know about are bad enough."

She started to talk, I gestured her quiet and went on.

"I don't see the thing he tells you tell me to drop the money, right? He hasn't got in touch with me, I don't know where to put it."

"He said just like last time."

I stared at her, eyes wide. "Just like last time, same hotel? Like last time, say it's for the same guy?"

She shrugged and nodded and then seemed actually distraught, said she didn't know then quickly added "I have the money, I want you to give him the money."

Set her purse up on the table, but the waiter brought my coffee—asked did I take cream, sugar, told him "No, no"—Helen put the purse back right in her lap.

When the waiter left, I rubbed my face, made a sad smile, shook my head.

"I don't think that makes sense, Helen."

And I didn't, even in whatever her imaginary scenario was—that this'd win my heart, that she'd set a trap and catch the bad guy—and especially not in the sense what was really she thinking about, here.

"I think it's a bluff, just he wants to grift whatever else out he can, we're not giving him any of your money and I'll take the consequences."

Darted my eyes to and from the purse—wondered was there money, who was putting who on, anxious about I was trusting what was being presented to me both knowing it was absolute fantasy and knowing it was coming from someone who know that too but really, really seemed she believed what she was saying.

Helen took a sip of her water, another, straightened at her hair.

"What if he gets mad at me?"

"He won't get mad at you, guy's a loser trying to scare you out some money he's not going to escalate."

"But even you said, why would he call me?"

"Helen, just because you're the only other interested party, guessing on your feelings for me based on he saw us and all, figured your take a bullet for me—you pay him, then he's likely he'll come back want more, twice as likely as he'll ever bother me, again, you do see that, right?"

I saw it, thought it was cleverly to point, honestly—not that there was anyone, but if there was that's just how they'd act and what they'd think.

"I have an idea," she said, like this is what she'd been waiting for, the script to that moment not going as planned so she'd just jumped track, her whole demeanor altered, her whole tone now like we'd already decided there'd be need for A Plan and this was just her offering. Wanted to tell her We don't need a plan, but instead waited through her pause—if I got evasive, told her a hard No, could be she'd move on without me, didn't seem she was in a mood to bow out so best to get her pulse.

"I should write a letter to your wife."

She looked at me, so I nodded, careful not to show encouragement or wariness, just a nod.

She went on: "Write her, say I had an affair with you, that we'd been together but you'd broken it off—you know what I mean? Write it like I'm the woman scorned, but at the same time make it clear that you dumped me."

"Helen."

"Say how it was a one time thing, you ended it off right away—you see what I mean?"

"I see what you mean, sure. I just think it's not so much a good idea."

"If you admitted it, he can't blackmail you."

Knew my eyes were open too wide, knew I wasn't blinking, was holding her fixed in just the wrong kind of glance, used a sip of my coffee as a moment's pause and thankfully managed to close my eyes, make it like I was taking the idea in.

"Then he can't come back."

"I don't think that'll work—I don't think admitting what I don't want to admit is exactly an out."

"You can control it, though, there's a chance it'll go wrong, but there's a chance it'll go wrong with this guy, either way—that's what you said, that you'll never know."

I nodded, my stomach felt like a swamp—not that there was an affair to admit and not that there was anyone to admit it to, just that the logic she paved was tight enough I knew she wouldn't relent unless I could counter it and not only that, but if I countered it too aggressively that might make her head off, take matters in her own hands, a prospect less and less appealing per sentence out her mouth.

"I tell my wife, then this guy gives the pictures—what'll that seem like?"

I was making this up as I went, but felt it, knew I had the tune and could tell Helen knew it too, look to her face like a trapdoor went open.

"My wife'll think I had you write some letter, yeah? Especially photos from a blackmailer into it, it's just two thing don't go together right, one thing too many."

She was nodding but I pressed on.

"One thing, the other thing, sort of fine, can work with them singular, but it's too much to go around with all the elements—I couldn't smooth over the mess, the air'd go bad, you know?"

Saw her hands tighten, both of them, to the sack part of her purse.

Two minutes passed.

My coffee was refreshed and since Helen didn't look up I said "We're fine" when the waiter asked did we need anything else.

"He wants this money."

She was looking up by the time I looked over.

"I want to give it to him. Maybe he will just go away if we do."

Somehow the restaurant'd gotten noisy, like a glop of something'd spilled in it, noise, people.

"I want to give it to him, Henry, I don't care."

I felt peculiar, but also light, felt outside the echoing hole the conversation had been, conversation one tenth real but also somehow eleven tenths make-believe.

"Did he leave you a number?" I asked.

She shook her head and I nodded at the same time, her purse now had straps back around her shoulder and her eyes were someplace I wasn't.

***

Getting closed back in the apartment, quickly closed back the room I rented, realized the whole trip back since Helen my mind hadn't settled on anything. Thing was, were I Helen it'd've made sense to've suggested the both of us just go out to the hotel—not that there was one—then and there, because according to her alleged instructions from the blackmailer this would've technically made the most sense. She, of course, knew there was no blackmailer—or at least knew this current blackmail threat was her own invention—so I'd dug some idea out my pocket how I'd need to call him if it'd be like last time, get instructions where he wanted me to ride out to after dropping the money before calling him so he'd know it'd be safe to pick up. Superficially, this made sense and since I'd told Helen to hold onto the money that took the curse off it she'd find it fishy—she was probably fretting I'd find out she was full of it, but she'd already tightened herself into a spot she couldn't exactly take the helm, basically she had to take cues from me, now.

I'd undressed, but felt too agitated to get new clothes on, couldn't sit and kept touching at my window blinds, no reason.

I really didn't think she'd have someone watching me, just couldn't see an angle in that, but still my mind tried to play out all equations with that in mind—too much, couldn't thread this with that, that with this.

There was five thousand dollars she was going to put in a room—she was going to let that five thousand go, for something she knew was nothing.

Mouth chattered while I smoked.

Why'd she do that?—because there needed to be a reason.

Figured it was something she wanted to stay in close with me, maybe even had machinations ready to break me up from my wife she didn't know I didn't have.

Found I was stubbing my cigarette after just three, four drags, tried to relight it but it'd got too fouled up, got another out.

Went out into the main area of the apartment, said Hello? a few times to be certainly guy I rented from wasn't around, took up the cordless phone and went through drawers until I came up with a phonebook. Dialed a few hotels in an area called Dover Wire, first two far too expensive, third too far out from main transportation, fourth one, a Ramada, seemed just fine.

"I need to reserve a room, but I'll pay in cash I get there, can that work?"

"Certainly, which sort of room?"

"Regular room, something up few floors if that works—it's interior access all your rooms?"

"Yes, sir."

Went through the general things reserving a room, gave the name Daniel Halbst—this was something off one of my many stolen IDs, just blurted into my mind when asked Under which name? hadn't even occurred to me I'd need to show ID until that second.

"There's someone going to drop off a package for me the desk, but you wouldn't give out my room number or anything right?"

"No, sir."

"I mean, not under this or that circumstance anything, someone came asking after me with some line?"

"Certainly not—we don't disclose any guest information unless there is notation to do so."

"Well, I want specifically notation not to do so."

"Certainly."

"I mean, sorry and I'm not nuts or something like that, not being rude."

"No, it's understandable."

"And when the package gets dropped, can it be left in the room—I give permission for that, you can do that?"

"We'll have it brought to your room."

"Okay—but not just right then, like after a bit."

The clerk actually chuckled, which I think might've been rude were I not so caught up in what I was caught up in, assured me the package would be taken care of discreetly. We went over the reservation, he repeated my instructions, we hung up.

Started dialing Helen, caught myself five digits in, set the phone down, went to stand in a shower but then changed my mind.

There was no getting around it that if I took this money, I'd have to split and leave the Henry Dollar name behind me.

Five thousand dollars.

I didn't care what Helen was thinking—and in every real sense, I'd left her alone, given her back her money before and broke it off with her sensible, at least according to what she was under the impression the circumstances were—none of my business she wants to take her gambit, here, whatever it is. None of my business and otherwise it was money'd be left in some room just wind up some stranger, because at this point even me coming clean or discontinuing contact'd just lead into deeper water, into murk, into things I didn't even want to consider.

Just wanted everything simple and simple-as-can-be was to jump ship, but not like some scardycat and not with less on me that I'd put in, already.

Got my box out the closet, unpacked it into my duffle.

If she were to have someone keeping an eye on me—or had already—this'd be the last time I could set foot in these rooms, this was endgame. Wrapped a few shirts around the box I kept my money in, my IDs, set the gun all bundled up on top of this, packed everything else in.

Stared at the bag, unzipped, looking right square back at me.

Gently, to not disturb the arrangement of anything else, I took the gun bundle out, unwrapped it, set the thing down on the bed.

Still loaded, still same bullets as always.

I didn't even know if this was my idea, anymore—didn't know what anything was my idea anymore, just knew that next time I'd be someplace else and I'd take better care.

For five thousand dollars.

Well, subtract the amount for the two nights I'd pay for this room—just to be safe—something four thousand six hundred dollars. Then subtract money from before, room at the Xavier Suites and all of it.

Shook my head and made cartoon silly windmill punches, tried to fake at least a halfway honest sounding laugh.

"So four thousand dollars," I said. "That isn't nothing. It isn't nothing."

Put gun to my coat's hip pocket just because if for nothing else it seemed a bad idea to leave it in my bag unattended. Was going to've put the duffle in a bus locker, but the phone call the hotel'd given me a more relaxing idea. Rode the metro out a few stops, found an Extended Stay Deluxe Suites, stood in line till it got my turn at the desk.

"Just realized I need to get a room, left my money and all with a friend isn't in yet. I'm meeting him for lunch, going out a bit, but could I leave my bag here, it's just killing me to lug it around?"

No hesitation, the girl working the desk took it, remarked that it was pretty heavy.

"And you'll put that in back, right?"

"We have an area."

"Great. And you wouldn't release it to anyone but me, right?"

"Absolutely we wouldn't, sir."

"Okay."

I gave my name, promising I'd be back probably that evening, but she assured me the bag would just be kept until I got in, nothing to worry about.

Walked a few blocks, nowhere, slow, sluggish, holding a cigarette didn't much bother about smoking. Did a little checklist like Was I forgetting anything? touched at my pant pockets, patted the front of coat, patted the side pockets, just tensing the briefest blink at the heft of the sleeping gun, there. Then patted myself absently everywhere, again.

***

Cab let me out in front the Ramada, glanced to the meter found the trip hadn't hurt so bad as I'd figured it would've. Asked the driver wait, I'd be just ten minutes or so— thought better of this, it'd mean the meter'd keep going and even if not it'd be too awkward to ask that, confirm. Told the driver Nevermind. Wasn't any reason to go around skimming off ten bucks here, ten bucks there for nothing, idea was keep things as frugal as could be managed.

Glad I'd decided against the cab waiting, line for check-in took awhile. I paid for the room, not even being asked for my Daniel Habst ID, got my room key, reminded the person at the desk about there should be instructions concerning a package being delivered—they scrolled down a computer screen, nodded, read back the notes'd been left.

To avoid any chance getting the same driver, walked down a few blocks, hailed a cab coming down the street, asked to be taken to the building I'd worked at, Delmore Street, from there I'd walk to meet Helen, more in keeping with character.

Struck me I might not be able to get loose from Helen, immediately—or rather that it might not be the best idea—so went into a bar, was pointed to a telephone back by the toilet, called about my duffle being held at the Extended Stay front desk, was assured that even if I didn't make it in until tomorrow, bag'd be held, only released to me.

Stood at the urinal but couldn't manage anything, bounced on my toes.

Why should this be making me so nervous? How'd it become so many component pieces, such a line done by a shaky hand?

Hadn't even done anything, but the nerves were all over me, nothing to do about it. Asked a glass of vodka, downed it almost while it was poured, waited for my change and was back out into the cold.

Say Helen had the money in an envelope already, not like I could ask Mind if I count that?

Obviously that was the thing, she wasn't such a lunatic she'd part with money over nothing, so why would I take this chance?

Cigarette tasted like my mouth after sleeping too long in a room too warm, smoked it anyway but kept rubbing my tongue along inside my cheeks, across my lips, wiping lips dry the back of my hand.

There was nothing left—money or not, I had to go, some creepy woman hanging around thinking up this and that was no good. Say she calls that private detective, say she does—it'd be a world of dirt down on me I couldn't even begin to get out of.

Helen was outside the restaurant, smoking her own cigarette, waved at me from me still a good way off, I just nodded kind of, hands down my pockets, one of them teasing the bulb of the gun handle.

"Is everything okay?" she asked, touching my arm, thought she was about to give me a kiss but then she didn't.

More worry on her face than I'd've figured showed—she was nervous, nervous her nonsense'd dissolved while I'd been out of her sight, was tempted to just call her out, split, but instead went ahead with calming her down.

"No one answered, number just kept ringing."

She didn't say anything, but I could tell she was relieved.

"Maybe he just wants you to go to the same place."

I shrugged, said it seemed so.

"Don't know Helen, but this is your money, maybe we shouldn't just leave it at the front desk some hotel."

"He gave you a name, last time?"

"Sure."

Now I tightened up, for some reason this little complication'd eluded me, no plan at the ready.

"What name?"

"Dempton," I said, right proud of that, too, said it again as a memory cue. "Dempton, last time left a package for Dempton."

I motioned we should walk, got a cigarette lit while we did.

So, now she had someone check out the place, they'd ask after a Dempton, they'd find no room for Dempton, which was how it should be.

Closed my eyes. Slowed my walking—took Helen a moment to notice, she drifted over to me.

"It's going to be fine."

Nodded.

She'd have someone go in once we'd gone, say they were Dempton, get the package back—provided there was anything in the package, which there probably wasn't. I felt sick to my stomach—no, I'd no control over this, this was all a mistake.

"We shouldn't give him all the money, shouldn't give him any money."

She looked at me, very odd expression, peculiar in its blankness, like she was looking at me but standing behind herself, watching the conversation like two other people were having it.

"You have the money on you?" I asked.

She went into her purse, took out an envelope.

"Why shouldn't we give him the money?"

She didn't resist at all, just let me take it, envelope wasn't even sealed. She touched my arm, wanted to know was everything alright. The money was all there—or at least a lot of money was, in fifty-dollar bills.

"I should just tell my wife, just end this all."

Was looking down, she put her forehead to mine, tried to nudge me to look up but I'd just move my head this way, that way, finally she put her hands on my face.

"We should at least try, okay. I want to at least try."

I nodded.

"I don't care about this money."

I nodded.

She kissed me on my unreturning mouth, kissed me again, would've again but I looked up, kissed her head, gave her back the envelope. Had to continue the line of drama, though, so I told her it's I was just nervous something would go wrong.

"It's better to pay him everything than just some," she said. "Just give him what he wants."

Didn't feel like disagreeing, kissed her head again, couldn't bring myself to do anything closer, more intimate than that and she didn't even press for it.

So, she had a name, of course she would—what'd that matter at all? Dempton, almost'd forgotten, nodded rapid taps of getting it in my memory. Dempton. Dempton. Was real money we'd be leaving, unless she'd try a switch up, but thing was I'd have a chance to confirm, we'd have to put the money in a box, wrap the box, if she tried to be the one to drop it off I'd know the thing'd gone sour, just take off, period.

She started putting her hand in my pocket, almost even let her before I realized it was the pocket the gun all bulbous down in it, took her hand instead, gave it a kiss, then her lips, slow, warm kiss.

"I'm sorry," I said.

She shook her head, smiled, brow creased while she rubbed mine.

"I'm sorry."

Kissed me, I let her, kept her hands in mine and when we started walking again switched which side of her I stood on. Looked over my shoulder as naturalistically I could manage, stopped for a cigarette, using the excuse to turn, have a careful look down the street behind me, up the street we were going. Didn't seem to be anyone except people seemed they ought to be there.

Helen asked for a cigarette, gave her mine and this seemed to make her happy, somehow.

***

Some middle aged woman working the front desk, gave her a nod, leaning to the counter while she finished out the phone call she was taking—reservation being booked—set the bubble mailer Helen and I'd picked out the drug store across the way, thing now all addressed to Michael Dempton. Way the lobby was set up, knew Helen couldn't see me, beside which she'd stayed down the way, I'd left her with a coffee and another for me cooling.

Was getting a rush of energy, but not enough the ride out to wherever I'd decide to place a pretend call that I'd have to say wasn't answered weighed down on me, quite a bore.

"Sorry about that, can I help you?"

She had a face it'd be a bothersome call, so I smiled.

"No trouble, I'm actually just here leave off a package for Daniel Halbst."

Held it up, explained it was addressed to Dempton but being left for Halbst, so she got a piece of paper, started writing down Halbst, asked me spell it.

"He's actually a guest, believe he arranged about you'd have it brought to his room."

She verified this in the system.

"I will send it up, presently," she said.

"Thanks so much, appreciate it."

Outside, ran myself straight into a cigarette fast as I could and since I still wasn't anywhere Helen could see I lingered through the smoke—even crossed my mind why'd I bothered with this charade, why not just've ducked out the back, cab to my hotel holding my duffle, but really it was best not to be immodestly rash. Smiled at that way of putting it, started another cigarette, made my way up where Helen was waiting, now smoking herself, stubbing it out as I got across the street.

She started to ask something—probably about had it gone alright—but I took her face in both hands and kissed her. Could tell she thought I was going to pull back right away, took her a moment to respond to my continuing kiss, her mouth opening, tongue meeting mine which'd been roughing against her lips, her teeth—kissed her long, too long, gesture even started seeming odd to me, my hands gripping her waist, moving around her neck, down her back.

When I stopped I was aroused, made her look at me, focus, though she was flustered and a bit lost for words, look on her like trying to think of something clever.

"Can we go to your place?"

She swallowed, eyes blinking three time, wider, wider, wider—puzzled look, I shook my head.

"He didn't answer the call, won't answer—just wants us occupied and I think we'll be occupied enough, yeah?"

She laughed, all through her nose, touched her hair but for nothing.

"Okay."

I kissed her again, this time she was eager for it, her hands getting under my shirt while I gripped the front of her pants, giving it tugs, felt her hand over my erection through my pants, felt how tight she clawed her fingers to it.

Noticed a cab, so flagged it, got in the door first, Helen giving her address while I closed my hand over hers. Caught my eyes, the driver's, for one glance in the rear view, Helen's shoulder nudging my arm, the top of her hair working up under my chin.

Closed my eyes for most of the trip, enthusiasm for the whole thing honestly beginning to wane very quickly—figured the money was in the room, Helen only just now knew which hotel, no way anything could've been arranged, money was just there, just sitting in an empty room.

When I stepped out the cab after her, Helen tightened up, stopped. I stood against her back and looking over her shoulder at me she said "That's my roommate's car."

"I don't care," I whispered, one hand in one of her rear pant pockets.

She asked if I was sure and instead of answering I started pushing her—we were into the row house, up the stairs, down a thin corridor and her door was barely closed before I had her shirt off, had her nude before she'd even got her mouth on me again.

Was surprised at the violence of the sex once it started, the intensity redoubled by Helen's odd kittenishness about making too much noise, my postures aggressive, holding her down, covering her face, insisting that she not stop, that she intensify her motions, choke me, claw, anything to prolong the thing.

Spent, we lay on the floor a long while—not a thought in my head, not a consideration even for Helen, her ankle over mine but her head far away, we'd would up on the ground almost foot-to-foot. Crawled over to where she was and she smiled, kissed me on the nose, told me close one eye and kissed me there.

"I'm sorry," I said, didn't feel like it was the words I meant and Helen poked my mouth, told me not to say that again.

"Thank you," I said and she smile, said that was better but also not necessary.

"I think there's a reason we met, Henry."

I nodded, looking at her, but before enough time'd passed it seemed appropriate to add anything, she sat up, told me I shouldn't be away from my wife, all night.

"Don't care about that, not tonight."

"I do."

"You do?"

She stood and dressed in just a t-shirt took up from a pile of clothes in a chair.

"I can stay."

"No. Get dressed."

It was an obvious out for me, but I was hesitant, made a few more protests, even started trying to work her up again which she responded to a bit, but in the end kept up on it about how I should go, went into the bathroom telling me Get dressed. I did, mostly—sat on the bed with my shoes in my hands, socks still on the floor at my feet, waited for her to come out.

"Everything alright?" she asked, giving me a kick then picking up my socks and throwing them at me.

"Starting to think someone ought to be blackmailing you, you're giving me the broom so quick. Got someone else I should take into consideration?"

She made a joke about that, first, then sat next to me.

"I don't know what's gotten into you, but I just maxed

out a credit card so your marriage wouldn't fall apart. No real point throwing fuel on a fire we just put out by having you out all night, right?"

Kissed me instead of letting me answer.

"Okay, security boy?"

"Alright."

"I'm glad we did this, but you're right we can't see each other."

Narrowed my eyes, but it wasn't something I understood why I'd protest.

She didn't walk me even to the front door, just gave a nod.

Was up a few blocks getting my bearings, realized somewhere in it I'd lost my cigarettes. It was tempting to flag down a cab, but managed to resist long enough I was down the metro train, corner seat, window rattling taps against my forehead.

Had a drink out someplace before I retrieved my duffle from the hotel, making apologies for treating them as day storage, the clerk hardly registering me at all except to verify the name on my ID.

Henry Dollar.

Had a few smokes, felt rather broken when I snapped the ID into pieces, littered them between four trash cans, pointless trips up streets and behind buildings between each. I was littering myself, discarding, stepping out of husk and same time felt like one.

***

Rode around the metro until I knew it'd be about to shut down for the night—timed it as much I could to get me out by the Ramada. Both compartments next to me were empty, mine was empty except for three people none of who were following me, just obviously weren't. Then out in the open air, still no one couldn've been keeping an eye—hint of orange to the sky like it'd snow, good mile walk from the hotel, nobody, nothing.

Going through my pockets for my room key, struck me how lucky it was the gun hadn't fallen out my coat at Helen's, shook my face around, rubbed at my eyes a long time, both of them watering, itching.

Got a little bit giddy when I was to the side door the hotel—absolutely not being watched and by this point, even were I, even was someone keeping an eye, they'd not know what floor I went to, room I went to, none of it—and Helen'd have to've had them shadowing me a long while, would've had to suspect this of me and why should she? She was already so finished, whatever her trajectory was veering off to its obscurity and well away, far far away from me.

No one in the corridor and then was inside the room, door closed, latched, everything to place. Strode across in the dark, pulled the blinds closed before ticking on a lamp. Right on the coffee table, just there, was the mailer, just there, like that.

"Hello?" I said, had a poke around.

Dug through my duffle for my flask, shook it a bit disappointed there'd only be maybe two mouthfuls, but drained it, sat in the lounge chair and got a cigarette up just taking my time with unsealing the thing.

Cash money. Counted the bills out. Full five thousand. Fifties. All of them.

Took a look out the corridor, closed myself back in, counted the money one last time but already wasn't so astonished. It was the money, thing'd worked. Didn't even add it into the box with the rest, just bundled it using one of the hotel pillowcases, tucked it away, shook my empty flask and lay across the bed.

Was a little while laying there realized I'd drifted off. Sat up and threw some weak punches around, got standing and drank water while I started the complimentary coffee.

Dialed down the front desk, was asked to hold, said No problem into the click of some recorded music starting. Pretty much right away, same voice was back on.

"Sorry about that, what can I do for you?"

"Just wondering actually—paid out for two days cash, but I'm just gonna need the one—I can get that refund right?"

"That shouldn't be a problem."

"Possible I could pop down there the next little bit, thinking for a train out pretty early."

He let a breath right into the receiver. "Cash I can't do right now, sorry."

"No?"

"Just did the drop safe a bit ago, no cash until the morning."

"Okay."

"I can do a check."

"It's fine. Which time the morning?"

"Eight, little before eight."

Told the guy thanks, I'd just leave a little later, didn't matter.

Microwave clock showed it was past two in the morning—even if I left now, I'd have to get to the train station, bus station, figure out about something and then I'd just be there. This new money didn't exactly boost me, got me ahead a bit, sure, but not much and even that was only if I played things right and playing things right involved not leaving off hundred, hundred-twenty dollars every which place.

Opened drawers until I had a phonebook, got the page out for train stations—felt more like a train than a bus.

Just to keep it from having to be a tremendous pain, booked myself on a train out quarter past one the afternoon, next earliest'd've would be a rush, that even provided my cash was ready prompt at eight.

Didn't feel like adding water my coffee to cool it, so set it the freezer, went around the bathroom to start the shower, undressed, examined my body, surprised at all the fingernail lines. I traced a few, pressed them and pressed some bruises on my side, my shoulder.

"You're quite a little thing, Helen," said to my reflection, pressed the glass where one of my bruises'd be were the glass really me.

Could hardly remember the encounter, already, even when I tried it made me drift, the energy of it'd spent total, nothing even left over for a proper remembrance.

Downed the coffee from the freezer at a go, poured another cup to cool on the counter while I washed, flipped on the television, stood clicking through channels until I was absolutely satisfied there was nothing on'd be enough to distract me.

Vaguely thought I should call Helen, give her a little kick—but why bother? Seemed that'd be mean spirited more than anything else. Thought I should call in to work, maybe, but again just why bother, why bother about anything?

Took out the Daniel Halbst ID, broke it in pieces so I'd not forget to, later—had plenty of other IDs'd to serve in a pinch, beside which I wasn't looking forward to having to make living arrangements, work arrangements, wanted to find someplace on the cheap, even live by burning down a few grand of my savings, someplace I could just hole up a month maybe more, get myself resituated.

My aspirations—life in a hole in the ground.

Shut off the shower, in no mood all of a sudden,

absently drank the coffee even though it was still hot and'd just wind up my bones even more—sleep seemed obscenely out of the question.

Emptied my coat pockets of everything, gun set gingerly on the mattress on the pillow I'd removed the case from, unpacked my duffle and rearranged things, refolded clothes.

Then—it shocked me how quickly it happened—thought I heard something in the corridor, was at the door, eye to peephole, gun gripped too tight, muzzle going tip tap tap just by the doorknob. Couldn't get my eye away, even though there was nothing, not a sound, not a movement.

Stared.

No idea how long.

Turned the coffee pot over my cup, again, downed the stuff, hadn't even let go of the gun.

"Are you going to shoot someone, Trevor?" I said.

Laughed, horribly phony.

It'd been awhile since I'd heard my name, even from myself—it seem artificial and ill belonging.

"Trevor," I said. "Hey, Trevor."

Put the gun down, brewed the packet of decaffeinated coffee just so I'd have something to drink, figured the caffeine from what I'd downed already'd keep me going well enough.

"Henry," I said.

Sounded closer to right.

Back into the bathroom, shower up, stepped in tense against what I was expecting to be too cold, was actually scalding, flapped at the wall, backing out, body stinging like it had been peeled. Shut the water off, used a washcloth at the sink, gave up after getting my face clean, my groin, my forearms.

Eventually, night'd end, knew that—it'd be tomorrow, I'd've picked a name, be someone. Tried to just settle into letting my head spin, to letting myself unspool enough to breathe.

***

It was an ugly morning all morning, filthy and ungodly wet, water spilling from everything and being ground through with tires—moments rain'd stop was louder, worse than the downpour. I was miserable and doubly out of sorts for my fatigue.

New coffee hitting up me by the time I was into the station, Wet Floor signs everywhere and a few custodians pushing mops around endlessly, mats that'd been set out to help with footing already submerged and gritty, mishappen. Hardly any line, at least, to get my ticket from the window—hem-hawed my way through having to show ID with some inane story I only halfway made up, woman working the window didn't seem to care, though did, kind of by rote, point to a placard that said Identification Required with some date this regulation'd gone into effect.

Still had a good while to spend, so ordered vodka one of the three bar areas, started taking it over to a bench, heard the bar tender calling after me—he was exasperated when I turned, obviously I'd not heard him trying to get my attention through a few attempts.

"Can't leave the bar area."

"Just over right there," I said, pointing, guy just tightening his face, giving me a look was I seriously trying to bargain this point.

I nodded, drifted back to where I'd been, sipped a few sips, downed it. Bartender came back over, asked him was there some way to get vodka in a To-go cup, something we could arrange—no laugh, so I asked what about if I went someplace, bought a coffee, could he turn the old blind eye I tipped the vodka in, we'd just agree like it'd be our little secret.

"You can have a vodka, here—you want to trick me, then you trick me, whatever, all your business but I'm not your pal, alright?"

Chuckled. "Yeah, sure."

"Alright?"

"Can I have a vodka?"

He poured one, set it down and turned away, shaking his head. Was thinking to hang around just to spite the guy, that or have a drink, go to the bench, come back have a drink, go the bench, but right away even the thought of such a persecution seemed a chore, what'd there be in it for me?

Opened random paperbacks a shop, then leafed through magazines, feeling the vodka getting a hold, amusing myself with how fascinating it was they sold pornography at train stations, magazines on the top shelf, placeholders high enough that only the titles showed—who'd go that gauntlet for a dirty magazine the trip out to Des Moines or wherever?

Paid for a bottled water and some gummie bears, loitered around by a little area with bushes and two fountains. Had a view of the bar I'd been sitting—saw someone was having a serious chat the bartender, bartender seemed to be pointing where I'd been sitting, telling a story, pointing off some direction.

I couldn't move.

The person who'd been talking to the bartender had a stack of paper with him, and when he stepped out of the bar area was met by another man dressed very like him, ordinary rack suit. Didn't even need the guns, the cuffs their belt loops to know they were detectives, but both those things were there—glimpse of this, glimpse of that they put hands to hips, pointed there, pointed there.

First instinct was move to the toilets, but straight off that was wrong—it was cinematically wrong, could almost literally see just what it'd be like, two men coming up on me while I was drying my face some cheap brown paper towels—second was to assure myself it couldn't've been anything to do with me.

Saw one uniformed officer showing a paper around, saw a member of station security talking to another, everyone pointing around at things—entrances, exits.

Could not have anything to do with me.

Pressed on further into the station, down a level, first side exit door I saw I took, was out in back, a parking area, loading area, rain an overturned pail all over everything and going all directions at once like dogs were shaking themselves dry of it, thousands, hundreds of thousands of animals with wet flung off them—couldn't even think straight.

Jogged all the way across to a sidewalk, headed down it, jogged a little bit faster and caught a cab.

"Sorry," I said, meaning about how wet I was, but driver just asked me where I was going, took a few drags from his cigarette and leisurely called in to his dispatcher before we took off.

Immediately I felt better, two traffic lights down I was even thinking to tell him turn around—no way at all it could have a thing to do with me, no way at all.

Few blocks further on, just wanted out the car, couldn't stand the touch of my wet clothing on me, wanted to feel my body moving, the motion of the cab just too sedentary, like it was a toy in the grooves of a track, chugging a few meters, chugging a few meters, resetting.

"Just here's fine."

"The corner?"

"That's fine."

"Or where? You tell me."

"Yeah, just up the next corner."

"Alright."

I paid, said sorry again about the wet, but he shrugged, pulled off and I walked up the block.

Could try at a bus station or just cab out to another city—waste of time, of course, but I could do it. Cab was the safest idea—bus station'd be trouble were the police looking for me.

Looking for me for what?

Annoying thought, as pretty much everything I'd done the last year was patently criminal, but at the same time none of it could connect to me here, just didn't see how.

Leaned to a payphone, started trying to get coins out of my pocket, already had the dial tone in my ear.

Was I going to call Helen?

I'd need to, get some sort of pulse off of her. Had something spooked her? Maybe, but just didn't see what could've was something it'd get the police after me.

Shook my face—dialed information for the number the train station, added coins to be connected.

"Hi, sorry don't know exactly who I should talk to about this, security I think."

"Security?"

Started to explain, but there was dialing in my ear, someone picked up.

"Security."

"Yeah, I was just leaving there about twenty minutes ago, was handed a flyer."

"Yes?"

"Didn't even really look at it until now—I know this person."

"Let me transfer you, please hold the line."

This time it was hold music and already my gut was tight and broken. So, it had been a picture of someone on that flyer, so great.

How long since I'd seen Helen last? Twelve hours? Fifteen?

"You said you know the man in the picture?"

"I think so, yeah, his name's Henry Dollar."

"Henry Dollar, that's right. Where do you know him from?"

"From work. He's security in the building where I work."

"The Croix building?"

I folded myself over the phone, rocked where I stood.

"Yes, that's right."

"When did you see him last?"

Couldn't think of anything else, just rocked.

"Hello?"

"Yeah, sorry. No, not for awhile, just he works there, just I know who he is."

Hung up. Let go the receiver, just tilted toe to heel, toe to heel.

Started walking, huddled down around myself, hoping I seemed faceless in the slop, faceless in the weighed down umbrellas and din and restaurant odors thinned with wet. Raised my hand for a taxi, seemed like on purpose none of them'd stop, like they were just making me stand there, hand up, illuminated.

***

Driver stopped at a convenience store, he'd asked me could he after giving dispatch a call, said it was for a cup of coffee and something. Seemed reasonable enough considering I was asking him to drive more than an hour out, city called Alster—only other city I knew was a good way off, only thing'd popped to mind when I'd asked You do long distance drives? Told him I'd direct him to an address once we were in town off the main highway exit.

Hadn't liked how he'd held my eyes in the rearview through our conversation, like he was looking at me, looking looking, not just some usual glance some guy sits in your cab—his coded talk to dispatch could've been anything. He was just in the store though, saw him pour coffee, select some sort of snack, didn't seem it was he had a mind about getting up to something against me. Not that it mattered—I needed to go, staying around just brought things up around me tighter and tighter.

Lit a cigarette the guy was still inside, rolled down my window the crank.

Could even be the police didn't have anything to do with Helen—likely they did, just I couldn't figure out what, so maybe not.

Say even she'd told them the whole, long, sad little story how I'd tricked her, I'd this and that, I'd taken some money's all it amounted to, didn't seem that was the sort of thing they'd be showing fliers at train stations and all of it.

Had they done a sketch? Did Helen have a photo of me?

Driver told me Thanks he got back the cab, asked me again Where to? but nodded even before I started answering. He asked did I mind the radio, watched me in the mirror I shook my head.

The name Henry Dollar, the Croix building on Delmore, all of that, while about Helen, could've also been just one piece in a puzzle—after all, I'd offered that up to the officer on the phone and all he'd asked was when I'd seen Henry last.

"It's alright I smoke, yeah?" I asked, having just dropped my stub out the window, getting another form my pack.

"That's fine, don't care."

He looked at me, watched me light up, so I kept my gaze out the window, not wanting little awkward clicks of him noticing me noticing him looking.

There was nothing, nothing I could think of'd add up to a net of police out trying to nab me up—and it couldn't've just been the one train station, why on earth would it've been?

What brings out a hunt like that? Catching a blackmailer? Catching an alleged blackmailer on the word of some woman?

No. Even if they knew about the stolen name, just didn't reason right.

Mind didn't want to play out alternative after alternative and soon enough didn't seem it'd matter.

"You sure the music's alright?"

I turned—driver was looking at me, floating eyes there the mirror and some of his mouth, nose in a slip of dark from a light passing over the car.

"I don't care. Music's alright, fine."

"Let me know, alight, it gets to be bad."

"I like it fine, don't worry."

He nodded, looked away and I looked away but got such a feeling of hands on me I had to slip a look to the mirror—he was looking right back.

But the highway was stumbling out behind us, each bit of it being left behind, car-less road, almost.

Whatever the thing was about the police, I got to realizing, if I was caught I'd be done for everything—not just everything lately, everything I'd ever done. I didn't have the resolve to stand up to anything like interrogation, keeping lines of deception going, stonewalling—and how long could it take until someone got my real name, traced me back, how long before Wynol and Klia and Herman.

And Norman.

Did that make sense? Could it be traced back to that?

They knew I wasn't Henry, so not like I could tell them forever and ever I was some make believe name, after awhile that wouldn't fly—and suppose they already knew I was Trevor, just the slightest hint in some detective's eyes about that and I'd blurt it out.

If I was caught, I was caught for everything. Maybe that's even why I was being looked for—for everything. That *Don't Call* sign Helen's office—say she had called, say first it lead to nothing but then all at once, just all at once somehow the P.I. comes up with something and just like that a bag of bricks's brought across me, just like that and now here I was.

Why would they be spreading cops out with pictures of me, though?

And I just couldn't get shut of wondering Which picture?

"Which exit you want for Alster?"

I blinked, took a pause to light a new cigarette, hoping he'd give me some prompt, but he didn't say anything, just looked at me.

"Main exit, just main exit."

"Fifty-four?"

"Yeah."

I nodded, reflection of his eyes seemed like he knew I wasn't sure, so I made it a point when I saw the sign for Fifty-four coming up to emphatically nod that Yeah, yeah, it's fifty-four.

Directed him down a few streets, then pointed to an apartment building, said to let me off.

There was mist in the air made it horrendous to stand around, but I chain smoked two cigarettes like I was in no hurry or anything, cab just idling there. Couldn't see in the window, just heard odd throbs of music and the engine chug, heavy scent of exhaust shivering in with the cold breaths up my nose.

Cab finally drove off. Waited until it was out of sight to start walking. Was at least an hour before I found a hotel.

Clerk was some kid seemed high or half asleep—combination of both—hardly even seemed he was putting me in the system right let alone concerning himself whether or not I looked close to the picture on the ID I gave—Theodore Brennon.

As soon as my room door closed behind me, started undressing, found the heater, toyed with the knobs, started a hot sower going.

Didn't matter why the police were after me—now I was gone, somebody else in some hotel someplace and by morning I'd figure out about transportation even further away. Didn't matter who was looking for me or for what because I had enough money on me I could hole up wherever for a year, I felt like it, see about what was what, take my time, relax through it.

Body sore from the shower water, I brewed coffee, turned on the television, started a cigarette, rocked on the hip of the king bed. It felt like sleeping would wake me up someplace else, past all this, and the pull toward the mattress was hard, terrible—let myself lay back, but right away groaned myself back up, made sure the door was locked.

It got where I couldn't really bear to think but just kept doing it, idiot impulses to call Helen, see if I could get it out of her had she'd anything to do with it. One reason not to make such a call, simplest one, was say it was to do with her, she recorded the number'd called—got area code, exact address—making the call'd mean I'd have to run and I just couldn't. Other reason—probably even simpler, uglier definitely—was that making a call meant admitting to myself thing wasn't over, something was still to come just out sniffing around to find the way to me.

Thing was, of course I knew something was coming, bearing down, but knowing it and making myself admit it were two different animals. I needed to be able to pretend, otherwise everything I did was rough draft for confession, everything something else could get me found out.

***

Not in the bed, but a chair by the window, towel draped over my chest, realized I was passing out between mouths of coffee, drags off cigarettes I no longer really registered. Got so I wasn't fighting it, deep dreams lasting something two minutes each, I'd dodder my chin to chest, wake up, shift around, lean my head way back, wake again to a stiff neck.

Room phone rang, jarred me, first ring getting me awake, tinny grumble in my head, second ring my eyes stung open and felt my breathing going hard, disoriented.

I'd been asleep full on, looked to the bed clock showed past three in the morning.

By the third ring, stomach upset panic got on me, started fumbling around for my clothes, head plump and groggy, footing and balance completely all wrong.

Not half minute after the ringing'd stopped I was dressed, duffle over my shoulder at the door, touching myself all over had I forgot something, was there anything even I'd forgot it'd matter?

Out the door, hurried down to the opposite end the corridor, hesitated going down the stairs just long enough to make a gesture like listening for something but my head wasn't awake enough anything'd've registered. Felt the shudder of my heels battering down the steps, falling more than walking, got out the side entrance, tense with the cold and the thought there might've been a camera over the door, not turning to look.

Was down two blocks I needed to catch my breath, pain too much, cold into my thick, dry mouth breaking me down, wheezing. Ducked into the space between two buildings—seemed like shops, maybe apartments above them but if so windows dark and curtainless—where if I peeked out could still see the hotel parking lot, area in front of the lobby entrance.

No reason for a call the middle of the night, knew just exactly what it was and no amount of trying to convince myself otherwise'd take the teeth out of the bite—clerk checking to see was I in, would I answer, police on the way.

Had to be.

Canvas'd led to looking into cabs, come up with some odd long distance fare, driver shown a picture or else was given little description of me and whap—couldn't't've taken some halfway clever policeman more'n two minutes to do the math I'd told the driver let me out just some random street, then few calls around to hotels, ask Anyone check in between X time and Y time? and even the sleepy little clerk'd hardly looked at me could answer that, didn't matter could he remember enough to describe me.

They were really looking for me and knew there were only so many places I could go, they weren't just going to stop because I wasn't sitting some coffee shop around the corner. What I'd done, come here this little town was paint a tighter corner than before—now they knew I was here, there was no space to turn around let alone hide and nevermind about get away.

Shivered, figured it was best to run, but same time what good could that do? If they were coming, they'd go knock on the door and when I didn't answer they'd open the door—worst case scenario—best case'd be they wait until checkout. Even if I ran the meantime, if they found me this quick here how much longer until I was done?

Cigarette couldn't hurt, but wanted a slap of vodka more, settled on neither.

Kept peeking around, looks to the lot. Soon enough, coming right up the street, passing right in front of me, police car—not in a hurry, but still a police car. Watched it slip lazy into the lot, lull at the door, uniformed officer got out, went in, other officer stayed put.

Looked over my shoulder and though nothing was there felt my chest well up, doubled over, sobbing, felt I needed to vomit but didn't, just spit a long string stuck to the pavement, maybe froze there a spot, a dribble that stayed attached to my lip even I shook my face around, screwing my fists into my eyes, shaking.

The fit passed, but I felt like a cloth sack weighed down with rotten oranges after, just couldn't make myself focus or think.

Looked back to the hotel lot and for some reason now the patrol car had it's lights going round at a clack, pelting the cold with purposeless colours, colours like they were looking for me to point at or else were pointing at me already waiting for someone to notice they were.

Went to the other side of the alley, across the street, through another alley, walked down a few blocks, turned, turned, another alley, finally tugged the door to an apartment building and when it opened I could feel myself about to start crying again just from the sudden change in temperature. I must've looked abominable—if anyone saw me, anyone, even forgetting with the police asking about me or showing a photo or a sketch, I'd be reported as some suspicious lurker. Up the stairwell, all the way up, pathetically up, hobbled by the time I'd taken the last stair and then just sat, useless as what spilled from a broken bottle.

They'd know I wasn't in the room, then'd do whatever they did about seeing if any cabs'd taken a fare and once they knew that hadn't happened—or even while they were figuring it out it hadn't—they'd start looking, patrol up and down the streets. By the time the sun was up, these apartments would empty, people would step out to be greeted with fliers my face on them.

Just sat there whispering to myself "Jesus Jesus Jesus Jesus Jesus," said it while my teeth chattered then until they stopped.

All manner of nothing went through my head—try doorknobs, see if they opened, wait until someone left, offer them money to let me in, anything, nonsense.

Then it struck me try for a basement room, storage room, swallowed and got stable best I could for the descent. Typical storage room down flight and a half of stairs from the lobby—not the same but no different than any I'd known before in my life, this one had big units and small units all behind wire caged wood framed doors, rooms full of nothing, gym equipment, boxes, fake Christmas trees, trashbags full of old clothes.

Made a circuit trying any locks with combinations, see if they were closed without being spun, then tried ones with key locks, too, tugs, jiggles.

No way in to any.

Little chance police'd search every apartment basement,

but also every chance they would—if they'd done this much already then why not—wouldn't even take long, could just call and ask the superintendent to do it for them, anything suspicious give them a ring about it.

Laughed, no idea was it real or not—laughed at how I'd buried myself down in a hole, now, laughed at that's just what I'd done, panicked and just started piling dirt on myself, figuring last place they'd look for me was down under my own grave.

Could break a lock—could dash to a shop, buy another lock, dash back, break a lock, get in a room, replace the lock with mine.

This was the best I could come up with—flawless in that it was imbecile drivel.

Nothing.

Little whistle of my breathing down my nose, five minutes.

In a bolt, unzipped my duffle and took out the suit, the tie, the nicer shoes. Stripped in stages, redressing to fit—coat off, shirt off, shirt, tie, suit coat on, shoes off, pants off, pants on, shoes on.

Took two packets of money out of the duffle, as much as would gently fit in the suit coat pockets, wrapped the rest in a few different shirts, chose the unit looked least likely to be visited, stuffed the bundles under the door. The gun I dropped down in the suit coat pocket, the duffle I squeezed under another unit door, the remaining everything spread between a few others.

***

It was thin sunny I walked out the building door with three other people, first few steps like my feet were tin cans, but up the block, once I saw an ordinary convenience store and the automatic door swung for me my gait became slow, hint of swagger I was going for taking hold.

Certainly not wanting to seem rushed, still went right for what I was after—shaving gel, pack of razors, container of pomade, cheap rectangular sunglasses, grabbed aftershave my way back down the aisle. Picked up two boxes of hard pretzels, large size gift-bag, roll of invisible tape, tube of birthday paper, three packets of decorative tissue. Didn't register what it cost, irrelevant, made chat with the woman ringing me, pleasant empty responses to the little questions she cooed at me about the gift material.

Out the door, biting the inside of mouth instead of taking even half minute to stop, start a cigarette up, immediately got back to the storage area. Opened the pretzel boxes, removed the plastic bag of the foodstuff, fished the wrapped packets of money out from under the door of the unit I'd stuck them, crammed the money still wrapped all in between the two boxes—crammed the gun on top one bunch of money—shakily wrapped the boxes shut, put both into the gift-bag and ruffled the decorative tissue as nice as I could around them.

Thought'd been I'd find a toilet some sandwich shop to do my grooming, but I felt safe where I was so applied the shaving foam and did the best I could mirrorless—could always touch up later—splashed on the aftershave, used two handfuls of pomade to slick my hair back and back and back, wiping the excess on the back of my shirt under the suit coat.

Sunglasses on, I shoved the accumulated trash under yet another storage unit's door, except the two plastic bags of pretzels which I just punted one into one wall, the other another, and my old shoes I just set neatly in a corner.

After not even ten minutes walking down the streets, no

particular direction, the distance this little diversion'd kept me from my situation started to lessen, head got soggy and jumbled with anxiety. Stopped into a coffee shop, directly to the toilet to recheck my shaving job, even though I already had done in five shop windows—touched at my hair, water to my face, brushed my shoulders, put my sunglasses on, took them off, put them on.

I certainly was a far cry from who I'd been scurrying around like a sick rodent, half hour back, felt I could walk around without concern, the disguise becoming my natural skin, the clothes my demeanor. I'd find a salon, get a dye job, some posh place wouldn't think twice about a well-dressed man dropping in mid-morning for such a thing.

A decently dressed man, anyway—but I'd nab an actual suit when I stopped for the brief case or nicer leather luggage to replace the gift bag, the weight of which reminded me I had money and considering the circumstances should consider it spent as much as it needed to be.

Circumstances—needed to decipher what those were exactly, still. Much as I felt I'd slipped free from them, it was just clumsy not to know.

There was a two level shopping plaza with a menswear shop—lazy three quarters of an hour spent getting sized and trying this and that got me back in my bubble, lost in the make believe of normal, left feeling crisp, new, invisible. Same plaza bought a nice leather bag—general travel bag, tight and sleek, nothing like the old bulk of my discarded duffle. In another bathroom, I unwrapped the boxes in the gift-bag, transferred the contents to the travel bag, took a moment to test would the gun fit in any of the pockets my new suit, chuckled at myself I hadn't bought a coat.

No coat, but maybe it was a good idea not to have one,

something powerful in the sight of the full suit, something so impossible to see as anything but what it projected, a coat'd have an element of hiding to it, waste the appearance I'd given myself.

No coat.

In the mirror, I wasn't anyone, now, not me, certainly.

At the plaza information kiosk, I was given a pamphlet of local businesses, woman telling me her preference in salons, mentioned one was a bit pricey, she'd never used it but her friends gushed about it nonstop.

"They take men, though?"

She laughed, touched my arm.

"I'm sure they do. They probably adore it when men come in, sign of good breeding."

Gave her a smile, said she'd sold me and hoped she was on commission.

Made an appointment the salon for early evening from a pay telephone, lit a cigarette which turned out to be my last, crumpled the packet, left it on the telephone top, thought better of this—stupid thing to be called out over—walked it to a trash bin.

Like a film—so much so it made me light headed—saw there was a flyer my face on it, unrumpled, just there in the trash, underneath some cardboard drink cup still somewhat full and this or that wrapper.

Took it out quickly, folded it and walked for a few blocks, temples throbbing, bottom of my throat tight and warmer with every step. City bus came along, waited in line to get on, lucked into a seat the far back, took up a newspaper someone'd left, wriggled the flyer from my pocket and unfolded it behind the spread pages.

Took me a moment to figure where'd the photo come from—it was the one'd been on my security badge, grainy from being blown up, printed out on cheap paper. Upset me that I didn't have a beard in the photo, but too late to do anything about it.

Have you seen this man?

Bus took an odd jolt, didn't move for more than a minute, but none of the other riders seemed to even register this so I slowly lowered my eyes back to the page.

"Henry Dollar" (may use other aliases)

There was a phone number to call *If sighted.*

Reward for information leading to the capture.

Seemed quite extreme, quite vague at the same time.

Considered dangerous, do not attempt to detain.

"Jesus Christ," whispered, chewing on the side of my lower lip.

Folded the thing back up, put it to my inside coat pocket, pulled the cord and got off the next stop—bus'd only gone a straight line so I just strolled back the way I'd come, discarded the flyer in another trash bin.

Odd I'd not seen a single policeman, now I started to peer around, very fact they seemed so absent off-putting. They either thought I was gone or else knew that I wasn't but that I'd have to try to get gone and there were only so many ways out.

It wasn't just blackmail, it wasn't even I'd stolen the IDs and been living fraudulently they were after me over.

Considered Dangerous.

Figured there'd be something in the newspaper about it, but didn't want to look, felt too morbid a thing to do and an odd tweak of cowardice made me tense my jaw. I'd already had to sniff around in rubbish to find out about myself, not gonna go put down a quarter to read about me on top, whole idea made me sting.

***

Held each drag the smoke in long, until it hurt and my breath out was colourless. Couldn't walk anymore, had come to rest at a row of payphones outside a gas station, cup of cheap coffee almost empty and sitting like a coil of worms in my gut.

Took up the phone—it just didn't matter—dialed Helen at home. Considering the time of day, was a bit surprised she picked up, a weak Hello, kind of froggy like a little kid playing hooky.

"What'd you do, Helen? Seems you got the bees awful buzzing over something."

Silence, a few breaths from her.

"I know who you are," she said.

It made me smile, hard, face disjointed and I leaned toward the wall around the side of the phone stand.

"Gave old Mister Beaker et al. a call, did we? Helen, Helen, why'd you want to do that?"

And even while the line hung silent it started crawling in my head just why—knew exactly the thing, what she'd done, it was like two hands'd took my face and made me look. Smile kept screwing itself, corkscrewing itself tighter, tighter, eyes squinting shut from it, my teeth like they were bared.

"Why'd you want to do that, Helen? Wanted to squeeze out the competition, get me all to yourself?"

"You're disgusting."

"Romp with the married fellow, wreck his hearth and home all up."

"You're disgusting."

"Right right—well, let's take that as read and get to a few other things, while I have you. Must've been a shock, right, you give up my old address, your P.I. turns out it's actually current."

"They're going to catch you, Henry. Or whoever you are."

"Thought you knew who I was."

"I know what you are."

"Think you forget, honey pot, I know who you are too, know what you are the same. Blackmailer called you, did he? Seems to me I had a wife, actually, that'd be interesting, right? Seems if there was a blackmailer to begin with, yeah? You've got your own little scheming to be disgusted about, way I see it. What'd you figure, tell me blackmailer's still out there then you drop the dime on me to my wife yourself, I'll think it was him, come blubbering to you all my woes and realize we're soul mates?"

"They're going to catch you."

"No, no and I think you know right well they just aren't, Helen, I think you know that same as me."

"They're not going to stop looking for you."

"I'll grant it does seem you've got folks all a big tizzy, seems a bit much over five grand—why don't you just let me in on the secret got's everyone working extra hours."

She laughed, pretended to, or just wanted to make a scoffing sound.

"You'll find that out when they catch you, won't you? And I'm glad I'll get to see your face."

"Ominous, ominous. Don't toy with me, now—not enough time you could've dug up something vintage, so I'm gonna ask you one more time what you laid out on me."

"I just told them what you did to me, Henry."

Cigarette was down to the filter, gave it a suck, dropped it and leaned all my weight down on my toe on it.

"Did I do something to you?"

Now she did laugh, like something had just popped in her, it was such angry giddiness it made me take a glance be sure there wasn't someone walking up on me while she just laughed what seemed way too long. Was just getting ready to try for another word in when she stopped, sharp breath in, little sound she was drawing in some spittle the laughing'd got on her lip.

"What did you do to me? Don't you remember?"

She took a pause, maybe really wanted me to say something, give her a stage prompt—my eyes blurred from being held open.

"Well, Henry, you raped me."

I swallowed, blinked once, then a few times, a flutter form the sting.

"Of course you're free to tell them otherwise when they catch you, but that might mean you'll have to answer quite a few other questions, right? I do make a very convincing little victim, all bumps and bruises and tearing."

"Are you joking?"

Was surprised at my tone, the seething of it, how elsewhere it sounded, more like a gurgle, sound of a cramp shifting.

"You can't do what you do, Henry, you just can't do that to people."

"Raped you?"

She didn't say anything.

Didn't say anything.

Got so I realized it was my breathing I heard coming through the speaker at my ear.

"They're going to catch you, Henry, and I think you know that."

"Helen."

"I know that, because I can't imagine you have anywhere to go."

"Jesus Christ, what do you want?"

"Well Henry—what's your name, really?"

The sentence didn't register right, it was too peculiar a combination of words, earnestly asked her "What?"

"I want to know your name."

Wet my lips, or tried to, tongue dry, felt almost like it'd split.

"It's Norman."

No idea why that name, every idea why.

"Well Norman, what I want is for you to find a lonely corner in hell and rot there."

Chuckled I went to talk, something, some sound that made me cough, brought my elbow around my mouth, wiped my eyes with my forearm.

"What do you want, Helen? I get it, right, I get you're not in the best of spirits but I never did anything about raping you."

"Turn yourself in, I'll tell them I made it up."

"You want your money back? Christ Helen, I gave you your money back then you called me, you started this so don't think it's in your court to get cute and holy."

"Bring me my money back, then."

Turned to look out at the street, clipped the phone to my shoulder with tilted head, got out a cigarette, couldn't get a match to strike long enough get it lit, flicked the thing toward the curb.

"I'll get it to you."

"Bring it to me."

"I'll leave it for you, hotel desk, leave you a message about which one."

"Do you think I'm bargaining about this?"

Again silence, the curlicue of my breathing in pops at my ear. I rubbed at my thigh, compulsive, pushing hard enough it felt like a bruise.

"Helen, I'm sorry. I am sorry for what I did. Please know that I'm sorry."

She hung up.

Got my travel bag strap over my shoulder, tried to walk but then just couldn't, actually stumbled back, knees bent and one shoulder to the wall. Three hard breaths, got myself together—exactly the thing I didn't need to be doing, nervous breakdown a gas station telephone, but true as that was just I couldn't walk, think, even feel my thoughts.

Sat. Closed my eyes. Counted thirty with them closed. Thirty again. Thirty again. Opened them and then closed them again counted thirty—don't know was I waiting for something to be different, look different I opened them, something even as simple as another car to pull in, someone to be walking on the opposite side of the road. Something, waited for something.

Got myself standing and called Helen back, let it ring and ring, ring and ring, her machine picked up and I told it "Please, I'm sorry" and then broke, slammed the receiver, punched myself in the leg enough my eyes watered, absolutely didn't care about a thing. But then, breath like hand to my throat, hit me Helen couldn've given the police the number I'd called from, right now they could know I was still in this city, at this gas station—I looked around for parking lot cameras, then knew that didn't matter because there was one inside where I'd got coffee.

Police'd show up, ask around, clerk'd've seen me out here, describe me, give them the tape, new picture blown up fuzzy to be passed around, printed in the paper, new paper of me dressed up polished.

Felt vulgar, a cartoon—felt I still looked like myself despite everything and always that's just how I'd look.

***

Apologized to the girl the salon about the amount of product in my hair, but she laughed, said it was fine, the shampoo'd cut through it.

"And you want a cut and a colour, just the colour?"

"Cut and colour. Blonde."

She said that was her natural and I complimented that the auburn she had looked flawless.

Asked if I could have my bag held behind the counter, she placed it in a drawer of her station, kind of winked, nodded at me follow her. The hair wash was relaxing, the roughing my head almost drifting me to sleep. Small talked through the trim, then was left with a magazine for the colour to set.

Leaving a tip, started getting curious as to how much money I'd been spending—was this all reckless, unspooling, tossing things overboard to numb myself of the inevitable hand coming down on me?

No. Way I looked it was impossible to think I'd be stopped, recognized, felt I could go up to Helen and start a new flirtation, even, I wanted.

Bought cheap cigarettes and a new flask, vodka to fill it, took a few mouthfuls but just those few, careful to prove to myself how I could control the intake.

Despite what Helen'd said, even if they were treating Henry Dollar as a rapist, even if they were scrounging around for every scrap of him they could find, even if they were amassing a file—my fingerprints, DNA—it didn't matter, they wouldn't find me and they would stop looking. Eventually, they'd stop looking. I'd be gone, they'd look a little bit more, but I'd be gone and they'd no choice but to stop.

But what'd it mean, they stopped?

Say I'm caught even something minor but enough to get

my prints took, this thing'd be waiting for me, big open mouth just waiting its chance to bite.

If I was ever caught, if this was ever put into my face as I'd raped Helen I might as well've done—denying it would lead to more, to everything I'd ever done and now that I was running, now that they knew the things they definitely knew I'd not have a leg to stand on to deny the accusation. Christ, even relating the facts, the real facts'd sound perversely imaginary—it'd sound like I was deranged, what I'd done sounded deranged as a defense to rape. There was no escaping this'd become a part of me now, this lie, this lunatic revenge was something tangible and breathing.

I ordered myself lunch at a crowded café, making up my mind it was time to tackle the problem of getting out of the area, straight on, this disguising was fine, but it'd get to the point it was just an extension of hiding in that apartment basement, just another layer of dirt I'd piled on—out in broad daylight I was nobody anybody'd think twice over, but some policeman saw me loitering around all hours, maybe saw me more than one place, maybe saw me at night then again the next day just doing nothing they might get thinking, concoct some reason to ask me this or that. It was something I just couldn't afford. Same time, I was too leery about trying for a hotel with no ID, wasn't ready to try long distance transportation, either.

I was hopeless, didn't know the town, had no reason for myself being anywhere, even if there was no reason I'd need to tell a policeman something they asked, if I didn't it'd look odd, they'd mark me and again, how would I explain I was just no place, all dressed up and no place?

No idea by the time I'd eaten, sat with a coffee—refill, refill.

They'd be paying attention the buses, the trains, all of that—obviously there was some bulletin out now with taxis, had to reason that any sort of hired transportation was being monitored.

Most that was, though, was my picture passed around, maybe a beat cop or two, security officer being a bit more vigilant than usual, could be I just walk on up to a ticket counter, flirt my way around I'd forgot my ID if it came up.

No.

Paid my bill, went to the toilet.

No. To try something like that and get caught, it was just too much. I just felt crippled and tired—that was the thing was I wasn't thinking proper, wasn't up for it. All of this doubt was ridiculous—they'd think I was gone, these circles I was making, this charade of dress-up and hair-cuts, was just my fatigue, mind churning on nothing, grinding in the dark.

Found my way to the station for the commuter train, consulted the maps, found it went out a long way, touched off the miles, absently, forefinger and thumb first to the scale measure then tap tap tap along the red line of the route. Next train out wasn't until early next morning, just a matter of keeping myself busy, overlooked the night then I'd mash myself in with everyone else. Gone.

Found there were automated kiosks set along the station, simple as feeding in money I had a pass. I'd just show up, hop on, ride out, seemed long enough a ride I could even get some sleep.

Started seeping in toward night, sharp to the air worse with every step, the reality of just how beat I was becoming more of an issue. Eyed side streets and parking lot areas—had to be someplace it was reasonable to assume no one'd poke around in until morning, some crevice I could wriggle in, insect myself away for awhile.

Knew these risks were imaginary, this idea that if I was

so much as noted, well dressed and tucked away, I'd be shackled, done in, but at the same time I couldn't stomach anything else, not one more risk, not one more risk with the weight of everything in my life tied to it, my whole self at stake.

An apartment building side door opened and I slipped in, nodding to the man exiting, dressed for a job, muffled sound from his earphones, the corridor no warmer than outside.

Middle of the night.

Middle of the night, I could wait it out in the laundry room or even stroll the corridors, up and down the stairwell, lean out the door for a smoke, time to time.

Nodded, nodded.

Go get myself a meal one of those all night cafes, a paperback novel, bear that as much as I could, reasonable length of time, then wander back over this stairwell, these corridors, just wait. It'd just be a few more hours, the building all sound asleep, just a jittering few more hours until I could take a seat on the train, pass out, not even stir until I was jostled by someone the final stop.

Nodded, nodded, felt around for a smoke, right then, nodding, nodding.

This all'd become a nightmare, the world turned broken and sagging down on me, but it'd be over, I'd be safe— few more hours, just same as every other hour I'd ever spent my life except I'd feel every second of it, every tick, feel the nothing of it all, horrendous but no more or less than any other time.

Cigarette went by, already, smiled at that, got another one up.

Nobody watching me, looking, counting how many times I paced, how many smokes I lit, stairs I walked, times I rubbed my eyes or shivered.

Cigarette went by, flicked it out the door.

"One more," mumbled to myself, "one more."

One more, then a walk down some restaurant, walk back.

Just the time it took to smoke half pack of cigarettes, have a meal, smoke the other half pack and I'd be free, not forgot but past that'd matter.

The Akerman Motel/Apartments
per week

I paid one thousand two hundred twenty-seven dollars and fifty-five cents. See my bulldog bite a rabbit and my hound dog's sittin' on a barbed-wire fence

BOB DYLAN, *Sitting on a Barbed Wire Fence*

Hundredth day, hundred-and-somethingth day in the apartment building of the Akerman Motel/Apartments still couldn't get over it must be a joke, if what I had was an apartment then couldn't imagine what'd it be like down in the motel area.

Closed the storage locker I kept out of town, thing ran me as much a month as the apartment, though I'd paid it all out in advance for six months first day I'd moved in. Skimmed the forty dollars pocket money off from the hundred forty I'd taken, rent due the morning and I liked to pay out for two weeks, made me feel less antsy—should really've just paid out on the room all in advance same as the storage, but there was no discount for doing that and had a feeling it'd be trouble wrangling out a refund things went I had to leave, some reason, all of a sudden. Had to or wanted to.

Hundred days was fourteen times this'd be I'd put in rent, or anyway seven times but I put in for two weeks each time, but this must've been the fifteenth time, fifty dollars a week fifteenth time, meant it was hundred and fifth say, hundred-and-somethingth day. Anyway, seven hundred fifty for the apartment so far, twelve hundred for the storage, I'd always dip in for at least another forty bucks each week on top of the forty I designated for walking around, so that was another twelve hundred.

Rubbed my face with the wrist of the hand holding my cigarette. Always did this same count every week because I refused to actually verify how much I'd spent, how much I had left, like keeping notes all in my head'd change anything—got excited times I'd mess up the count, think I hadn't spent as much as I'd thought, always come down from that hard even though all the while I knew how underneath I was.

Spent the rest of the day sipping from my flask, wandering the aisles of shops not feeling like swiping anything, just looking, looking. Looking.

I'd overheard someone say that none of the pawnshops around'd take anything from the local merchants, wouldn't take anything they knew was kept in stock around. Never yet got up the nerve about verifying and anyway even in the worst case scenario my reserve could last me another several months, no need to worry about getting drawn and quartered over six bucks for a mini-television or anything.

Office of the Akerman was its own little building really looked like a miniature house, someone there all hours but'd only come to the window if you said something they thought worthwhile into the intercom. 'Rent,' usually worked, said it with a sigh and rubbing my lower back and having a look around. There always seemed to be somebody else at the window, strangest thing in the three months I'd been there, no chance at a rapport or anything and here it was again I was explaining all to someone new I was paying for the two weeks, because if I didn't say it, didn't insist on it, I knew they'd take the hundred, mark down I'd paid the one week only and what kind of a position was I in to argue that with them?

There was a cigarette machine at the base of the side

entrance stairwell, something I always gave a kick vaguely hoping a pack'd fall into the collection drawer, never did. Started my ascent leisurely and at the landing to the third floor stopped, leaned to the wall, took a particularly deep drag. Caught out the corner of my eye a woman I knew lived down in the motel—knew her name was Kathryn, I thought—peek her face to the widow panel the door, move away, second later door opened.

She caught her breath noticing me, laughed when I said "Hello, sorry."

"It's fine, no, I'm sorry."

I nodded as well, looked like she was going to maybe stand there long enough some small talk, but then she didn't, just ducked her head and down the stairs.

Finished my cigarette, started another before I went the next four landings up, stubbed it on the wall by my door I went in. Poured a tall glass of vodka, dumped what was left of a fruit juice bottle in on top of it, just a mouthful, turned on the television, giving it a nod as I always did as though to remind myself it was worth the extra five dollars rent per week to have the thing. Sat, looking at the screen with the volume muted.

Stood long enough to refill my glass after downing the first faster than was necessary, back to my chair. Thoughts drifted maybe I could try for some work, get something going—nothing official, certainly I couldn't chance that— maybe see if some of the other residents worked odd jobs on the cheap, or maybe just place an advertisement I'd be up for anything, moving boxes, cleaning, see if the ad ran a week and I got some response.

Didn't remember turning off the television, but when I drifted awake, still in the chair, the room was dark enough I noted licks of colour in slaps to the outside of my drawn curtain. Used the toilet before taking a look out, two police cars parked in front, little mash of people around talking. As an ambulance was pulling in to the lot I lost interest, padded around in the dark for my cigarettes.

If I weren't so inebriated, so beat on top, the police presence'd have me more on edge—but I was still pretty drunk and'd gotten used to the fact police'd come around for this and that, they didn't seem to bother with anyone in the Akerman except just whoever might be involved in whatever specifically brought them out, usually domestic quarrels, drug busts.

Chuckled, drinking water from the tap, it'd probably be more trouble than it as worth for police to talk to residents, must be an alarmingly high felon rate the Akerman and pretty obvious anyone wasn't a felon yet just hadn't been nabbed up, would get the distinction soon enough.

Took a last mouth of water, swished it, spit it, went back to my chair.

Came awake again to the heat of the day in through the blinds, scent of cooking dust and whatever food was maggoting its way through the walls. Had a quick shower, put the same clothes as the previous day back on, made sure I had my forty dollars, put twenty in the kitchen drawer, hesitated, took it out and left, locking up, scoffing as I always did the flimsiness of the door, that if I leaned on it too long lock'd probably pop free.

Right away down the stairwell knew something was still going on with the police, voices echoing, swirling up the well, general sounds of feet scuffing and vague taps of door knocking.

Just passing the fourth floor landing, heard someone call Excuse me, turned it was some guy cheap suit.

"Yeah?"

"What's your name?"

Stared at him a minute, on principle. "Why, what's going on?"

"What's your name, you live here?"

"My name is Terrance Wales, yes I live here, on seven, seven H."

"You going out all day?"

Held another stare. "What happened here?"

"Were you around last night?"

"Sure."

"You're on seven?"

"Yes."

"You were in all night?"

"Yes."

"Seven H?"

"Yes."

That seemed to be all he wanted, just turned away like it obviously wasn't worth it having a word with me.

It was the third floor where the main concentration of activity was going on, took a peek to see how far down the corridor, maybe in apartment three D or E. Out the door, now there were four police cars, two other cars probably belonging to detectives, mild crowd of people milling around, some talking to police, police taking notes, uniformed officers knocking on doors the motel area.

Lit a new cigarette as I cut through, trying not to feel like everyone was giving me a hard glance.

***

Nothing so much in the paper about odd jobs, or there was but I'm sure I'd be passed over—even construction, putting up walls, people around here'd done things like for ages, even knocking down walls, I'd show up, get a look up and down, only in a last ditch situation'd someone give me nod. Looked at the Models Wanted ads a little more intently than usual, knew just what it meant but tried to entertain the idea maybe not, maybe it just was someone wanted a subject to paint, to photograph.

I'd been avoiding the fast food place, local thing called *Howya Likeya Burga?* where I'd left my number with the owner about cleaning the place up at night, dirt cheap, figured no call meant he'd found someone else or decided it didn't matter or decided I was up to something. I loitered around in the parking lot of the liquor store across the street, waiting to see about did the owner's car show up. Probably chose the wrong spot to wait around, after hour-and-a-half the pull of a cheap bottle of vodka bled me off six dollars and I was dull minded, slightly sick to my stomach.

Spent the rest of the day up till evening doing about nothing except I managed to misstep up a curb and turn my ankle around the wrong way, found myself limping worse as I got near the lot of the Akerman, enough I didn't bother with the stairs, leaned to wall, cigarette fresh to lip I didn't even feel like.

Right away, few half drags into the smoke, knew the guy crossing the lot from out his parked car was aiming for me, but preoccupied all by my hurt paw didn't occur to me this was still about there being cops around until he smiled and called me Seven H, little click to it, half a question but same time he seemed pretty certain.

"Didn't realize we'd got to first name basis," I said, actually chuckled, no mood for this but still always proud to be funny, got me down again when he chuckled just as much, though.

"How are things in Seven H?"

Small talk sort of scene, terrific, rolled my head around could we cut past it he didn't mind but, no, he wanted to keep it up.

"You really pay rent by the week?"

"Me personally? What do I look like? Pay by the fortnight," I said, thick long pronunciation to the 'fortnight' but I don't think he got the thing I was basically flipping him off.

"Been here long or what?"

But I just bet he knew all about this and so skipped to telling him how I took it there'd been ugly bit of bother night before, something that I couldn't have less to do with, on top couldn't care either.

"What time were you in?"

"Might not believe it, don't own a watch. Late. Past midnight. No idea."

His eye went up a tick down a tock at something in what I'd said, same time I turned and there was a peek of someone's head at their motel room curtain. Kathryn. Curtain didn't close, not until I'd looked until it did, felt my gut go tight from all I'd eaten all day was cigarettes, kind of cramp like a rib aching back around my lung.

"What've you got going on around, just out of curiosity?"

Told him "Looking for work," but told him still while looking the motel window—didn't know what I wanted, the curtain to peek again, the door to open. Made myself look up the sky, same time not looking down I dropped the stub of my cigarette'n gave a random step of my toe I could feel didn't find it.

"I bet if you could loan me one of your cigarettes, there" pointed to the fat pack of his front pocket "I could tell you all about my hopes for public office, all of it. What're you interested in knowing?"

Another swell grin off the guy, he handed one right over, lit his own, took a stance like all of a sudden he was more playwright-doing-research than murder police or whatever it was he was. Just asked why I'd stayed on so long, he couldn't tell what people had going on with the Akerman, no other guest had stayed more than two weeks except a couple dozen who'd been there more'n ten years. Funny, this actually made me feel awkward, like it was something peculiar about me, identifying I'd never've thought to think about.

"That so? I mean, yeah I'm here awhile, but I couldn't dream of ten years on."

"Didn't used to be motel apartment place, just apartments, but things took a bad turn this part of town. I once dated a girl lived here, back then."

"She one of the lifers?"

Whatever reason, he took ill to that, the whole time I wasn't even being mean with it, kind of just wondered.

Door opened at Kathryn—no, her name was Kaitlin—at Katilin's motel, she just stepped out, lingered around the ashtray between her door and the next over, stole two glances at me I avoided except passing eyes over her, blurry eyes.

I asked the cop did he need anything else, that I wasn't going anywhere, if that was his clever trick to figure out with being my buddy and all.

"You should get a watch," he said, looked at me like he wanted a retort, but just gave him a bob up down of his cigarette my lip, almost winked but managed to not.

Stared at him walking until I could manage to look away, giving a hiss that Kaitlin was still over there, loitering like I'd agreed to something.

I got up to my floor, lame pathetic lean to the railing whole while, looked down my corridor remembered I'd meant to take a look down the corridor of three.

Must've been murder police, obviously the thing if he's gonna make sure he sticks around his car out in the lot until everyone is nice and accounted for, at least in some rudimentary way.

Sure, there he was still, at least his car parked, exhaust out the back, probably for his heater, the night turning chill as rock as soon as the sun got lost in the city skyline other end of the canal.

But, Kaitlin, she wasn't hanging out anymore. Put the spook in me for the next hour, two hours, that any second there would be her knock to my door and it'd be something I'd have to deal with no matter how much it was something couldn't matter to me less.

Soon though—soon a bit to drink, soon the kind of tired I let it feel more tired than it was because why bother not making the most of it—I was more thinking it made sense what the cop'd said, how these used to be apartments, actually. It'd always seemed to me the motel rooms, they seemed like the whole row'd used to be a carwash, an autobody shop, something, probably they were converted, whatever they'd been, when things'd headed south and the apartments went from proper rent to cavities not worth the fifty a week the dinge who'd rent them were made to cough out.

***

Woke up tired from the night not being good for anything. Stood in the shower, but it was pointless, I could feel the granules in the stream I'd always known were there but just never thought about, scabs either just from the inside rusting up of the pipes or else, all I knew, from the dirty pond the pipes were sucking out.

It was on me more'n I'd've been thinking it was, these police—as much as plenty of them'd been in and out of the Akerman the time I'd been there, this was something else. Noon two days since the thing and here I looked out and there were still some there, cop car even, that and the plain car I thought was that cop I'd had that delightful exchange with, guy was maybe camping out for the duration.

It just wasn't I could see who'd been got dead in the Akerman this sort of peek'd be made into what'd gone on. Had my little theory, obviously this'd been some guy done in not from the Akerman, this theory on account of one, if it'd been a guest, they'd've caught the other guest most likely behind it as quick as they did anything else, any other crime they'd been around for last four months, and two, on account of the Akerman seemed a sure thing people'd wound up dead here, time to time, but something about this one seemed a real surprise to all involved.

Figuring to have some smokes out in the fresh air, by now must've been plenty to read about it in the paper—wanted something, something to get myself feeling it'd be all done, that the cops weren't going to be pressed to start turning over every rock, poking their sticks everywhere just on principle, glad to step down on whatever else scurried loose, related or not.

Muggy but cold, worthless kind of afternoon, got the train out to some shops more proper in the city. Knew it wasn't because of some fairy tale about the pawnshops I was so reluctant to make a swipe anyplace, it was all just because when was the last time, really, I'd nabbed anything? It's the sort of thing a touch gets lost, I'd no bearings any more how things were protected, would likely get strung up I tried to sneak a single stick of gum out a pack, put it back the shelf. Anyway, paper I'd snuck from a table the fast food restaurant some guy'd got up for the toilet had nothing on the Akerman, whole thing a great big secret. Political scandal. Hollywood star found out on the skid.

Chuckled at myself. Was I trying to boy detective this out, cash in on the reward, key to the city?

So much I wasn't paying attention to anything, it was only while I was rounding one aisle to another an all-purpose store—thinking maybe a suitcoat or two could get me a few bucks at a secondhand shop, places never really asked many questions—that I took notice there was Kaitlin, hanging back. Knowing it wasn't any kind of mistake her being there, headed right out through the door, nodding deep to the security man leaning against a row of shopping carts, lit myself up cigarette and wandered around over by the drink machines to wait out her catching me up.

She didn't register surprise to hear me say her name behind her as she stepped by, squint like she was trying to figure out had she seen wrong which way'd I gone—no surprise of any kind, even so much to the degree she smiled and corrected me her name was Corrina. I remembered that, soon as she said it—we'd spoken what'd it been, the once? I'd been figuring out about the laundry in the basement didn't work, she'd directed me to the Laundromat I'd've found myself, no trouble, it being half block down, I saw it every day.

"What brings you out this way, Cor?"

But no, she had something set to her eyes, wetted her lips I could see suck the moisture in dry just quick, wetted them again and moved in close, finger wiggle could she bum a smoke. I lit her one off mine, mine almost out so then lit myself a new one from my old.

"I can't pay you," she said, out breath of her first drag.

Nodded, held in smoke, almost thought I actually might want to know what specifically did she mean, but instead, still not having exhaled, told her "Don't worry," she didn't owe me for a thing.

Her eyes went hard, perfect look an angry woman can get and same time knows it's an occasion keep her mouth shut. "You'll have to do whatever you want, turn me in, or we can arrange something else, maybe. I don't know what you want, but I don't have money."

Scratched my cheek all through her saying that, one eye squinted and gave my head a shake. "Didn't tell the police I'd seen you that night. That it? That's just because they're the police, okay? You don't owe me on that."

But it caught up to me she wasn't thinking about I was going to come at her about wanting something, it was that someone else already had done and she thought it'd been me. Blew smoke down my nose and she got a look like she could tell we'd gotten to the same page, though still distrust in her, like I was playing pretend.

"How much money is it I want?" I asked, tone like really I was trying to remember, maybe because I was sort of trying to guess how she'd answer, same time.

Uncertainty, freckle hid by her eyelashes visible even in the shadow from her brow. "I saw you talking to that detective and then he didn't come talking to me."

"I told you that already, he's not my good friend just because he had to ask me about things it's his job to go figure out on his own. I'm not your trouble if you've got trouble and I'm saying that and now I'm leaving." But I didn't move, felt my face tight a smile, one side, gave my nose a rub of thumb knuckle. "How much do I want?" I asked again, a bit more kitten purr.

This time, make believing herself confident but touch to ear showed otherwise and the way she did her shoulders was all wrong, she told me "Twenty-five hundred dollars."

"Corinna," I said, flick of cigarette right in the collection slot the soda machine, "Corinna, it'd been me asking and you've done what you've done, I'd be thinking brown penny more'n that, I can assure you."

Again those hard eyes, but not angry, hard like she didn't want me to see she'd cry later remembering this exact moment, my blank face, taste of cigarette off me haunting her, indelible ink.

"You don't know what he did to me," she said, mix of choke and stage whisper.

"Can't imagine I'd wanna envision it, one way or another, you not quite being my flavor, Cor. But either way, I'm explaining to you I don't care. Someone wants loose change from you over you asserted yourself to some fella, my advice is I'd pay them."

"I told you I don't have anything to give you."

Nodded, nodded, faked a big smile, breathy laugh, and did her an aw shucks, we have nothing further to talk about shrug and said "Hey, maybe we'll have a drink, laugh about this mix up the whole thing blows over."

Maybe not so right to put a poke to her that way, but turned and left her to ponder it all a bit. Walked fast even though I knew she wasn't following and, a little silly, felt tense and like I didn't want to look behind me she might be firing off a pistol on account she thought it was time for a last resort.

***

Already out that deep in the city, grabbed the subway all the way out the Orange line, deciding I'd take a few more bucks from storage, even thought so far I might take a proper hotel out, splurge a night, glut myself on delivery pizza, actual bottle of actual bourbon, pass out sloppy with the television on, still damp in a real bath towel.

Last thing I wanted rattling in the background was this woman thinking I'd something I wanted out of her—even the idea I could play her to get some whatever made me cramp up where it might've once made me anxious to see what play I could run. She'd gone out of her way enough to follow me, get me alone a minute to plead her case, showed herself at least something of a planner, someone trying to get the pulse of a situation—planner just a shade lighter from schemer, schemer the last sort I needed getting a fixation on me. Thing with her, she'd have every word of our exchange going through contortions, the dot-to-dot of my having seen her right after she'd done whoever in and then my not mentioning peep about it the cops while meanwhile someone who'd seen her also'd gone ahead and asked some money off her, sure thing I could see how she was thinking it was something to do with me.

Shook my head and put hard butts of palm against my eyes, pressed till black went red orange green and when I opened everything was under a fade. Stepped out the train, changed back in the opposite direction, transferred Orange to Blue and got out three stops shy of the Akerman, same as always and same as most of the time blew five bucks on vodka and downed it with a chocolate bar, bleeding through three cigarettes, as well.

What'd happen'd be whoever was making their play, they'd either not get a buck so forget about it or they'd not get a buck and so do whatever else they felt like. My own take, I couldn't see them much pressing hard enough to bruise her, considering she really couldn't pay out—figured most they could do was say they knew Corinna and whoever'd been lovers, been in the room together, something corroboration of'd be impossible, as far as I could make out, add up to nothing but a headache she'd squirm out just fine.

The drunk sloshing shoulder high, I was relaxing in to

this line of thinking—of course I was going from the idea that whoever was pressing her'd been doing it based on seeing her coming out that apartment on three. From her point of view, yes, this was something to be antsy about, but something I could only ever leverage as threat not cudgel were I the one squeezing her, follow through'd not be worth the trouble

Only other angle, someone knew something more and could prove it out, but they'd have to show their hand on that, which'd put me out of her mind, I could go back to being nowhere, nobody, left alone.

My next thought, coming into the Akerman lot, was going to be that third possibility existed, possibility the cops'd just nab her, but this got stalled by my hearing Hey, Seven H.

Turned to see that cop rolling down car window, leaning across passenger seat, causal wave. I gave a deep nod, kept walking, heard him say Seven H, again, that he just needed a question.

"City can't even shell out put you up in a room?" I slurred, not exactly approaching the car, loitering pointed in its direction.

"Don't think I'd take them up on that even had they offered, no offense."

His smile seemed so sincere, like he was glad we'd found simpatico by way of sense of humor and booze roiling in my ears making me grin right back like he was a laugh, at best, at worst like putting up with a sales pitch.

He started his question, then rolled his eyes, motioned couldn't I just come to the window or else he'd have to get out and the cold wasn't to his breeding. I obliged and he passed me a fresh lit cigarette I took without blinking.

"I needed to ask you again about what time you got home, the other night."

I let out a sour breath, half cigarette half vodka belch, head drooping forward. "Not in the head for it, man, you got what I told you, it's all the same. Anyway" I motioned vaguely in the direction of the apartments "I have to piss and it's been awhile I've had to, so just gonna see you later."

He told me to go ahead have a piss, he'd wait, head bob like he really sympathized with my plight. But I explained I meant I'd be in no shape I'm gonna walk back down seven flights after I'd drained, to which he chuckled, pointed out the driver's window at the partitioned dumpsters, told me have a piss there, he didn't see the harm.

Actually having to piss, I pushed away from the car, went right ahead how he'd suggested, in behind the partition, far in the corner as I could, odd puffs from the cigarette while getting my pants undone. I muttered Jesus to myself, froth of urine likely surrounding my shoes, I wasn't paying much mind. Was still zipping up I tapped the driver's window, he rolled it down asked me "What about it?"

"About it? The time? Man, it was late is all I know."

"Past midnight you said you think?"

"I guess."

It was like I was faking tummy ache get out of having to wait for the school bus, some morning.

"What'd you been doing before?"

"Drinking."

"Bar? Someplace maybe if you think about it you might remember the time, ball game on the TV, something?"

I drank mostly in parking lots, I explained and, anyway, he got done with his toying me about, let on the thing was he'd had to ask around and had it from two points of reference I'd got in the sun was still up, somewhere closer to seven than other side of midnight.

"Well, yeah maybe, alright, if someone saw me."

But he held up a finger, got me quiet, said reason he'd had to look into it was it seemed the victim—first time he'd said anything like that, like I knew the song as well as him—had been dead around then and police'd got called, shown up ten.

He looked at me, but I was thinking harder how to be clever about telling him screw off than bothering to get the weight of his pause.

"See, cops were watching the doors, taking head count, names and all of anyone in anyone out. No listing of you in and then there you were, out the next morning. But you tell me you'd only got in past midnight, I had to look at that funny because of my job and all, right?"

Stared at him, legs were ready to give out, holding me up about as well as dishwater might, but got it together enough to get up my hands he'd caught me. Told him I'd got in maybe around six, just meant to make his job a mess however possible, policemen not my favorite men despite their knowledge of civics and such.

"You were just saying it, you mean?"

"Yeah, that's what I mean. Could've said two o'clock, could have said million o'clock, alright? Mind I go up to bed now?"

He shrugged, asked me could he ask if I happened to've noticed anything, seen anyone, something didn't look right.

"Anything did look right, I'd notice that a beat quicker, officer."

He chuckled again, like he would've written that down, tell the wife, he'd had pen and pad handy.

"Get to bed," he said, a winking sound of tongue to teeth. Then double quick, pretend afterthought, asked me

"If I happen to have another question or anything, you'll still be around the fortnight, nothing new to report there?"

"Still the fortnight," I said, throat a fist. Almost added I'd be pulling up tent after, but thankfully mouth shut before stepping into that one, as well.

***

Middle or early-afternoon, woke up thinking I was answering a quiet few knocks at my door, impression they'd been knocked few times I'd been too still asleep do anything but ignore them. No one in the corridor, even walked kind of toward the stairwell could I hear someone going down, gave up, closed myself back in.

Washed my face rough at the kitchen tap, even rougher rubbed at it the one dishtowel I'd dried face, hands, forearms, dishes with no idea how often. Found two cigarettes left to a pack, got one lit, stick of smoke right away in my eye making me wince as I paced around, dab my fingers at the watering that got worse with each touch.

Only thing to carry anything with in my room was a small backpack, majority of my belongings with my money in the nice carry-all I'd bought for it before winding up the Akerman, that all tucked up snug in storage. Walked the apartment gathering up things weren't perishable—clothing, toothpaste, brush, even my two few-times-used fifty-cent shaving razors—when it got on me what I was doing was thinking I'd be heading out, but really I couldn't head anyplace.

Second of the cigarettes, sat to the bathroom sink, blowing smoke to the open toilet bowl, the scum of the shower floor.

Couldn't head out anyplace.

Tried to laugh at myself thinking on this, but instead it

made me feel used up, feel I'd lost all perspective about my situation, about myself, like a kind of senility'd doddered itself in me.

Why'd I told that cop I paid rent two weeks? Why'd I told that cop anything?

And now I'd told him twice and knew he'd be checking up—any day went past he'd be sat out there in his car and not see me in or out he'd come poke around, having it somehow all in his head I'd to do with his beat.

I looked out the window, down the lot, spot where he tended to park, kind of diagonal by the corner of the offices, nothing there—no cop cars at all, either, which I wanted to feel relaxed about, instead couldn't get a pulse on feelings concerning it one direction or the other.

Looked over at the front door to Corrina's motel room, stared at the window of it a minute, then stepped back, lump of myself down like a broke egg to the short sofa.

Last thing any good for me'd be to stick around, now especially Corrina with it in her head I'd something to do with bleeding her off money—she gets in a tight spot or gets thinking too much, one thing or another thing, she'll point me out, mention me, and with my position even a mention was more'n I could honestly stand for.

Got dizzy two ways, all of this in my head, sobering into headache.

All she'd have to do, it occurred to her, tell the police she'd seen me in the stairwell and then tell them I was giving her toothache from blackmailing her, figured this'd give the police the right to string me up, get my prints at least, run me down on everything else there was to run me down on, even if they did detective it out I was nothing to do with Corinna or whoever got dead down on three.

Full truth, I couldn't even hit back, couldn't deny, couldn't threaten—hadn't not told the cops about Corinna on account of my caring what happened to her, hadn't told the police because I couldn't have them asking me for so much as a driver's license I didn't have.

Could be even Corinna'd told that cop I'd been in the stairwell, the first place, what'd I know about it?

She'd done in whoever on three on account he put the hard line to her one too many times about his bedroom preferences, well and good, but that's nothing I wanted to be the one to go mentioning, that'd only do me any good to bring up I could prove it and somehow doubted I could do that and who'd come to back my word? She got smart enough, she could go ahead say I'd done the killing, threatened to put the frame on her for it—ludicrous, but even her saying I was maybe something to do with it was, for me, as bad as if I was.

No.

I felt insects under my skin, this was not good and the deep underwater of it was getting all over me. None of this would go away and I couldn't leave, now, not for nine, ten days, not without my new best friend detective wondering where'd I go—and as he already had an idea he liked me for this killing, doubt he'd just shrug and think guess I'd nothing to do with it, just decided to ramble on.

Horror, because for all this thinking there wasn't one thing I could do but run, but I was already running, I'd run myself all the way down the Akerman, figured to blend in, be no one, all of a sudden I'm what everyone is looking at and any more running, this time, whoever was behind me would clean catch up.

I started packing up again, just everything, would've shoved in apple cores, banana peels—I could at least go for a walk, think about it with the expanse of the rest of the world in front of me, thumbed-ride away, bus fare away, didn't have to sit inside a headache inside a sour smelling room some flea hump apartment some city I really wasn't even sure which one it's called.

Made a last pat around myself and scan of the room for cigarettes, happened over by the window, parted the blinds for another look, not meaning to, but saw there was a car now out in front Corrina's room—first thought being it was the cop, but wrong color and three times too clean to have anything to do the Akerman, cop or not. Watched to be sure it hadn't just that minute pulled in or maybe it was there about someone else, but it just seemed it had to do with her room, way the faded stripes for spaces mapped out the pavement, anyone there for a visit either room next door to hers'd've parked nearer to whichever.

Something in getting caught up thinking about this car got me even. Calmly left my room, bag just still on the counter—if I did run, didn't need any of that stuff, no need to look I was bolting, the off chance it made some cop pop out put questions to me.

From ground floor, light of the sun making my one eye start to water raw again, was obvious the car was parked for Corrina's and the light off the clean of its paint, the wax of it made it look almost absurd.

Still didn't see my cop buddy's car around, so made a long loop around the lot, came back very on purpose to pass by Corrina's room door, figured I could pause a listen, ear to door, maybe get some idea what was the business she'd have the car's driver.

Turned out, no need to even slow my stride—the door thinner'n receipt paper, the windows more or less plastic wrap, the sound of the moans and bodies thumps all over each other all over the unwashed carpet was more than audible even by the time I'd stepped down the curb the end of the row.

***

Gas station convenience store, one of the few places around'd let you use the toilet, no questions except did they have the key you could use, though for me it wouldn't've mattered, I was buying a pack of cigarettes, asked once the transaction was over, I was slapping pack to palm. Stood around in front when I was told toilet was occupied and another guy was pointed out who was waiting on next.

An older guy getting out of his car, he was giving me a squint and as he got closer, slowed, pointed a finger at me, my face going just slightly he should take a walk but then big smile and handclap, he pointed at me jab jab jab said "Terrance, right, Terrance?" It was the name I was using, but still I didn't hear it often enough it to sound natural, even had to double check with myself was that what I was going by.

"You never came back by," he said, said he heard I was still looking for work, maybe we could talk about it.

"Sounds good, man. Heard I'm looking for work from where?"

Told me some cop'd been in show some pictures around, and when he'd recognized me'd mentioned I'd asked about being a cleaner after hours, cop'd in turn told him about I said I still needed something.

"I'll be honest, you know, I was fine you not coming back because I don't like to hire from around unless it's with regular contractors sort of thing, but he said you were alright, looking to stick around and weren't having luck."

Couldn't work my head around this angle, did my best to seem nonchalant.

"Why'd some cop got my picture?"

"He had lots of pictures. But not just some cop, he said you'd spoken a few times."

I made a roll of my hand, sure, I knew which cop, kind of had to say Yes about I'd be interested in the overnight gig it was on offer, we agreed on it if I could come out, even that night, he'd be there until closing and we could work out exactly what it'd be, what it'd pay.

Still needed a toilet, but decided enough was enough, I'd wait things out my room, get proper rest, not move an inch until I was in my clear head. About a block back in the direction the Akerman though, it was like the breath drooled out of me, found myself slowing, would've just stood still if not I saw a tailor shop to get around behind, relieve myself, have another smoke.

All I'd done was walk up the stairs. It was all I'd done. That and I'd walked back out, the morning. Now one minute this cop is prying out of people what time did they think I'd come home, another minute he's vouching for me some nighttime janitor work—I mean I got the picture, I'd landed in his line of sight, but how little did he have to go on that my giving him a line about when I'd got home was enough to get me top dog his suspect pool?

Furious, I spit, then spit, spit nothing, huffs of air, tightly brought my arms around myself, tensing biceps like I'd be punching but too self-conscious about making a scene, even started hissing out my nose to keep my lips pressed tight in case anyone—I don't even know who I was thinking or what would it matter—was watching me somewhere around.

Like a lost sock, cop's car was back the lot but he, I could see, was chatting to someone over by the stairwell door up the apartments, someone he broke off from the moment he saw me, gave their arm a pat, started in my direction.

"You my social worker now? My agent?"

He laughed, kind of shy raise of one shoulder. "You get the job?"

Knew just exactly what I wanted to answer, but wasn't so much a drip I'd let this nonsense get me tripped up. "I got the job, sure, and look don't think it's anything I don't appreciate it, but the same time can't help but admit I wonder why're you showing me off around and asking after me?"

Face like he was my girl and knew why I was upset, he put on soft tone and explained it wasn't anything specific to me, he wasn't badgering, owner of the burger place'd just responded to my photo, thought he'd put in a word. Much as I appreciated that, I explained, would he mind not acting on my behalf, again, and since he was so understanding about my having the wrong idea, maybe he could do me a favor, right there and then, tell me exactly how I could best help him out with whatever he was doing, what did he need to know about?

It was getting to me, his reactions—now he was head down like I'd given him a spanking he's six-years-old mouthed off to me.

"I'm not meaning to pester you. I understand it's delicate around here, I do appreciate that, and I'm not looking to ride you. Okay?"

I nodded, made a sound of parting my lips but nothing to say.

"If I could just ask you—do you know Arnold Houghton?"

"Arnold Houghton? I don't. Why would I?"

"No reason you would, I'm just checking on some things."

"Who is he?"

He blinked a few times, made a thumb point up gesture, told me it was the dead guy from three.

"You didn't know that was his name?"

"Why'd I know some dead guy's name?"

But all he'd meant was it'd been in the paper a lot, lately, he just thought if I'd been browsing the Help Wanted I might've come across it, something, or else maybe I'd just been curious why the cops around.

"Cops around same reasons everywhere, I'm not interested unless it's to do with me."

"And this time it isn't."

Again his tone didn't match—wanted to use that remark as an excuse to storm off, but he got the perfect smooth to the words it'd seem I was suddenly angry over nothing, enough it'd be reason him to look me up again later on, excuse to go digging, see what might've been the matter.

"I don't know him."

"Do you know someone called Kyle Beeker?"

"No."

He nodded, burrowed tongue to the inside of his cheek. "What about—you know a woman named Corrina Eastbridge?"

Managed not to betray any pause or fakeness in admitting I thought I did, pointed nose the direction, in general, her room, asked "Doesn't she live here, or did anyway?"

"She still does. You know her?"

"We met. Talked once, don't know, way back I moved in, talked about where'd I do the laundry."

He nodded. "And you remember her? Got" he pointed directly at her door "to know where she lives?"

But I wasn't having this cute bit either, told him I'd seen her around awhile after we'd first talked, even found her dandy looking and'd daydreamed a bit, maybe, but then thought better of it on account the Akerman didn't seem like the best place to meet a girl interested in Betty Crocker.

He laughed, head jiggling like he knew all about it and his air, after that laugh, was relaxed, like a doctor done touchy-feeling couldn't wait for me get my clothes back on.

Kept my face impatient, asked him was that all.

"We're all done. I don't think I need to ask you anything else, I know where you are if I do."

"Wonderful. Gonna get some sleep before I see about the job. Wanna thank you again for that."

"It was least he could do," he said, especially as I was being so helpful, added in. He said no one else in the Akerman'd tell him squawk about a thing, he maybe just kept finding reasons to chat with me because I was so forthcoming.

***

Before the burger place shut off ovens and all, owner had them make me whatever I wanted, which'd be part of my pay, he explained. Other than that, pay was fifty bucks per week, I could take as long or short about it I felt like each night, as long as things got done—any of the more heavy duty cleaning stuff I only needed to bother with every other night, third night, and anyway a lot of spot cleaning happened during the day.

Was left key to the place, immediately started in thinking I'd move in there, out the Akerman, sure if I timed it out right I could clean, have a sleep the rest of the night, be well out the back by morning whoever it was showed up to open. This job, it'd pay for my rent, keep that neutral, but work it out right, instead I could have a trickle of money in, no more of the slow bleed through my reserve, always waiting out the last crumb feeling starving already.

Had a laugh at myself over this plan, sat out back the place, work done the night, smoking through a chain four five six cigarette—I supposed it felt like shedding the room the Akerman'd have me shed the whole place, but it wouldn't, even I took a train the city all day, came back to sleep on the floor, I was just as much stuck, not free from a thing.

All this thinking was just, I knew, only to distract me off the tension building in me each breath closer to next sun up. But also it was that with this job, this room the Akerman, I really was set up as perfect as I wanted to be, everything how I could live with it, no concern—except Corinna, cop, pokes, prods.

Flicking the last cigarette I felt like smoking then right away lighting another, standing, heading back the Akerman I muttered, clownish It just isn't fair, is it Trevor? sucked up rough phlegm and spit, new suck to cigarette. It was genuinely miserable, though, it not being fair—everything behind me was a mess, the things I'd done, even, were just as much things I hadn't done, no one wanted to remember them or else the ones who did for the wrong reasons, anyone I'd wrong'd likely see something fitting me winding up some dinge like this, satisfied to let me lay.

This was where I could be, now I just had to leave but now I was stuck, couldn't go. Funny, funny.

Kept my head down, the cop's car parked as usual, engine cold, windows I couldn't see through, made a line for the stairwell door, same time had to notice that car was parked out front Corrina's, again. Past four o'clock—my first thought was fellow was making a night of it, but just as much I figured second later he might've been the early worm, come to get his bird.

But in the stairwell, the dark of it—no inside lighting, just windows every second landing—the quiet of it except me, I got on guard maybe he was here on behest Corrina, waiting to brain me. She'd gone ahead told him she was in some bind—certainly not what bind—he'd decided to be the upstanding sort, see could he put the fear to me.

No.

If it came to that, she thinking I'd name her out she'd done in Arnold the third floor, it'd have to be the guy'd do me in, straight out, and somehow doubted whatever feelings Corrina inspired were enough to get some man able-bodied enough to afford to wash his car regular to commit brazen violence—even I'd never done violence toward anyone, though probably I'd had reason enough to, few occassions. And even if he wanted to have some stern word with me, show me his weight up close, he wouldn't because a scare might get me skittish enough to forget the money they thought I was after and just pull the plug. Corinna was smart enough she was still breathing motel air rather than the alternative, must be smart enough to know not to go out of her way to bite at the hand holding the stick that was prodding her.

Not, I reminded myself, stepping to my door, key to lock—actually had to remind myself, a minute—that I was that stick, but she thought so, anyway.

Inside I felt a sensation like relief, some thought beginning, dream of it all over, but then could tell my toe hadn't stepped down the tile inside the door, something else. Looked down there's an envelope.

Hadn't turned up my light, poured some of the last vodka I had left—warm, bottle left out and open—then instead drank what was left in the bottle I hadn't poured, flicking at the side of the glass, hesitated, downed it, too.

Light over the stove, skinned knee more'n any real color,

I could see the envelope wasn't white and had the words *Give me a call tomorrow* and a telephone number written under.

Empty pack of cigarettes the counter, I fished the almost empty pack from my pocket, let the stove coil heat enough to light it, took the three crisp pages out, folded not creased, leaned a squint to read.

Scott, the writer was addressing, *you won't understand this, but I wanted you to know from me before you heard anything, wanted you to know what I did, really, and why.*

I made a glance toward the stale curtained windows, almost convinced myself I saw someone there, but was just me starring—thought I could hear things move out the hall, the air vent, snoring from other rooms, people shumbling out or home, drunk or about to be.

Things weren't right I exactly felt like reading, just looked at the pages, wondered—stupid thing to wonder though it might be—what the meaning of it could be, if maybe on top of everything had someone slipped parting words to Scott under the wrong door, everything in the world piling on me from everyone else.

Thing was signed—and noticing this, noticed also the pages were photocopies—*Corinna.*

Thing was signed, *I love you* and then *Corinna.*

Those words, numbers on the envelope, saw them I reached for the glass now empty, took the pages and moved to the window, thinking I'd take a peek out, but too beat, sunk to the sofa, found remote to get the glow off the television, more light than I needed to read, shadows off everything, off each letter, words were fidgeting, poking, rolling shoulders, animal, pensive.

First page about the ins-and-outs Corinna and dead man Arnold bored me, really, despite it was pleadingly graphic, really she wanted Scott to understand not only what had

Arnold done to her, but why she never told, how exactly so much it was Scott meant to her.

Was grazing the second page—it was expected, but still I tightened jaw, narrowed eyes on it to be sure—and there was my name. She was explaining why the letter, why she was turning herself over the police, explaining it was on account of not wanting to suffer the indignity of my forcing them down on her.

Terrance, a man I know from the apartment building, he sold me the gun when I asked, but then afterward he came to me, told me he knew everything, all about Arnold and me, had known since maybe the beginning, everything, and he did, enough he could prove everything. I don't know how, but he had the gun.

A numb twist of grin, dog gums, crossed my face—the flourishes she'd added were almost lovely to me, most of all how she'd left out the money part, found such a neat tweak to wring as much victim out of herself as she could.

He told me how he'd always watched me. And now that Arnold was gone, he told me what he wanted.

Almost wanted to whisper to the page "Well, bravo"— or maybe I did. Next I realized it, the room was lit enough by day it was bright and I'd been pacing, the letter there the floor across the room.

***

The platform waiting on the metro into the city, felt Corrina's little confession all folded tight down my pant pocket. I'd called the number on the envelope twice, now, nothing except it rang and rang and rang, which could've meant something, could've nothing, meant anyway I'd have to keep calling it.

I wasn't going to leave, didn't think I was, but still I was moving in the direction my storage locker, my money, everything I was.

If Corrina'd wanted the spook in me, it was in, but even still my head wouldn't stop with puzzling it around. I understood this was her way of telling me she could make it hard on me things went hard for her, but of course she had no idea how hard on me it'd actually get—I needed to get a pulse on how she had things lined up, how this made sense from her side of the fence, knowing nothing, I'm just someone random an apartment she lived in the motel at the foot of. Might be she figured anyone in the Akerman had something to hide, any investigation'd turn it up and so I'd back down on that account, or maybe more straight forward this was just her showing, regardless, she could do something to hurt me if it got grim enough she felt she had to.

It didn't matter, because the flat fact was there's more than enough to turn up on me, she knows it or she doesn't, and there was no way I wouldn't be brought in for a close look the cops snatched her up she either told her tale or—better, which is how I thought it'd go—for effect the mysterious Scott showed up with the letter, all postmarked, back dated, beautiful time capsule I'd have to explain myself out of conspiracy charges, at least. And in the meantime, my fingers'd go to ink, one way or another, things come demolishing down around me.

Without thinking, I'd got out some random station, walked the platform, but another train came by I didn't get on, just sat, wanting a smoke I didn't have, not bought new pack yet, slipped my mind, as well.

Fingerprints'd turn up the business with Helen, but meanwhile had no idea what else'd accumulated around that. Maybe fingerprints'd be enough rake up every old grave, all the way back. However far that was. Norman. Farther. Everything. Even just Helen, the certainty of Helen, it was enough to do me in for good—that plus whatever'd go down here, Corinna, no way out but I'd be put inside for all day.

Left the station, bought pack of cheap smokes, last fumes of the money I'd taken the locker, what'd it been, just a few days ago, top of the week? Went back in the store, broke a bill for coins, asked about nearest payphone but clerk'd no idea, figured probably close by, though. I walked by two phones, ginger time of opening the cigarettes, stick-figure matches lighting in pops, diffusing immediately, six down before I got the flame to take, then stopped at the third phone, receiver from cradle, left it dangling while I dialed, number still not memorized, uncrumpled envelope from my pockets.

After five rings, woman came on and straight off said "Hi Terrance."

"Hi, Cor," I said, but wasn't sure, she sounded different or else I didn't know so much what'd she actually sound like, couldn't concentrate, either way, on account the tang of the cigarette smoke had my stomach the wrong way over.

"I don't want to take up too much of your time, so I'm just going to tell you how this is going to go."

"That's cute, but thing is I get the idea I'm missing something."

Overtop the last of what I'd said, she was already in with "Whatever you're not bright enough to understand, this isn't a Q and A."

I liked her trying to steam roll, so started in on top with "Cor Cor Cor, all what I can tell is you're threatening to turn yourself in, which you just aren't gonna, so sure tell me all about whatever's in your pretty little head, but you're way turned around here."

She sighed, like she wanted to retort, but wasn't going to get that easily unfooted, just a chuckle, fake but she didn't care. "Terrance, you read the letter? Remember that gun it mentioned? I'm humoring you, a moment, because I don't need you thinking that you're smart enough not to do what I'm going to tell you to do."

Her voice was my thumb caught in a closed drawer, I swallowed wrong, eyes watering up from holding it trying not to cough—could tell she had something up I hadn't even been considering, so I just muttered about I remembered the letter.

"What you need to ask yourself, Terrance, is where might that gun be and who is it gonna seem put it there."

I nodded Yes, then the line hung silent, so eventually I said "Sure, yes, I see how that's something to think about."

"You're going to give me five thousand dollars."

"That'd be a marvel, I can't see how you've settled on that's gonna happen."

But she wasn't listening, this was a speech, could practically see her grinning, pacing her squat room or wherever she was, barefoot, schoolgirl playing a trick on her best friend. "Seemed a good number—brown penny more than the twenty-five you were after, isn't that right? You have three days to get it together if you don't have it now. You get it sooner rather than later, you give me a call at this number, I'll tell you where to put it."

"Can I point out I'm not even the one was blackmailing you?"

I didn't care, like all the wind was out of me and I was asleep falling from a rooftop—I was smiling, hand wrapped around the creases in my forehead, twisting last of a cigarette into the brick of the nearby wall.

"Don't think of leaving, Terrance. I want you home in time for supper, every night, and if I get the feeling you're aiming to leave me, it'll be both of us going down together."

Her tone was corkscrew, both giddy and a bit put off, enamored by her cute lines and bored by the surrounding stuff.

All I could say was "Yeah, okay. But I don't have it, now." The line went quiet again. "Corinna, it wasn't me trying to bleed you out that money. I didn't tell the cops anything and that's all I did. You don't need to do this."

And I was thinking she might actually be listening, that I might get her to focus on thinking straight, thinking had she heard anything else along the lines of the original threat, maybe she'd see it'd been hot air, she'd called the bluff not even meaning to, but then she let out a low kind of breath, long, too long, told me she didn't care about anything, but just she needed to get out of here, this was her way and it was the same to her as any, said I should just consider it like I'd drawn the short straw. Then her voice went back to crisp lettuce, she told me figure out about the money and the line was dead right after.

I left the receiver to my ear until it beeped, waited through the beeps until it started ringing, listened to the recording all through at least dozen times about I needed to hang up and try my call again and did I need assistance I should dial the operator, then I just left the thing a dangle, wandered a few steps off one way, stopped, walked back, hung the phone up and leaned there trying to strike another smoke with matches burst like blown fuses I skid them across the rough of the matchbook.

***

The storage unit I kept was in a complex generic and sprawling and outdoors, unit about the size of half a closet, the lock I'd bought requiring combination and key. Really I'd lost track when it'd been I'd just been to it get the money out for rent, it was something I never remembered, no need much for time the way I lived, but slogging in, roaming the complex just to avoid having to face my thoughts, roiling the long toilet hole of the place, it seemed even more in the ether—few days at most, couldn't yet've been the week.

Unit was deep enough I could stand inside, bulb for light so I shut myself in as much as I could, knelt, unzipped the luggage bag. Setting the shirts and clothes on the floor, one at a time, first other thing I uncovered was the gun—my gun, Norman's gun. Been a long time since I'd laid eyes on it, usually just burrowed hand down under the clothes, grabbed out some money, burrowed excess money back under. I held the thing, pointed it limply, wrist lolling like a bobbing boat, then set it down on the clothes, covered it with the rest I took out.

Money was in a state of disorder, I just stared at it and then dug further down under it, all the way into the corner the bag, took up the rumple of paper I'd balled pill tight and stuck there. Carefully unfolding the thing—things, really, thing I wanted wrapped in two restaurant flyers—I looked down at the artist's rendition of my face, way Helen'd described me to police she'd figured out what I'd been up to, or figured out some approximation of what I'd been up to, anyway. The paper wrinkled to the point I could hardly make out the letters of the large word Wanted, it made me think the drawing looked even more like me, didn't seem to distort it, smoothed it right to grotesque perfection. It's what I looked like, I thought, blew air down my nose and had an actual smile on. Then I squinted until I could make out the writing describing me as Dangerous, as Violent, that I should not be approached, that authorities should be called.

Crumpled it, abruptly, held the fist hard as I could, but

when this didn't seem hard, when I didn't feel the least bit strong, just rolled the paper back to pill-ball between my palms, wrapped the fliers back around, tossed it to the corner, heard click click of it hitting wall, cement of floor.

I couldn't take any chances. Corinna could have her money, she could have it. Jesus, any breath of suspicion on me anything, anything I'd be locked up, I'd be over— Corinna planting a fired gun on me, gun that'd done in some hump didn't even matter who, that on top of Helen on top of everything, I'd be over and done.

I wasn't even angry—it was just fact and the only way it'd go that way, only way I'd be strung up was to tie my hands up my own, didn't matter what'd I tie them to—this money, some apartment, some job—anything I could do to stay free was just what had to be done and everything else I'd figure out some other time.

Piled the money out by denomination, not counting a stitch of it, thoughts in repeat cycle—half thoughts, really, half thoughts'd get going then blink like dead televisions back to where they'd started.

Four thousand six hundred fifty-four dollars.

Four thousand six hundred fifty four.

Four six five four.

My face was contorted, felt like a crab. I counted the pile out, no distinct thought of exactly why this was troubling me, just a blank state of something wasn't right, mind shrinking from it.

How is this all I had left?

I unfolded out the clothes, rubbed each bill as though another might've flatted to it like paste, went through pockets, patted around the concrete floor.

How was this all I had left?

I began crying, bubble pop, had to cover my face in hands, practically choke myself to stop the blubbering—

even then had to keep my neck tight, twisted, eyes fixed on the soft blur of light the bulb overhead was, bright of it not enough even to sting my rigid eyes.

Whispered Fuck and it brought me out of it—repeated fuckfuckfuckfuck in sets of four, taking out from the luggage everything but the money, all else left on the floor, then shut up the unit, got a cigarette lit and stood there, no place.

I lingered through the one cigarette, starting in the direction of the facility office during the few drags I took of another, stubbed it appropriately in the ashtray stand by the handicapped parking, went inside, electronic bell chiming.

Some young couple was having a lazy discussion about which sort of cardboard boxes to take for a move, the man working the office seeming relieved to see me, asked could he help, leaning good to the counter his elbows.

"I rent a unit here, paid out for six months few months back, wondered could I change that, end it off end of the month, get whatever refund?"

He nodded, like he was considering some fine point. "We could do that, sure, but we'd have to charge the full month's prices for how long you've rented—you paid the six months at a discount, I take it?"

I nodded, said it'd be fine, what'd that make the refund?

Had to give him my name and all, he pulled me up the computer while fielding a few questions from the young woman, the young man at a dawdle looking at car air fresheners like he was awaiting instructions.

"You'll have to pay all the way through this month."

I nodded, said "It's fine, still wanted to use it until end of month."

"That'd make it four months total you're paying—so two hundred you'll get back from the twelve you paid."

I must've had a look I was trying the math, though I certainly wasn't, because the man explained the six months prepay made it two hundred a month instead of two-fifty.

"Sure. That's fine."

"You paid cash, but I'll have to cut you the refund as a check."

Blinked, nodding like this was alright then caught up myself, too forcefully shook my head and held up a hand like he'd pulled something on me. "No, no. I need the cash back." He was shrugging, real sorry look his face but I kept on that I got what he meant, but no check'd do me any good. "Just something's up and I don't need the unit the six months, so why can't I get cash back?"

His eyes must've met those of the young man or the young woman, blip of silence I realized I was breathing hard out my nose, apologized.

I turned to the woman, "Hey, let this guy write you a check two hundred dollars, you have any cash you can give?"

Hadn't let her answer—her eyes going to the young man, dubious—asked the clerk'd that be alright? He didn't answer before she was saying about how she just couldn't do it, she didn't even have that much cash free.

"Alright, come on—lucky day, okay? He'll write you the check two hundred, you give me one fifty."

Held her eyes—couldn't get a bead on how she was interpreting me—almost said Please.

"I have a hundred out in the car."

I didn't say anything, heard the young man asking the worker was it alright about writing the check and as soon as the worker'd said it'd be fine, woman repeated she had the hundred, I wanted it, best she could do.

**

I drifted to sleep again and again on the metro, couldn't help myself—not even I was trying to sleep, it was like I wanted to keep to that tick of space, that catching my thoughts drifting, realizing I'd lost them, some drool maybe over my lip side, head noddering, sniffles, rubs to nose and closing eyes hard, they crunched.

When I got off the station, had to find a place to stand, get myself together—my thoughts were waterlogged, couldn't even steady myself enough to tell myself steady myself. Got a cigarette and the smoke creaked back into me, out, swivel of lightheadedness it struck me when'd been the last time I'd had anything to eat? Must've been before cleaning up, ate what they'd made me the burger place, couldn't't've been that long ago—awhile, but not enough to justify this soupiness, body like an empty pant leg.

When was the last time I'd eaten before that?

I couldn't remember.

And before that?

The sunlight felt worse for being back behind some overcast, I made my way toward the Akerman, then turned away from it a block off, walked instead to the burger place. The lot was full, which I'd never seen, but I supposed I'd never really paid attention either, scanned for the owner's car and when I saw it, slap of relief, hung back for one last smoke, focus as much as I could possibly manage. I kept tapping the side of the luggage bag while I stood, tense each time the door the place opened someone'd walk out, nerves that the owner'd be slipping out home or something and last I wanted'd to be accosting him at his car window—still, for all the nerves I stayed until my cigarette was smoked, pale orange between second, third finger and pinching the stub between second finger, thumb stung.

Owner was at the booth furthest back, one by the toilets, had several newspapers out, making notes of something in a little memo book. I slowed, hoping he'd get an eye of me from a distance off, give me some indication come over, instead he only looked up to my quiet Hello, stood right there at the side of the booth. He gestured me to sit, so I did, right away he told me I looked terrible, was I feeling alright.

Bolstered myself with a breath, took advantage the curve of sympathy to him, he was full attention on me, said "I was hoping I might ask you a favor, but I don't imagine you'd feel comfortable about it."

He didn't answer anything, but lips parted a bit, head motion I should go on.

"I know it's not your problem and you've already helped me out this job, everything, but I was wondering isn't there maybe some way could I get an advance of a week or two, just anything you might be able to? It's some things, I'm behind the eight, you know, figured—"

But he stopped me, changing his posture to sitting upright. "I don't need to know the details of it, I can't think that would be comfortable, going into anything private. You're behind, I'll try to help out how I can. How much money do you need?"

Felt right away I was being set up, powerful sour of paranoia went right in me, but he went on that he would be glad to pay me in advance, but if there was some amount I needed, within reason, to get me on my feet, we could work out about payments and all, but he'd prefer to help as much as he could, right away, instead of having me still underneath and having to go door to door.

My eyes ticked few ways—really I was just trying to do math, for whatever reason not wanting to overshoot this, but thinking I might manage the last of the gap to five thousand plus have a few dollars my pocket for afterward—and before I really'd thought it through said "I need three fifty, three hundred fifty dollars just to take care of some things."

And I'd taken breath to go on when he stopped me, again, told me to stay there, he'd be right back. While he was away in the door the rear office, helped myself to some of his fries, a sip or two his coffee, the taste of which, thick with sweetener, cream, turned my stomach.

Had my head watching out the window someone pump their gas the station, owner came back out, discreetly handed me an envelope which I put into my bag, head bowed, couldn't meet his eyes, didn't even manage a Thank you. He told me not to worry about cleaning up, that night, and that so I wouldn't stay behind, wouldn't have nothing for the next weeks, he was just going to pay me forty the week instead of the fifty until the debt was evened off.

"Yeah, or a few bucks less even than forty, I'm under your thumb, you know?"

His eyes went even softer, told me not to think about it like that. He said it turned out I was screwing him about, he knew just the cop to have me straightened out proper, to which—though the mention of my good friend the cop had me ready to return the money—I nodded, shyly smiled, said "That's true."

Maybe to save me embarrassment, he excused himself, papers and all, back to the office—I'd wanted to ask could I still get my meal for the day, but the thought of knocking on the door or of explaining myself to one of the cashier's, having them go back and ask, it seemed too much.

Ducked into the toilet, closed myself in one of the two stalls, opened my bag. I'd hoped the owner would've slipped in a bit more than I'd asked, but it was the three-fifty only, bringing me to five thousand, one hundred and four dollars.

Everything.

Which meant I had one hundred four dollars left after paying out Corinna.

I was one hundred four dollars. All I was.

But there was no way out of paying—it was better for me if Corinna had the funds to run off, get out of here, it was better. Either way, I'd have to leave, as well, no way I could keep around, but this way, at least, I could well and proper disappear again someplace, not have new dogs on my heels, not have new sniffs of crime hanging all over me.

Left the toilet, the place, started in the direction of one of the shopping plazas I knew had a bank of phones outside the nail salon, took one of my four singles into the cigarette store next door to it, broke for coins, fished the rumpled envelope the telephone number out of my pocket.

Thought could I tell Corinna all I'd managed was four thousand? Cash money to her, right then, she could head out, get wherever it was she had to go?

Line clicked on. No one said anything, so I almost started talking right off I have your money, but instead asked "Who's there?"

"Do you have it?" Corinna's voice, hushed but easily recognizable.

"I've got four thousand, and had to pull some tricks to get that much."

"Get back to tricking, then, Terrance. Deal was—"

But I cut in on her, told her I had the money, could we just get it over with.

"The five?"

"I have all five. Corinna—this is everything I have and I

had to go hat in hand so can we just cut to the end, just have this done, alright?"

There was silence. I wanted to imagine her sitting the bed, half dressed, half packed to go, little blush of sympathy come over her, instead she told me if it wasn't five she counted when I dropped the money she'd leave, but leave the gun behind, if I got her drift, and it'd be me there all alone to weather whatever went down, after.

"It'll be five. I can bring it to you, right now."

Don't even know why I'd said that, she even laughed, said I'd do no such thing, that I'd call her from the metro station next morning, the line clicked off.

***

The cop's car was parked in the lot, I purposefully having come around the Akerman in such a way as to note this before any possibility of being seen, and it being there made me turn around, walk off in the direction of the same plaza I'd just telephoned Corinna from. I read magazines in the franchise drug store, got a coffee from the sandwich shop and hung around in the parking lot behind until it got dark.

I spent the night in the bathroom of the burger place, maybe got a good amount of sleep and maybe not—no real way to tell, I had to take a look out the door every time I popped awake, even a bit, get an idea of the color of the sky—but was able to have a good stomach full of hamburger rolls, saltine crackers, poured myself a large soda from the fountain before leaving, but three swallows into it, not even the other side of the lot, sun just properly up, I tossed it aside, already feeling ghastly and leeched from the syrup.

There was a kiosk set up across from the metro I went to, fellow brewed coffee, sold it properly on the cheap, got it fresh, pot just changed, and blew at the steam rising a circle from the Styrofoam cup.

Went to a pay telephone in the mezzanine area the station, commuters in queue for passes, echoes making it hard to hear even the ringing from the line, receiver cupped to my ear. Corinna didn't answer first two times I called, spread over an hour, but each time, though it oughtn't to've, the phone captured my coins so I had to break a bill off a random person, the station attendant sluggishly informing me it wasn't her job to help in such situations.

When the fifth call, still another hour later, didn't go through, I swallowed last dribble my coffee, was thinking to head back to the kiosk, but the phone rang. I answered dubiously, it was Corinna.

"What station are you at?"

I scanned around, spotted the name on a sign, told her.

"What do you have the money in?"

I stammered. "A luggage bag, like a duffle suitcase thing."

"What you need to is get on the Yellow Line toward Yardsend. Do you know what that means?"

"I know how the train works, yeah, I got it."

"If you're at Bailey, there should be a train about to leave in five, six minutes. Don't get that one, get the next."

She paused, so I waited a blink or two, told her I was following her, she still didn't come on the line a moment, maybe verifying something.

"You there?" she abruptly asked, part clearing her throat.

"I'm here," I said, air out my nose. Silly, but the call was making me impatient—I knew I wasn't going to play games with her, even I really could just hand over the money, face-to-face, but I could see she had to be on her toes.

What would she do if I slipped five hundred, one thousand out, kept it as traveling money my own? Decided on testing the water about that, last time.

"I only managed the four thousand, Cor."

"I imagine you're joking, Terrance, which is not a good idea."

"Christ's sake" I actually gnashed, furious in a single pump of blood "I had to kill myself even get this four— what you think you can pick random tenant some flophouse he's got five grand laying around?"

"I think if I picked one who has four thousand laying around and who's on the phone to give it to me, then I picked the one who doesn't want the trouble of not also having five. And from what I hear, you've hardly been killing yourself over anything since last I heard from you."

"What's that mean?"

But whatever slip she'd made, nerves on her part, into the more conversational bent was swallowed back up—she coldly told me I was to get the Yellow the direction of Yardsdale, take the front car—meaning front car in Yardsdale's direction, I didn't want to knucklehead this up—and I was to sit in the seat behind the conductor's area, the one partitioned off, then leave the whole duffle on the floor, tucked back in under the seat, when I got off at Howard.

"Do you understand?"

I told her "No," and it was true, I really didn't. "What if someone's in the seat?"

"Hope someone's not."

"Jesus, have you even thought this through?"

"It's the next train now, Terrance, should be leaving

your station in ten minutes or so. We're getting off the phone. You take the next train after straight back and you give me a call from the exact phone you're on now—I see a different number, I won't be happy."

"Hold on—what if the conductor, something, takes a little break for a smoke, pops out his room, sees the bag or how about someone else gets on?"

"I appreciate your concern" I actually laughed over her, told her Yeah, because she was bullshit at this and this was still my money, she just continuing on though my blurt "but I'm hanging up. Get the money to the train."

Hung up few seconds after she had, ran my hand over my face, another surge of Wasn't this my chance to run off with the money, it'd seem something'd gone wrong?

No.

Gut sunk that I'd better cut it out with thinking anything like that, I paid for a pass to Howard and back, bumped turnstile turn with my hip and walked up the escalator to the open air platform. Yellow towards Yardsend was seven minutes out, platform deserted, got a cigarette going.

Sure, Corinna'd know the general way the train went around here, it's why she hadn't answered at first I'd called, too busy with the commuters—and sure she wasn't in her room, on a cellular phone, she'd be waiting whatever the next station out from Howard was, just that little span of secured time the bag was unattended, she'd be waiting for the door to open, in she'd pop, maybe even ride the train out the airport, it was on this line or something.

Three people were in the front car as train pulled in, but two of them, young guys, got out and the third was a potbellied foreign woman looked in a coma seated about the center.

What was to stop me leaving off the bag, jogging a few

cars further down, keeping a sly eye did Corinna get back off after nabbing the money, keep cool and give her the follow?

Again, clenched my jaw, forgetting the side of the stick was up me, the moment.

I'd do what? Follow her? Attack her? She didn't get the money here and now, she'd end me. I wasn't ringing her up inside twenty minutes and she got the right number coming up as Incoming, she'd end me. This was me doing as I was told, this was me I'd better get it straight double quick who and what I was this situation, because anything else'd taste ugly I didn't want to find out how.

In the span from the station before Howard to Howard, I stood and moved away from the bag, checking be sure my own money, short of one hundred now, was in my pocket. Stood at the center door the train, in front of the foreign woman who was dead asleep, overturned soda can having leaked damp circle around both of her feet, one in a cast, the other bare and calloused.

Doors rattled open, I stepped out to an empty platform, found a seat and watched the sleeping woman continue to sleep as the doors closed and the train slipped back a little, got traction, got momentum, hurried on and out of sight.

Facing the other platform, saw a train back to Bailey was fourteen minutes off, lit a smoke, slouched where I sat.

"Good boy, Trevor," I said, mocking, but then, like I was a father figure assuring myself, said "No, no, it was what you had to do."

Rubbed my eyes some smoke'd wormed into, stood and stretched to tip toes, flicked cigarette, only half gone, to the tracks, lit another.

Found I'd got thinking of Norman—him staring across at me his apartment, me my knees scooping up the money he'd thrown like a handful of dry dog food on the floor—

and I whispered "Good boy, Trevor, really. Let her be her bag of money"

***

The Akerman was of course just where the Akerman always was and I sleepwalked the same exact path, most likely, always I did, even turned eyes over lot—spot where cop car normally sat, no cop car sat, window of Corinna's room blinds done as always—but it seemed cankerous now, just a sore but not a threat.

The fatigue in me up the stairwell, a group of three overweight men passing me on their way down, was so extreme I decided to lay to sleep on my floor, was there, thoughtless, maybe a minute or maybe most of the evening, came awake though on the sofa in a mechanical seize, patted for cigarettes which there weren't any, made my way to the kitchen to see from the stove clock I had an hour before I should be to the burger place, or I could just head over, straight away.

Drank from my hands from the bathroom sink, back to the kitchen saw money, rough lump of it, the kitchen floor, took it up without counting, shoved it down my pockets, left.

The staff the burger place apologized the ovens were down, pointed they'd just made me my usual thing but it was cold, all of which confused me but I nodded a vague Thanks, ate while they finished the general work, turned out the lights. While I ate I was too conscious of the slosh of my chewing and of the click of my jaw I couldn't get gone no matter how I manipulated my mouth to eat.

I didn't clean a thing, hardly imagined there'd be any noticeable difference—I did toss the already gathered and tied trash bags into the three quarter filled dumpster, touching myself all over again for smokes the moment I hit outside air, skunked my way back inside with venom at the reminder there were still none, it seemed a direct insult.

Woke on my sofa again, it was already afternoon, had the sensation I'd not gone to work, absolutely knew I had at the same time. Ate two of the burger rolls I'd swiped a bag of and brewed a pot of the cheap ground coffee I'd filled a take away bag with. Stood in the shower, only the flimsiest thoughts of my situation holding up a moment, flopping, sulking down the drain with the water that left me halfclean at best, who knows considering the last of the cake of soap'd been used up just to lather my underarms.

Eighty-two dollars and coins was what I had it was impossible, but there it was—and doing some faint calculations meant to relieve myself that my situation wasn't so grave, provided I was left alone by Corinna, an honest anxiety started.

I was only receiving forty per week now for the cleaning job, so my rent wasn't covered. Even if I lived on literally nothing, I'd have to dip in the eighty to keep afloat, ten dollars a week. My debt, at ten dollars a week, it'd take coming up on a year to get even. The thought of finding a grift to pull, anything, it was too much to bear if it was necessity—if stealing was needed to sustain me the balance was off. That—though I tried not to think about it—and the fact that I was dead caught over everything, same as if Corinna'd made an accusation against me, over everything I'd ever done if I so much got nabbed trying to slip baggage off the cart the train station, the turnbelt some airport.

I should never've paid, I thought, no energy and thinking it I moved to the window, touching the blinds to one side two fingers have a look out. Midafternoon, snake-tooth sunny, saw Corinna's door, like another, was propped open, her windows open full, same as another room, watched both until I saw the movement of the two foreign ladies on cleaning staff step out Corinna's, light up smokes. It was the bed sheets smoothed out, hit with freshener, quick once through to make sure nothing was left stuffed in a pillow, under mattress, hour long air out that served, as far as I'd ever been able to tell, as the new vacancy cleaning for the motel—something as often as not, time I'd been here, seemed was left off entirely, that only if a guest stayed more'n a week would they bother much.

I stared, chewing on the knuckle of bent thumb, working it into the space of my missing tooth, pressing it into the jags of the two neighbor teeth then sucking on it once it hurt.

Cop car wasn't down there any more, either. Clicked a look was I sure it was Corinna's room, but yes I was and had been.

Away from the window, took another burger roll out of the bag, downed new coffee, cooled a bit with water from the tap, couldn't exactly figure how this had gone on so quickly. Good job was, I suppose it meant I was left alone—she'd scampered with the money and maybe it didn't mean anything the cop car wasn't there, right now, it wasn't always there. Or I suppose she could've been arrested, but figured that'd make the room, at least a day, a crime scene, added to which where'd the arrest've been made, not her room?

Thought ambled through my mind that the cop car not being there could be my good friend was out digging up the gun from wherever, getting ready to come get me, but this, again, didn't make any sense—she'd have to plant it here, my room, which was an easy enough thing to manage, or else what'd it have to do with me?

Convictionless, made a search around, cabinets, under things, normal places someone'd think to hide a gun, then clevered out a few places else I might tuck something if I really needed to keep a gun after using it.

Nothing.

Or say she'd somehow rented a locker or something under my name? That'd never work though—and I swung my arms around what was I thinking? She was gone. I was just irritated by it. There was nothing left to do, to leverage, to imagine. She took my money and left, never coming back, now I couldn't really leave if I wanted, because the best bet I had, pathetic it was, was the Akerman—room, job, weather it, figure something out.

I was eating another roll, swallowed rough, the bread doughy, sticking to teeth and wedging up under between lips and gum, decided I needed to cut it out with eating, save these things—I could handle getting food and all, free meal and steal some rolls beside, but couldn't do it so much the theft'd go noticed, would need to ration.

Jesus, I sighed, shaking my face, unable to remember the last time anything in the world'd seemed so sour as me.

Well dark, I left for the burger place, again, Corinna's room door closed, but curtains opened—I gave a little nod, tried to make out my reflection but the light wasn't so that there was one.

Kept my eye on the spot the cop car'd park, straight glare, whole time I made my way through the lot, but it wasn't there—just a spill of dim light, almost green, from one of the bulbs each corner the Akerman office, light showed some dead insects, general rubbish, cigarettes stubs, and something I saw looked like a coin but when I went for a bend it was the tab a soda can under the remaining slop of a dead leaf.

***

Finished up mopping, took a seat, determining fully I wasn't going to do anything else, even if they came in, the light of day showed the place a mess, this just couldn't fit me anymore, nothing to be done. Spread myself out in a booth, watched out the window the cold light of the gas station shut down the night, could tell the wind was picking up from the frequency of peculiar shadows shot every direction things winking past the various hanging lights the station lot.

It was a bad idea to stick around, as much as there was probably nothing to worry about—not knowing the fallout of things, even where Corinna and the cop were, I'd never get right in my head and why live inside a loaded gun? I had money enough a bus ticket, or anyway could get a few bucks, enough the ticket combining in what I had on me with selling off the worthless clothes I still had in storage, could get someplace new, be derelict until I could figure something out.

I tugged the mop bucket out back, poured the used water, left the bucket in the storage room the toilet and gathered up the trash, all left neat and tidy for me. Noticed in one bag there were newspapers, probably the owner's, so when I opened the back, threw away the trash, I kept this bag and tore into it, same time scanning the ground for cigarette stubs—I'd been distracted enough to've gone without smoking all day, but it was on me hard now, I was having trouble from keeping my head rolling, feet always heel to toe or else just heel grinding or tap tap tap in place if I sat.

Papers were wet from coffee, stained from mustard or something, didn't so much matter to me though, I arranged them out—two weren't local, wouldn't do me any good, the third was the Sentinel I always saw the stands for, street advertisements, signs up you could rent out slots the bus stops you gave the Sentinel a call, put up some ad, a service it seemed no one much thought was a bright idea, only ad ever up being the ad for ad space.

No idea what else I expected, only bit I found about what went down the Akerman was thin quarter column, bottom of a page—same page spent a full box, two photos, on a story about the vandalism to the front window a strip mall shoe store. The gist was an arrest'd been made in the death of Arnold Houghton—seemed a young man, unnamed, from Alemore West, wherever that was, had done the deed on account of Arnold being the steady boyfriend of the woman he was having a step out on his own wife and kid with.

So, that was that—could translate well enough the woman was Corinna, figured the young man must've been whoever's car that was those time, probably more times than I knew. No telling what was what, actually, considering of course the guy didn't do it and Corinna's gun she'd put the hard word to me with must've been what'd hung him up.

I reminded myself, saying it aloud, I didn't really care and now it was nothing to do with me.

Except thinking to leave out the door—maybe not even back to my room before taking off for keeps—the thing wasn't shut off in my head. Corinna had my money, off she'd gone, so what in Christ was the point in putting this kid she'd been seeing over a hump? Especially since he hadn't done it, on top he had a life his own, he'd raise some fuss about his innocence, which'd just bring the world back down on Corrina.

The puzzle of it, mattered to me or not, was a balm, I relaxed, sat on the cold pavement out back, again, with my legs out—it wasn't even I was thinking how'd this turn around against me still, it was just fixation, hungry and tired.

Must've been she'd thought it was a good idea to have the crime over and done with, figured whatever evidence she could plant on the fellow'd be enough to get her out of it anyway. Paper said she'd been Arnold's lover—different song than she sang, but suppose she could change her voice to hit those notes it served her—so Arnold's her steady fella, the boy-toy she has on the side wants more quality time with her, does Arnold in, boy-toy either tells her or else she puts two and two together, however she wants to spin it, and she turns him in herself.

I was nodding.

And my money paid off whoever it was had witnessed things otherwise and got Corinna traveling money into the bargain.

Except—I was still nodding—that didn't make sense.

I stood, pretended to laugh, told myself not to apply to the academy any time soon, following this wise crack up with the fact I didn't understand was all the more reason to leave without even locking the door behind me—this arrested guy gets a chance to air his side, more investigating has to start, how long until my door Seven H gets the knock and my benefactor has to put more questions to me? How long until Corinna realizes that swell as it was of me giving her money for nothing, she can still make life just as bad for me I don't do whatever else she asks.

And just as my mind was turning to what a cold poison Corinna was, meaning I couldn't help but admire her in the rhetorical—another chuckle at myself for that word, there—got stuck about thinking of my door getting knocked on. Cop called me 'Seven H,' I always about called him piss off, never called him anything, just some cop.

Lifted myself over the lip the dumpster to take the paper back up, brought it inside, sat back to the booth. Article told that in the yesterday early morning detectives Chris Stans and Scott Howard'd made an arrest of a young man from Alemore West in the murder of Arnold Houghton at the Akerman Apartments—no mention the motel portion of the name—and then went on the two choppy paragraphs after the same as before.

Physical evidence obtained in the home of the Alemore West man, paper said, but I didn't care, eyes back to the detectives. Didn't understand a thing any better than before, except the name was Scott. Put my hands through my pockets, only thing in them what was left of my money—letter Corinna'd left under my door in my storage unit—so I stared at the printed 'Scott' in doubt, thinking maybe that wasn't the name in the letter, but it was.

Car pulled in at the closed gas station, obese woman got out, tried the door, could hear the crack of her swearing and flatting palm to the glass, watched her trod back to the still open car door, yelling at whoever was in there, car pulled away.

But it was like I couldn't get my eyes back down from the window to the paper, anything, just stared.

Say it was Scott, same Scott—said all this at the window glass, trailing off into just thinking it but tight like I was still talking—what'd been the thing with her writing him out a confession, he's a cop all along, not exactly one to be friendly with her way of handling whatever it was Arnold'd put her through?

Letter given to me'd been to get me to pay, obviously it'd never been delivered to anyone, but if had been it'd've been to him—things went inside out for Corinna, she wanted to unburden herself proper to someone and that someone was detective Scott—forgot his last name, didn't recheck—and I was not only too worn down to get why, also didn't see it much made a difference about what letter was to me now. Really, didn't even know if it was what I wanted it to be, but felt myself smile hard enough up one side that eye shut.

***

Though there would've been someone there anytime, felt it better to wait until middle of the day to head up to the window of the Akerman office, shift most likely someone, when they did come to window, would have to be awake enough, in general, they might put up with some question outside of the normal run.

Got some rest up in my room after a long shower, lukewarm, each minute feeling less to do with anything, my purpose in Corrina's game done. My part in the cop's game, too, thought crossed my mind—and though I tried to dismiss it with telling myself 'Think straight, he'd just been doing his job, putting his questions to me, and only reason he wasn't around anymore was because case was closed,' I knew this shoved in awkward.

He must've known. Known about the planted gun. Known it'd been Corinna'd done the thing. He must've been helping her as best he could.

It was just why would he've been?

And if he already knew the shot from bang to bang, what'd been all of this in Corinna's letter—the thing'd been wrote like it was telling him the news, but he knew it from way back.

All of this enough to get me antsy, needing movement, I made a once around the apartment, found nothing worth bothering with, drank a handful of water and downed the stairs, crossed the lot the office. Said 'Rent' into the little intercom, waited for maybe two minutes it opened, some chewed lollipop stick thin woman, tan the color of rust, asked me which was my room, was I motel, was I apartment.

"I'm apartment, but look, just realized I still need to cash my check."

Her eyes got a muddy impatience, but I pressed on, asking her did she know whether or not the cop that always hung around—I pointed to the side, to where he was always parked and she rolled her eyes, nodding—left a card or some number to get in touch with him.

"There another murder to report?"

She wasn't being cute, but I smiled, said it was just I had something I wanted to tell him, nothing bad, and figured it'd be easier than tracking down his precinct or whatever and being routed around. She was already opening a ledger, didn't care what I was saying, cut in on me with did I have a pen. I hadn't, so she snapped a Post-It note off one of three pads I could see, stuck it on the sill that served as counter, set down a pen and turned the ledger around.

Detective Scott Howard, I copied off the card that was stuck in the ledger page with invisible tape, very careful to get the telephone number correct, even asked the woman could she read it off one last time I turned the ledger around to her, handing it back.

"Do you think you can answer me one more thing?"

"Depends."

I could tell she meant that fatally, wet my lips like I was considering was my question so important, after all, but being light with it, nonchalant, then asked "There was a woman, Corrina Eastbridge, she lived in the motel down there, just moved out, right?"

Woman moved like she was going to shut up the window in my face, said "I can't tell you anything about people."

"No no, I get that. I'm not asking anything, you know, not really asking anything."

"Then what are you asking?"

Her look was so severe, I reached into my pocket and came out with some money, jumble of it looked like kids' lunch money. I said, holding up twenty dollar bill "All I need to know is had she lived the Akerman a long time? I don't need to know where'd she gone, I'm not looking for anything other than had she been long term?"

Woman didn't consult any ledger, nothing like that, took the twenty dollars off me and told me "Yeah, Corinna's been here a long time."

"Thanks." I stood nodding, woman just staring at me, hard to make up my mind had I just handed her twenty dollars for no reason or did I trust her she was being upfront. "Can I ask one more thing?"

"I thought you weren't asking anything."

"I'm not really."

I held up another twenty, but she'd started in while I did with "Seems to me you're asking about the police, you're asking about Corinna and there's been something going on about that around here. Maybe it seems you really are asking me something."

"I'm not," I said, tapping the air with the twenty, tensing my jaw but trying to look like it didn't matter. "I just wanted to know if you maybe could tell me about did she used to live in the apartments—back before, like did she live there once, maybe transfer down the motel or something?"

"Is that all?"

"That's all." But she kept her eyes trained on me, long

enough it got awkward, realized when she widened them she'd been referring to the twenty dollars she still hadn't taken. "That's all, yeah—until payday, you know? Not asking this costs more than not asking the other thing?"

"Seems you're more interested in not getting an answer about this."

"Right," I chuckled, pushed tongue hard to the roof of my mouth and, still casual charm as much as I could, put another ten with the twenty.

She took the money, said she'd double check, but that she was fairly certain Corrina'd lived in the apartments a long time, growing up, that maybe there'd been a span she'd lived somewhere else, but then had taken the motel room—maybe not even a span, though, maybe just the move the one to the other.

Watched the woman go to a filing cabinet, poke around in it, no idea what was all that about since I'd never filled in so much as a form to get my room, but maybe something'd been different back when the place was legitimate—either way, she peeked in some folder, not even taking it out, stood and told me that Corinna'd lived in the apartments, yes, but she wasn't telling me anything else about anything, adding that this shouldn't bother me seeing as I wasn't asking her anything, anyway.

I'd intended to give a Thanks, at least, a cute retort if I could manage it, but she closed up the window and I headed out of the lot, around the corner, walking fast in the direction of the nearest shopping plaza.

I didn't even think about it, not about anything, bought a pack of cigarettes from the drug store, asked for two books of matches, they didn't give books of matches told them Never mind then, bought a lighter from the little stand set up, bought a chocolate bar, as well.

Out in front, leaning to a wall by the trashcans, I ate the

chocolate in three bites, was chewing the overflowing mash of it in my mouth, getting plastic from the cigarette pack off, slapping pack to palm, had one lit by the time I hadn't even swallowed.

Cigarette down me tasted like me, harsh but easy to breathe, the tiptoe giddiness of the first rise of the high before the smokes would become background, sludge, blood, had me tight and smiling and just my right color.

***

The tone of Corinna's letter still confused me, something between writing to an old friend and to a current lover, but when I thought maybe she'd figured I'd known this Scott was Detective Scott it made cleaner sense, at the time'd been her way of showing me both that she could turn the tables around on me and how. In fact, I kind of felt an idiot thinking back on Corinna threatening me—she must've been under the impression I'd known she meant she'd have Scott on her side about finding the planted evidence, whole time I'd just caved at the loosest version of her threat.

Lit a cigarette off another, chuffing down my nose that, really, I'd've caved threat or not, she could've threatened me with anything.

Shut up my storage unit, had the long walk back to the nearby town and made one photocopy the letter, only, thinking maybe I'd even only copy one page, save myself a few cents, then had the long walk back to tuck the copy Corinna'd left me with back in the unit, then the long walk back to the town wait on the cheap bus into the larger city.

It wasn't until evening, almost nightfall, I made it to the large train depot, place I could not only make my call but be indoors the night—it kept catching me off guard to think I couldn't even afford an economy seat, hardly a subway pass for that matter, because I had the feeling on me that another advantage of the depot was if I got creeped too bad I could just disappear, be a country length away from any of this in a few day's time or blot myself out into the landscape anyplace in between.

Made a few trips to and from the toilet between trying to linger through two cigarettes at a time, ration them out, in the toilet wetting my hair, slicking it, trying to change the part with my fingers, no success, trying to push it all the way back, flat it all the way forward, something it just stayed how it was, no matter what.

There we telephones everywhere, but I used one on the lower level, the few food stands and shops closing up, clack of a few luggage bags being trailed, an odd hush that made me feel I might be asked to leave, though same time saw an old man reading newspapers, had a stack like he hadn't moved all day, at one of the tables, three chairs turned upside down on it, the one he was sitting on the only chair not that way in the plaza, in fact.

Tapped my forehead on the cold of the two prongs of the cradle, dial tone in my ear, clunked my coin in as slowly as I could manage, already my rehearsed bits slipping out of my thoughts. It was unexpected, the call went straight to a voice mail almost immediately after I'd dialed the final number—I bolted up, awake, sat back, hung the phone and heard my coin swallowed, flop onto others in the belly of the phone case.

Pressing in and rubbing hard my forehead with the knuckle of a curled forefinger, put cigarette, unlit, to my mouth and head went in tense twitches like I'd be giving myself either a pep talk or a dressing down, but wordless, just twitching at a telephone a train depot.

Lit smoke, new coin down, dialed and waited through

guy's voice saying how if I needed something urgent I could dial separate number for the precinct and that if there was an emergency I should consider calling the normal emergency number—odd message, made me worried this was not a personal phone he carried on him, like calls might be routed somewhere else—hung up again.

But what did I care it routed somewhere else?

New coin in—three actually, had run out of single coins enough to do the call their own—dialed and tucked phone to shoulder with my ear, one hand pulling cigarette away for a breath out, other one a claw scratching at my chest, arm up underneath of my shirt fabric.

Message finished, three electronic tones, waited a beat then said Hi Scott—this is Terrance, you remember you got me job at—name slipped my mind—burger place? Really appreciate that still. But hey, actually calling about something a bit more pressing, if you catch my drift, about that thing we talked about a few times. Something kind of important, I'd even say really urgent, has come around to my attention, so I need you to know I'm gonna give you a call tomorrow, noon, one o'clock but I can't call later than that. It's really important you take the call, man, and this is the only number I've got to reach you. I mean really important, like otherwise I might have to find someone else to tell about what I know, if you catch my drift.

I fumbled over how to end the call, finally just hung up, face a snarl thinking about the ten seconds of odd silence he'd wait through before the thing clicked off he listened.

And burst out laughing—laughing at myself—even hit my thigh, hard, then leaned elbow down on it, still sitting in the little portioned area of my phone.

No one else was going to screen the calls and so now Christ knew what I'd sounded like—maybe he wouldn't even catch my drift, and then I'd be completely over it, have to find another way to contact only he'd have wind I was looking around for him.

Laughed more, but fake now, not even morose like the previous blat.

It just didn't matter—the letter in my pocket, keeping it from being entirely comfortable for me to sit, just didn't mean anything.

Now I was sitting here waiting to make another call—and I would need to leave if it got much past one o'clock next day, I'd just not be able to take it. This in mind, I wandered out the street, thinking I probably could scrounge up enough from selling the clothes I had, maybe swipe a piece of luggage or two the depot, just enough to get a ticket together, be on my way.

Went into an all-night drugstore, not even thinking to steal, really, but immediately felt myself clam up like the cuffs had my arms around tight up behind my back. Pathetic, I stared into the soda case, the frozen pizzas, the chips, the magazines, thinking I needed just to take something, prove I still understood that I could.

In an aisle with picture frames, film, photo albums all along one side, the other side, right by the shoe polish and all, there were various packages of cigarillos—not in any case or behind the counter, just there—and I took up three packs, six cigarillos in each, wandered back in the direction the magazines.

From what I could tell, it was only mirrors up to keep the place safeguarded, and this hour it was the same guy stocking the shelves as running the till, or maybe someone else was in the office, too, would be out in awhile, but doubted if they were in there it was to monitor security cameras, if there were any.

Slipped the three packages, all at once, down tight my pant pocket, stood there, eyes unfocused on the page of some film magazine, then realized I honestly was reading the article, actually finished it and put the magazine calmly down, walked over to the guy stockings shelves, put it to him did he know if the place was hiring. He didn't think so, told him Thanks and he said maybe it would be best if I tried back in the morning, he could leave my name if I liked.

***

Good job about train depots is nobody bothers you much about sleeping overnight, provided you're gone by morning, the commuters start filing in—or even then no one really rushes you out with a broom, they just take note, maybe direct you someplace else for a few hours if they can tell you're derelict, no ticket to show for yourself.

I woke stretched long across a pew in the main waiting area, far corner, like a crumb in the crease of a cathedral, woke and stared at the skylight, listening to the hectic mess of noise get thicker and thicker, finally stood to get water on my face when the bustle hit peak, figured noon must be coming on.

It was raining outside, which struck me off because I hadn't been able to tell from the skylight, not even that it was going to be overcast. Lit one of the cigarillos, but like the two I'd spent down before passing out, there was something off about the whole rhythm of it, and I was only tentatively taking any smoke in my lungs, unsure if it was safe to do, if it would double me over.

Tangle of hunger up me, took handful of packs of crackers from the salad bar one of the station restaurants, headed down to the lower level—just as packed as the upper—took a seat at my same phone, three others in the line occupied, but nothing to be done about that.

Dabbing the cigarillo out in the coin return, I put in money and dialed, realizing I never had checked the time—head still fogged, wanting more sleep, more food—but didn't so much suppose it mattered.

Straight away in my ear were the words "This Terrance?"

"This is Terrance. This Scott?" I had a pointless grin and was shouldering the wall like I wanted a cuddle from a half asleep lover, also using shoulder top to scratch my ear. "Hello?"

"This is Scott, Terrance. What exactly can I do for you?"

The trick of his voice, he really sounded busy with something else, like taking the call was him humoring me maybe I needed another favor off him or something, hard to get footing so I just butted ahead with "Did Corinna ever tell you how she got me to pay her, what she did to get me around to doing that?"

I was braced for him to play pretend what was I talking about, make believe the part in case he was being recorded or something, but just as off putting as his first tone of voice, now he straight said "No, Terrance, she did not. And nor did I ask. And nor do I care."

"How's that work, all the while you're a policeman?" No response a minute, then I went on. "You'll change your mind, probably, I tell you. She wrote me a letter—wrote you a letter, but slipped it under my door. Love letter, in a way, but the kind where she confesses she killed someone and that gosh she just wants her old flame Scott to understand—only person she wants to understand in case things veer Southward, get what I mean?"

Letting out heavy breath, he said "I think so."

"You want I could read you some of it, some turns of phrases I like especially?"

"You don't need to read it."

Now I paused—his last sentence an absolute blank got

me off track, asked rather than told him "You didn't know she wrote it?"

"I didn't know. I didn't know anything about it."

"Interesting thing, I have to say, in it she mentions I gave her a gun, that she figured she'd got rid of it, then I show up with it, put it to her she's going to play kitty on all fours in heat whenever I fell like she should, and that she couldn't bear it, being used again, was going to turn herself in. Lot of things, really, it goes on. But then it turns out, in reality, that it's case closed, she didn't kill anyone—did I read that right in the papers?"

"What do you want Terrance?"

Couldn't help myself snapping at him, I was leaned forward, shushing the back of my free hand against my cheek while I spoke, words growing quieter but sharp, bricks crosswise against bricks. "Am I boring you?" No point my saying that, clenched my toes, had to wait on him responding with 'I just want to get to the thing' before I could press on, redirect back to where I'd been going before the growl. "The thing is your childhood sweetie took a lot of what was mine—screw, I'll be straight with you, she took everything that was mine, you understand the extent I'm angry right now—and I'm going to need you to get it back my way or else a lot of people will have their hands on this letter and not so much as two of them would need to be the curious sort to open up a whole lot of questions about What does it mean? Me, I'll be in the breeze and even if I'm not, you get any idea try something funny, copies of the letter get out to everyone, I've got a scheduled pick-up and I'm not there to stop it off they go—do you follow all of this?"

"Why don't you come have a drink with me?"

It was a sad, but oddly friendly, way the question came out, but didn't fluster me this time, told him I'd prefer it we just kept to the matter at hand and not have to give each other dirty looks, on top.

"Well, I'm just around the corner and I'd really prefer to have a drink with you, we'll get this settled."

Neck tensed, hurt to turn it but I scanned the din of people at the eatery tables, looking for someone lingering, particularly giving me the eye or particularly trying not to.

Must've been staring longer than I'd meant to, Scott came back in my ear and said "It's just me, I didn't bring anyone else—you're at the depot, right? I'm just down the street, I have a booth a place called Salazar's, corner pub by the little clothes boutique, you'll see it—out the main entrance, block down."

Weak, I'd let him have his whole piece off before clearing my throat, said "I'm hanging up," but didn't, felt myself cramp like I'd needed to piss for three hours.

"It's just me, Terrance, alright? I just want to get off the phone. I agree we have some things to talk about, it's not going to do me any good to have you picked up, right?"

"No it isn't." I tried a tug of tough guy, but chest felt like kid who's mom'd just slapped the dinner table, told him Eat.

"I'm hanging up, Terrance. Get yourself together, have a smoke, I've got a booth toward the back, you'll see me."

He hung up. I shut my eyes while he did, but had to open them I got dizzy and somehow felt I'd lost footing, tensed to catch myself though I hadn't moved to stand.

Wriggled a cigarillo out of my pocket, leaned to wall and lit it between four different strikes of my lighter, thumb raw from not being used to using one for so long, hurt to keep the flame held up. When I turned my head up, saw the old man with all the newspapers—still same place as the night before, now with coffee one hand, half sandwich the other—looking at me, not shying away when our eyes locked, it was me turned head down, stood and headed for the stairs.

On the way up, got in mixed behind a slow young couple having some sort of friendly debate—I just didn't want to change path to get around them, was in no hurry, and cigarillo'd gone out by top step due to my lack of interest in it.

***

Salazar's was busier than I'd've imagined for the time of day and weather, but not so much I had any trouble at all seeing Scott at his booth, deep in back—the moment I walked in and got an eye of him he was busy reading the menu, as though earnestly considering just what might hit the spot. A hostess asked me how many in my party, I just finger-pistol pointed back in Scott's direction, she told me enjoy and that some woman named Cynthia was the server off in that section.

Scott got sight of me just as I was sitting down, kind of playful double take at my all of a sudden lumping myself down the booth corner, one leg draped out full its length.

"What would you like to drink?" he asked, touching two fingers to the lip of the empty glass in front of him.

"I don't think I need to be here that long."

"Have a drink," he said, pointing, getting the waitress' attention, his other finger pointed at me in a kind of fish flap while he explained I'd like a drink.

So, I asked for a double shot of bourbon, found it a little funny she didn't ask me to specify a brand, noted Scott was nodding approvingly while he pointed at his own empty, gave me quick lick of smile.

I took the letter out of my pocket, meantime, set it on the table in front of him. "None of this seems to be upsetting you," I said, slow, even wary, tapped the envelope for emphasis then leaned back into a pile, again.

He held up a finger, waitress back with the drinks already—his the same as mine and she took his empty—held up his glass like I was to give him a clink and said "To Corrina." He waited a second while I neither touched glass nor repeated the toast, downed his while I didn't do anything, then I set mine down.

"She seems a fine gal and all, it's just I don't see I'd go putting my career on the line on account of her figure or anything, planting evidence at her behest, but that might, I admit, just be me."

He'd started slowly shaking his head while I'd said all that, long move of his tongue over his lips and a look into his empty glass like willing a mouthful back in there—I almost offered him mine—then when I stopped talking, he looked at me straight on, told me he hadn't planted any evidence.

"I know you've got enough of an idea and something that can cause a real mess" he tapped the envelope, acknowledging it for the first time "but we don't need to pretend like you've solved the puzzle, Terrance, and you don't need to waste time guessing any more letters, alright?"

Made a face, blew air down my nose, but also rolled my head and after a sigh said "Sure thing, Scott, sure thing. And you're right, I think we can move to matters more pressing—you want to give that a read?"

"Your summary, before, was fine, Terrance, I get the point. What exactly is it you think I can do for you?"

"I think you can pay me some money down, something to even out my temper."

"How much money is that?"

Stared at him, eyes narrowing tight like they were one

straight line across the two of them. "I'm not in the mood for your cute act, Scott, you wouldn't be here if you didn't know just what the thing was." But in his face I could tell everything was all cross wires, got nervous now if I said the wrong thing it might betray I didn't have so much the upper hand I thought, which itself was hardly an upper hand at all. "It's five thousand dollars."

His eyes widened "She got the whole five out of you?"

Knew a look confusion and curiosity was all over me, didn't care, shrugged shoulder up and scratched my nose to give myself a clean transition into "She did, she did just that."

"You had five thousand dollars?"

"Well, doesn't everybody?"

"And you gave it to her?"

Downed my drink, rubbed my forehead while I swallowed hard, then abruptly looked down the barrel of him, snapped my fingers, lips tight to snarl. "Good talking to you, too, detective, blah blah and all of it—now tell me how you're going to have my feelings feeling better, tell me just how you're going to do that."

"I can't get you five thousand dollars any more than I could get it to Corinna, Terrance."

Nodding nodding, said, not without irritation coming through "Well I more than take your point on that, officer, and seeing as time is of the essence and everyone shares a common screw, here, I'm making today chock full of discounts—you can get this clog out of your drain for half price."

"I can't do that."

Didn't even let him finish, went right overtop "I'm going to leave this table with you having told me where I can pick up the money, otherwise I'm going to leave this table with a violent urge to tattle-tale."

"I can get you one thousand, Terrance."

I tensed up—he was standing, he was shifting and standing up from the table, but I couldn't think of anything to say to keep him there.

"I can get one thousand dollars for you. And I think we all understand each other that this is the best any of us are going to get out of things. You think about it—give me a call by this time tomorrow if you're interested or else just split, take off, I sure won't come looking for you on any account."

He took out his wallet, dropped two twenty dollar bills on the table.

"I tell you you could stand up, we're done here, sometime I wasn't paying attention to myself?"

But he didn't even register I'd spoken, just finished out his piece with "I don't hear from you in twenty-four hours, Terrance, I'm taking that to mean I have to take my own precautions, which I am perfectly capable of. Corrina'll have to understand that, only so much I can do."

I watched him leave the place, not even so much as look back at me, took me a full two minutes to turn my head from the door, when I did noticed the copy of the letter I'd put to him was still sitting there. I brought the envelope across and though I could tell just from fingers pressing it either side, took the pages out, to be sure he hadn't taken those and only left the envelope.

Quickly took the forty dollars off the table, ducked it in my pocket, craned head around until I got waitress' attention. Pointed at my drink, she nodded.

Noticing the toilets were just there beyond the booth, off to the left, I stood and got in the men's room, to the sink mirror. Not surprised—I was even amused—that the expression my face was a gargle of baffled, anxious, like dog that'd been kicked, saw boot raised and'd tensed but the next blow'd not yet come. Opened the faucet, but closed it right away, got two fingers wet enough off the basin to wipe at my lips, tongue then touching out against salt.

My refreshed drink was there at the table, I took it standing, this time in two shorter mouthfuls, set down the empty and set a coaster on top, making a clear show of getting a cigarillo out and to my lip—waitress happened to see me, so I pointed from cigarillo to the door, gave her a thumbs up gesture to which she nodded, and I also pointed to my empty, again, to which she nodded double nod.

***

Sat at one of the long benches facing the main line of cashier windows the bus terminal portion of the depot, giving last puff to the cigarillo I then extinguished, certain my next move would be to the kiosk I could see, pack of cigarettes, book of matches. There were buses, tour buses mostly, I could afford, buses that could get me more than far enough away, this could be finished. Stared at the prices, eyes ticking between the bottom two listed a particular tour, knowing all but for certain I wasn't leaving.

If it'd been on Scott's mind to do something to me, he would've done it, any last niggle of doubt I had about that was thinning to flat—even if he'd wanted to meet with me it in mind to get an idea just what exactly did I know or did I not, one, he'd not even read the letter and two, he hadn't exactly chit chatted enough to be certain I'd not been playing the fool to flip the same trick back around on him.

He'd give me the money.

He'd give me the money, the thousand, which was more than I'd need.

Lighting the first of the fresh pack of cigarettes, walking

down some random block just for motion, sense of detachment, invisibility, it didn't seem bad at all, starting up again—the money in my pocket could get me crumby bus wherever, I'd have one thousand in my pocket to get temporarily set, wouldn't even have to dust off some receipt grift, nimble up for pickpocketing, nothing. I'd been feeling under the thumb of everything when I'd shown up the Akerman, never even bothered much about finding work, but I could find work enough I felt I wanted to, enough to get a similar set up going as I had the Akerman, if not a better one, could rent a room a house, share an apartment, all of those things I'd done before, set myself up nice as well as that.

"It's not like there's a way to angle one red cent more out of the thing," I muttered, tired of walking, leaning to the wall of a steep hill beside a bookstore, view of an artificial canal, some tourist little paddle boat tour passing by.

And it was true, for all I knew, in fact Scott'd be in the mood to change his mind any second, maybe figure out just how bluster I was, have himself a laugh by telling me he'd drop the money, then just not.

Though it'd be my show, I'd be the one telling him where the money was to be and when—don't know why I had it the other way around in my head, this clarity making me feel lighter.

He wanted to keep Corinna clear of everything, that much was obvious, so I doubted he'd be planning a bust, setting me up—probably true he could take precautions to keep himself out of trouble, but it'd seemed he'd said it with regret. *Corinna'll have to understand that.* Like Scott was so understanding of her letter—she'd had to do whatever she'd had to do, play whatever angle, he'd have to do likewise.

I had a picture in my mind saw Scott would've given her the five grand, whatever she'd needed, just honestly he couldn't—wife'd notice the bank withdrawal, or someone would, no criminal consequences, just consequences to his life, or even possible criminal consequences later, something he wouldn't let hang over him.

Kind of a joke that I'd had five thousand to give, cop a steady job didn't just due to circumstances, except not as funny considering it was every last stich of me and I'd had to beg half-thousand of it between strangers.

Maybe it was even Scott'd offered Corinna one thousand, she'd not taken him up on it right away because he'd told her it was last ditch offer and she'd marked me or they'd marked me together as someone to milk—Jesus, I felt a mental cripple it only just now hitting me really there'd never been anyone else blackmailing her, just crocodile tear nonsense to feel me out, get the depth of me, what'd I have to hide since everyone the Akerman had something.

And I was so forthcoming, as Scott'd told me, shooting my mouth off, thinking I'd a perch above Corinna'd I'd given away more of myself not thinking than I could even give away I tried to set it down five paragraph essay for someone.

"Jesus," I spit the word out, flicking a just lit cigarette into the street, then telling myself shut up, didn't even know what I was talking about. Just like Scott'd said, I was pest enough he'd pay me but I didn't know what in hell was happening and by this late in the day found it didn't matter, either.

What could it possibly matter to me, any of it?

I'd gotten lazy, sloppy, I'd let my guard down, forgotten who I was and stepped in it both feet, pants down.

"So what?" I said, starting to walk again, as standing in place I was finding it harder to keep my thoughts internalized, would wind up jabbering there same as some hobo.

Crossed the street to get to the phones outside a gas station, two of the three out of service—receivers not even there, in one case a cord, minus receiver, at least dangled, in the other case just nothing—the dial tone of the one I lifted faint, but I dropped coin in, pressed a finger down to ear not at the phone after dialing number from quick reference Post-It note, Scott coming on immediately.

"What's going on?" he said as though in a group of people, or maybe I perceived it that way due to how anemic his voice was, like the only volume this phone could manage was half sheet paper thick.

"I'll take the thousand," I said.

He asked "What?" and I got worried the reception was just as bad, his end of things, but when I repeated it he said "I gotcha," reinforcing my thought he was in company.

"I'll take the thousand," I said a third time, nothing else coming to mind. This time he responded "Absolutely" and I, clenching my jaw just because this whole call seemed degrading to me, some reason, said "I'll call you in the morning, early, with the how and where, so be around, right?"

He didn't respond and I guess took me not saying anything further as signifying we were through, hung up before I did, me leaving this phone dangling off the hook, head down, moving away from it faster than I probably needed to.

Went into a fast food restaurant, some franchise I'd never been in before, ordered chicken sandwich turned out I couldn't stand two bites of, sat with my coffee and fries, sulking in a seat underneath a mounted television playing some news program or another.

It was for the best—and made me smile—the call to Scott'd gone queer like it had, seeing as I'd not bothered coming up with the how or when he'd drop the money. Large part of me thought I'd just tell him to meet me, hand it over, but figured that wouldn't fly, would make me look up to something, besides.

Had to come up with something else, at least surface level clever, thought through, come up with something to give the appearance to him I at least cared enough to take the time or else he might get thinking I didn't much care so he didn't much see why should he, either.

***

I shut the storage unit behind me, pulling shutter closed down so that just a clipping of daylight from outside got in, crumpled immediately by the murk, sat down without pulling on the bulb overhead, closed my eyes.

The forty dollars I'd taken that Scott'd left on the table was already dripped down to just under thirty, so I decided against counting it as part of what I had—I'd start with the thousand dollars, even, if not I'd start with nothing, just couldn't stand counting halfpennies with such an empty stomach, such a bloated head, aches and anxieties. This would work or it wouldn't, I just wasn't going to embrace the part of measly little beggar.

I packed everything in tight the backpack, surprised that it wasn't even stuffed three quarter capacity. Made a careful inspection of the floor, all the way back to the wall, very glad I did because I found the crumpled Wanted poster inside the two crumpled restaurant fliers, just there, just sitting there for anyone to pick up and have a look at.

There was the first twist of nausea through me, the first click of thought about the implications of this absent-mindedness—when had I even tossed this in the corner and how could I have ever been so stupid?—but I shook my head, opening the shutter, pulling it closed behind me, scrambling combination on that part of my padlock, turning shut key and removing it after. Two steps in the direction of the office, stopped short, tensed, eyes shut they felt two bruises, turned around and put the numeric code for the lock back in, proper, put in my key just to make sure it was correct, popped the lock, shut it, took key out, left the numbers be.

Middle aged woman in the office I came through, loud car commercial the television by the circular table, three soft chairs for folks to wait around in—must've been for people transacting whatever other business this place did, couldn't see the need for chairs just for renting out a storage unit—she told me could I wait just one moment, she needed to send a fax, I told her certainly.

Went to a knee, took the envelope from the copy of Corrina's letter I'd made, put the extra key to my padlock in it, was standing, licking the adhesive V of the envelope flap when, laughing, the woman came back in, telling me she hated sending faxes, just never trusted they went anywhere, didn't understand how they were meant to work.

I shrugged, said "Search me, I'm with you on that," then asked "Hey, I rent a unit here and was wondering, I have a friend coming by, he's a policeman, a detective, I need to leave him this key, would that be alright?"

Held up the envelope, scanning around for a pen.

"He's a police officer?"

She noticed my eyes settle on the pens down on her desk, handed me one.

"He's a detective—not a uniform cop, but he'll have badge and identification. It'd be okay to leave this here for him to pick up?"

I could tell she was intrigued, not worried at all, and she reached to take the envelope without even looking at it, asked me what was the detective's name.

"It's Scott Howard," I said, giving the envelope a point, getting a shy smile and a self-deprecating head jiggle from her. "He'll be by this evening, late tonight. You could leave a note for whoever's on shift, could you, in case he can't get by until late?"

She was nodding, made a motion at me could she have the pen back. I smiled, giving it over and she immediately started writing a note. "He'll come in asking for it?"

"He will. He'll know to show his badge and all."

She was nodding, though, like this wasn't at all irregular, just a bit exotic due to the detective side of things, maybe. "And do you two have a code word?"

I loved that, huge smile across my face I just couldn't help it, was slapping cigarette pack to palm and I said "Sure do, sure we do—code word is Loverboy."

She blushed, though that was silly, repeated "Loverboy" like I'd said something kinky and I thanked her so much for her time.

Noticing a pot of coffee the corner, other side of the television, asked if a cup of it would cost me anything, she said to feel free to it and I could help myself to any of the pastries that were left, as well.

By the time I'd gotten up the road—nearest payphone in a public park I always passed on my walk to and from the storage place—the coffee'd corkscrewed down through me, had me stomached and needing to piss. Due to the placement of the phone, around in a secluded area—trees, picnic tables, grills, none of it looked hardly ever it was used—I just unzipped and relieved myself onto the cement an arc out toward the grass, took the Post-It with Scott's number out of my pocket as I zipped up.

Scott came on the line very formal, though as soon as he heard it was me his tone dropped casual, I could tell he was sipping something through a straw while I spoke. I explained that he was to show up to the storage facility, gave him the address, my unit number, the code word, explained that I'd left the combination part of my padlock with the code in and so he just needed the key I'd left at the desk to get inside the unit—he was to leave the envelope with the money on the floor in the unit, simple as that, and then was to drive away.

"Sounds good," he said and the manner was so casual I almost felt I was talking to a friend. "When do you want it by?"

"It better be in there by tonight, man, and don't think about anything cute."

"Terrance" he said my name heavy, like it wasn't even him talking anymore or else like it was the first time, right then, I was hearing his actual voice "she did tell you, you do know what Arnold did to her, don't you?"

"I'm a bit more acquainted with what she did to me, sorry to say, though I'm sure it's a three hanky story, she and Arnie. Meantime, you want to tell someone the sad truth of it all, why not give a call up that young stud you've got stitched up for the whole mess—Corinna ever tell you what he did to her? In case she didn't mention that, Scott, it's nothing, he did nothing to her and neither'd his wife or kid, into it. So let's get this perfectly clear that all you've to worry about is drop the money, I don't even want to get the feeling something else is going on and the last thing I think you'd want is to try some sweet talking me into finding my conscience, don't you think?"

Heard him let a few long breaths, but not any emotion in them, it didn't seem, pace breaths, putting a little distance between what I'd shoved on him there and what he was going to say. "I understand, Terrance, I'll get it there tonight."

He hung up on me, I could tell, but still asked "Scott?" into the mouthpiece a few times, shook my head, hung the phone back to cradle and spit in the direction of the puddle of urine I'd left.

***

The night seemed to go by without my even thinking, and by midday, buried somewhere in an offshoot town, doing nothing but walking odd lines and finding places to sit around, I began questioning whether my plan to wait until nightfall again before emptying the unit was necessary. Of course I was in no rush, but the time, the time, every inch of it I was arguing with myself that it was more likely—not less, not less likely—that something could be set up against me at the unit the longer I waited. It wasn't as though if Scott had someone else watching the unit for me to show up, keep tabs on me, they'd just scratch their foreheads, give it up when I didn't show, immediately, they'd not convince themselves I'd spirited into the facility and out around their surveillance.

I really made it all into a boogey man, lack of food and sleep grinding my bones harder with it—at one point, even thought to myself It's only one thousand dollars, is it even worth this? a question I'd answer No if not for the answer really being Yes.

It was everything, might as well be me in that unit, coffin, waiting for me to bodysnatch myself out.

Thing was, Scott was so disinterested in the letter, hadn't

read it, hadn't taken the one copy I'd made away with him, even—only sense I could find in this was a way of him playing it cool, lulling me he was just going to pay then send me on my way when all the time he was trying to get a sniff where the copies of the letter were and once he had them give me a smash, heel grind the bug of me, twist me past I was dead.

The alternative?

He took me at my word, translating to he knew I wouldn't risk burning myself down over any of this nonsense—if I got my money, I'd be gone and not come back.

"Which way do you strike me, Scott, which way do you seem?" I hummed to myself, made a tune of it like some spearmint gum jingle.

Both ways at once, that's how he struck me, worse thing, he struck me both ways, either, neither—and he was right I hadn't a fingernail dug in to what was going on with any of the moving parts, much less did I have a grip on any of the levers.

Gave up by evening, had to eat, found a family pizzeria, sat myself by the window and gorged. There were kids hanging off each other around some generic pinball machine, cussing with their parents not around, mixing the types of soda at the fountain—they wouldn't stop laughing, really seemed they wanted to screech each other like jabs, overpower each other. I let my mind drift, wondered if they were even playing pinball, if they had a coin for the machine between them.

After choking down the third mouthful of dough past too much, I groaned, moved to the pinball, asking Excuse me and dropping in a quarter, all of them gone quiet, or at least whispers, oldest one kept giving the game a nod as I played as though to show his place to the pack—if I lost a ball, he'd cuss for me, blame it on the machine, explain to the younger ones the machine was a waste of time and when I lost he asked me if I was going to play again. I told him Naw, went back to my food, they went back to their bullying each other.

Had no idea what I was doing—just wanted my money, be away, gone, have my money, be gone from all of this, find someplace to rest, hole up, didn't even care.

Bus back in the direction of the unit, got off a stop early but regretted it when I realized I was much, much further off than I'd been thinking, took an hour to walk to the start of the thin road would get me to the facility and I'd no idea how late it was when I got there.

The person working the desk in the lobby area I had to pass through seemed to wake up at the sound of the electronic buzzer of my opening the door, look of almost anger like why in hell would I be there—made me feel good though, oddly, feet nothing was set up if this poor kid humping the graveyard just wanted to be left alone.

I smoked three cigarettes, wandering the lot—if someone was watching out for me, it'd've been easy enough for them to stay hid, as wide open as the place was there were two blocks of units set in the center of the others circling around, I could wander one way, they hang back, peek around corner.

But there wasn't going to be anyone, I could tell from the air, the moisture in the air, I was alone, might as well've been unpacking worthless stuff to move back into some apartment for all anyone cared about me. Scott was nowhere, gone, whole thing behind him.

He'd scrambled the numbers on the code part of my lock, a gesture I nodded at with a chuckle, got the numbers in, key, shutter opened.

Even without the bulb on, moon was out enough I

could see the envelope where he'd tossed it—he'd tossed it, it hadn't been laid down, was almost against the wall, set at odd diagonal.

One thousand dollars.

Ten one hundred dollar bills.

I touched fingers over them, held them up for a look— far as I knew they were genuine, added in to which why wouldn't they be?

Nothing written on the envelope, nothing else inside. I turned on the bulb just a moment to see was there maybe anything, but no, just the envelope I dropped again, going to one knee, burying nine of the hundreds down under the clothes in my backpack, shoving the other in my pocket.

I got it clear enough that just the money being there all on its own meant Now get out of here, meant If I wanted to, Terrance, I could have someone follow you, make certain no letters are sent anywhere, got it all fine and almost felt chummy with Scott over it, like we read each other, knew just the limits of each other, had made a pleasant deal.

Gas station shop across the street wouldn't break any bill more than twenty, but didn't matter, all I wanted was coffee, candy bar, still had enough and got enough in change from the purchase to use the phone out in front, one I'd not noticed there before, maybe'd never looked. Got the Post-It note out, phone receiver tucked under my arm while I got a cigarette lit—occurred to me I'd no reason to call Scott and kind of blah crawled up me, inhaled, blew smoke out quick, hung up the phone.

Car pulled into the parking space right in front of the phone though the whole lot was empty, bass-line of music and mash of words shuddering through the closed windows out into the cold—I turned my back, but the headlights didn't go off, didn't go off even when I heard the car door open, someone get out, laughing drunkenly, slurring something to the several other voices still in the car. I managed one quick glimpse over my shoulder, surprised someone was sitting on the hood of the car smoking, looked away, I hoped, before they'd noticed my glance, then leaned forehead down, touched it to lip of the enclosure housed the phone.

Closed my eyes the ten more minutes—until the music behind me receded, headlights letting go of me, yawning, unwinding out and away—whole time no idea what I thought I was hiding from, just kind of felt there'd ought to be something.

***

I'd fallen asleep, few times, spurts of it at the picnic table where I'd been sitting, head down on folded arms—kicked awake at thoughts of bugs on me or at half-dreams that my backpack wasn't at my feet anymore. Stood to get my head working, watched two men out jogging stop at a water fountain, not able to make out details due to the light of the sun coming up filtering through the tree line, there, that and from my face needed a good wash before I'd see anything without some smear of fog over it—watched the men and set backpack on the table, unzipped it and dug for the nine hundred, which I put in my shoe, having a chuckle about this move but still feeling comfortable it was safest.

Did an inventory of the rest of my belongings, shedding a few scraps and receipt papers into the grass, wrapping the gun a bit more properly tight in two shirts, pair of pants around it—found rumpled bag with two more rolls from the burger place, hard as stone, gave them a weak toss out into the grass same moment around the perimeter of the lawn area sprinkles came on, louder than it seemed they ought to've been, hiss and rattle like cicada mixed with tapping sound of a rotary dial.

I started a cigarette as I opened one of the two copies of the letter Corrina'd slipped under my door, without even thinking struck a match and set it on fire, first giving the growing flame tiny breaths to stabilize it, then jogging few paces off to a grill set up for community use, tossed the now alight pages down, watched them roll and tighten and disintegrate.

Took envelope with last copy in it, struck a match, blew it out and sat, opening the pages but not reading. First was thinking did I need to keep the thing on me as a kind of insurance, but no, couldn't see a point there, then thought was there any way else I could wring a dime or two from it, some trick I'd missed, new way to blossom something out of it now I could at least temporarily breathe. Wasted some time arguing with myself who'd wound up where in the power game between Scott and I, to call it that, and where Corinna fit in, but all of that seemed to have consumed itself, no other movement was possible.

Occurred to me, sure, I could redact my name, black pen it out, make a photocopy—whoever it was was taking the heat for this, maybe get his wife to spread out a few dollars for me, or some other concerned party, as even if I didn't stick around but I played it right it was true that the presence of this letter, even with redaction, should be enough to give a leg up the man's defense if the defense weren't faring so well. Scott might take that as a mean spirited lunge at Corinna, my part, and in that case get wind he'd got a stake in it, put a fresh hunt after me—always that, new description of me and couldn't be hard pull fingerprints, especially Scott was the spiteful sort.

Then again, even if I redacted Corinna's name, even if I

just sent in an anonymous note explaining what the letter was, that it was true and some names'd been removed due to their implications, it could still be viable, give doubt, give credence to some storyline the guy was innocent, something was being done behind the scenes.

-Makes sense, I said, makes sense makes sense, repeated, rolling head around, mumbling that the letter was a negotiable paper, at least—I wasn't promising anything anyone wanted to buy, caveat emptor, it just had to seem a good idea to someone desperate and wanted a crack at this poor bastard out breathing real world air, again, and there'd have to be at least one or two such people laying around I could get a word in their ear, give them the sales pitch.

It was just how could I work that to be a quick turnaround, money in my hand?

It'd have to be full exposure on my part, show the letter, give the terms, drive to get the money straight out, no way imaginable to play around with some other drop-off flimflam, not with things already in motion—this wasn't someone's guilt I was dicking with, they'd not be shy, this was someone's innocence and folk can tend to get prideful and blabbermouth about things they don't want people not to know.

Things'd all quagmire too much around, even catching sight of Scott just a glance he'd know I was still around, something, things might get edgy—I couldn't do some dwindling thing I teased an interested party and trust they'd keep it to themselves.

No.

It was worthless, letter was worthless. To do anything with it, I'd have to poke my toe in, hope someone had the money to spare, hope they saw it best not to involve the authorities, all too much, all too much.

Thought about the fact that, to Scott, letter was still just as tight a spot as ever it'd been, maybe wait a length, show up again, give him another squeeze, but again the uncertainty and who knew if he'd be willing, if the letter would still have any bearing—Christ, I didn't know if the letter had any bearing at all, already, it was worthless, I was lucky it'd been some swallow could cause bellyache enough to Scott he'd given me his thousand dollars, probably cash advance against some credit card.

Moved back to the grill, poking at the remains of the burnt copy, snapping some of the crisps left, no words on then, roughing the mess up with a hand I then wiped on my pant leg. Put the pages of the last copy in the envelope, struck match and set the flame, struck another two, just for fun, to two other spots, watched the opening holes of combusting paper move toward each other, crash, vanish, the flame lick up and sideways, tilt of it reminded me of the graceless way a shirt looks falling from a window, being blown across a yard, something.

Letter burnt gone before I'd really realized it, roughed the new ash, dusted hands in claps like halfway an applause for the whole situation. Only thing left was bus out—or train, which might be best they had discounted enough seats, better to just bury myself in for days at a time, little mobile world, bus too much temptation to wander of at any stopping point, wind up Christ knew where and with what to work with.

Thousand dollars.

Say I had eight hundred, just say that was what I started with—two hundred I should spend however it was I felt to get the taste of these past weeks out of my mouth, off of my skin, two hundred so I could feel even for a few days, like it wasn't all a continuation, not feel I was some crumb still in a pocket after pants're cleaned and hung a month in a closet. Two hundred to make this feel over, because when I came up to breathe it was going to be a grind, it was going to be tottering on the lip of empty, again, no way to sort that otherwise.

Eight hundred.

"Sure," I said, but still didn't know did it mean I'd take a bus or a train, blew long air out my nose, zipped backpack shut, put it over my shoulder, didn't like that, dangled it dangling from end of my limp arms, fingers hardly curled tight enough to keep it from falling.

***

Tour bus got me at least into another state and I'd found a ticket on severe discount, even wandered around the little historical villa awhile before moving off my own direction, found the town, city, whatever it wanted to call itself, good few hours walk some country roads, place'd serve well enough as anyplace. In fact, got the heaviest feeling I'd been there, stopped off for some reason before, turns around buildings felt I'd done them, into and out of a takeaway shop for a hamburger felt I'd eaten same hamburger before, and when it started to snow got the actual scare I was being watched, had bumbled my way back over some old tracks I'd left half buried. Got out of the main drag of the city, things evened out more to just look like any generic anyplace—shopping centers, highway onramps, few theme restaurants, mini-golf—the unease off me when the place seemed should be familiar because it looked like nowhere.

Made a distinct point of choosing the more expensive of two motels that glared at each other either side of the six lanes of traffic, right at the entrance up or down from the highway, not just to feel moneybag, but because the cheaper place was less by only two dollars and a quarter, just seemed idiot, didn't want them to think that strategy'd worked.

There were a few families filling up the lobby, I waited my turn, looking at the pictures on the wall—what the town'd looked like frontier days, plaques which year motel chain'd won this or that award or seal of satisfaction—and in the rack of brochures even found one for the tour I'd just rode the bus for, gave it a read twice through, my body already acting like it was asleep, could smell the antiseptic of the tight bedcovers waiting, taste the cotton mouth I'd wake with from drinking the tap water, feel the way my eyes would sting from the cheap soap and spray from the showerhead.

Got my turn, I asked did they have weekly rates.

"We do, but there's a two week limit."

"Is there?"

Got a dull nod, like this was something got brought up a lot, bone of contention with contractors, truck drivers, something, I raised a hand like to make it clear I only needed a week's stay and how much.

"Two fifty, unless you have a discount club card."

"I don't."

"Do you want one?"

"Sure. Does it cost anything?"

"No."

"Then yes, sure—and it works right away for this stay?"

"It does and you can earn free nights, the more you stay."

Nodded nodded, and when he told me the price was a clean seventy-five dollars cheaper I just laughed. "Does anyone ever not take a discount card?"

"You'd be surprised, some people just hate having cards, some people won't even let me just apply it to the one stay, not even take the card."

"I get an actual card?"

"In the mail, but we don't need to do that."

"Let's not."

He just needed to see my identification and by rote I did my dance it wouldn't be a problem but then acted as though it struck me, broke down look, all of a sudden that I'd left my larger duffle bag with my friend who'd dropped me off, it had all of my stuff in it.

"I have cash though, that's not a thing." But his face was puckered, that fearful look of hotel worker facing down unknown public. I made myself seem soft, fatigued. "What is it?"

"I can give you a room for the night, but weekly it's required to get an identification, computer won't even let me proceed past the first screen."

"Can't you just—what? it needs a number? You can't just make one up?"

But no, he couldn't—not because he'd be bothered to, but because computer somehow knew if a number was legitimate, he'd never been able to put in just some random number and have it work—and he joked that he'd also tried, for fun, just adding in random last four digits of credit cards, but somehow that never worked, either.

Smiled at him, "What's the rate a single night? Like out on the sign?"

"Yep."

I pointed out that this was like losing the equivalent of four nights—price out front times three was the discount club price a week.

"Do you think your friend can get back?"

"I don't think so, man, I was going to have him mail the stuff here. What if I get in touch with him, he can fax a copy?"

"That would work."

"But meanwhile I can still pay the weekly rate?"

Guy let out a breath, paused, shook his head. Best he could do was, when my identification got there, go back and retroactively change the thing, update my stay to weekly, prorate the remaining days, some such rubbish I don't even care if he knew what he was talking about.

Told him I'd have a smoke, see about what could I do, probably be back by later. Figured I'd try the place across the street before moving on to other places, though really just wasn't in the mood for any sort of grind.

Recognized a franchise doughnut shop I'd not seen one of in forever, wonderful bland of it there, and just like the specific one I was thinking about, even the people behind the counter were smoking cigarettes, dough and frosting of what I bought had that scent, taste laced right in—ate until I was sick to my stomach and then downed two coffees on top.

Started to snow harder. I watched through the window everything get quiet—by the time it was dark and whatever shops had lighted signage lit them up and a few parking lots got their streetlights at least burbling, snow was everywhere maybe two inches of it, wet liked it'd freeze solid the temperature kept dropping the way the wind against my back as I made my way back to the same motel I'd been in earlier seemed to be suggesting it certainly would.

Girl working the counter, I introduced myself, explained how I'd had a spot of bother earlier trying to get the weekly rate on account of having left my identification in my bag, a friend's trunk, friend on his way cross country back home, was there anything she could do to help me out, I just needed to stay the one week and didn't want to get gouged.

"Because—what happens if I just stay for seven days? I can do that without I.D., yeah?"

She wasn't sure, but it seemed to both of us if I could stay one night, then it wasn't like they'd kick me out the next night and so on, so what could the thing be it mattered I paid the discount all in front?

"Or I could just put in my I.D.," she said, looking down, then followed up saying she'd just try, because she didn't think the computer really cared what number, as long as it was legitimate.

"Can I smoke in here?" I asked, clearing seeing two full ashtrays saying I could, but she nodded it wasn't a problem, typing, and asked could she have one.

"You're much better at working in a motel than the guy, earlier."

She nodded, still looking at what she was typing, telling me I was in at the discount week, and told me Francine I asked her What's your name?

"And what's yours?" she said, both straight asking—eyes on mine long enough to distinctly shy away—and also needing to type it in.

Told her something and then I spelled it when she asked how.

this gun from
Norman Court

So I remember ev'ry face
Of ev'ry man who put me here

BOB DYLAN, *I Shall Be Released*

It was the microwave hamburgers were a step too far—
impulse to take them I even noted was the kind should've
been ignored, kind the rule was to ignore—but took two in
basket, wandering the drugstore to the magazines, leafed
through same entertainment tabloid I'd flipped through all
week. Went to a knee, I figured discreetly stuck the burgers
in my backpack with the various other spoils, then walked
around with the basket full of the dummy items I'd leave
off at the counter, saying I'd forgot my wallet could they
hold the things I'd be back ten minutes lived up the way—
move I only used when nabbing an armful, otherwise it'd
get old fast despite different clerk on duty every day.

Knew just from how he took one step a bit fast then
suddenly lingered at a display of shampoo that I'd been
spotted by this guy—shabby beard, cropped hair, gut but
over abs seemed probably worked out regular enough, all
the appearance of off-duty cop—so tightened up and gut
did a rollover twice.

It'd been ages since I'd had to unpack a swipe, not since
I'd been a kid, practically, knew I was screwed so figured
just try for the door, casual. Did out my bit with the front
clerk about leaving off the basket, just finishing up when
sure thing the guy I'd marked stepped in, gave the clerk a
smile, said That' alright.

All I could think was to give the guy a Hello, word came

out my mouth all consonants, his hand went to my shoulder while he asked could he trouble me to come to the back with him, just a minute.

"What's the thing?" I said, going to my pocket for cigarettes.

"Come on, sir, let's just go."

Clerk watched, eyes big but more than halfway disinterested, guy moved hand from shoulder, took my backpack with it, told me, again, just to come on.

There were some clerks, maybe one of them in the fancier uniform a shift managers, sitting at the break room table, one stood at the punch clock, all of them looking I was marched past—recognized one of them, one who made eyes at the guy walking me.

As soon as I was sat in a stubby office, door closed, asked was it alright I smoked a cigarette.

"Sorry, can't back here." Guy sighed, not sitting his desk, holding my backpack I tried not to eye too intently, not to betray the actual pitch of my dizziness at seeing it, everything I had, at a limp sway by his pant knee. He asked me "Do you have anything you want to tell me?"

So, I sighed too, went out with "You know the thing, alright? Look, man, just cut me loose, take the stuff back, I'll be off, not back this way for forever, okay?"

He jiggled the backpack, getting the heft of it, told me sit there, he'd be back in a few minutes with some papers I'd need to sign and out he went, backpack now cradled his elbow like some sleepy infant.

Only decision I made was not to run, simple because I had nowhere to run and it wouldn't help anything, best I could keep my head together, hope it went slap on the wrist—total amount of merchandise couldn't be even north of twenty dollars, but what did I know from drugstore loss prevention, how this would go?

No sense how long had it been since first look I'd gave to the wall clock, but it went another almost ten minutes'd passed by the time guy came back in the room, set backpack on the table, took a seat.

"You can have a cigarette," he said, which made my heart sink past sick, but still fished one out of my pocket, lit it, he smiled asked me had I paid for the smokes.

No point saying anything, but said "No, man, didn't pay for the smokes, well done. But you'll have to do the legwork on your own to figure where I got them from, they aren't paying me enough do your job on top of mine."

Guy smiled, asked me my name, did I have identification.

"I don't have I.D. Jesus, man, just let me walk out the door this place—I promise I've got it bad enough, that'll be the end."

"Bad enough, how?"

He was really asking, so I made double quick not to pause like I was sizing him up, played myself most pathetic, hoping to keep any whiff of grifter off of me. "I'm staying at the shelter on Pearle Bridge, alright? There or some of the other ones—Swan Street and one on, I don't know, like the Youth Center, at night it sometimes has the basketball court set up halfway for overnighters."

"Bowler Street," he said, whole time he'd been nodding.

I took his chiming in to barrel forward my apologetic best. "Bowler, right. Okay? I won't come here, again, I promise you about that, believe me. I just wanted to have some stuff on me, I don't know, not feel like everything was a handout. I even work, shelter on Pearle, just it's they pay you by they let you have some better clothes, not even five bucks cash my pocket for carrying shingles up the roof all day, okay?"

I looked around for an ashtray, he noticed and moved the squat little wastebasket out from next to the desk. I ashed and meantime he said "What's your name?"

"My name's Stuart Bells."

"I like that name," he said, "but figure I'd like to know your real name."

"Stuart Bells is my real name" blew smoke down my nose "but I can give you an alias if you like."

He was chuckling, handed the backpack over to me, I hugged it in my lap. "I ask around at the shelters, they'll tell me 'Yeah, Stuart Bells, good guy, sometimes carries shingles up the roof and we give him secondhand sports coat for his trouble?'"

I didn't answer. We held eyes—can't exactly say, knew I was getting off the hook, but was trying to same time mark was it because this guy he'd known someone wound up down on their luck or else was it he'd been a drinker, sometime the past, liked handing out second chances now he was put together.

He told me he'd left as much in the bag as he could, but I needed to understand two things, these being, one, he couldn't leave it all as I'd been marked taking the shaving foam and, two, that I couldn't come back to this shop, better make it the shopping center. Then, head tap, directed me the door, turned around to his desk.

I made the walk out through the overhead announcement being made that some cookies some caramel bars were on sale if one had a store discount card, was out in the open air and around a corner before I remembered still had cigarette my hand, gave it sucks to keep it going.

Took a seat on the concrete base of a streetlight bloomed up over me, heat of day making for patches of gnats everywhere, I could see the gatherings of them moving in closer like short breaths.

Guy had left the burgers, left the plain crackers, left the short bottle of vodka, even. But more important, I dug down into the clothes—my clothes—and at first tensed, then let out a long breath I could feel the solid fist of the pistol there, wrapped in the undershirts and balled socks.

Batted at a waft of gnats just outside of arms reach, tried to flick my cold cigarette stub at them but it went way off one side, so I settled for lighting another, blowing hard out first drag at the things, no idea they registered it or they didn't.

***

Because I'd burnt through my stolen vodka, didn't even bother with bumming for bus fare or hangdogging for some driver to get me back to the shelter on Pearle Bridge, instead got to the line outside Swan just as the doors were opening and got in third from they had to start turning away the people showed up in back of me, about half a block of people none of whom put up a stick of resistance, though one of them, I saw, decided to have a piss next to the trashcan in front of the shuttered up tailor shop partway down the block.

Swan Street was the worst, the guests all inebriated, a lot of them putting up fronts about not wanting to sign in the log, like they should be recognized, it was something to respect they'd been there so often, most of them straight up ex-cons, no down-and-outers proper, no one there on a spot of bad luck or've been screwed around by the intricacies some system meant to do right by them. Also, no one got anything at Swan, it was just a depot, some three day old donation food, not even bins of socks to rummage, not even brochures on programs to get oneself right by detox or therapy or church—certainly none of the perks someplace like Pearle, no movie each night, no this or that volunteer group bringing something hot, no slackness about lights out time and at Swan it was for certain if you leave out the door so much as a smoke past X hour it was too bad you weren't getting back in.

Discreetly asked the bloat of a woman at the log desk, her mouth like teeth were larger on one side, if there was a microwave I could use. She signed, asked me what did I want to microwave, told her two hamburgers, she said No, we don't have microwave for that.

So, I found a cot and lay wrapped around my backpack, twitched through a night of more sleep than I tended to get when I wound up at Swan—grimy dreams a lot, sleep half-awake needing to piss but just tightening down against the stale air breathed out gravely by everyone else, and sometime woke once, quick eyes open to a see two guys, nude, coming back toward their cots, one of them itching at their scrotum whole time, brief pop of flatulence as I snuffled face into cot flat.

The morning, last call about everyone being shooed out, I like usual hung around until last, then quickly ducked into the toilet, had a piss, splashed various water on my face, not much bothering with soap—figured to do a more proper wash some bookstore toilet, later, frowned at remembering it was the shave foam guy'd had to put back from my theft, previous day—same time tossed the two microwave burgers in the trash, thought about it, took them out, figured what could it matter, considering what they were, that they'd gone unrefrigerated awhile, nothing like I hadn't eaten worse.

Heat was atrocious, already, not even eight in the morning, but seemed maybe cloud cover would keep it just humid rank, none of the blinding sun off pavement and all tended to do my head in, make me feel exhausted out in it even ten minutes.

Lit up my first cigarette, noted how I'd enough left the pack I'd need another by evening, so was making itinerary of how I'd scrounge up the few dollars for the off-brands I could get the kiosk outside of the Olive Street metro—combination of conning someone I needed one more coin for a phone call, begging fifty cents more for a train pass, all these kids game that'd take hours to add up but always would, just I kept at them.

Was about to head off, I saw him there—store detective, bus stop bench, there, paperback and cup of coffee—saw him a tick before he raised his hand to me. Nothing better to do, I gave head nod, deep, got down to a knee, a poke through my backpack to get a breath. No point trying to avoid him, of course—flicked the zipper as I zipped it back up—he'd obviously come out to see me and he obviously couldn't do anything to me, so I waited out a beat of traffic, crossed over to him.

He stood, handing me a coffee, which I almost told him No thanks until he right away moved to pick up the other coffee, his, from the bench—just left the paperback there—asked me could he borrow a cigarette.

"I'm a little bit tight on those, you know? You made me see the light, yesterday, your spontaneous kind hearted gesture, so I can't go around stealing another pack, right? Gotta make these fiends last until I'm gainfully employed."

He chuckled, paly-paly best friend, told me just give him a cigarette, he'd get me a pack of something real when we stopped, he'd just forgotten the pack he normally kept in his car—he pointed to some lousy, green thing parked a few yards off, meter showing Expired—and wasn't in his plate until he'd had a smoke.

"Were we going somewhere?"

He looked at me, waited until I relented my glare, was getting my pack out to say "Speaking of gainfully employed, I thought that's what we might have a talk about."

Chained his smoke lit from mine, handed it over with a theatric grin, eye wink, asked if the thing was I'd become store security with him, use my obvious expertise to give him the leg up in the industry. Seemed to like that, said it'd crossed his mind, just that very thing, but went on he just did the loss prevention gig as a sideline because it got him decent benefits, what his tip actually was was private investigator.

"That so?" I eyed him, trying to feel out the actual angle. "Which has about what to do with me?"

"Has a place to say, few bucks walking around is what I think it could have for you. Better off than this" he pointed at the Swan Street shelter sign "better off than shoplifting five and dimes, too, right?"

He let me size him up, let me all I wanted and sizing him up as far as I got it he was serious and this was the time I needed to say how it'd be, I was on board or I was humping it to beg coins then pretend soda machine was broken.

"What was my getting caught over hamburgers a job application, a referral?"

And sober as the clouds breaking, heat getting lit and nauseating, he told me "It was a reminder" repeated that, even more grave "it was a reminder. And I figured I'd ask you you wanted to try something out. You don't, you don't. And it might not work out, but let me know and we can talk about it in the car."

He tipped nose at the coffee I was holding, got me realizing I was actually holding decent, actual coffee, got the lid off to drink proper, mouth wide over the cup lip. Started putting lid back on—stuff was too hot—he touched my shoulder, told me Come on, few paces getting him to driver's door he opened, leaned on.

Swung my backpack over my shoulder and soon as I took a pace in his direction saw he was down his seat, closing his door, leaning across passenger side to lift the door lock, his elbow accidentally sounding the horn as he wriggled back to his place, adjusted at the rearview.

***

We pulled in to the lot of an office park—seemed most of the spaces rented by either cleaning supply companies, hiring offices for security, companies something to do with computers, also seemed quarter of the spaces weren't rented by anyone—after not having spoken much the ride over. In fact, it was with a laugh that the guy, already the driver's door opened, mentioned that his name was Leonard Bellow, little cough, added he supposed he figured I'd gotten that when he'd nabbed me for the shoplifting, but now thought probably not.

Occurred to me, watching him unlock the door his office space—L. Bellow Investigation stenciled on it—that I'd kept so to myself due to undercurrent of figuring this was no legitimate thing, but seeing the generic layout of an office room, two offshoot rooms behind doors both opened a sliver, filing cabinets, licenses on the wall, got me thinking the job offer was actual, so kept on quiet as not to queer it, still couldn't focus right why it was being put to me.

"I have coffee, but don't think I've emptied an old pot for almost a week, who knows what's growing there." Kind of wondered why was he saying that, as I still had my cup from he'd given it to me before, but he also wasn't looking at me, just moving some folders, taking a seat. Continuing, he said "I don't want you to get the wrong idea about this, I can't promise you this is going to work out official and there's the matter of you're not licensed to actually do legal investigations, so what we're going to do is a kind of trial period, see how it goes, then we'll hit the ins and outs of seeing is this something you'd want to pursue and all, licensing wise."

As this relieved me—I'd been preparing a speech to squirm out of anything necessitating fingerprints being taken—I told him "So this isn't on top of the table, exactly, but still sort of is?"

"Exactly," he motioned I should sit, little finger waggle to pull over one of the two comfortable chairs from what I supposed served as his waiting area, giving a halfhearted apology he had no idea where the client chair was, he normally met people only on appointment so would be more together when they showed up, "that's exactly right. Which is what I meant, that I can't cut you a paycheck, put you on official rolls, but I have a set up."

"What's that?" I disliked the last two words of his statement, twitched a grin. "You'll just pay me out freelance?"

"Something like it. Basically, I'm going to have you cover some what could be termed grunt work—keep an eye out, stake some things out, time consuming stuff that if I were able to get someone to cover, I could take on twice the work, not have to turn away some easy, quick dollars for being caught up with things a bit more intricate."

I nodded, his face going like I was objecting.

"Yes," he said, patting the air with both hands like I should stay seated, "in a way it's like getting cheap labor, I admit that, if I took on someone proper it'd be less advantageous to me. But like I say, you'll get a room, your own room, and a weekly stipend, a percentage of the overall fee."

"Okay," I said, didn't care so much for the fine print, his awkwardness putting me at ease, the menace of him being the guy a day ago could've ended my life proper without even meaning to effaced, replaced with someone seemed more pudgy than firm, looking for a way to take advantage for a sneaky bit of extra cash.

"Great," he said, but gave me a look made me think I should act more invested.

"So nothing official, you tell me watch someone, get their picture took or whatever, I do it, you slip me something for my trouble—maybe it seems we work well, this is mutually beneficial, you help me with the exams?"

Something there made him laugh and he admitted about how getting licensed wouldn't be trouble, anyone could basically pay a fee get a paper sent, so really I should think of it like a kind of interview period and if he felt like it things might get more regular, I'd get a better slice of the overall pie.

"What room?" I changed the subject, this the part I was mostly interested in, though pocket money and all was a perk.

"Hotel room," he said, business again, some of the luster off his eyes, the sheen probably'd been mostly nerves and now we were past what to him'd been the out-on-a-limb. "I've got a room out at a hotel, always, hardly use it, now it'll just be yours."

"What if you need it for whatever you keep it for?"

Big laugh, he said in that case then he'd get another room, but what he might need it for wasn't something so likely to come up—he almost winked like we were sharing an in-joke.

"You just give me the key? I need to sign the guest log?"

"I just give you the key, don't bother about putting your name down, you know, maybe better if you don't. We're not doing any paperwork, yet, this is going to be you doing me a favor."

"What is?"

Awkward look between us—I'd taken his phrasing to mean he was putting something specific out, he'd actually just meant it generally.

Blink blink, he shook his head around, pulled out a folder from a pile, replaced it, pulled out another, gave it a peek, handed it across. "You take that, this is about as easy as it comes. Two love birds—free agent fellow, the woman with a husband, kids back home."

"Husband wants to know is she going out a side door on him?"

"Actually, mother of the fellow—he's a young guy— mother has it in her head he's in with the wrong crowd. I got on to the woman being his poison, but this sort of thing is where client wants proof."

"Proof?"

He told me he'd get a video camera out of the back for me before we left. This was a situation, he explained, where the client wasn't paying for any frills, but now that he was in the position to do what he termed a Reveal the thing was he would explain that he could affirm the kid wasn't a hoodlum, but if the mother wanted to know what the kid was, instead of a hoodlum, it'd be an extra whatever amount of dollars.

I nodded.

"I play that part by ear," he said, like showing off, "see how I can pump it. Now, usually, this is bit of work where all I'd get would be the base fee, I'd do a few paces of leg work, tell the lady I've not noticed anything funny, she'd want nothing further."

But I agreed with him it'd be easy enough, me on board, to milk these situations, told him I totally understood—meantime, I asked, he was busy with other things?

"I am. But, if it turns out you have the knack for this, I intend to take on more of these busy work gigs, and sure I think you'll be doing the initially follow-arounds, which is why you'd get paid more than just a bit of shutterbug work." He put his hand out for a shake, time to make things as marginally official as they could be made. "Can't do anything about a car for you," he told me, standing, but said he'd spring for an all-purpose city transit pass—bus and train—he was sure I could make due.

"Hate to ask it, but have to admit, especially a night of Swan Street, it's got me salivating a bit—walking around money is how much?"

He stopped—I was just leaning into the door, outside heat half on me, stale of unused office so no air conditioning on the other half—shook his face again, said he needed to get the camera, too.

"It's two-fifty a week for this kind of thing and depending what mommy's willing to pay to know her boy likes them her age, you'll get a piece of the final payout, too."

He gave a motion I should wait outside and, sweating from just a touch of the sun, one eye wincing all the way closed from glint off another office's window, I lit a cigarette, already pretending I was tasting the cigarette I was going to buy just as soon as I'd been rinsed off a cold hotel shower.

***

Leonard dropped me off outside a hotel—chain hotel, diner across its parking lot—told me there was five minutes walk to buses and metro, that he'd work out about the transit pass he'd mentioned in the next week, skimmed an extra twenty dollars off a money clip, told me it could cover transportation, the meantime. I was walking away from the car when he sounded the horn, quiet and quick, saw him leaning to tap on the passenger window, rolling it down as I re-approached. Real air of embarrassment, he handed me a mobile phone, told me it was mine, but the plan was limited so I shouldn't go racking up calls, it was basically to communicate with him and so he could communicate with me—all of which I nodded to, slipping the thing down my pant pocket, gave a wave and got into the hotel lobby.

My room was on the third floor, so I made straight for the elevator—didn't even see a clerk at the front desk though the phone was ringing—rode up letting out a long breath, rubbing my face, trying to get my backpack to settle right over my shoulder, it always slipped off.

Had been expecting, whatever reason, there to be evidence of Leonard in the room, but nothing, antiseptic room, like no one'd ever been in, this making more sense considering how Leonard'd painted the situation, housekeeping'd've cleared up any incidental mess from his last stay, even had it been recent.

Set my backpack down on the bed, glanced around.

First thing after shower, after cigarettes, after decent meal, I'd rent out a box someplace, not comfortable with leaving my bag in a room someone else had access to and didn't want to keep lugging it with me everyplace.

Turned on the television, let it sound out some adventure film and commercials while I was around the corner at the sink undressing, getting the shower running, touches at the water to get an idea how best to set the temperature. Last decent shower I'd had'd been months back, even the shelter on Pearle Bridge would only allot a few minutes and the water stood room temperature, at best, showering always a decision between a full lather, leaving residue unwashed away or else washing the skin clean of just a slick of suds from a soap cake rolled in hands a few turns. Still, I didn't luxuriate, just washed, soon was toweling myself partway dry and spreading myself down an X over one of the two double beds, covering my face in a pillow I unearthed from the rigidly tucked comforter.

Started in thinking about how I was going to handle the money—two-seventy I had, all of a sudden, and as much as I wanted to believe in this good thing, I more than that didn't want to take it for granted, splurge, turns out Leonard cuts it off with me next week, whatever reason. Obviously I didn't need the full twenty for transportation only one week and only one place to go, so say I used ten, had a total left of two-sixty—find a thrift store for some new clothes, sick to death of the few things I had, maybe forget about the celebratory dinner, instead grab bread, peanut butter someplace, one pack of decent smokes, carton of cheaps just until the next payment came in, until I'd seen was this all doable.

Woke up'd been having a dream I'd worked out how I'd actually overlooked an extra five hundred dollars, knew from the saggy feeling of my still shut eyes I'd been out for hours, lay wishing I could get back to sleep, into the feeling of being flush just a few more minutes instead of having to somberly tell myself I'd get there, that this gig'd go at least a month, at least a clean thousand bucks and on my feet to think straight before it'd go bad if it went bad.

It might not, too, I tried to admit, but not quite ready for that.

Getting dressed in some things out of my backpack—no cleaner than what I'd removed before the shower, but somehow seemed to be—decided it was just the gun I needed to worry about holing up, everything else I could keep in the room, worse things coming of it I had to take off without retrieving I'd have enough in my pockets to replace it all. Looked around for something to stick the gun in, not wanting to chance just using the waist of my pants, some nonsense like it drops out and I get asked questions, settled on the backpack, everything else emptied out—as the backpack was the second most valuable thing I had, anyway, would want to be able to take it with me I had to leave.

Front desk, asked did they know was there a post office or the equivalent, somewhere close, young woman told me she'd be more than happy to mail something for me.

"Thing is I need to rent out a box, you know? Anyplace around?"

"We have a few safes, if you'd like, there's no charge."

But I shook my head, politely smiling "Nevermind," but she caught on, told me she was sure there was someplace just in town and if not then just a bit further into the city.

Don't even know why'd I asked, other than maybe because I wanted to seem normal, not have to act like a derelict for two seconds—went so far as thanking her she handed over a phonebook, I leafed through, asked for a pen, wrote down some random address and phone number, left with another, kind of flirted, "Thanks a lot, I appreciate it."

It was dark out, the lights of the diner, only a handful of cars parked around it, beckoning me I had to steel myself to walk past.

Figured buses and all must run at least another few trips, I could get my bearings, and walking to town also found myself thinking how it was pleasant to think I had a room to go back to, that even if I missed transportation, had to walk for hours, end of the line would be bed, television, vending machines, end of the line would be sleep I'd not be woken from unless I felt like it.

Figured best to treat Leonard halfway he was a threat, not enough to start making rounds in my head how I'd keep a step ahead of him based on it, though—so far, really, he'd given me money and a room, nothing else, and so far I could leave, keep walking, I was in a better place than I'd been in for months, had some weight, some sense of myself.

The nearby town was actually full enough with shops still open—strip malls, few streets with residences above boutiques—that I didn't bother with the bus or anything, sprung two dollars for cheap slice of pizza a takeaway place, ate it even feeling the stomachache tightening with each chew, each swallow.

It was kind of a haggle to get rented out a box at a shipping store, usual thing about my not having identification, but the dance went about the same as always, I signed a form explaining I well understood if I did not make prompt monthly payments the contents of the box could be immediately thrown away, auctioned, whatever, was given a key, a spare, given a combination written in bad handwriting—I had to recopy it myself—on the also badly handwritten receipt.

***

Morning, woke thinking to myself it was kind of funny this was my second time waking up the hotel, only my first morning—not so funny or even odd I got a bit more awake—shook my face around inside slaps of faucet water, dressed quick and left the room barefoot, double, triple, four times checking I had my key, last thing I wanted some absurdity of having to ask another and it being recognized I wasn't Leonard Bellow so what was I doing in the room.

Didn't find any toothpaste, toothbrush in the vending on the floor of the hotel my room, took the elevator down to ask at the desk, saw a buffet set up, full breakfast, in the common area.

"That's free?" I asked, middle aged woman giving a quick look halfway up, eyes back to the paper she had in her hands.

"Sure, help yourself, breakfast goes until ten, every morning."

"A wonderland," I said, to which she, still not looking up, had a real chuckle, me asking "Do you happen to have little tubes of toothpaste, didn't see any in the machine upstairs?"

She pointed off to one side, then seemed to snap out of whatever she'd been concentrating on, told me toothpaste was in machines on main floor, but she'd just get me tube, did I need anything else.

"Shaving foam?"

"You need a razor?"

Thought, nodded, blew a little laugh out my nose, nodded and said needed a toothbrush, too, actually, she said it'd be no trouble, left, came back with a little bag had a bunch of stuff in it, told me not to worry about it with the vending machine, I needed something else just to ask.

Made myself two sandwiches from English muffins and bacon, took a cup of coffee, got back in my room, shut off the television, but turned it right back on, found I liked having the sound, made me feel more alone for whatever reason.

I'd left the file on the desk in the corner, opened it and gave a look through for the first time, proper. Seemed Leonard'd done pretty much all there was to be done except videotaping the forthcoming rendezvous—had no idea if he knew, exactly, it'd be the coming weekend, in two days, they'd get together next at some hotel or if this was a just a general thing to try, but as far as I could tell my job'd be get there early, stake out, film them together as much as possible, hopefully get something clearly, without doubt, indicated the relationship was sexual.

The woman was called Lara Daye, guy was called Gregory Murfin—unless that was a typo—twenty-two year age difference, he'd just graduated high school start of the summer, she'd been married almost as long as he'd been alive, her own kids just a step younger than he was.

I was impressed with all Leonard had in the file, especially if I was reading it correctly that this had been on his agenda only since the last two, three weeks, all sorts of things, car makes, licenses plates, addresses for home, work, addresses for other parties associated with both Lara and Gregory, general schedules—more for Lara than Gregory—information on at least a few times they'd met up the hotel, some photos—not that Leonard'd taken, but from various sources he'd come across for Lara, probably Gregory's mother'd given the ones of him—and a whole mess of things I didn't even dig into.

Made the decision, as long as the breakfast was free each day, I'd not spring for anything but cigarettes, maybe some vodka, not until second week's pay got in—things like new clothes, though appealing, weren't pressing, and all closed in the room, away from anything, away even from exhaustion, it clicked the right way that money was first priority, this was not a chance to squander.

Heard an odd bit of music going off from around the

corner, realized it was the mobile phone I'd left on the bathroom counter—took it up, flipped it open, looked was there a button to press but heard soft of voice asking Hello?

"Leonard?"

"Okay, great, you're there."

"I'm here. Sorry, had you called before? I'm not used to having a phone, left it in the room."

He chuckled, told me Jesus and I needed to get used to it, phone should stay on me at all times, I should pick up anytime he called or else he'd have to get the impression I'd taken off.

"I'm not taking off, was just leafing through the file, actually, then I'm thinking to watch television."

He laughed, said "Sounds great, man, I see though my money is well spent, I should find you other things to keep busy with, maybe use you to wash my car or something."

We politely back and frothed, leading to him wanting to make sure I had everything I needed, had I tried out the camera—I lied that I'd tested it, all was good—asked me I'd be able to find my way to the hotel just fine.

"I'm all over it, nothing to worry about. We're pretty sure they'll be there?"

"All but certain, things like that aren't too hard to count out—the event they don't show, we'll try a plan B, and if not we'll scrap it, move on to something else."

After hanging up, decided I should take things a bit more seriously, tested out the camera—glad I did, too, as this was the first I'd taken it out of its case, found the thing was smaller than the flat of my palm, took me number of trials to feel confident I understood how it worked just fine—even called the hotel I'd be staking out, asked what was the best way to get there from public transit, made notes, leafed through the file some more.

Found a page dedicated to Lara's husband Marcus, found he was younger that Lara by almost twelve years, himself, had been married once before, the divorce coming official just right before the marriage to Lara.

Got me wondering who was the father the kids, as I saw they were thirteen and fifteen, but nothing I came across got so clear on that—Leonard must've either thought it wasn't worth it on the strength of what he was getting paid, or it was that if the information wasn't readily available he just did without. Did find it clearly noted it was Lara's first and only marriage, she'd only once been engaged, before, long time back, probably around she was Gregory's age and Gregory wasn't even out of the womb yet.

Spent a few hours watching television, but knew I wasn't much paying attention, thoughts kept drifting into imagining myself in the scenario of Leonard having the chat with the mother.

What would he say to get her to pay out to see the tape? Would she just be that interested, despite being relieved she was having it confirmed to her that her son wasn't out flushing his life down with crime and drugs or whatever she feared? Was it that Leonard even had to play people like Gregory's mother—or anyone, for that matter—that it was just innate they'd pay because they had the opportunity to know something they hadn't really the right to?

It made me laugh, how I felt, in my pretending, kind of sketchy, tentative, like I'd have to soft-sale the thing, like I was inherently taking advantage of someone, tricking them, while Leonard had full license and law to do what he did—all it was was putting a question to someone, all it was was taking a few bucks and telling something he'd seen, something I'd seen, something anybody'd seen.

Didn't sleep much that night, lay watching all three installments of some cut rate science fiction franchise movie, took a shower after, slept until afternoon, woke up and had another shower, only regret was I'd missed breakfast, but after a minute didn't care, started regretting, instead, I'd not bought cigarettes the previous day, would have to leave to get them when all I felt like was laying down until I had to leave, next morning.

**

First thing struck me about the Queen's Lodge Motel was it was four steps down the chain from the room I was staying in, sort of place I'd've stayed in, in the past and to my own devices, and second thing I noticed was three of the room fronts on the lower of the two levels, corner of the parking lot, had tarps covering their doors, pavement out in front jackhammered, seemed'd been like that a long time.

There was only parking out in front and the way things were set up, hill then shopping center across the way, it'd be no trouble to sit, film with the rather surprising zoom the mini camera had—I'd spent the night toying with it, discovered all manner of sophistications, not the meager point, press, film gizmo I'd first figured.

It was mid-morning, so I had smoke, walked down the block, came back around, decided just do a close in walk around, get a feel for the nooks, where was ice, where was vending, was completely caught off guard to see that the young man's car was parked in the lot. New smoke going, took a minute, verified from the little slip of paper I'd transferred what I considered pertinent information to that, yes, the guy's car, he was already inside.

Why this surprised me I didn't really know, and it also got me worried about were they both already inside and if so how was I to figure out which room in order to get some kind of footage of them together—not to mention how would I be sure it'd be anything along the lines I was supposed to get, kissing, touching, the lot?

Muttered some Goddamnits, moved across to a spot on the hill, obscured by some dumpsters, made sure I had a surveyor's view of the whole motel front. I'd take it for granted she was coming in her car, so relaxed, but then thought it just as likely she'd park someplace else so as not to have her car distinctly spotted on some random accident a motel lot—she'd be able to explain it being in the lot some shopping center or outside whatever one of the the nearby buildings, at least would be able to explain it better.

Relaxed.

Then it hit me why wouldn't she meet the guy someplace she easily could explain her car—metro station, even leave her car home, meet him she's out for a walk, something—they show up in only his car?

Of course, then I'd catch them leaving, getting in the same car.

I was wound up over this, got on me how much I was making it mean, a test I'd not studied for, pitfall'd show I didn't know what was what or have the knack Leonard'd assumed.

It was a few hours later by the time another car pulled in—there'd been no movement from any of the rooms—this car parking right by the office, flabby foreign guy getting out, going inside, twenty minutes later still wasn't out figured he was evening shift.

Zooming in the camera on the guy's car to have a look—verifying the plates for the fortieth time—was the first time it crossed my mind what was the difference between how Leonard had things set up in a situation like this and just asking a few dollars off from the parties involved? The thought was at first kind of scoffing, like in make believe I was having a laugh at Leonard, but then it got solid, I really wondered. It made more sense, purely financial, to run a little investigation like this, find something out on someone, give a report back all was clear but then go ahead and keep an eye a bit longer, take a stab at the interested parties.

Or, it kind of made sense.

Guessed from Leonard's perspective, his job being legitimate, it could go funny too many ways dicking with people like that—something went southward, someone got thinking, it might lead to some investigation or another, make things blaringly obvious to anyone half a wit it was a private eye making funny with the client pool.

Nodded to myself, eyes more peeled, more intent on the lot, sun starting to go down proper, all the street lights'd already lit up half hour back.

In this particular case, though, it seemed no harm no foul. This wasn't the husband wanting to know was he being made cuckold, private eye says he's not, husband finds out later whole time he was, wife says someone bled her off some or such amount of the savings, line goes straight point A point B—no, this was oddball, was some mom wants to know her boy's not making poor life choices, this was something just keep mum the affair angle then make it a suckle one's own sweet time.

Might not be worth it, still, not worth it to someone like Leonard, license at risk for at best some few grand when the case probably pays few grand to treat legitimate. Not that I was Leonard, I was thinking—me, I could give full report to Leonard, even turn over home video, just not before I got a camera of my own or maybe made copy the contents from off his, keep in my own little file.

Nodded.

Even the mother decided to do what she did to the son, figured it stood to reason it wouldn't go so far she'd get to screwing herself into the life the woman he'd been trying it on with—and even if the affair ended, affair's not something a husband'd like to find out even good number of years after the fact, was sort of thing, instead, the sting stuck just as raw, whenever.

Car pulled in the lot, parked right next to Gregory's, lights went out and same time door the top level the motel opened and my finger went to the record button—zoom out, zoom in, zoom out, zoom in, whole little chorcography of Gregory over the railing waved Hi, Lara did obvious Hi hi back, Greg leered behind his cigarette at Lara making her way up the stairs and, presto, Lara takes his cigarette, sips a drag, flicks the thing over the railing, her tongue driving home down his mouth, his hand cupping one half her ass, arms obviously the type worked out enough just his gripping a squeeze's enough to lift her brief off both feet, inside, door closed.

Could tell from the zoomed image on the camera screen that even were I to get right up, in physical person, to the window the room it'd be no dice on getting a glimpse inside—and even if the ruckus could be heard from outside, wasn't sure the risk needed to be took.

Crossed my mind to maybe call Leonard, give him the update, even ask his opinion did I need to stick around until morning, get the shot of the two of them leaving, but the figured all of that went without saying—needed to remember Leonard was footing my bills, last thing I wanted to seem was lackadaisical.

So got comfortable, smoked through half pack, every once in awhile glancing at the room rates on the dingy lit sign—thirty-nine for the night—thinking I could ask the room next door, maybe be able to get some sleep.

By around eleven o'clock, door to the room opened—got a swell shot of Gregory, nude, hair fresh perspiration to it, Lara stepping backward out the door, not the steadiest on her feet and touching down at her skirt absently, Gregory bold enough even he stepped full out the room door, leaned to railing, watched Lara—real gentleman—all the way until she was in her car—she giggling to find he was there when she looked up, rolling her eyes, too.

Lara's car was out of the lot two minutes, already, when Gregory finally pushed back from the railing, stretched to tiptoes and closed himself back inside.

-Well bravo, I said, camera off, slipped back to pant pocket, same pocket took cigarettes pack out from, got one lit and first puff out said Bravo a few more times, raising smoke up like some wineglass.

∗∗

I'd woke about two minutes before the mobile phone started its little song, probably quite early still, the television had on some infomercial for an abdominal workout machine, I squinted at the fellow demonstrating as I reached to the bedside table, unwound myself from how I'd wrapped legs around pillow, top sheet around legs.

Made no attempt to act less groggy than I was, Leonard laughing after my Hello, he asked how everything went, emphasized he wasn't being a micromanager about anything, just figured it'd be good to see how I'd gotten my footing or not.

"Oh, everything went perfect, man, think we got more than enough, more than enough."

More laughing, but also business, he asked "That so? They got the room?"

"Sure thing they did" yawned, yawned again, propped up because honestly felt I was falling right back to sleep "got quite a show for my trouble."

"No kidding? Not the shy types, right? So that was a titillating bonus for you."

Now I chuckled, mouth tasting of cigarettes and tap water. "Well, not so great—only thing parental guardian would've been required for was the cock and balls, sad to say."

Big laugh, he told me he was sorry to hear it, but that I'd be surprised how often that'd turn out to be the case.

"No worries," I said, giggling proper, Leonard's wide awake jumpstarting me. "But as to our needs, got about all that could possibly be needed to make the mother right proud of the boy she raised."

Leonard asked me I meant I got enough on film, I said "All of it," asked him was it a thing I should bother about going back or this was just slam dunk.

"Stake it out, again, the more the better, especially if it's a same-girl-every-time scenario, that way less questions and it makes us seem thorough."

"Right."

He wasn't sure did they have the reservation for another night, kind of surprised me, I asked how come.

"There's ways to get information like that, of course, but no need to go that route if it isn't necessary. Think of it like line items on an invoice, you know? We've done enough work, don't need to waste talent on glissandos."

"Sure."

But still curious, I casually asked he had tricks for getting information like that, he told me he had tricks for everything but he'd teach them to me on a come-as-they're needed basis, might even see how well I could improvise, be there the whole time hold my hand, best way to learn a trade.

He didn't need me to come by the office or meet up, hung up after a few more remarks, little bit of ribbing me about I better make sure not to tape over anything, said how it could be a problem with the digital camera—I assured him I'd put in the training, got myself a feel for the thing.

Only took a brief shower, as I felt so awake, made it down to the free breakfast in plenty of time, ate in the dining area watching some medical drama two desk clerks had the television on to, no one manning the desk, other than me no one but them around, laughing loud, bad mouthing the hotel and the hours they had to work or couldn't work and all.

Kept my eyes down, started running it through my head about would it be best to try my thing with approaching Lara or approaching Gregory—on the surface, same thing either way it cut, but settled on I should play which song I felt safer with, this all being a trail run, just to try back my sea legs.

Lara, she had an actual stake, meant she had more a likelihood there could be blowback from all manner of directions—say I put a scare to her, then Gregory's mother gets it out of Leonard for a few bucks, or even gets it out of Gregory, who the lady in question is, where she lives, makes some approach of her own, then Lara makes a fuss over not believing Gregory would just make a straight betrayal for nothing, then mother for whatever reason starts thinking it was Leonard who leveraged Lara when Lara confronts the mother, Lara thinking the mother'd sent me just to dick with her and it all gets to be a huge mess where Leonard'd be the wiser man and know I was double dipping, then due to this all being his proper living would have to either let me go or, worse, get thinking he should look in to me.

Hated that thought, stood, refilled coffee, back up to my room.

No, anything that could lead—however paranoid that 'could' might be—to Leonard thinking it better to get the scoop on me more than I was a stumblebum shoplifter was no good at all.

In the file, found where Gregory worked, waited awhile to give the shop a call, learn he was on shift until four o'clock and'd get in at eleven—asked which bus, which metro could get me there easiest, then thought things over on the toilet and taking another shower, more lingering.

Fair odds had it that Gregory wouldn't peep so much as a funny question to Lara, as he clearly knew her deal as happy housewife sort and was fine with it—it'd end between them both, one day, he'd have it at why rush it to the finish line, especially considering a guy who liked to get some married woman'd be likely to like even more having the reiteration how much power he had over her, all things considered, pump him up he could flatten her she stopped giving him his jollies.

Didn't even towel off, smoked, soaking the rumpled comforter, looking at the television, now a military movie some kind, bombs going off while some soldiers played guitars and looked at crude nudie pictures.

Even if Gregory didn't need to get off feeling the man with the upper hand to the nth degree, he wouldn't tell just because there was no reason to—I wasn't going to hit him for anything bad, was treating it more like a practical joke than anything, most important thing was to test my perception, see if the flab was where I thought, the lean where I wanted.

Clapped my hands, started getting dressed, then right away stepped free from pants around just one ankle, removed underwear, shook it across the room a foot waggle, paced around with hand gestures, full talking aloud in half speeches about what this was, what it meant, how I'd work it, how it'd work. Reminded myself this wasn't to set myself up—emphatically, redoubling this with widening my arms open, turning a circle in place, surveying the room thinking I am already set up—this was just a formality, a way of putting my stamp on things, getting out from the headspace of caught petty crook into the one of free roamer.

Down the lobby, helped myself to last coffee, found the breakfast hadn't yet been cleared away, all of it thickening stale, the two clerks now smoking cigarettes out in front, nodding to me Have a good day when I stopped a few steps off from them to light cigarette of my own.

The heat of the day had me soaked through by the time I caught a bus and it got no better during the ride, thing crammed full with body odor and no air conditioning, just stream of heat from windows all cracked down part way— I could smell the coffee wafting from my pores and moving my tongue over the front of my teeth, working tip into the empty space my missing tooth, found spit thick enough I could collect it, stagnant, into piles, manipulate it into balls and chew, swallow it, it flowed straight right back up.

***

Kildarby's was a clothing boutique, nothing I'd ever wear though the disheveled yet tailored look of the window mannequins was eye catching enough and I liked how the display had suitcases strew and burst, letters falling out, artful in clumps stuck to the windows or in arcs up from the floor, illusion of suspended in space despite the violent set to them. Could see in, marked Gregory arranging things on racks, folding others, and once I'd confirmed his being there setting myself up sentry across the street with fruit juice, cigarette, candy bar after a stroll around to confirm there wasn't a rear entrance, or not one, anyway, I was betting was used by employees after clock out.

It was only three when he exited, put on dark glasses and stopped to arrange his shoes better around his sockless feet—followed him from other side of the street, dubious at first, maybe he was just on a smoke break, until I eyed he was heading for the metro station, a choice on his part made me glad one second, nervous the next, one hand I liked I'd have him contained, other hand worried train'd be too busy to get proper word in his ear or else might make it easy for him to make a scene he turned out to go that way in cases of awkward confrontation.

Turnstiled in right after him, escalatored down to platform two people back, entered train car from another door, car not even quarter way full and those it was quarter filled with all students buried in distractions, glum workers starting to read newspapers, obviously fighting sleep on account of being beat and the heat of the day, on top.

"How's it going?" asked to him, sitting across the aisle, our seats facing the same way and not so much turning in his direction, he giving me kind of friendly enough smile and nod like I was just making random talk, he'd put up with it he had to but making no indication it was particularly welcomed. "I'm a friend of Marcus," told him next, now pointedly turning, legs in the aisle, his eyes going squint, little shrug, still smiling like it was great I was friends with Marcus but I should understand from his expression he did not know what that meant and that I could well have him mistaken for someone else. "You don't know Marcus?"

"Naw man, don't think so."

He'd said this expansively, scratching his neck and turning face from me, not turning to face back. "He's Lara's husband, you understand? I'm friends with Lara's husband."

This got a straight up look out of him, but if he was taking measure of me he wasn't making a thing about it. Let it stand that way a moment, then leaned forward, doing unnecessary shifting where I sat, lacing fingers, patting knees, lacing fingers, patting knee.

"Nothing to worry about—Marcus is a dickhead, maybe you don't know because you don't know him. I'm his friend and all, but frankly he is a bit of a dryhump."

Had him, could tell—he just didn't care about this, it was a curiosity as far as it went with him, so I decided to stick with the surreal tone I'd hit.

"You and Lara don't talk about him or anything? She didn't come up to you 'My husband's no sixty minute man, you seem like you might be' nothing like that old scenario?"

"Nope," he said, air like he'd buy me a drink or whatever except for us being on a train. "You wanna know about it, I went up to her. Didn't take but two chats worth of convincing, doesn't seem it mattered her husband could float her or he couldn't."

"Just drawn to your boyish charm, is that right?"

He laughed, "I'd seen her lots before, actually, even told her that, figured why the hell not, right?"

"Right," I nodded, nodded. "I wanted to ask you something, something I always wondered, having known Lara since she was first making eyes at Marcus."

"What's that?"

"Is she a bit unkempt with herself you manage to get her to lose the clothes? Always seemed to me she'd be, but Marcus says it doesn't go that way."

"Can't speak for Marcus, then, sure never thought about Marcus, but as far as letting herself unwind, yeah, Lara's a regular old workaholic there's a task at hand, you know?"

He eyed out the window what station had we pulled to a stop at, trickle of commuters in, some few making to sit by us.

I gave a gesture Gregory should follow me a bit further back the car, held my eyes to say there were a few more things I wanted to explain and he moved right with me, even sat legs in the aisle just like me and it was him who started talking again, first.

"It doesn't surprise me, though, man, I'll tell you that. Lara, as much as it seemed like sometimes she's surprising herself, got the distinct feeling her heretofore untapped assets were ones she had particular alone time wishing'd be tapped, if you follow what I mean."

Told him absolutely, let long breath down my nose and went on in to he must understand I was talking to him for a reason and he might've taken note it wasn't to give him a lecture.

"You have to understand" I just cut to the chase "much as Marcus is my friend and I think little of him, certain information comes my way I'd be remiss not to take something for myself."

He made a face, got the drift from him he was of a mind I was asking could I ante in, so I waved some fingers at him effeminately, shaking my head. "Wouldn't impose myself, wouldn't impose myself, Greg. Funny thing is, my girlfriend, she has a hankering for this suede jacket on sale, so then I thought wouldn't it be a hoot you lent me the money for it, same time we have this little good natured gossip about the state of the happy couple, right?"

"You want me to buy a jacket?" he said, knowing I didn't want him to buy a jacket, look he was making sure I knew he was being fatuous, maybe enjoying this all more than I was, myself.

"Jacket's two hundred dollars, figured hard working kid'd be the sort to do me a solid along those lines."

He asked, flat out, was I blackmailing him, odd spring of giddiness to it, cut in on top his own chuckling to ask me what was my name. Told him don't worry anything about my name's this or my name's that, and also corrected him that to be plain I was technically blackmailing Lara just through the intermediary of him, this getting a genuine laugh and he shifted like to take him wallet, same time like it might be a pretend move, but then wallet came out.

"If I don't give you two hundred dollars, you'd drop this to Marcus? Are you serious?"

Told him I was, even same time he was opening the wallet, plenty more than two hundred there. He skimmed off set of twenties, recounted it on his knee—it was too much, he put three back—looked up at me.

"Of course, you might tell even if I give you the money."

"Never," I said, taking it—he let it go lighter than air— putting it to my pocket.

My head was light when I stood up, noting the train slowing, the pillars of the station we were entering whipping by the window, slowing, slugging beside us, and Gregory was looking almost like he was a bit put off I wasn't sticking around—maybe both of us with it in mind had what happened just happened.

Even after the train'd pulled gone, Gregory not so much as looking out at me—and I was out of the station, just walking off random, couldn't get my head exactly settled how I felt about the whole thing, the ease of it obviously elating, same time the ease of it puncturing the skin of the view of things I was creating. I hadn't even done anything, so this, win though it was, was based on nothing, just the whim of some kid obviously fond enough of whims.

***

Rounded through the shopping plaza, slowly got up the hill for a view of the motel it was already dark—really I'd been there a few hours, wandering the plaza, a bit further off until some bridge, turning around, had smoked through more than a pack. I wasn't putting off the moment I'd see had Gregory and Lara showed up, but was in no hurry for it, crept as much as I could, silly thought that Gregory might be keeping his eyes out for me—ridiculous, no reason for that, but still I'd be embarrassed somehow it went that way, maybe wanted to stay ethereal to Gregory, some guy came out from no place slipped back no place, someone he couldn't find me if he gave it best effort.

His car was in same space as night before and he was inside it, slither of exhaust out the back and I could hear the murmur of talk radio or something.

Went back down the hill to fiddle with getting the camera set, kept it recording as I got back up the hill, down the other side, snuggled in by the dumpsters.

With the zoom, it was easy enough to tell he was in the car, paying nothing any mind, might be it was marijuana he was smoking, especially considering how long in he held the smoke, pointlessly slow he let it out.

Shut off recording, got in back the dumpsters and had another smoke of my own, spent the time dragging it down to the stub thinking about the four hundred and change I had in my pant pocket, how long it'd been I'd had anything near that—felt whole, like I could strike off in any direction, renewed, like I was rebuilding myself out of pure will, this train of thought sputtering into self-mockery, but none that I dwelled on.

Trained camera back on Gregory's car, not hitting record, now thinking why was he in the car and not the room? Was it Lara who was paying and it was on a time-by-time basis? Was it he'd forgot his key?

Intent on this puzzle, didn't notice until her car was already curling to its spot that Lara'd arrived—Gregory'd noticed and was already out of his car, leaning against the rear driver's side door.

Settled the zoom in tight, Lara moving over, nothing to her, even sweet, like she was apologizing for being late, Gregory not moving a tick until she was in front of him and then, quick as it takes to shiver, hooking his one hand over inside the front of her skirt and pulling her forward, no resistance her part, just the opposite, after the jolt of the jostle her both hands up into the short shag of his hair, he busy getting her top unbuttoned enough to uncup her breasts from bra, both of them exposed, turning to have her back pressed against the car, ducking down his mouth to take more than her full nipple in his teeth, then quickly the other. This all seemed to suit her fine, though she was having a look around, something he noticed just as it was obvious from the push and strain of her skirt fabric that he was hooking fingers down around the fit of her panties. He suddenly backed off, having a laugh I could hear easy enough, but I could only guess, my lip reading not perfect, that what he said next was Leave them out, when Lara went to start doing up a button. They stared mouthfuls at each other, Gregory breaking gaze first, turning, no ceremony, moving off in the direction of the stairs, Lara staying put until he finally did turn, just about to head up, and I had the camera on her to see her face in a kind of sarcastic smile, last beat of play pouting, she started in his direction, breasts out, almost a strut for him, but not unselfconscious, tippy toe quick steps to catch him up.

Stopped recording just as soon as the room door opened, shut, stood wiping an itch that'd started on my chin with the shirt fabric over my shoulder, absently camera going back to pocket, cigarette pack coming out.

Apparently, whatever little shock I may've been thinking I'd put into Gregory hadn't thrown him half step off his game, fact which almost made me proud, except I couldn't properly remember had this been how I'd assumed he'd get—pumped up, big man on campus—or had I been certain he'd be on the verge of calling it off.

Either way, my move'd worked, meant future moves'd be possible I kept my eyes open for them. This, I'd got few extra dollars, but still the main thing was I'd also done good by Leonard—he could work his take on Gregory's mother with ample evidence to back his case that the boy was just hurting in the natural way, nothing to worry about, and that he at least had the sense to go with an older woman'd have sense enough to take precautions to high hell rather than screwing himself into every pretty classmate or gal he met at work, who knows what'd be in their head.

I was walking back toward the train to get to the hotel before I even knew it, licking my lips at every fast-food place I saw, promising myself that soon enough it'd be no more subsisting on free breakfast and also deciding, just as fast, that prize to myself would be to splurge this two hundred, proof positive it hadn't mattered and I didn't need it, just I'd splurge in a way that's build me, not just get me glut on hamburgers, bellyache I'd regret.

Found my room just how I'd left it, even television still on, cold so much I almost set the thermostat higher, but then didn't bother, undressed, socks soggy, crotch of my underpants actually damp.

The money.

Didn't count it except to segregate the two hundred, leave it on the corner desk pinned under the weight of the ashtray—looked at it from across the room, drifting but never going full asleep, thoughts fade in and out of same thought like nothing was happening and never would.

Decided to run a bath, settling myself in, television volume loud enough on a comedy talk show I could hear without straining, kept bathroom lights off, ashed my cigarettes right into the water and felt the little nip of energy each inhale gave me, the doddering lilt of my head with each exhale.

When I got into bed, volume back down on the television, I lay with my head at the foot, feet buried under the pillows, comforter bunched into cushion for my head, two sheets and a towel I took up from the floor as blankets.

Vaguely thought about Gregory, Lara. Were they spending the night each other? Was Gregory spending it himself after she had to get back home? Would he be thinking about Marcus? Would he have made a sly question or turned a joke or put Lara on the spot to give a comparison how he sized up, prowess, physique

Would she care? Would this be the last they saw of each other, Gregory's little show of ownership—show only I'd seen, which maybe he kind of hoped was how it'd be going—something he was making to leave her in a state of feeling discarded, feel same as the dampened tissue plopped to waste bin she'd cleaned herself up with it?

Looked at the money. Two hundred.

Knew it was nothing like that, Gregory and Lara. I was thinking about this more than both of them combined, same as I always thought of everything more than anyone—they didn't care, only I did, and I only cared to lay, gloating over my little treasure, slipping asleep in television grey.

***

Recalled the place—didn't see a name, just signs over and over reiterating suits were two for one hundred dollars, four for three hundred dollars, this type, that type—from days spent walking around between nights at the shelters, like a closet thin slip in a row of legitimate shops. The woman working, probably who owned it, didn't look up I browsed, the racks so packed I took anything off couldn't fit it squeezed back right, some racks up high enough couldn't figure how anyone'd get to them, no step stool even around.

Eventually, had to ask her about how did I know about prices, the question taking her away from some magazine, printed on paper kind of lemon colored, she disparagingly pointing to the obvious sign showing the suits were color coded, stickers on the sleeve.

I had a real hankering for a brown suit, but everyone I found had an orange sticker, two for three hundred, one for two fifty—odd price breakdown, but they were all broken down like that—finally asked did she have any suits, brown ones, with the white stickers, two for one hundred.

"How should I know, you see all these suits? I don't remember them from color. Must be some around, I don't care if they're brown, brown isn't special, I don't price because something's brown or something's not brown."

She looked back down, forcefully rereading, it seemed, what she'd just read.

"Sorry, can I ask something else?"

No answer, but could tell she wasn't reading, passive aggressive about yeah I could ask so why wasn't I?

"This one" held up a brown one I wanted "it has an orange sticker, but maybe I can get it, just the one, for one hundred?"

"Orange is one for two-fifty," she said, not looking up.

"I understand you, and you're right, of course, but I was thinking that might be, like things sometimes are, flexible?"

Someone called to her from the backroom, but she didn't bother answering, not even at all, told me the orange were how they were, the whites were how they were, she had nothing to do with it, she priced them how she wanted and so that's how it went.

"I was thinking since you give two other suits for one hundred and I'm offering one hundred for just one suit it might be a deal, you know, for both of us."

"It'd be a deal for you, you win one-fifty, not for me, I lose one-fifty."

Which was true as much as it wasn't.

I noticed she had on some face cream of sorts, clumps of it at the creases of her ears, the dangles of the earrings with some of the gunk long caked.

Mobile phone went off in my pocket, so I made way to front of the store, Leonard giving me an expansive How's it going? before I'd even said a word, guess he could tell the call was through.

"Fantastic, man, I'm haggling for a suit with a real venomous one, but I have faith."

"Suits a good thing to have, no question. I take it things went well, again, with the lovebirds?"

Told him things couldn't've gone better, that between the two nights we had more than we needed—even added that this time I'd got full monty off the woman, not a sniff of the fellow's contraption even to sour it.

"Fantastic, fantastic. After your suit, come on down to the office, bring along the camera. Some other things to discuss, another bit more involved bit of business I have for you, think you're my man for."

And a few more casual remarks, he hung up, I rolled head around shoulders, moved back to the woman, asked her again how about a deal on the suit.

"What's the matter with the other brown suits?"

"I don't find any in my size and none that are white stickered."

"In the whole store, there isn't a suit cheap enough for you, no brown suit?"

Pep from thinking to meet Leonard, close out the first bit of work, get my hands around something thicker, smiled like the lady wasn't some bad tinkered piece of work but a sweetheart, told her "How about a compromise?" Again, she didn't answer, just went still, eyes wide and irritable could I get to the point. I suggested that I pay two hundred, but for the brown suit and another suit, white stickered. To her logic, though, this was a big trick I was trying to pull, because white suits, individually, cost one-fifty, so a white sticker plus an orange sticker made it five hundred—she meant four, but I didn't press—and she wasn't an idiot, said if I was chincy and full of tricks how about I didn't get any suits.

I laughed—just couldn't help it—tried to get her to see the mathematics in mixing the combined stickers for a middle price, but she retreated into her magazine, told me she put stickers on things, posted the sign so she didn't have to deal with people like me. That was her final word.

"I'm going to look for a different suit, then."

No reply.

Spent twenty minutes engaged in what if she was paying attention'd've seemed a thorough search, same time peeled the orange sticker from the suit I wanted, a white sticker from another, swapped them, almost giggled, more interested in how she'd react she caught me out than the child's game actually paying off.

Not wanting to wait all day about getting to see Leonard, found a grey suit, my size, white stickered, went back up to the woman with a face on like she'd bent me over but I'd buy even though it wasn't what I wanted.

"One hundred dollars," she said, tip tap inspection of the sleeves, looked at me a moment enough I got there wasn't going to be receipt or cash register involved— probably a sign about All Sales Final and As Is someplace in the mess.

Paid her with five twenties, money going down a pocket the side of her skirt. She didn't offer me a bag, told me leave the hangers—I did ask could I buy them for an extra five spot, she repeated to leave them—then draped the coats and pants over an arm and headed out back to the metro.

I called Leonard back when I was to the hotel, just to apologize for the delay, explained I'd meant to tell him I needed the camera from the room first. He told me not to worry, he wasn't even at the office yet, I had time, also told me not to worry office was locked up I got there, though probably he'd be in by the time I got there the bus.

Rinsed myself quick in the shower, dressed—no proper shirt for the suit, but I kind of preferred it with just the patterned tee underneath—really wished I'd done laundry as I pulled my underpants, palpably damp, itch starting immediately, the soap fresh skin in contact with the swamp.

Next thing'd be I'd get a haircut, promised my reflection aloud, unlit cigarette on lip, tip of it actually to my mouth as the back end'd come loose, flecks of tobacco loose, the paper a slight tear.

Put camera the inside suit pocket, my cigarettes the other one, looked around like did I need anything else, but left out the door before even halfway'd considered, elevator down dreading the heat and how it'd sour the new feeling of me inside five minutes—same time, honestly, kind of liked that, and liked that I only had white socks and that my shoes were hideously worse for wear, didn't know last time ever I'd taken a stich of notice of them.

***

Traced fingers over the lettering on the door, pushed shoulder my way in, found Leonard there standing, office ice cold, loud from the air conditioning, he taking one look at me, my skin sopping, soaked hand over mop water forehead, bursting out a laugh, asked me how I could wear suit it was whore's blood outside. I just shrugged, he directing me to a seat at the desk where I noticed an iced coffee, plastic cup sweating worse than me, made a shy point at it was it mine, he nodded. I took the thing up, had a sip through the straw, turning chair to face him, elbow on the desk.

"Have the camera?"

Took it from my pocket, set it on the desk, he nodded, nodded, let out a breath and moved toward the door, beginning to talk with his back still turned.

"Told you what you did was you reminded me of

something, Trevor, that you reminded me of something, you remember that?"

I set the cup down, slow, careful, touched forearm sleeve to brow and cleared my throat. "I do remember that, sure."

"You pick up on how I called you Trevor, there?" he said, grin like a kid made a dirty word out a regular one, proud of the crudeness.

My mouth didn't want to say it, but told him I'd made note he'd done that because it was the observant sort of person I was raised to be, this making him swing his arms, air from his nose like he was going to get the giggles, then he did a quick face shake, totally composed.

"What you reminded me of is that opportunities are there and to be taken. Could be good opportunities, bad, all kinds, but they're there if you look for them or they're there if you just find them."

Somber tone, he pinched nose to index finger with pad of thumb, squinted he was thinking his line.

"Awhile back, kind of opportunity was presented to me, kind that normally is not my thing—person who presented this, while they hoped I'd be game, more than that I think they understood right away I was the sort of person who if I didn't go for it I'd be fine to let it lay, none of my business."

He sat in one of the comfortable chairs, moved it not quite to face me, crossed his legs, decided against it, leaned back, forward, stood.

"I'll tell you, Trevor, when you came into that store, when you came in to nab your shaving foam, your chewing gum or whatever it all was, I really thought to myself I was going to use you, make an effort and string you up all for something you didn't know a thing about. Not straight off, but when I found that gun hunkered down in your bag it clicked in my head and then the look on your face, how I knew you weren't feeding me a line about the shelters and you'd never come back to the store—you looked such a shivering puppy I thought I was going to frame you into something you never even knew a thing about, blindside you you wouldn't even understand."

He paused. I hadn't so much as moved, only enough I was fixating on the drink I'd set down, watching the wet building under it—nothing for me to say, I was too choked to bother remembering about needing to breath.

"Let's be upfront, though, Trevor, it's not like the television, the movies make people believe—I know that, know it's complicated to do something like that and as much as I didn't have it in me to take this opportunity myself, I much more didn't have it in me to take chances with something like that. Stupid—he chuckled, kicked at my shin—stupid, right? How does someone really do something like that? It doesn't work like that."

I nodded, earnestly, because I agreed, wanted to say I agreed, felt adrift in this talking, like it was still something good from where I was sitting, something I needed to loosen up about, that Leonard wanted someone to just agree, tell him Yes, he was exactly right and that was all.

Then—I hardly listened except I spelled every word, too, while he said them, heard them so hard I could feel the warmer of them in the artificial cold—he told me how the serial number on that gun, he took it down, just a thing to check, how that gun it'd been registered to a man called Norman Court.

"Norman a guy" he told me like catching me up I'd missed the first act "who'd misread the dosing instructions on a few bottles of pills and'd gone the wrong way for it. Norman a guy, it seemed, wrote a note out all about a woman called Klia—Klia who'd cut her wrists in a bathtub just a little bit before Norman self-medicated. Note was also about a man named Trevor English. That's you right?"

But he didn't wait for me to say Yes and when I did say it he was already moved on.

"Trevor English" he pointed at me "had been twisting Klia's arm for money, twisting Norman's arm for money, twisting" he added like it wasn't so interesting "some other guy called Lawrence's arm for money, though Norman" he held up his hands like wanted me to understand a subtlety "didn't know that part, that wasn't in any letter from Norman, that was in another report from a police precinct where Trevor" he pointed at me "had once been sat for some questions, some file complied by some busy body cop" he shrugged, actual note of contempt.

I nodded, which seemed to make him glad, like he had it all straight.

"Anyway," he went on, "there was also a thing about—this was a while later—some guy named Trevor English had tried to extort money from a high school teacher called Wynol. Seems it didn't work, but Trevor did extort money from Wynol's wife. Well, things went bad, family unit and all suffered, and Wynol found himself miserable enough to report some gory details to the police, kind of spiteful, and to bother his wife to corroborate her side."

"And then Trevor disappeared," I chimed in, reached for the drink but couldn't lift it when I touched it, heard it slosh louder ten times than I should've.

"For awhile, yeah. Except he turns up again, calls himself Henry Dollar—a great name, better than Bells or whatever you're on to now—and it seems some very very nasty business goes down on account of he wants more money and tricks some lonely lady for it and then she gets wise and when Trevor learns that she wants to be made whole he goes and treats her very poorly, gets his picture around town as quite the violent sexual offender."

He told me, abruptly, that he had a file, odd the way he said it, like he remembered he wanted to be showing me visual aids but now it was too late, he was on his roll.

"I never raped Helen," I said.

Leonard clapped, pointed at he with the clapped hands. "Helen, that was it, Helen. Well, so anyway, then poof, again, Trevor, Henry, gone."

He stared at me.

"Poof, again."

He stared at me. Pointed at me.

"Poof."

He grinned, bored seeming, but then face went tense.

"You notice how I'm calling you Trevor?"

A jab of it this time, the question said as swagger, but then an almost embarrassed look over his face like that was too far, no need to be mean.

"The long and the short is, Trevor, I got to figuring that rather than making pretend that you did something but having to do it myself, I'd just have you do it yourself—I mean, you can see that, I'm sure. It's one thing you just have a gun, it's another thing it only takes me a few days and this is what I find out not even straining with the lifting—you can see that, yeah?"

He flopped back into the comfortable chair, let some phlegmy breaths through his nose, patted his knees, slouched back almost he'd slide to the floor.

"I mentioned it's something involving you using your gun, or had I not gotten to that yet? Sorry, I'm a little bit nervous, wanting to make sure I'm getting you to understand me."

Told him I understood him, he'd done great about that, asked he had a tip jar or something for the show, this bringing a grin, grin immediately went worm squiggly mouth.

"I mention you're going to use that gun to put a bullet in a guy's name's Lester Grove?"

He was pushing his tongue, almost sexual, this cheek, that cheek, clucking it like he was waiting to poke me some more, now he'd had his fun I was just there to kick.

Not wanting to hear anything else out of his face, bit my thumb a nibble, said "Yeah," pointed finger at him, little cops and robbers pistol shot, told him "Yeah, you'd mentioned that."

***

I sat in the chair, facing away from the desk, third cigarette and finally drinking from the thin of the coffee, ice melted all but a few pieces felt more like film against my lip, warm like peels of skin. Leonard'd had to make a few calls, nothing to do with me and him, had asked me to have a seat one of the comfortable chairs, but when I didn't move he just told me I could suit myself.

Between the first and the second call, he'd handed me a photograph—man in suit, hardly looked like anything, sideburns maybe a bit too long but not like they were noticeable unless I forced them to be—on the back, pasted on, typewriting on an index card the name Lester Grove, two addresses, a telephone number, a date just shorthanded to Thurs 11, two days off.

Leonard's calls were hypnotically banal, one just some ins and outs of what seemed a run-of-the-mill thing he was taking on, another something about the company he had to handle invoices, then a call in to some store—maybe where we'd met, funny as it now felt putting things that way—asking if he could confirm his scheduled hours.

When it went quite, when I noticed it'd been for awhile, I turned, found Leonard'd picked up the camera, was watching playback on its screen. I stared at him, the little changes in his focus, expression, must've been two three minutes before he just happened to sniffle, took a look up more like he was considering shutting off the air conditioning than he'd wanted to take note of me, and he smiled, setting camera down, I could tell images still moving across it.

"Funny thing about it," he said, getting cigarette from the pack—mine—out on the desk, lighting it from a book of matches he took from his shirt front pocket, "is that I'm forty-six, but I still consider myself as having a thing for older women." He chuckled. "Obviously, that's all I can get now I want them or not, but what I mean is I get this kid all too well. Kind of sad to me, makes me a tragic case that I can get what I want but I'm not who I want to be to make it what I actually want." Then he let a sigh, squinted at the screen, daintily pressed a button to stop the playback. "Isn't that funny, Trevor?"

"It is," I said, took another of my cigarettes for myself.

"How about you, you like an older woman?"

Shook my head, eyes unfocused, had trouble making them sharp again, said "I don't like anybody."

Leonard nodded, scrunch of mouth like that was my loss, and while I relit my cigarette that hadn't taken right, he pointed at the photo I had resting on my lap.

"First address is where he lives, second where he works, he takes the train point to point like any old working stiff."

I nodded. "And Thursday is my deadline?"

"And let's be clear about that—that's the drop dead line, which means he should be well dead before then, but if he isn't, definitely, by then it's all the time I can waste on you."

"Sure."

He gave me a stern look, leaned forward, crossing his arms, head going tilt, centering. "I'm going on the strength that you're a smart enough person not to think about doing anything smart. Would you say I've made a fair assessment of you?"

"I would. I'd say I'm exactly that smart and no smarter, never having much call to be."

Cleared his throat few times, leaned back, told me I was a wonderful guy, asked had anyone ever told me that before.

Not sure I'd got his drift, said "Sorry?"

"You're really a wonderful human being, Trevor—hasn't anyone ever told you that, before?"

Thought about it, or made a face looked like thinking, said "I suppose someone or another has, here or there, someone must've, yeah."

"Good. That's good."

He stood and went into back room had the door open, heard a refrigerator open, he came back in with a bottled water, chewing something I couldn't tell what. I was starting to feel like I should leave, like it was what was expected of me, didn't feel I was holding up any end of anything by staying, but instead of moving I asked him was the thing it was necessary I use the gun, was that important.

He said it wasn't, I could do whatever I wanted, though he couldn't imagine what'd be easier than using the gun.

"And other than society makes it I'm strung up by the neck, what happens if I don't kill this guy?"

"If you don't?" he swigged water, could read the genuine question in his eyes he swallowed faster than he normally would've.

"To you. If this guy doesn't get killed."

His face lost interest, almost his eyes rolled, said he supposed he'd have some egg on his face and he could forget about referrals, but nothing the party in question could do except not pay.

Then he got an expression, sitting back down, grave, thoughtful, spoke looking away, then turned his head to me, soft eyes at the end. He said "I think I could kill someone. I do. Kill them. If I had to or if it came from something in me, something in me made it so I, personally, wanted to kill someone, then I could do that, I think so. But for some money, I couldn't do it. I don't know anyone who could do that kind of a thing for money." Big smile then, he flicked a finger at me, like little brother being pest, going "So the good job about this situation is I'm not paying you a thing, you won't have to go around with that banging around inside of you after, right?"

I found that curiously humorous, it knocked me loose, realized only then how sunk back in my head I'd got, like I'd been looking out my eyes with eyes.

I asked if he might be good enough to give me an advance against my cut of whatever he got off of Gregory's mom, pointed at the camera when he didn't seem to follow.

"Can't do it, can't do it. The coffers and bare, it's all on a royalty basis this business, sorry."

"What's to keep you from turning me in even if I do it?"

"Nothing. Nothing's to keep me from it, Trevor. But don't you start talking that way, you've got time to work your head around it, just take care of it, off you go, we both know you're instinctually driven enough to get and stay as far west of me as possible this plays itself through."

"Where am I supposed to go, exactly?"

But he was done with it, maybe had been since I'd started posing the questions not just sitting good little mute. Looked at the door behind me, said almost a mutter "What should that have to do with me? Piss off back up the asshole your mother birthed you out, all I care."

Empty, I just stood, considering taking off my suit coat as I got near the door, but couldn't bring the motions, would rather just shoulder the heat and peel myself out of all the gunk seeped out of me, later.

"The phone," Leonard said, snapping his fingers and I started my hand into pocket for it he said "No no. The phone—you keep it, it rings, it's me, you answer."

"Yeah," I said, pulled door open, left out it thinking maybe he was saying something else, maybe not, ears hollow, blood coiled in them.

Only got as far as the end of the office park before drooping, more or less falling to a seat on a curb, surprised I was still holding the photo when I looked down and I was. Shut my eyes but they wouldn't keep that way, so I pierced them hard at the image of Lester, held him up in front of me, put my thumb over most of his face, clicked it aside, covered it back over him, clicked it aside.

Eventually probably I'd decided to stand up, walk, found I was walking, had been, bus coming in, I was in line with whoever else.

***

Sometime, three o'clock, past three o'clock in the morning it first hit me it was Wednesday, technically, meaning Lester needed to be dead by tomorrow—one of those odd tricks of time, seemed I had one day, really had two, two felt like one, everything last minute.

I'd blankly watched all of some interview with either a film director or producer, couldn't tell, sat naked on the end of my bed, had my laundry going down on the main floor, now drying, everything but my new grey suit and a filthy t-shirt I'd just throw away.

Lester's photo was on the bed next to me, couldn't bring myself to look at it—seemed I shouldn't have any problem looking, no thought in mind to do anything about killing him, but it was almost enough my stomach'd snuffle around like dog trying to settle to sleep I even thought about Lester.

Shut off the television, turned up one of oddly placed lamps on the wall—wincing away from the sting off the bulb, saw the file on Gregory, Lara, took it up and walked with it to the bathroom sink where I'd left my cigarettes, lit one off one of the last three matches left in the booklet, letting the match burn out full in the sink basin.

As of my last count, had little north of three hundred dollars. In a pinch, it came to it, I'd take off with that, even pay it all out for a ticket someplace get myself lost, once again back to zero and nowhere—but if I could, without too much bother, get some other few bucks more, didn't reason I should pass up trying.

Lara.

Squeeze just something, nothing much, just something out of her, enough to float me awhile.

Lara.

Thing was, of course, it was that Leonard was watching me, so if it started to look fishy, he'd drop the ax. Even this hotel, it struck me—wandering in the gloom of the one light, opening the room curtains full for a view of the lot and, in the distance, some sign of the city—was set up like a cage for me, no real way to slip out unnoticed. Basically, there was one way to walk from the lot I wanted to get anywhere, one place to get the bus or the metro, and that a good mile or so away—even if I slipped out one of the several entrances, awful thing was it wasn't the entrances Leonard'd have to have eyes on, just the road in and out, so if he situated himself from some vantage, binoculars, camera, I was just a crumb in the bottom of a bowl, he'd see me no matter what.

Took a minute, breathed false, controlled, even, tried to pretend he wasn't watching me, tried to make that reasonable, but this only got myself in a tailspin of thinking. Maybe he had someone else watching me. So what was the difference? But it he had someone else watching me, maybe then did that mean did they know why they were watching me? But what could that matter? And, anyway, he wouldn't have someone else watching me, he'd be watching me. And if he was watching me, even if I did kill Lester, sure thing was two seconds after I'd polished off the deed it'd be Leonard calling police down—or even waiting for me to get as far as the bus station, close myself inside a rolling coffin, authorities waiting the other end to just scoop me up, easy as pie.

I stopped cold, watched my reflection, the eyes set to some thought, the slug heavy tongue move across torn paper lips, watched until I got the impression it was the reflection watching back at me, giving me the thought it's found.

Leonard was watching me. Meant I needed to behave. Meant behaving meant I needed to seem like I was trying to kill Lester. It meant I needed to seem to have a plan. I didn't need to sneak anyplace, needed to seem like I wasn't doing that at all, just trying to cover my bases—anything else, his alarms'd go shrill and he might get premature in finishing me off.

If I was going to kill Lester, it served to reason I'd have to set myself up an escape, otherwise what'd I bother about killing him for? If I did it, I needed to get away with it or else I'd just be even in a worse screw than Leonard had me in already. What did it matter even Leonard sees me go to a bus depot? As long as he sees me come out, it'd look I was making steps in the right direction.

Paused up a minute with considering about what'd it look like to him he saw me bleeding few bucks from Lara?

But still it didn't matter—as long as I didn't make a beeline back the depot it'd, again, even more, seem I had my focus in.

Leonard'd want me to take care of myself.

All I had to do was think.

Told myself in the mirror, mirror told me back "For once think, Trevor—once in your life actually, honestly think."

I nodded.

I nodded.

Nodded.

And first thing I thought was that to put him at ease, Leonard'd better see that I had the gun on me, see me empty my box the shipping store, put everything in the backpack. I needed to have the gun, even, just in case he decided to spot check me—silly as it sounded, I needed to be who he wanted me to be.

My clothes weren't completely dry, but I brought them back up from the laundry room, folded them—noting the brown suit pants probably shouldn't've gone in normal water wash, decided just leave that suit behind—packed them all in a pillowcase when it was either that or a flimsy little trash bag.

Was staring at the pillowcase, might've be awhile or not, it was like medicine head I came awake, eyes focusing hard, went crossed, resettled. Knew I'd been thinking to myself So why not just kill Lester then, so much I have to act like it?

Why not?

Otherwise, it'd come down to what? I'd follow him? Go in his apartment? Gun to him? What?

So, I don't kill him, just go in apartment building, wait around awhile, when Leonard sees me come out he's going to confirm, there and then, is Lester alive—and Lester's alive, cops called, I'm done.

If I killed him, it'd be murder on top of a pile that already had me humped flat, but also it'd be a chance I'd run away and maybe maybe not get caught out for it later, along with everything else.

What in Christ's'd be different leaving Lester alive, murdering him dead?

So 'I kill him, Leonard turns me in, maybe,' or 'I don't kill him, Leonard turns me in, certainly' is the same as 'I kill him, Lester turns me in, certainly,' and 'I don't kill him, Lester turns me in, certainly.'

Shook my face, said aloud "Stop it," then said aloud "You're not fooling anybody."

Puzzled what'd the second thing mean, but only long enough to dismiss it.

Started dressing, full grey suit, though button down shirt was stale shabby and necktie had creases, deep permanent wrinkles. Looked at my bare feet, over to my shoes, sighed, sat on the mattress, lay back.

Even doing something wasn't doing anything. Sitting in this room and waiting out the clock had every exact advantage as not, staying resulted in the same as leaving and somehow the different versions of the same result— get caught or escape but be running, again—each felt worse than the other for all they felt the same.

Smiled at how myself that made me feel.

***

Shipping store didn't open for another hour, something completely took me off guard though, standing there, tugging locked doors limply, it was more like a punch line, something I'd no reason not to've expected. I crossed the street to a drugstore, bought cigarette, asking three books of matches, stepped out into the bleary overcast, soap scum humidity, giving glance this way and that.

How would he be watching me, how would he be able?

Figured part of it could be his taking it on faith I wasn't going to just split, but same time that couldn't be all. People follow people, watch people, it was his profession, I'm sure he had all sorts of tricks—adding into the mix that I was on foot and had extremely limited resources, must've been a cakewalk. It was deflating, remembering my spike of panic overnight, a good half hour I must've been plotting some intricate way to wriggle a getaway, thinking every turn I'd come up with'd been stroke of unexpected genius when all the time not only had I not done them, but had I they'd've been exactly things he knew like from a workbook to be on the lookout for, could picture him having a laugh I'd tried X or Y, tsk-tsking me for being so unoriginal.

-You're no wild card, Trevor, said with a swirl of cigarette into the air that seemed to sponge it up.

The grey suit was much looser fitting than, according to its size, it should've been, the pants especially it was like I had them hobo-cinched, checked my reflection expecting to look a shipwrecked sailor, but nothing so bad and the length being a bit long took partway the curse off my deplorable shoes, my white socks buried, even sitting crossed legged that'd not be a thing.

I couldn't concentrate, things like that—whether someone'd have a laugh at me about socks—creeping in, though I did justify that it wasn't pride or vainglory, just I knew certain things'd make me stand out more, should know what they were, know how I looked abnormal.

I entered the shipping store right behind the opening clerk, smooth talking that could I just be two seconds, get at my storage box when he told me they weren't open for another twenty minutes, yet—clerk waited, leaned to the open door, actual sick of nervous on him like maybe it'd been I'd scared him with my pushiness, he was bracing for the worst. Didn't say a word, even look at him, when I left, already stuffing the pillowcase filled with my clothing into the backpack, shrugging it up over shoulder, letting it slide off like always, taking it by the scruff and wandering down the street.

All of this, imagined Leonard watching—imagined he knew already I'd taken the locker, but even if not didn't see the difference. I wanted to take the gun out, right there, walking down the street, hold it long enough he could note I had it, was doing what I'd been told—instead, went into a coffee shop, waited my turn for the toilet, letting the two people who wound up in line behind me go ahead, shy nod that I might be awhile when they tried to insist I go ahead on the strength of having got there first.

Gun was never how I remembered it, this time wasn't how I remembered it felt bigger, heftier, maybe the reality of the bullets in it burning hotter in my head, the reality I might level the barrel in someone's direction and the swift of fear that I might, in that moment, feel compelled go ahead, depress trigger, take what'd come, run—pull the trigger, run, see how far.

I pointed the gun at the wall, watching the odd three shadows, each a different dark, made over the wall by the toilet lighting—pointed it at the toilet seat, the hand dryer, trashcan, door. Then turned, lowering gun, looked my reflection, shaking my head with a tried on smile, mouth evening to nothing. I regarded myself, suit, hair still seeming kempt, hair I added several more laps of water to, forcing it back and snakeskin smooth as much I could.

Bundled all of the clothes out of the backpack—just didn't want the cumbersome feeling—forced them down into the small trashbin, filling it, just one brief moment of hesitating maybe I'd keep something, then no. Almost I left the backpack, but figured I'd need it, better to keep the gun there than my odd pockets the misfit suit.

Had a piss, flushed, quick double check the picture of Lester and file on Lara were still in the front pouch of the backpack, left the toilet, passing line six deep of people'd been waiting, buried looks of irritation from them all, but nothing worth they'd bother me about.

I wasn't going to shoot Lester Grove.

Waiting out for a bus into the city, whispered the thought to myself—peculiar, as it wasn't even Lester's place I was on my way toward, was Lara's work, but my reminder felt distinctly pointed, like I could see myself doing it, could do it by accident, could do it and somehow not notice until after, hand slapping forehead, what'd I just done?

Took a seat in the bus, furthest back, head vibrating against the window, dead insects, live insects down in the groove where window sunk into window base—certain parts of the road, things got jittery enough there was no difference, looked even the live ones were confused, spooked, uncertain of the approach of the carcasses. It was fun to watch, think about. Anything was.

But soon dissolved in to pointless musing that I could approach Lester, tell him I was supposed to kill him—that someone wanted him dead—that only chance we had was make it look like that was happening. Pictured it Lester goes along with me, lets me pretend walk him to his car as though leading him off to privacy, but really I take him down some lonely road, meanwhile'd asked him to've called a friend to meet me with another car. Thought about I'd fire off a shot after leading Lester in through some tree line, he and I'd switch outfits, he going back to his car, driving away out of state like as though he was me making a break for it, while I hop into some stranger's car, they'd thank me for taking such a risk with myself. Thought how Leonard'd no idea how it was I'd managed to get him so duped until it was well too late and how he now knew Lester knew who he was, knew what was up, how Leonard'd know and investigation was coming, knew how he'd kick the wrong patch of ground when he'd turned me over.

"Jesus," said, snapping my head like I'd been nodding off, knowing full well it was all wide awake, all that nonsense wide awake no matter I wished it'd been vomit of half-asleep anxiety—it was really what I'd been thinking.

Because the bus got caught up in some kind of commuter traffic, knot of unmoving vehicles seeming it'd never untighten, I got off just a the next place it pulled over. Stared at the unmoving clot of cars, trucks, vans, ambulance—if he was in that, Leonard, he couldn't follow me, not without abandoning his car.

Stared.

Stared.

Turned and started walking, sidewalk in the direction well away from that congested street, whole time picking up speed, slowing, picking up speed, slowing. If he was in there or not, truth was I should be hoping he didn't lose sight of me, should be angry at the traffic if Leonard hadn't planned for it.

And still none of it changed the fact that even if it was just a matter of police being informed that Trevor

English—full file on me handed them—was in the city and looking to leave, or had recently left, how long before the clamp would come down?

Stopped where I stood, closed my eyes, started off again at a stroll, fishing telephone from my pocket, pressing in Leonard's number.

***

Office building where Lara worked was generic, same as buildings either side and across the street. Set myself up in a bakery café around the corner, coffee I added water to from the pitcher set up by the napkins, a cigarette out on the table I dabbed fingertips at. Also had out the mobile phone, kept giving it flicks, wondering did I want to use it or did I want to wander over few blocks more where I saw cluster of payphones—finally just took out sheet from my backpack had Lara's work number on it, dialed, clearing my throat, one last swallow the coffee while call rang only once before her This is Lara Daye.

"Hi Lara, glad I caught you. My name's Trevor" that slipped out, hadn't meant it, but what'd it matter? "I need to ask you about something."

She was clearly focusing also on something else, slight sign of dubiousness to her voice she asked me "Alright, what's that?"

"Need to know what's it worth to you keep your husband from knowing about your younger model you like to have a roll around with?"

Only the briefest pause, not much in the way of concern, she said "Worth to me, what?"

"To have Marcus stay blissfully in the dark about other intimacies of yours—let's cut out playing dumbbell each other, okay, I'm on a schedule."

And still calm—too even her voice, made me want to hang right up, felt air shifting around inside me like everything'd gone loose—she asked me was I the guy who'd taken money off Gregory the other day.

"No I'm another guy, Lara—yes obviously I'm that guy."

"Where are you?"

Hackles went up, felt everything soft under me, like chair'd give way, like ground wasn't there, sinkhole. Told her I was on the other end of a telephone I was about to call her husband from, told her last chance to forget with the interview bit, I was really losing patience.

She let a sigh first, hard to get what it actually sounded like from the static quality the reception so much breath, told me "Marcus knows about Gregory, but you can call him if you want."

Chuckled, sniffled, stared at my coffee, some little speck floating it in tried to stick to the cup inside a tap of my finger. Was about to press in with calling her bluff, but'd stayed quiet enough I guess it unsettled her to go on, her tone quiet, direct.

"My husband knows all about it. What is it you want?"

"Your husband knows all about it?"

Detested the sound of the question, my voice so beat.

"You want some more money? Gregory told me he paid you?"

Tried again the speck in the coffee, making a Hmn sound while I did. "Gregory paid me, he did do that, yeah. Thing is, it isn't so much Gregory was the fellow I thought to stake the whole amount actually I need, wouldn't seem fair, right? You husband knows about it, that's what your telling me?"

I wanted to hang up, winced eyes shut so hard it was as though they'd closed sideways, around, upside down—no sort of idea was she playing at something, was it straight truth, all of it was a buzzing, gnat got all the way down my eardrum set up house.

"How much money do you want? Are you there?"

I took a swallow the coffee, crumb still in it after, grit teeth they slid, top off from bottoms, slight bite to inside lower lip.

"I'm here."

Didn't know that I was though, just gazing out across the bakery, didn't feel there.

"Where do you want the money? Where are you?"

Repeated her, Novocain mouth, "Where do I want the money?"

"How do I get it to you?"

Slow, felt it slithering up like from underneath my feet'd started to sweat, heel tapped, squirmed in my seat and chest went big breath out, eyes narrowed. Nodded to myself, pudding head, even morose grin trying to take but kept slipping instead just to slight pucker, twist side to side my lips.

"Because you don't want Gregory to know Marcus knows."

I said it, dreadful apparent it'd just struck me right then, blew laugh out my nose, sure the ship was capsized, Lara just about to get the hint, put a growl to me and hang up.

But nothing.

Tested things out—nothing better to do—starting "How much's that worth to you, in today's currency? Keep your tiger thinking he's not just the in-joke some freaky old couple?"

"How much do you want?"

Could tell her voice it wasn't worth all that much, but worth something not so inconvenient she'd take a real hit.

"Five hundred."

"You only asked Gregory two hundred."

Burst of laughing, knew a few other patrons looked at me, I slathered "Are you being serious?" legs of my chair giving squeak they scraped the rough tile floor. "Five hundred," I repeated.

"How about three?"

"How about three? What? Because that's five total? Is this what you're thinking?"

Another sigh from her, followed by "How about nothing?" but the question seemed halfhearted.

Likely, there was more to this turn than the hassle of her not getting a young one up her, she was contending with some other slant, nervous. And next blink. I had better footing, stopped playing the stooge and found the right groove to press down in, get the sound I wanted from her.

"Five is the thing, Lara—hundred rather than thousand is on account this is Wacky Wednesday, you get a discount, alright? Otherwise maybe Greg'll think he's been played around and doesn't so much like it, might be he's the sort not to take to that and want's to poke around you're playing house the hubby, home with the kids. I'm trying to be polite on account of I like an older woman myself, but don't press your luck."

No more sighs from her, no more quick chiming in, just whole good twenty seconds of telephone silence, me with cigarette to lip, standing, getting out the door. Had match booklet out, ready to strike, got the "How do I get you the money?" in my ear, again, this time ringing correct. Took my time striking matching, swallowing first drag, invisible letting it out my nose after holding it down long.

"Bakery café downstairs, around the corner. You know the place?"

She said a name, I turned my head to verify, told her

"Yeah" and told her "Don't be an idiot" she asked she was supposed to meet me there.

"You have that cash on you, right now?"

She said there was cash machine the lobby of her building, I told her she had two minutes to be at it, I'd be watching.

"Where are you?"

"I'm everywhere, far as you can tell. What's more important's you're going to be popping in the café with the money, you're gonna be buying a coffee you empty out, you put the money in the empty, you walk back to your office, you leave that cup in the trash right outside the door. Easy enough?"

She made a hesitant sound. "How about I put it in a cup from right here on my desk, just open the lobby door, leave it in the trash, turn around and take the elevator back up?"

I blinked, felt my eyes tick side tock side, movement of them distinct enough it started hurting.

"Or I'll just hand it to you," she said, still hesitant but like she was maybe thinking million times more clear than me, maybe knew she was, even second thoughts about she'd go along.

"You can just meet me downstairs," she said, bit more confidence, adding that she'd just give me the money.

"Bring a cup, put it in the trash," I said, snapping phone shut.

I'd stopped moving at the curb, crosswalk, stood watching the indicator on the other side count down to zero from fourteen, just as it did steeping down the curb, loitering traffic at the light all sounding horn in odd sequence while I ducked head, holding hand up to the side, little wave of Sorry, sorry.

***

Lara, she didn't even so much as look around she stepped out the building, cup to trashcan. I'd made no effort about making myself hidden, had expected some eye contact, some look up down, an assessment in whatever expression she'd give me, but nothing, even the cup into the trash had no kind of emotion or identity to it. I waited through a chain of three more cigarettes before a casual stroll past the building doors, glance inside to empty lobby, stroll back to take cup, feeling there was some weight in it, didn't open it until few blocks later, arbitrary turns this way and that.

Five hundred dollars. Twenty-five twenty dollar bills.

I walked with it still in the cup another few blocks, then transferred it to my pant pocket, taking stairs down into a metro station where I stood against a wall, watching the seep of few commuters, some attendants mopping the beige-red tile, setting up signs warning people to watch their footing.

Felt fatigued—more than that, completely emptied out—only thoughts toward a room, a bed, even just a seat on the metro, head to window, eyes closed, a seat a bus across country, even just a bus three hours away, I could close my eyes and wake feeling in a new moment. That was the trouble, I felt in the same moment, even the new money in my pocket nothing, no accomplishment, no finalization.

Stared bleary at the map of the various metro lines, had to ask an attendant which one would take me near some bus depot, train depot, felt a right idiot when they told me, polite as can be, I wanted the Green Line would take me to a station named—bold, big, prominent lettering on the map—Huxley/Downtown, clear parenthetical beneath it this was also the central transfer station for out of state transportation.

When I got on the metro—Blue Line—I didn't take a seat, though the compartment I was in stood all but empty, I wafted in place, holding the high railing, center of the aisle, eyes tight to the posted map, to the station called Billington where Blue joined Yellow and Green, all directions.

My impulse, as trodden down it might be, was to take the first bus, any train I could. It was impossible that Leonard was following me, I didn't care how experienced he may be—there was no absolute way to follow someone and there was no way for him to know where I was. When I'd called him, just one hour, two hours earlier, he'd hardly registered it, just listened to whatever nonsense I'd told him how it would be tonight things would go down.

Though, this was as off-putting as it was reassuring.

Wasn't that just what someone trying to sound convincing, all the time being full of it, would say? Hadn't that likely, moreso even than not hearing from me, put it in his head to take precautions?

I couldn't even understand why I'd done it, hardly seemed I'd even made that call, the more I thought on it, the more absolute the reality of it crawled on me.

Transferred to the Green line, this train swarmed with people, everyone cramming on, bodies against bodies, my nose just over the tip of some lumbering fat man's shoulder, the man every few seconds nosily sucking on his thumb, the skin of which—I couldn't keep myself from observing—was wrinkled from the length of time he'd been moistening it, flesh around the thumbnail chewed, deeper here than there, some points tips of hot soft pink, the rest of it sucked pale, dead, waiting to harden and be bitten, chewed, swallowed by the man, later.

I closed my eyes when it got to be too much, when the train slowed to a halt in a tunnel, announcement coming on that it and another train were sharing a track for part of the route, voice with no identity apologizing for the continued delay.

Occurred to me, again, Leonard didn't have to keep an eye on me, so much. Really, if I wanted to leave town there were only so many places I could go, so many ways out.

What could I do? Train? Bus?

So, even if I slipped out, the station cameras'd be examined, my picture shown around—simple as two is one plus one I'd be tracked, nabbed right up even if I ditched mid route.

Or a taxi? Pay for it to take me out of state?

Same thing—record of my travels, driver to identify me, trail to be picked up.

It wasn't like I'd be able to keep running, couldn't keep coming up with clever subroutes and feints, eventually it'd all come down and I'd be approached, brought down.

How had I ever gotten away from anything before? Series of ridiculous luck? Apathy on the part of whoever might've been pursuing me?

Didn't understand how I'd got where I'd got—not even I didn't know what'd brought me there, it was just simply I didn't get how was it possible I'd been able to ooze along so far as this, why the end was waiting instead of already behind me.

The Huxlet/Downtown station was enormous, the yawn of a church, walking in the doors it was almost too much, my head drowned as it was, to figure out where were the ticket windows, to read the schedule boards. Everyone was looking at me, no one was, some people were for a minute then stopping, the moment they stopped other people taking a turn, turning away.

I vomited in a toilet, heard the shush of dozens of other people queuing for the urinals, tapping the faucets on, tugging more paper towels than they needed, depressing buttons for air dryers, blowing noses, flatulence, voices, clacks of heels. Flushed the toilet, kept to my knees, stared at the cusp of water down the bowl, hands to the side of my face like the addition of the shadow'd make it possible to see my reflection.

Standing in line to purchase ticket, sudden grab of panic had I left my backpack somewhere, was surprised to find it was gripped in my hand when I swung that hand up like to find backpack over my shoulder, made sure to chuckle at myself, roll my eyes when attendant at a window called me to come over, obviously'd been looking at me this whole odd display.

"I need a train for tomorrow," I said, "just something cross-country, preferable leaving around eight o'clock."

"In the morning?"

Took me a minute to respond, shaking head too much "No, no. At night. Sorry."

"I have a train to Virginia leaving a nine."

"Nothing earlier?"

"To Massachusetts at six-forty."

Swallowing to try to get my ears to pop—they'd clogged, soft ringing—I said the Virginia'd be fine, cringed at the price of it, but laid the money out.

"Do you have identification?"

Grimaced. "Do I need it?"

She let a defeated breath, didn't even answer, typed hard at her keyboard, presented me with something to sign, though I didn't know what it could be about on account of I'd paid cash.

"It'll be the main terminal", she said, did a nose tap in some direction.

But I was already turning, ticket in my teeth, opening front pouch of backpack, making for the exit back onto the street, needing air, cigarette, to breath.

***

Spit a string I couldn't get to break even by spitting again, finally grabbed at it, ran hands over my shirt front, my pant leg, wiped mouth against my shoulder.

Getting my bearings was an impossibility, but still I looked at the names of the cross streets and down at the two addresses typed to the card stuck to the back of the photograph of Lester, turned the photo over, gave the man another look.

Seemed the bench I'd found to sit on was at the outskirts of a dog park, intermittent yaps making me jump, yaps or handclaps of owners proud their animals'd done this or that.

Was just realizing the pack of cigarettes I had was empty, crumpling it, glance around in case some uppity person'd bother me for when I discarded it off into the grass—when I did, with a graceless, girlish toss—the mobile phone sounding from inside my suit coat. First impulse was to snatch for it, get it to ear immediately, but got hold of myself, leaned back, legs long and searing from being stretched out in front of me, and I waited until the little tune went through four times to open the thing up, give a bored Hi Leonard.

"I'm starting to get worried about you, pal."

His voice was terse, but shy of aggressive, I sucked on the inside of my cheek making sour eyes. "Nothing to worry about. All according to schedule, you know? Thing worth doing, someone once said something about it."

I could picture Leonard nodding slow, taking stock of

what I was saying, imagined him sat at his office, takeaway sandwich on a plate, sipping from a fountain soda.

"You're not looking so well, Trevor, I have to say, you're really not looking so well."

Didn't bother to even have a lazy turn of my eyes around, just mumbled I couldn't be bothered with keeping up appearances, he'd just have to take my word this was how I got things done, style and strategy I'd been developing for years.

"I see, I see. Because I'm starting to think this might be all done, between us. Tell me I shouldn't think that."

"You shouldn't think that," I said, clicked a smile at my shoes, feet scrunching and relaxing inside them, toes aching like all of them'd been stuck with pins.

"Where's the ticket for?"

I looked up—just deciding wherever he was it was someplace looking up made it like I was looking at him—made my face sober, somewhat irritable over the prying. "Ticket's for Virginia, Leonard. Am I not allowed to plan an escape? I don't remember agreeing to get caught in with what else I agreed to."

He told me that was certainly fair enough, that he was, all things considered, glad enough to hear I was thinking ahead, but then voice got colder about he needed, of course, to be sure about exactly what it was I had it in mind I was escaping.

I watched a man throw a purple ball, two medium size dogs go tear after it, ball hitting ground near the base of a tree, both dogs overshooting it, clumsily changing inertia, each rounding the truck different side in tandem— probably should've been giving Leonard an answer, though he didn't seem put off when after a few more seconds heard him ask "What's in Virginia?"

"I've no idea. Nothing, probably."

"Read me your confirmation number, whatever you have like that, the trip number, departure time, bus number."

Couldn't help it, I laughed inside of stomach cramps, leaned down to open backpack, mumbling "Gosh, Leonard, if it's going to be like that."

Took a second to examine the ticket, read him a bunch of information, most of it probably he didn't care about, but I wanted to be transparent I was really looking at a real ticket, telling him things I just couldn't make up.

"You know if I check that and it's not legit, I'll have to take offense."

"Can you see me?" I asked, almost overtop him, now just curious, even turning around where I sat.

"I can see you, Trevor, don't even think for a minute I can't."

"Alright. And can I ask a question, as long as I have you?"

My casualness, akin to giddiness, kind of alarmed me—touched myself to see did I feel feverish—but if it did the same to Leonard, he played it room temperature, told me ask whatever I wanted, he'd answer if he felt like it.

"How much are you getting paid to kill this guy, to have me kill this guy, what's it costing someone?"

"Just about what you'd think, Trevor. You know how it is—not as much as I ought to be, considering, but enough that it's enough."

"I just want a number. It'll make me feel good about myself."

"That right?" He sniffed, then it sounded like he was wiping his mouth, lips smacking—maybe the sandwich part of what I'd pictured was accurate, just he was parked in a car, napkin on his knee. "Seventy thousand dollars."

"Seventy or seventeen?"

I'd heard him fine, first time, but wanted to hear him say it again, then said "That's nothing to sneeze at" when he did.

"How much did Lara give you?"

If he wanted that to spook me, it didn't, but he probably didn't want it to spook me, just figured he'd get as much data he could data to make whatever decision he was making about my state of mind.

"Just five hundred. Hey, you know her husband knows all about the kid?"

"I did not know that, no. Funny thing, isn't it, what people do when left them to their own devices? So she paid you on account of what?"

"She didn't want the kid to know the husband knew."

He laughed, said it was terrific to hear people taking so much pride in their complications.

"Leonard, you remember you said how you figured you could kill someone, just couldn't do it for money?"

No answer, but no answer in the way he knew I wanted the dramatic pause much more than a jump line.

"I think I could kill someone for money, Leonard. Before, I didn't think that. But I think I could, I do, in thinking about it as much as I've been. I think if someone put money in my hand, just about I'd put a bullet anywhere they asked."

This next pause he made I didn't like, it stung in my ear, made the phone seem hot, so much I held it an inch or so away, rubbed the side of my head with my free hand.

"I hope you get away, Trevor, I want you to know that."

"I appreciate that, Leonard."

But he'd hung up, which I did, too, after a moment, touching myself for cigarettes, remembering the empty pack I'd just thrown, scanning the ground around for it, seemed it'd vanished.

I made my way to the metro station, sluggish, all sense of urgency, of need, of persecution gone—knowing Leonard was there, that he'd been there, it made me feel at ease, a mechanism that was functioning, no chance something'd jam up, that some innocuous bit of rust on me'd bring me grinding dead before the revolution of me went full. He'd give me until last minute, verify it I went wrong before packing me up, not just make a decision from remote based on his imagination.

I showed the attendant in the booth down the station the address on the typewritten card, asked could she direct me closest station to it, she was able to like by rote, hardly giving what I was holding a look, even told me what the fare'd be and pointed out I'd want to get a pass in the next few minutes, before the rates went up to peak time.

***

The humidty'd gone rotten, some odors from someplace'd taken root in it, from the moment I'd started up the stairs from the metro it'd gotten a rank feeling on me, so I stepped into the lobby of the building where Lester worked, tucked myself to the wall by some plants and took mobile phone from pocket. Lobby wasn't entirely free from whatever it was stank outside, sips of it must've gotten in every time door opened, glass just permeable enough not to be full security from outdoors, but the air conditioning had it chill, somehow just the look of polished tile floor and large brass placard with slots for names of the businesses up the elevator added to the feel of refrigeration—bearable, fine, anything better than outside, that air.

Took backpack up to take out Lester's picture, again, dialed up his office, plugged his extension in when automated voice was through with introducing the company, started giving me options. Man came on the line just with Hello, so I playacted I was calling for someone called Henri, he told me wrong extension.

"Who's this?"

"This is Lester Grove."

"Is this accounts payable?"

"It isn't, no. I think you might have entirely the wrong number."

"Henri isn't there?"

But I didn't let him answer, told him Nevermind, to which he didn't say anything and I hung up.

Nodded like I'd accomplished something, glanced around, let myself sink, leaned hard to the wall, to the floor, first keeping knees bent, then letting them splay. Only rested just the one moment, real effort to get myself standing, had to shake around a lot to get my focus back.

There were kiosks on the street, bought a bottled water and candy bar off one, situated myself back in the lobby, walking bored circles of it, checking the time.

Considering how much information I'd had in the Lara Gregory file, it irked me to only have these barebones over Lester—seemed Lester was deserving of as much thoroughness as possible, especially the job being farmed out. He could get off work any minute, could get off five o'clock, might be he had to stay late—I should know which it was.

My mind drifted, nothing else for it to do, keeping tethered in the current situation, stopping blind thoughts about things forthcoming from winding me up, wearing me down.

It had to be someone who knew Lester, whoever wanted him dead, so seemed they should be able to have some intimate detail—might very well be a co-worker, in which case I'd expect a breakdown of Lester's workday by the hour, give me as much to plan with as possible.

Though, not necessarily a co-worker, and maybe the work address was secondary, because his home, he in his apartment all alone, seemed the more sensible place to do a killing a killing was going to get done—even then, though, an outline of his usual activities, other places he tended to go, anything might be useful. It should be up to the party doing the killing to decide what was pertinent or what a viable time and place, not the party just wanting man dead.

"I'm really disappointed in your lack of professionalism, Leonard," I whispered, definitely feverish or something, just glad the manic episode from earlier didn't feel it was coming back on me.

At various points over the next few hours, elevator doors'd open, whole clusters of people coming out all at once, I'd assume a more thoughtful posture, like I had actual business in the building, watch everyone file out the lobby doors, growing sensation of anxiety that I might be missing Lester walking right past me, didn't feel I was recognizing anyone, getting good impression. When end of day came around, though, there was Lester, easy enough, he and two women passing right by me, casual chatter, one woman going left once out the door, Lester, me, other woman going right, other woman dropping off just half block down, veering to head around to a parking structure.

I'd marked, from before, that there was only the one metro station Lester'd be at all likely to use, so him heading in that direction, I kept hung back, watching his legs, watching him untuck his shirt as he walked, loose his tie, all funny to see from behind, things so easy to watch that to him, to anyone, were so unconscious figured no one'd ever look if they could—he seemed alien, houseplant that could walk, mound of soil that suddenly yawned or blinked its eyes.

On the train I was close to him, no way not to be, especially as I was not confident forcing myself through a crowd to get off some station—he and I were back to back, or almost, were side to side. I watched his reflection, noted he was keeping track of some redhead, not trying to catch her eye but not being covert. When he shifted his position, facing her direction, full on, I turned to look the same way, watching her over his shoulder, tried to make out the title what book was it she had, becoming disinterested, turning to look out the side windows at the flicks of light and the stop motion appearance of coming into this station or that.

Lester rode almost full out the end of the line, exited at an above ground station—it'd rained either while we'd been underground or in this area of the city, sometime earlier—and he and I along with few dozen others sort of penguin walked on account of not knowing how slick had the water made the steps, the tile.

His metro card wouldn't let him through the turnstile, so I got into the lobby, first—fuming at myself why did I still not have cigarettes?—saw him grumble his way to the machine to add on whatever amount he needed to add, how he snatched his card out once it was viable, big huff to him he wanted to make a grand show of slamming his way out the station, the mechanism how the turnstile worked not allowing for anything like that, his shoulders eventually slumping into pile of seething.

Even though Leonard'd not mentioned anything about car or that Lester took a bus after the train, I tensed up as we made our way across the damp parking lot, pass the line of loading buses—lot of drivers in a bunch all smoking, one of them pitying me enough to lend me cigarette, the rest giving me glares like I was just a lousy person, didn't understand how many people'd come up to them, every day, thinking they were the only one's coming up to beg their little smoke.

I tried to make the cigarette last, but it was gone by the time we'd crossed a pedestrian walkway over lanes of traffic, so I kept eyeing every little shop we'd pass, willing didn't Lester need something out of one of them, quick stop in, but he just lumbered along, sometimes taking odd steps, quick tights of hands or arms like he had some little scene playing out in his head, real caught up in it all.

Maybe I looked just like that to anyone else walking by, to Leonard if he was watching me still—he was, this was the time to be watching me, after all. Maybe I seemed like drifting daydream of man with gun down my pocket, in my bag, pretender pretending cigarettes and murder, maybe I was whispering everything I thought I wasn't.

Lester went into his apartment, I crossed to the other side the street, eyes narrowing his entrance was a door needed key or being buzzed in, something I'd have to contend with.

Cleared an ear out with my little finger, head lilting back in the direction I'd come, calculating how long it'd take me I went at a jog to the last drugstore, two or three blocks back, what was the chance Lester'd slip by, wondered would Leonard give me call he did.

***

Last breath in, a little one, I put hand out in front of me, open palm, looked at the ridges of veins my hand back, closed fingers, rapped on Lester's door. Could tell his eye was to the peephole, took him a moment though, until I'd knocked again, to ask me could he help me.

"Yeah, hi, hope so. Sorry, I live downstairs, man. Do you have a leak or something? I've got water soaked my living room, man, something going on."

Another pause—I was keeping my face a smile, but brow a furrow, hoped I looked I was just feeling awkward for the oddness of bothering him, not that I was about to pass out, way it felt I was already falling.

"I don't notice anything," he said, peephole dark again from his eye.

"Are you sure?" I tightened my hand around the gun, out, ready at my side. "It's coming from the ceiling, you know? Don't know what else except maybe pipe or something."

And I was continuing with could we just have a look because it was really bad I heard the latch open, some second lock. I pushed forward hard as soon as I saw a slip of his face. He hadn't been too knocked off balance, was about to say something, shout something—I could tell from the hulk of the inhale he was taking—before he saw my gun out, at him, went stiff and small, took two silly teeter-totter steps no direction, I got the door closed, locked behind us.

Motioned he should step back, got him in his living room, had a look around, asked was anybody else at home. Shook his head, lower jaw going a quick chatter, shook his head more.

"No one is here? You need to tell me, now."

"No one," he managed to get out, then like he'd swallowed a damp glove all at once he choked up, seemed he was trying to keep from gagging.

"You need to listen to me, Lester."

He didn't move.

"You need to listen to me."

His head moved, I supposed a nod, he made a twitch to

rub his nose, look of panic, the hand going up, then flat hard to his side.

"I do not mean to alarm you, but unfortunately have to burden you the bad news someone wants you dead."

He stared, eyes focusing on the gun, me nodding, giving barrel a tiny waggle, repointing it blunt.

"I'm supposed to be the one doing that, so it's pretty important you nod that you understand you'd better do everything I say you don't feel like having that happen, here, now."

He didn't move, I repeated he needed to nod if he was getting my drift. He nodded.

"Lucky day for you, I got a better idea in my head than killing you, Les. But it's not a free pass for you, follow me?"

He nodded, though it wasn't a point where I really cared did he or didn't he.

"Because I'm being paid little more than a half dollar to do this thing, what's gonna make it worth my while not is to is I'm keeping the money I was given to do it and on top I'm taking the money you're about to give me for not."

When he didn't respond, told him he needed to nod, now. He nodded. Again. Confusion getting all over him it changed his complexion, he asked "What money?"

"Your money, Lester. Everything you've got."

I realized I hadn't even had a proper glance at the room, tried to avert my eyes off his, couldn't, then after a second noticed he was pointing to a wallet on the kitchen counter. I stepped slowly over, flopped the thing open, taking what seemed the maybe two, three hundred dollars inside.

"This is a start, but I'm going to need whatever we can get off your bank card, alright?"

He swallowed, pale of nausea over him, looked he was about to cry, lips starting to shiver, I told him calm down.

"I don't have any credit cards."

"Credit cards don't matter, just what we can get out the ATM."

But he was pointing at the wallet, head moving around, nod, shake, quiver—I touched around the wallet, turning the center flap, locking my eyes on him and telling him to get the cards out, moved back a few steps.

"I don't have any cards. I don't have any."

Immediately I knew he was not playing at anything, and whatever expression got on my face made him start to blubber, he actually clapped his one hand over mouth, eyes all apologies, but I was busy touching through he wallet, verifying it really didn't have any kind of bank card, credit card in it.

"Are you kidding me, Lester?" I brandished gun, tapped it his forehead, stepped back. "Are you out of your goddamned mind, Lester?" Grit my teeth, that last burst escaping me loud, knew I was becoming unspooled, no thought catching any other. "Where is your money?" Put the gun back to his forehead, away, back to his forehead and hissed "Where is your money, Lester, I have exactly no time for any of this."

Hyperventilating almost, some kind of something like a fit, he stammered he didn't have anything but the cash, something about being on a budget, something about only his planner had access to his accounts, paid his bills, gave him cash for the month—I knew I was smiling, maybe laughing but without sound, forcing the gun back to his head, finally, just to get him to stop.

I couldn't think of single thing to say, do, mind just blinking noon again again again again, I swayed back until hit against a wall, hand not holding the gun turned to hold me up with what was left of the strength in my legs. No idea how long before, but Lester was looking at me, horror on him, everywhere on him, I had the gun out full arm's length, he was halfway doubled over like ready to shield his head in his arms.

"How much did I just take?" finally managed to get out, he just crybabying Please don't do this until I'd ask him four more times and touched him with the gun, again.

"Three hundred and something, three, three hundred and something."

"Three hundred dollars?"

He looked up, making his eyes the shape of Yes and the shape of still Please please don't shoot him.

"Three hundred dollars you think your stupid little life is worth?"

He just broke, started crying, sound like a train was rattling the room above us, the room under. I kicked his ribs when he went to his knees, covering head, kicked his leg with the toe of my shoes, felt hornet stings of pain up me, kicked him again.

I wheeled to the door, put hand to knob and stopped, a clap of everything gong quiet, enough I heard every inch of breath I was making, every rumple of the cloth I was wearing. When I turned, he was still huddled all into himself, must've still be wailing, I just couldn't hear, things had all go inside out, spilled, wrecked.

"Lester," I said, even, heard the word out in front of me like pronounced by typewriter keys. "Lester, I have the very real feeling that someone is going to kill you, very soon."

He was crying, could tell but couldn't hear—maybe he'd gone past the point of being audible, completely upturned, nothing.

"When that happens, Lester, I just want you to know it wasn't me did it. I never did that to you."

And after saying that, don't know how long I stayed just

staring at him, putrid little writhe of him, broken like some pair of rolled up socks. When I did turn to leave, took me halfway down the corridor to catch I still had the gun out, walked the rest of the length to stairwell not watching where I was going, just fixated on the bulb of the revolver, like it was floating, crawling, pulling me along.

***

The pedestrian traffic started to get thicker as I walked, the sun now down, but just only, music from this restaurant, that shop, lines outside of certain establishments. The gun was down in my pant pocket, I could feel the touch of it with each step, each time I stood still at a crosswalk or just because I found myself not moving, no idea why.

Outside of a certain bar, taxis kept pulling in, letting out patrons, filling with others, pulling off—I stood in one spot, outside the doors of a closed for the evening florist, watching, eyes drifting to my backpack, thoughts to the bus ticket inside. It may well've been that I'd managed to, for the moment, slip Leonard or that maybe his plan was, really, to have my name, description around, authorities stationed at any likely exit from the city to pick me up. If he, himself, hadn't apprehended me, which I realized is how I'd expected things to've gone—to've pushed out the rear door of Lester's building, find Leonard idling, gun at his hip, smile. There was the chance it was a bluff game— good on him if I did kill Lester, he'd get lump sum of cash, if I didn't, then no bother to him and he knew it I'd scamper, no second thoughts, leave me to do that.

I nodded to a cab driver, guy right away dabbing his cigarette on the cab top, opening rear passenger door in same motion as he moved around the driver's, car honking from his not looking to see were things clear, slur of profanity from him, out in general ,and he was still complaining about whoever'd honked he got in the car.

"Do you drive out of state?"

His eyes wrinkled in the rearview, then he shifted to face me. "Out of state, not so much usually. Bus might be cheaper, I can take you to the station."

Told him no, it wasn't a matter of it being the cheaper thing, it was a matter of leaving right away. Little mouth Hmn from him, he figured that made sense, supposed he could take me, it depended how far I meant out of state.

"Can I just give you some money, you drive the highway until money runs out?"

Tensed against this raising some alarm, or a flat denial, instead he explained it'd cost me fifty over the meter, but he could drive me wherever.

"Drive me wherever, then, that sounds exactly right."

"North, West—what're you in the mood for?"

"I'm not in the mood, just someplace."

He started the motor, made me tighten when he called in something to his dispatch, string of words I didn't understand, then he sounded the horn for no reason or else at some people crossing in front, ten yards off, perfectly within their rights.

Turned, he said "Now, you said you give me the cash I go until it runs out, you have the cash?"

I shifted, took out what I'd beaten off Lester, counted off two sixty, reduced it to two—did some kind of count of what I thought I had left, full amount, other money and all, but no idea what my thoughts were accurate to— handed it up and showed him I had more, so he didn't need to account for the extra over the meter in what I'd just gave.

"How far does that get me?"

"Gets you someplace else, anyway, man, gets you awhile."

So I let myself feel swallowed in the dark, closed my eyes, but hand on my shoulder'd happen each time, finger to my side, eyes jolt like something'd clapped in my ear, so I moved to sit more straight, watch what I was passing.

For an hour, highway traffic was thick and there were odd patches of rainfall lasting no more than fifteen second, driver of the cab moaning each time these happened, but never turning on the wipers, even a lick. Soon after, traffic thinned, everything moving, trucks taking up miles of the far lane, stretching ahead as far as I could make out at each rise in the road—thought about that might be how I could do it, thumb a ride some truck stop, something that couldn't possibly be checked, real disappearance, no worse the wear than when this horror show'd started what felt forever ago, felt yesterday, the end all of a sudden and also like it'd taken forever to come.

"Do you think any of these cars are following us?" I asked, didn't want to say the words, but also did, needed some release valve.

"Following us?" driver laughed, said if I'd wanted to know about that, I should've asked him to keep an eye from when we left, how was he supposed to know now, laughed again.

Had follow up questions I wanted his thoughts on, but instead just chuckled, made more of a game of looking out the back window than I needed to, maybe wishing he'd ask me did I really think we were being followed, offer some trick to lose a tail or at least verify one.

A cramp up my neck, it occurred to me about maybe the mobile phone could be used to track me—no idea how, but anyway it was something that was Leonard's, still on me, and even if it wasn't as ridiculous as it could act a homing beacon, how was I to know from could he give it a call, police use that to sleuth out my position from where the call bounced around or whatever it did.

Took the thing from the smallest pouch of the backpack where I'd stuck it—felt, distinctly, the lump of the gun press up my leg as I shifted around—opened it up, shut it off, stared at the husk.

"Do you have any cigarettes?" I asked—he'd lit up at least half dozen times so far we'd been on the road.

"Sure man, two dollars."

But he laughed, right away, handed one back, a lighter.

I lit up, handed back lighter, cracked my window more than I needed to and first time I went to tap ash out, had the phone palmed, dropped it out, not hearing a thing of it falling if there was anything to hear—it was hard not to whisper some mockery at myself for the covertness, but the road moving under me, actual sensation of being away and—to judge from the meter and the possibility of the rest of the cash in my possession—feeling of soon to be well away made me hyperconscious, even wishing I hadn't said the thing earlier about being followed.

I must've started to drift, because I came to focus, driver obviously repeating, maybe third fourth time, should he be on the lookout for some specific sort of place to pull over, hotel or something, or did I just want literally to left out the road when meter got two hundred, which was just twenty dollars away.

"You can go a little past two hundred," I said, slurred, eyes gunk wouldn't get pen right. "At two, start looking for next gas station or hotel, whatever."

Seemed there were no cars around, just proper dark, though sure someone with the headlights off could be anywhere. The dark, really, started to make me feel worse, less hidden on account if I could cover myself in it, anything else could, things could already be hiding I'd intrude on them, they'd see me coming whole long way off.

I had no reason to think Leonard, cops, anyone was poking around for me, but, just as much, ugly fact, I had no reason to think anything at all, just couldn't quit.

***

Gas station about a mile down a road off the highway someplace—wherever, didn't even want to know—I lingered in the lot, nothing else around, except slight indication of lights in the direction the signs across the road indicated there were two hotels, a diner, fast-food. Station had a decent sized shop area, its own small restaurant affixed, or the shell of one, place looked closed down permanent.

I went inside, made a round for coffee, two glazed doughnuts, poked through a magazine while I ate, having clearly shown the attendant what I'd taken, he knew to keep it in mind, add to my total. I waited out a line three deep of patrons, people seemed local, just in and out, all of them kind of chatting, not really, got to the counter I eyed the rows of cigarettes.

"You actually have Daphne Durants?" I asked, not sure, the package seemed different than I remembered, however long back it was I'd smoked a Durant, these might be some new bastardization, some different thing trading on the name.

Clerk just nodded "Sure," said they were the same as they'd always been, as long as he'd known, just regular Durants.

"I'll have a pack," I said and he rung it up, usual high price showing higher probably on account of this was some no place gas station they might as well charge just whatever they feel like a given day. Told the clerk "Hold on," took a look at the off brands, asked how much.

"For the cheaps?"

I nodded, he ticked off three prices for the various kind, told me the one hundreds were no different.

"I'll just take a pack of those then" I pointed, shaking head when he pointed at one pack, nodding when he pointed at the next, added that I'd take the hundreds, but then said "No, forget it, the Durants, I'll just take the Durants."

"Sure?"

"Yes, sorry. I'm just beat, thinking I'd probably not have the energy even I'd taste them, why waste it, but it's still a Durant, I guess."

"Sure," he said, ringing them, again—didn't seem he'd punched the doughnuts in, me of no mind to remind him about how to do his job.

I did ask "You from around here?"

"Yeah."

"Know anything about the hotels, that way?"

He kind of made a face, funny quizzical, shrugged both shoulders to his cheeks, goofball smile said "They're hotels. I don't think there's anything to know about them, you know?"

"I mean are the expensive? Are they local owned?"

He gestured no idea, so I dropped it, asked for key the toilet, he said it just pushed open, pointed back past the coolers.

The was no knob to the door, someone'd stuffed it with toilet tissue, this kept to place with invisible tape, various graffiti overtop, nothing especially clever in the parts that were at least legible. No mirror, either, so I just splashed water to my face, swished some, spit it, mouth felt dry from it, so bought a fruit juice and wandered back out front the shop, sat on the ground by the ice cooler.

Somehow I'd wound up below three hundred dollars, total—counted it too many times to trust myself about that, though, didn't trust myself about verifying anything, tucked it in my pockets, stood and dumped the Lara Gregory file and Lester's picture out in the trash bin.

Not even three hundred.

Still, it had me ahead of where I'd been and I supposed there were shelters all over the world, I'd just make an effort beg my way far enough a bigger city or else see what I could see down the road, maybe little town I could get a room, tuck away, figure out some way to ingratiate myself with someone long enough to get in proper they set me up room and board, little job or something.

Police car pulled in at the pumps, me still stood by the trashcan, new cigarette just lit, head swimming from the quality of the last four I'd chained. I stared, could tell enough there were two officers inside, neither getting out, didn't seem either'd marked me or had a mind to. I turned to the side, gauging distance to end of the lot, the road, the tree line, how long to get around in back.

Twisted cigarette into the rough concrete façade the shop front, took one step, not even sure I really'd heard it, from the pumps handclap of my name "Trevor English?"

Let my eyes steady on the cop in front, hand at his sidearm, but just a saunter to the two steps he took—other officer'd started causally moving around in the direction I'd been looking off, hand just as at the ready. I set my bag on the ground, could feel heft of gun in pocket tugging at my pants the same way.

"You Trevor English?"

Nodded. "Sure, I'm Trevor English."

Cop made some gesture his pal, same time asking me it

might be alright we had a word—I bolted toward shop door, was through, gun out of my pocket but concentrating on getting it out lost sense of anything else ran straight into short rack the candy bars, wind partway knocked out of me, staggered, some sound coming out of me like a stuck balloon not gored enough to pop, then was through the door the toilet—no latch even—moved the waste bin in front, backpedaled until I felt the sink against back of my thighs.

Trained the gun on the door, wasn't a minute even until I heard my name being asked through it.

"Don't come in here," I yelled, almost like just informing them it was occupied, they were thinking to come in, bully me for a laugh. "I have a gun, don't you even get near the door—do you hear me?"

Whichever officer said "Sure, sure," said he heard me just fine, no one was going to open the door, but maybe I just should come out, he didn't see what much choice I had in it.

Two minutes, something, I stood, just staring, gun not even pointed, my name being asked every few seconds.

Trained gun back on the door, then slowly moved it to side of my head, instant it touched like whole of my body, testicles to inside my eyes, seized up, despicable, stomach tangled felt like broken fingers done in knots, I slumped to my knees, tipped to side one, elbows, retching, scooted back toward toilet bowl, raising gun a moment the door, then couldn't hold it, set it down.

"Trevor?"

Note of concern, cop must've heard something he thought maybe he could try his way in.

"Stay away from the door," I screamed, pointed my fingers like pistol, arm held strained so tight it vibrated, made me bounce where I sat.

Felt my face groping its way into some smile, my breath coming out the sound a coin spinning to stop on a table.

Looked at my fingers, bent the thumb like gun hammer banging down, did it twice, three times, chuckled.

"Trevor, are you alright in there?"

"Don't come in here, don't even think about it, I'll shoot you right through that door, man, I even decide to think you're thinking about it even if I know really it's you're not, you get what I'm saying?"

"No, no—nobody's coming in. Just are you doing alright?"

Moved fingers to side of my head, loosening my necktie I'd no idea why I was still in, scooted back another bit or else just rubbed against gut of toilet bowl, stared at door, brought thumb down, again, this time like Click.

***

New voice the door—I'd stood, been standing, moving the one wall, the other, sometimes footing a bit noodle, leaning hand to wall the toilet jutted from—was deep, same piano key the bottom of the lowest scale just clunked again and again. I didn't say anything to the volley of questions this new voice made, just tried to work up to warn them not to try this, not to try that, but thoughts no further—nothing about how they should let me go, how I'd explain to them I went figuring that'd ever conceivably work, didn't want them to start thinking me halfwit, snickers the same time they were working their extraction.

In a regular speaking voice, facing where mirror ought to be, facing sink basin by the end, asked "What are you arresting me for?"

"Is that you, Trevor?"

Sniffled, turned, cleared throat, then tad louder repeated

question slow "What is it, exactly, all of you are thinking to arrest me for?"

"I think you know that, Trevor, come on. Why don't you tell me, it might be better?"

"I'm not telling you, man, you tell me."

I'd set the gun on the tank of the toilet, leaned to the wall far from it as possible, let my eyes go blurry while the voice told me, first of all, they had several warrants, one of them over violent sexual assault, that I knew that as well as I knew the rest.

"You see? Man, I never raped Helen. This is just the thing, okay? I mean I know the rest of it, but same time you're out there on that and that's something I didn't ever do to begin with. No. Come on."

But straight off, not treating me some sucker, voice said "Alright," said it was just answering my question, that was the warrant, one of the warrants, so as far as voice was concerned cops were just there about serving the warrant, I could explain about whatever, that was another thing.

"Another thing?"

I moved to take up the gun, let it slouch my shoulder arm that held it, stood square at the door, directing my voice to the toilet tissue clogging the space there should've been the knob.

"I get to explain it all, is that right? That's your offer?"

"It's not an offer, it's what happens. I'm just here to get you out of there, Trevor, then these guys take you, it goes on from there."

"Sounds great, yeah, that sounds really good—but what about I save us the trouble, put this gun to use?"

"Trevor," the voice said, real tone of I was talking wrong, needed to think, started in with telling me something else but I was already going on my own piece.

"I'm telling you the truth, all you can tell me is some

nothing, all kinds of it, every kind. Man, I didn't rape anybody. And you know what else, it's Norman he gave me this gun, wanted me to do somebody up dead and I never did, I never have—I never raped Helen, I never killed anybody, not for Norman and not for anyone else thinks they see me I'm some scum who's the one just waiting for all of that. How about I explain that to you, but same time what do I think, you're going to believe it? Not for one minute, man, and don't treat me like an idiot, don't 'Trevor' me, don't tell me I get to tell you things like it means you'll listen or any of all that, like something's the matter with me I'd believe you ten goddamned seconds, right?"

I looked around the room for where I was casting a shadow, but it didn't seem to be anyplace except when I'd lift my feet there'd be a kind of blob on the stained tile. Fixated. Had to get my hand or knee or face all the way up near the wall or the door to get sight of any shadow of mine—mind just locked in on this, couldn't get shut of it and voice wasn't saying anything else, like it knew I was roiling, guy in toilet sniffing after shadow.

Finally, voice came back with "Trevor, I'm telling you the truth, too, and I never told you you'd get to talk to me. You won't. I'm not lying to you, I just want you to come out of the room."

"To go to jail?"

"Yes."

Laughed, opened and closed and opened and closed the faucet.

"Fantastic. So whyn't just I'll stay in here, right? What's the difference we let this be jail? Just go away, brick me up all I care, I don't even want to look at you."

Was expecting another calm agreement or sidestep, instead voice told me to think about it that if they had to open the door, if I pulled on them or did myself dead, I'd not get to tell anyone anything, just whatever anyone said would be it—it could be a million times worse, I should think about it, think about not even getting to have a say about anything.

This got me centered. I started, torrent, jabbering at the door about if I was being arrested, then same time just as much a guy named Leonard—couldn't think of his last name—a guy named Leonard, some private investigator, some store detective, he ten times, hundred times as much should be so why wasn't he in jail.

"I don't know about that, Trevor. See? That's something, see? Nobody here knows what that means."

"That's exactly right," I said, gesture with my hands as though it was obvious, proved my point, my face a screw of sarcasm.

"Why don't you tell me?"

"You found me someone told you about I'm here, isn't it? Or what else? You just stroll to gas stations some bumblefuck no place and ask after Hey are you Trevor English? and chase people into some toilets they say Yes?"

I laughed more, almost thought I heard the voice laughing too, like on the same page.

"We were told where you were. That's right."

Even more forceful, slapped the door few times, I charged along that reason they were here was on account of Leonard and Leonard knew about me from way back, had got all the dirt on me and told me go kill some guy, no reason even, just told me do it or else.

"And I didn't do that—that's the thing, see? You're here because someone wanted me do someone up dead for them and you're here only on account of I didn't do that."

"Trevor."

"Don't 'Trevor'," I shriek, felt myself beginning to break

apart, tears streaming. "Man, it's why I'm here and you're here and you can say anything you want about it but who's going to go out get him, alright? What it's gonna go like? I come out, whisked away, tell you Leonard told me to kill someone and when I'd had enough and didn't do it he finked me out to you for nothing?"

I stumbled back, swung up gun form toilet, got fingers at the edge of the door enough to get it opened, man who'd been talking to me stepping back—officers behind him at their guns—and I put my gun to my head and stepped out.

"So, go home. I'm out of the room, go home."

The talking man was dressed some suit, semi-bald, looked a thirsty old cat eyeing bowl of water through glass window.

"Trevor."

"What?"

He put hands up, palms out, peaceable, little move his head made all present lower down guns.

"Trevor."

I made hideous mock out of my voice, repeating "Trevor? Trevor?" then demanded he tell me what I was supposed to do or was the thing he was just going to say my name all night long.

"I want you to put the gun down."

Our eyes locked, his wide, mine like they wouldn't stop bouncing, pressure they were coming loose I wanted to bludgeon them in my thumb knuckles.

"I want you to put down the gun."

Everything slipped out of me, my arm spooling limp to my side, sticking where the gun ended otherwise arm would've piled in a mess on the dry mopped tile the store.

Talking man was nodding, telling me I was doing good, saying Thank you to me for lowering gun, but I needed to put the gun down, all the way down.

"No."

"Trevor, I need you to give me the gun."

My head was nodding, but like it wanted to be lighter than it was, float off, was drifting like one thread held it, thread cut it could go.

"I want you to give me the gun," he said, step closer, step closer.

"You're going to have to take it," I said, and my wrist of the hand with the gun went as much around one way it could, as much around the other.

"Don't make a mistake now," he said, another step in, look on him I knew he just was pretending like fear and sympathy in his face. "You're thinking right, now. You don't want to make a mistake, Trevor."

He glanced to the gun, not moving, looked at me until I met his eyes, held the look—and like what he'd just said caught up with me, I stepped a step back, coughing to get my voice and moistened my lips.

"I just mean I can't give it to you."

"Trevor."

But I shook my head, cutting him short. "You have to take it. I just can't give it to you."

His breathing, my breathing, they got the same until I only knew his, mine someplace I never wanted to know it, wanted it lost to never come back. He took two steps, had gun from my hands, turned his back quick, never another look, and everyone else, guns up, came down. I closed my eyes hard, sour of every blood in me filling taste the inside my head—held my eyes closed so hard just to be sure if the talking man was looking again I wouldn't have to see him, and I choked some sound—meant it to be a word, but just wheeze from my nose—something supposed to be maybe my telling him "Sorry."